Given In Marriage

by

B. M. Croker

Given In Marriage
by B. M. Croker

ISBN: 978-93-61423-48-2

Published by

DOUBLE 9 BOOKS

2/13-B, Ansari Road
Daryaganj, New Delhi – 110002
info@double9books.com
www.double9books.com
Tel. 011-40042856

ABOUT THE AUTHOR

Bithia Born on November 6, 1849, Mary Croker, sometimes known as B. M. Croker, was a British author who died on October 20, 1920. During the late 19th and early 20th centuries, she was a well-known and prolific writer who was well-known for her captivating novels and short stories. Croker lived a significant portion of her life in India, where her husband was a British Army soldier. Her experiences there had a profound effect on her work. Her paintings frequently portrayed the life of British expatriates in India, providing realistic depictions of the people, customs, and natural surroundings of the area. Croker's writing was distinguished by its intricate character development, captivating narratives, and vivid descriptions.

CONTENTS

CHAPTER I
A STRANGER IN THE LAND

"I say, did you hear old pensioner Jones, jawing away to Haji Aboo about the gold reefs, that lie round Tappah?"

An eager young planter put this question to his companion, as together they—or rather their horses—toiled up a sharp ascent.

"Oh yes, *I* heard him," grunted the other with a shrug.

"And what did you think, Ted?"

"That the old boy was drunk as usual," was the uncompromising rejoinder. "Filthy Bazaar liquor; some of these days he'll snuff-out!"

"Well, of course it's Shandy, but I've a notion, there is something in his story. No smoke without fire! Eh? He swore that one or two of the estates were chock full of gold."

"Oh, there's gold enough in coffee, if you know how to work it," declared Ted Dawson, an enthusiast at his trade.

"Yes, but why not the other sort as well? Imagine two heavy crops—the berry, and the nugget!" urged his partner. "I've heard that lame Maistrey— whose ancestors lived here when these hills were opened up—say, that the first planters were granted immense tracts for a mere song, and that one or two of them like Pattador and Fairplains—run right down to the low country, where there are old workings, smothered in jungle."

"Bosh!" ejaculated Ted, "I've heard these fool stories, but there's nothing in them;" and he ruthlessly turned from this ever-dazzling subject, to an unromantic discussion on bone manure and sulphate of ammonia.

The two planters, accompanied by a pack of dogs, were riding up the steep, short cut leading to their joint estate, which was situated on the western slopes of a hill range, in Southern India. Edward Dawson, the elder of the pair, was a big, loosely put-together man, of five and thirty (he looked considerably younger, thanks to his round, beardless face), with almost lint-white locks, and candid blue eyes. His clothes were decent—which is all that could be said for them; a cotton shirt, wide open at the neck, canvas breeches, leather belt, and a battered topee, completed his kit.

Dawson was the son of a retired Indian general, who had wisely invested part of his savings in coffee, when estates were cheap; and had thereby provided for an heir of simple and bucolic tastes—a good, honest fellow, who loved the land of his birth, was keen on his job, and spoke Tamil and Canarese, with effective fluency.

Nicholas Byng, his companion, cousin, and partner, was a slight, young man, with neat features, quick, bright eyes, and a remarkably clear idea of the importance of appearances—especially of his own appearance. He wore a well-made drill suit and polo boots, and rode a long-tailed, useful-looking, bay thoroughbred, bearing the discouraging name of "Mad Molly."

Byng, the darling of a widowed mother, had been intended for the Army, but was "spun" so repeatedly, that his failure appeared to have become a confirmed habit. The death of his parent put an end to further efforts, and a certain high-handed uncle then deported him to the Chicknabullnay Estate. Here, for the first time in his career, he put his unaccustomed shoulder to the wheel, and, after a year's apprenticeship, became partner and sub-manager. He liked the life.

Teddy, for all his unconventional, "jungly" ways, was a good sort; a strong man, who kept the reins in his ugly big fists, and was master. His partner enjoyed ample liberty and holidays—oh, it was not *all* "coffee"— and Nicky was able to disport himself in Madras, and fashionable—alas! rather remote—hill stations; he got a bit of shooting, was making money, and, on the whole, the billet suited him down to the ground.

The couple had been to the foot of the ghât on business connected with the transport of their crops; every yard they now travelled carried them further and further from dense, tropical forests, sweltering heat, and swampy valleys, and nearer to the quiet beauty of the grassy uplands.

Turning a sharp corner, they debouched into a little glade where three tracks met, and here, with a slight shock of surprise, discovered that prominent figure in early Victorian fiction, known as "a solitary horseman."

Dawson, who was still expounding on the scandalous price of bone manure, broke off his sentence with:

"I say,—who's this?"

"Hello, good afternoon," said the stranger, raising a smart topee, "I heard your voices, and waited. I don't know these parts, and I'm afraid I've lost my bearings."

The "lost one" was a well set-up, self-possessed individual, mounted on a fine waler cob, and accompanied by a wiry, and more than half-naked syce.

"I expect we will soon put you all right," said Byng, —ever the speaking partner—"Where are you bound for?"

"A place called Fairplains; the estate of one James Fletcher."

"Then you are just five miles out; you overshot the mark by that native village among the plantain trees, near the bridge. Why didn't you stick to the road?"

"Well, I suppose because I'm an adventurous idiot," was the modest reply, "and I was told that a bridle-path cut off seven miles."

"So it does,—but it depends upon *which* bridle-path. This one has put you on, a good ten."

"I say, what a confounded nuisance!" exclaimed the wanderer, looking down at his blown, and sweating, steed.

"Our place is barely a mile from here," announced Dawson, speaking for the first time. "Come on with us, have a drink, give the gee a feed, and a rub-down, and we will send a coolie to put you on the way to Fairplains—unless you'll stay the night?" he added, with true planter's hospitality.

"Thanks awfully, but I'd better shove on. I'll be glad to stop an hour at your diggings, and give the cob a rest—he's pretty well done."

"Not the usual 'Hirling,' I see," remarked Byng.

"No, I brought him from Cananore; he is awfully soft—that climate is only fit for horned cattle!"

"Yes, beastly wet," agreed Byng, his bright eyes taking in the well-knit figure and military bearing of the cob's master. "Your regiment quartered there?"

"It is—my name is Mayne—Derek Mayne—an uncle of mine is a pal of Fletcher's, he invited me up for six weeks' shooting—and naturally I came like a shot!"

"But Fletcher has gone home—went off ten days ago!"

"What do you say?" cried Mayne, reining up his horse.

"It's a fact; he has been rather seedy, and ran down to see a doctor in Madras, who ordered him to start then and there for London—it was a case for an immediate operation."

"Poor chap! I'm most awfully sorry. Well," after a reflective pause, "I'm in a pretty big hole. I had a line from Fletcher three weeks ago, and I've got my leave all right, and have written to announce my arrival, but the shoot is off! I suppose I must make for one of these hill stations. I can't tell you how I've been looking forward to this shikar trip—my first."

"Oh, I expect you will be all right," said Dawson reassuringly; "Fletcher is bound to have left instructions; he is a most reliable old boy. Let me introduce myself. My name is Dawson, and this," waving a huge paw, "is my cousin, Nicholas Byng. We run a coffee estate known as Chicknabullnay,— but called by our neighbours 'The Corner.' He is the ornamental, and I'm the working partner."

"Come, I like that!" broke in his cousin: "I live with my nose to the grindstone. I've been on duty since six o'clock this morning; down at Burliar, making a bundobast for our crop."

"We would give you some shooting," continued Dawson, "but nothing like what you'd get at Fairplains—that has always had a Shikari owner, who knows the best grounds, and beats in the low country, as well as he knows his A B C, and can call out any amount of good, plucky beaters."

"Well, I sincerely hope it *will* be all right, as you believe, and that the manager has been warned by Fletcher; otherwise, it's no great matter, as I am a complete stranger to them both. I say, what a mixed multitude!" pointing to the pack.

"Yes, all sorts and conditions," replied Byng, "and a real good specimen of an average planter's pack, only ours are absolutely healthy—no red mange."

"But what variety!" said Mayne, turning in his saddle to survey them. "A fox hound, three beagles, a deer-hound, half a dozen fox terriers, several—any other sort—a bull terrier, and what was once a poodle."

"Yes, and the poodle has the brains of the lot. You see how it is; people going home are glad to leave their dogs in a good climate. Most of ours, have a history! The deer-hound was given to me by a girl, the poodle came from a French priest at Pondicherry, the fox-terrier with the black head, belonged to a poor chap who died. They get on together fairly well, all being fond of sport, and they have a rattling good time."

"Lucky dogs!"

"Yes," put in Dawson, "hunting, drawing sholahs for sambur, and pig, and at home, there are rats and bandicoots. Two dog-boys feed and brush them—and a few live indoors."

"A *few!*" echoed Byng, "make it a dozen! The poodle and fox-terriers,— like the poor,—are always with us, and I've found a couple of beagles in my bed before now, and"—as an old retriever came slowly towards the party, "here comes a pensioner to welcome us. This is Chicknabullnay."

For the last quarter of a mile, the journey had been on a well-metalled cart road, and through a crop of dense green coffee bushes; now, a sudden curve brought the back of a long, low bungalow with adjoining gardens, stores, and stables, into sight. As the trio rode down a steep slope, dog-boys, and syces, hurried forward to claim their respective charges.

The guest dismounted rather stiffly, and was escorted by Dawson straight through the house, and into the front verandah. Here the view that lay before them was startlingly unexpected; low hills to right and left had, as it were, been cleft by some volcanic convulsion, and disclosed a far-away, and exquisite, blue panorama of the plains.

"Oh I say!" Mayne exclaimed involuntarily.

"Hits you bang in the eye, doesn't it?" was Dawson's complacent rejoinder. "Most planters manœuvre for a fine outlook—the one up at Fairplains is the same—but Fletcher swears, ten times better. Now come along inside, and have a wash."

CHAPTER II
"THE CORNER"

For a bachelor abode "The Corner" proved unexpectedly comfortable, and well-furnished.

"Wouldn't you swear a couple of old maids lived here?" said Dawson, as he ushered his guest into the dining-room. "This is all Byng's doing," pointing to a precisely-laid table,—where four little hill-ferns, in four little white china wheelbarrows, supported a central ornament. "He found things pretty rough and tumbled, when he joined me three years ago."

"You may say so!" corroborated his cousin, now entering sleek-headed and refreshed, unfolding a smart silk handkerchief as he spoke. "Why, there was hardly a sheet or a towel—nothing but rags—only one tumbler, one breakfast-cup, and two plates, both cracked!"

"Oh come, draw it mild!" protested the other. "Anyhow, the Missy—I call him the 'Missy'—gives picnics and tiffins, we have an ice machine, a piano, and lace-edged tea-cloths! Now sit down, I'm sure you are starving."

A black-bearded butler brought in a substantial cold hump, salad, roast potatoes, bread, butter, cheese, and a huge cake; whilst his satellite, an attendant chokra, supplied each of the company with a long and well-iced peg.

"Not much of the old maid in this quarter!" remarked Mayne, when he had swallowed a few mouthfuls, indicating the splendid tiger-skins, and heads, that surrounded the party. "That bison—I say, what a fellow!" surveying the trophy with eyes of envious respect.

"Yes, a good specimen," assented Dawson. "You should see those at Fairplains. Travers is the finest shot in Southern India. Have you ever done any big game shooting?"

"Nothing bigger than a hare! I've always been mad keen on trophies, and when my uncle wrote about this invitation, I nearly stood on my head. Supposing Fletcher's manager has received no instructions, and gives me the boot?"

"No fear," rejoined Byng emphatically. "Travers is the great shikari in these hills, a magnificent shot, and absolutely without a nerve in his body. If you are a keen sportsman—a red-hot enthusiast—he will love you as a son, or brother."

"How splendid! What's he like?"

"I'll tell you all about him, when we adjourn outside. Have one of these Trichys?"

With a Trichy between his fingers, Mayne followed his host into the verandah, and there, subsided into a deep and seductive chair. His eyes ranged over the unfamiliar outlook, of rich green coffee bushes, heavy forestry, and vague, blue plains, as he meditatively rolled the cheroot.

"It's rather a painful story about Laurence Travers," began Byng, blowing a cloud.

"Then—er—perhaps you'd rather— —"

"Oh, it's common property—no scandal. Travers' father lived to spend his last penny, and left nothing but debt for the family. So Laurence, instead of going into the Army, came out here when he was two and twenty; he had a little capital, and started coffee planting at Fairplains. After a good season, he went home on three months' leave,—and got caught, coming out!"

"Caught!" repeated Mayne.

"Fell head over ears in love with a fellow passenger; a young governess bound for a situation in Melbourne. She had not a penny, needless to say. They were married, and lived very happily, in spite of the wrath of his relations,—whose chief asset was family pride. Mrs. Travers did up the house, started a garden, rode about all over the place, and made heaps of friends; she was Irish, very pretty, lively, hospitable, and an immense favourite. Those were fat years for coffee too—and Travers prospered."

"Oh, get on!—don't be so long-winded!" growled Dawson, who was nursing a fox terrier, whilst jealous dogs of various sorts surrounded his chair.

"Well," resumed Byng, "after a good while, there was the usual baby—a girl. Travers was in the seventh heaven, but Mrs. Travers somehow began to go down hill, though she would not give in; other people saw it, and urged her to take a change, or to go home. She stuck it out, that she was as strong as a horse. However, when the child was about a year old, Travers, coming in late one afternoon, discovered her sitting in the verandah,—as he supposed asleep,—with the baby on her lap. When it turned out that she was stone dead, he went nearly raving mad; in those days the place was a bit isolated, neighbours were far off; not like it is now,—the Ffinches and Hicks within a couple of miles. Strange to say, the servants had the sense to put away his razors and fire-arms, and to send for the nearest doctor. He gave Travers a sedative, and found that Mrs. Travers had died of long-standing heart disease. She was buried in her garden.

"After this blow, Travers appeared to have no further interest in anything in the wide world,—bar the kid. She had a superior English nurse, and the most wonderful frocks, sashes, and dolls, that had ever been seen on these hills. Travers could not bear her out of his sight, and brought her about with him everywhere,—even shooting. When Nancy was six, she got typhoid—our crystal clear streams are deceptive—and she nearly went out, and had to be sent home. Her father took this separation terribly to heart; after her departure, they say, he used to sit for hours, in a sort of dream, just smoking, and staring into space! Some people thought he was going dotty; and it sounds a funny thing to say, but in a way, the child was his *ruin*! An irresistible magnet, that drew him to England, and often at the most critical seasons. There, he had no occupation; here, his coffee estate was going to pot. Other planters warned him, but in spite or all they could say, he would leave as manager, one, Doria, a cunning half-caste,—such an oily persuasive rascal,—to take on his job.

"There had been bad seasons, and losses,—common to the whole community, and this fellow urged Travers to raise a mortgage, and Travers, who wanted ready money, and was dying to be off home, agreed, and departed. Then Doria, left to his own devices, set about to rob and plunder in the most shameless way; he pocketed a whole season's profits, also large arrears of debts—and cleared out, leaving no address."

"I believe he is in South America," interposed Dawson. "Go on, Nicky— you'd make your fortune in the Bazaar!"

"I think," resumed Byng, "that it must be nearly five years since Travers returned, and found himself completely smashed. He made a desperate effort to pull things together, but it was too late; the coffee was neglected, and blighted, the bungalow full of mildew and cobwebs,—and the mortgagees were calling for their capital. I must say, they behaved infernally badly; would not give Travers a dog's chance; foreclosed, and sold up Fairplains. Fletcher bought it, lock, stock and barrel, and kept on Travers, as his manager. He has a bungalow, and four hundred rupees a month—and is worth *double*. When Fletcher is away—he is boss, and lives in the big house."

"Where he was once lord, and master!" exclaimed Mayne. "What frightfully hard luck,—I wonder he stayed on."

"Hobson's choice! He'd got to live, and to pay for the kiddie at home. Now she is grown up, and out—and——"

"Do you mean to tell me," interrupted Mayne, pushing back his chair, "that there is a girl at Fairplains?"

"I am thankful to say there is! She is the life and soul of the neighbourhood. We should all be uncommonly dull without our Nancy— she is full of energy, and true *joie-de-vivre*—does everything bang off on the spur of the moment, and is the apple of her father's eye."

"And mine," supplemented Dawson, "apple of both eyes."

"Yes, she put new life into Travers," resumed Byng, "he is like another man; goes all over the place to picnics, and tennis, and takes an interest in his personal appearance—not like my cousin here," with a contemptuous gesture of his thumb.

"Oh, go on!" grunted Dawson, "*I* haven't thirty-eight ties hanging on a string—I've no red silk socks—and no looks! Travers, though he is nearly fifty, is far and away the handsomest fellow in these parts; he's like a king! I suppose it's the old blue blood—and one of the best, into the bargain."

Mayne listened with ill-suppressed impatience to this long eulogy. What were the handsome planter, and the apple of his eye, to him? His programme must be entirely revised.

"But I say," he broke in at last. "It's one thing to go shooting with a bachelor, my uncle's old pal—but another pair of shoes, to quarter myself on his manager, who has a grown-up daughter—even if he wanted to go for a week's shikar, he could not leave her at home alone."

"Oh, she goes with him," was Dawson's staggering announcement, "she's an A1 shot."

"Then *that* settles it," declared Mayne, rising to his feet. "Two is company! Only my baggage is on its way to Fletcher's, I'd ask for a bed here, and start down the ghât to-morrow. Anyway, I won't stay at Fairplains more than a couple of days."

"Oh, *won't* you?" said Byng, with ironical emphasis, "I advise you to 'wait and see.' Nancy won't be the fly in the ointment—she's a rattling good little housekeeper, and will make you uncommonly comfortable. She does not always go out shooting; sometimes Mrs. Ffinch comes over, and keeps her company—they are tremendous pals."

"Yes, if you are really anxious to see first-class sport," broke in Dawson, "don't let a scruple, or a little girl, stand in your way. Take my advice, and make no arrangements, till you have seen Fairplains for yourself."

"Well, I daresay you are right," said Mayne, after a weighty silence. "It does seem rather rotten, to have taken this long journey, and be, so to speak, headed off by a petticoat. I—might be sorry afterwards."

"You are bound to be," rejoined Dawson with conviction.

"All right then, I'll push on. Have the Travers any neighbours besides yourselves, and this Mrs. What-you-may-call her?"

"Oh, yes, the Ffinches at Clouds Rest, are within two miles—there are only the two of them. He, given over body and soul, to money-making, and coffee—otherwise just Mrs. Ffinch's husband! She, is our local dynamo, and keeps everything going;—extraordinarily clever woman, absolutely wasted out here;—would make a great Prime Minister, or Secretary for Foreign Affairs. Then we have the Hicks'. Dr. and Mrs. and two girls; he was doctor on board a liner—and picked up a lady passenger."

"More of a passenger, than a lady," corrected Dawson, "but a rare good sort."

"And the girls ditto," continued his cousin. "These are our nearest— if not dearest. You'll soon get to know everyone, and everyone will know you,—and give you lots of sport."

"Well then, I think I'll make a start, if you'll send for the cob, and syce; it's seven o'clock."

"It's a fine starlight night, and no hurry; only the Travers' are early birds," said Dawson, when Mayne's cob was led up. "There's a coolie to guide you. I expect we shall see you pretty often—mind you look in, when you can."

"Upon my word, I don't know how to thank you! You have been most awfully good in taking me in like this," said Mayne. "Perhaps Fletcher has not written; and you may have me back on your hands to-morrow morning," and with a laugh, and a salute, he sprang into the saddle, and cantered away, closely pursued by syce, and coolie.

"A real cheery chap!" remarked Dawson, as he looked after the parting guest; "no 'haw-haw' nonsense about him. I like his eyes,—and he laughs like a boy."

"Boy! He must be seven or eight and twenty," said Byng, "may be more. Money, I should say. I noticed his watch, and he paid a smart sum for that cob. He's not a bad-looking chap—I hope he won't turn the child's head?"

"Not likely!" rejoined Dawson, "Nancy's head is too well screwed on, and she has no room for anyone in her thoughts, but her Daddy—as for that fellow, his one and only object in life, is to bag a tiger!"

Having pronounced this dictum, Dawson flung himself into a long cane chair, and picked up *The Planter's Gazette*.

CHAPTER III
THE GIRL AT FAIRPLAINS

Proceeding through the coffee estate at a sort of dog's trot, Mayne was sorely exercised in his mind; being filled with serious misgivings concerning the planter's daughter; probably a pert, autocratic little minx, after the manner of the usual "apples of eyes," who would no doubt prove—as far as he was concerned—a real spoil-sport! For days he had indulged in glowing visions of a rough outdoor life; of camps, long marches, exciting stalks, heavy spoils, and freedom!

Could a manager leave his estate? and if he did, and brought his encumbrance, how hateful and irksome to have this girl tacked on to the party! Well, he could soon see how the land lay, and if the outlook was too discouraging, would hurry off and spend his leave in Ceylon—where he might,—with any luck—get an elephant or two.

It was a lovely starlight evening, and after the hot and clammy atmosphere of Cananore, the thin cool hill air, with its tang of eucalyptus, was as refreshing as a draught of spring water. Up various steep coolie paths, bordered by clumps of aromatic blue gum, and ragged bushes, and round many sharp corners, Mayne followed his light-footed leader. Presently they came upon a good metalled road, running through coffee, and above them, on a raised plateau, stood Fairplains, with lighted windows, and lanterns flickering like fire-flies about the premises.

As Mayne approached, the barking of many dogs was deafening, and he halted just below the bungalow. When he did so, the majestic figure of an elderly butler, appeared at the top of a flight of stone steps, brandishing a lantern in one hand, and salaaming profoundly with the other.

"Is the sahib at home?" inquired Mayne.

"Yes, saar, please to come up, saar?"

Thus invited, the visitor dismounted, and ascended to the verandah; and as he did so, caught sight, within a room, of a girl reading. By the light of a shaded lamp, he invisioned a wisp-like figure in white, and a bent head crowned with a mass of hair.

"Francis!" called out a clear young voice, "why are those dogs making such a noise? Is it the panther again?"

"No, missy," replied the servant reassuringly, "no panther to-night—only one gentleman."

Missy lifted her head, and beheld Mayne standing in the doorway. As she rose to her feet, he discovered that the word "little" did not fit Miss Nancy Travers, who was rather tall than otherwise.

"I hope you will pardon this late and audacious intrusion," he began, removing his topee as he spoke. "My name is Mayne—Mr. Fletcher, my uncle's old friend, invited me up here for some shooting. I only discovered a couple of hours ago, that Mr. Fletcher has gone home, and had no time to make other arrangements—but——"

"It is quite all right," she declared with serene composure, "this is Mr. Fletcher's bungalow, and naturally you are welcome. Francis will get you some supper at once."

"I suppose you had no letter—you did not expect me?" he inquired, advancing to the table.

"No, but that makes no difference. We are accustomed to stray visitors, and always glad to see them. Planters, doctors, chaplains, and missionaries, drop in from time to time. Won't you sit down?" indicating a chair; a half-finished game of chess was on the table between them. "Father and I were playing, when he was sent for to see to a sick coolie. He will be back in a few minutes."

"Did I hear you say something about a panther just now?" asked Mayne abruptly.

"Yes, they come down from the rocks above us, and prowl round after dark, and carry off dogs if they can; last week one of them took the dhoby's best goat!"

"Then the shooting about here must be good?"

"I'm afraid father has not left much in the immediate neighbourhood; for real sport, you have to go down the ghât—I mean for bison and tiger—hereabouts, there are only sambur, and wild pig."

"And panthers?" supplemented Mayne.

"Yes, too many of them! Such treacherous, cruel, brutes, and very bold. More dangerous in their way than tiger—Father says the tiger is a gentleman—the panther a bounder."

"I wish I could get a shot at one."

"No doubt you will have a chance. Did you come far to-day?"

"From the railway. I arrived from Cananore last night, and stopped at the Dâk bungalow. My guns and traps are following me, but I really don't like to billet myself on you, and your father."

Since he had been in the company of Miss Travers, Mayne had been anxiously endeavouring to distinguish her appearance; but a heavily shaded lamp left, beyond the mere outline, everything to conjecture; and, save an impression that she had a small face, large eyes, and a thin brown hand,—the lady's looks, remained an unknown quantity.

At this moment, Travers, who had been prescribing for a stomach-ache in the coolie lines, reappeared, unaware of the arrival of a visitor. As he stepped into the verandah, he heard talking—a strange voice, vibrant and attractive,—the voice of a gentleman; and there, sitting in his own pet chair, was someone whose sleek dark head, and white collar, appeared above its cushions.

He entered promptly, received a hasty and apologetic explanation, and became at once the cordial and hospitable host. The dark-haired young fellow, was evidently an Army man, with pleasant easy manners.

A description of his journey was presently cut short by the announcement that "Supper was ready on the table," and as Travers hurried his guest into the dining-room, the young lady disappeared.

Supper was laid out with an unexpected display of fine damask, cut glass, and shining silver, and the new-comer did ample justice to an excellent meal of which the *pièce de résistance* was cold hump. There was a sameness in the planters' homes, not only confined to food; here again were dead trophies, and not a few live dogs; but dogs, trophies, and surroundings, were all on a superior, and more imposing scale, than that of the *ménage* at "The Corner."

Travers, noticing his guest's attention fixed upon a valuable old sideboard, said:

"I see you are looking at the Chippendale! This place is no mushroom, and been established over eighty years. I took it from the executors of a very old planter, who started it, and collected no end of good furniture, plate and glass, from auctions and sales—the break-up of families, who were pioneers in these hills."

Presently the conversation turned to the subject nearest to the wayfarer's heart, "shikar." On such a topic, the two were in the most profound, and, so to speak, deadly sympathy. Mayne listened enthralled—to an excellent supper—to vivid descriptions of beats and bags, "near shaves," and glorious triumphs. Afterwards the sportsmen smoked in the verandah, and exchanged views on a surprising variety of subjects, from the stars in their courses, to the preserving of skins, and the imperative use of arsenical soap.

Later, as Travers escorted his guest to the spare room, he said:

"I expect we shall be able to show you some fairly good sport."

"I'm sure of it," responded Mayne, "but by no means so sure, that I ought to trespass on your good nature. For all *you* know, I may be an impudent impostor!"

"Oh, I'll risk that," replied Travers with a hearty laugh, then as he turned to withdraw, "Make yourself at home—and sleep well."

Next morning, the dâk-wallah's brown leather bag carried the English mail to Fairplains, and among papers and advertisements were two or three letters for Travers, including one from Mr. Fletcher. He wrote from a nursing home in London, and gave a belated notice of the prospective arrival of the nephew of his old friend, Richard Mayne:

"I don't know the young man personally," he said, "but if he is like his uncle, he will be all right. Mayne is in the Porcupines on the West Coast, is mad keen to see some sport, and could not be in better hands than yours. His father is dead, and his mother has married again. My friend, a bachelor, is a man of large property, and I fancy your visitor will be his heir. He has a little money of his own—and they say, brains. Let him have my guns, and the brown pony, do your best for him, and don't let him flirt with Nancy. I'm not much better, and the doctors talk of having another 'go' at me. How did our ancestors live without these operations? They died, I suppose. Well, we must all go—sometime——"

The remainder of the letter was filled up with business directions, suggestions, and interrogations.

When Mayne came out of his room in the morning, he sat on the steps, and greedily devoured the delicious pearly prospect; it was similar to the one from "The Corner," but finer, and more extensive.

"Isn't it lovely?" said a clear voice, and looking round he beheld Miss Travers.

Seen by the clear and impartial light of day, her appearance was disappointing; a tall slip of a girl with deeply sunburnt face, in which was set a pair of wide-open grey eyes; and Mayne was struck by the intensely youthful expression of these eyes—that now regarded him curiously; her hair, very thick and wavy, was of a tawny red—almost the same shade as her complexion; a white linen frock emphasized a slim, rather boyish figure, and made no attempt to hide a pair of surpassingly neat ankles. Nancy's age was possibly sixteen, and to sum up her personality in one word, Mayne's hostess was neither more nor less, than a happy-looking, well-grown flapper!

"I never tire of it," she resumed; "if I am bored, or in a bad temper, I just sit here and stare—and it always soothes me."

"Are you ever in a bad temper?" inquired Mayne, who had risen, and was looking up at her.

"Don't ask *me*—ask Daddy," she answered with a gay smile, revealing a set of perfect teeth, "I'm afraid he will say it's—fiery!"

"May be your hair has something to say to it?"

"Probably! When I was a small child, it was much worse,—other girls pretended to warm their hands on my head. It has grown deeper in shade, and I have hopes, that it may yet be black."

"It will be white before that."

"How smart of you!" she exclaimed, seating herself. "How did you sleep?"

"Like an infant."

"Really? Sometimes they scream all night! 'An infant crying in the night,'" she quoted. "And so you lost your way yesterday?"

"I believe so—and only for two good Samaritans, I might be wandering still."

"You met Mr. Dawson, and Mr. Byng?"

"Yes, they were kind enough to put me up, and to lend me a guide. I say, what an oddly-matched couple to run in double harness!"

"They are; but it's so good for them; they counteract each other's failings, and get on splendidly—the same as people who marry their opposites."

"Do they? I see you know all about it!" said Mayne, now sitting down beside her, and warding off the attentions of a fine bull terrier.

"Go away, Sammy," commanded his mistress, "I'll talk to *you* by and by." Then to Mayne, "Are you trying to be sarcastic?"

"Perish the thought!"

"And I *do* know all about it—within our small circle, every married person is the exact contrast to their partner. You will soon be able to judge for yourself—as for Teddy Dawson—we are all christian names up here——"

"May I call you by yours?" asked Mayne audaciously.

"In a few days—perhaps——"

"Thank you; and you were speaking about Teddy Dawson?"

"So I was; he is so practical and hard-working, and loves coffee-planting, but is rather rough and untidy. If you had only seen 'The Corner' before Nicky arrived! The Bungalow was crammed with sacks of coffee, tins of kerosine, and packs of dogs—scarcely a chair to sit on. Ah! here is father at last!"

As Travers dismounted from a shaggy estate pony, and approached, Mayne realized that he was undeniably handsome; dark, with finely cut features, and noble bearing; the gallant air, that descends in certain families, from generation to generation.

"Too hot for the steps, Nance!" he said, laying his hand on her head, "and no topee! Away with you into the verandah." But Nancy merely lifted a slender arm to thrust back a hair-pin. "How are you, Mayne? I heard all about you this morning."

"*All*, sir? That's rather a large order; but I gather that you have had a letter from Fletcher?"

"Yes, poor old boy, I'm afraid he is in a bad way. He is anxious you should have good sport. I believe I can manage a big beat next week, and I've arranged to draw a small sholah this afternoon." (A sholah is a deep fold in the hills indicated by trees and undergrowth). "We may get a jungle sheep, or a pig."

"Anything will be a novelty to me," declared Mayne.

"I can lend you Fletcher's rifle, till your own comes up; in fact, he said you were to use his battery and——"

"But, father," interrupted the girl, "you have forgotten that this is tennis day! The Hicks, the Ffinches, and the 'Corner' boys, are coming."

"Oh, by Jove, yes! but you will be all right without us. You can tackle more than that, my little Nance." Aside to Mayne, "She manages everyone."

"Now you are thinking of Mrs. Ffinch," protested Nancy, "what excuse could I offer? You know Captain Calvert is still at 'Clouds Rest,' and with the Hicks, Andrew Meach, and the Pollards, she said we ought to make up three sets."

"To-day or to-morrow is all one to me," was Mayne's generous announcement,—for he was secretly longing to be off within the hour.

"Oh, well, Mr.—or is it Captain—Mayne?" He nodded. "I will try and arrange the tennis somehow, and let father carry you off to draw the 'Bandy' sholah."

The immediate result of such magnanimous permission, was an animated dispute; each party clamouring to yield to the other; finally it was decided, that the sportsmen were to remain at home.

"It will give you an opportunity of meeting some of our neighbours," said Travers; then turning to his daughter, "Nancy child, five minutes ago, I asked you to go in out of the sun."

"Yes, dear, but you know very well that my hair is as thick as a roof thatch, and my skull is bomb-proof."

"Ah, I'm afraid this is a day, when you don't feel very good?"

"Oh, Daddy—please——!"

"Come along," he interrupted, taking her gently under the arms, raising her to her feet, and drawing her into the verandah. Then to Mayne—who had followed them, "When this sun-worshipper was a small, and unruly mite, she obligingly prepared me for the worst, by announcing, 'Daddy, I don't feel very good to-day.'"

"Oh, that story has been told all over the hills since I was two years old!" protested Miss Nancy. "People are always quoting it. Don't you think, Captain Mayne, that it is too bad of Daddy to give me away?"

"Make your mind easy, my dear child, your old Daddy will never give you away. Now come along into the dining-room, and give us some breakfast, and let Captain Mayne sample our famous Fairplains coffee."

CHAPTER IV
THE COFFEE ESTATE

The Fairplains coffee, fully maintained its high reputation, and the accompanying food was on the same satisfactory level; fresh cream, bread and butter, apricot jam, and new-laid eggs, grilled ham and chicken—what a welcome change, from the sodden West Coast fare, to which Mayne had been accustomed. Besides the menu, he could not help being impressed by the deep mutual affection, existing between Travers and his daughter; how quietly she forestalled all his requirements, how his dark eyes softened, when they met her glance, and how the pair laughed, and chaffed, one another with light-hearted enjoyment.

Mayne cast a thought to the domestic atmosphere of his own home. What a contrast to this! There, a fashionably youthful woman of fifty, shrank from the too convincing appearance of a son of seven and twenty, and her early morning manner was particularly chilly and acidulated. Breakfast was never a convivial meal.

Lady Torquilstone, an only child and heiress, among her many suitors, had, to the disappointment of her parent, accepted handsome Derek Mayne, a mere officer,—and not even an eldest son! and accompanied him when he joined his regiment in India. As soon as the glamour of a new life, and a new world, had worn off, the lady drooped. In India, she found a dreadful spirit of equality—no nicely partitioned sets, only the sternest rule of "precedence," in short, from her point of view no "society" whatever!

Money failed to give her the prominent position she considered to be her right, she was merely Mrs. Derek Mayne, a Captain's wife, and one of the herd! Unfortunately the marriage was not a success; the heiress was discontented, and irritable, she snubbed and tyrannized over her good-natured husband,—and spent most of her time in England.

Captain Mayne died in Jubbulpore of cholera,—when his happy wife was dancing at a London ball,—and within the least conventional period, his widow married Lord Torquilstone, an elderly, but well preserved peer, and hardened man of the world; they shared the same tastes—particularly racing, and Bridge—and lived for eight months of the year in a gloomy, but imposing house in Mayfair,—where it required a combination of three men-servants, to open the hall door.

Derek Mayne Junior had never been permitted to become "an encumbrance"; school, Sandhurst, and his Uncle Richard, lifted the weight of child, boy, and man, from his mother's shrinking shoulders,—and he made only an occasional and brief appearance at his so-called "Home."

"I'm afraid you will have lots of spare time on your hands," said Travers to his guest. "This is our busy season, and I can only get off for a shoot now and then,—but Nancy will take you on, when I have an extra full day."

"What do you call a full day?"

"Well, when I start at seven, with roll call of the coolies, am out till twelve; after a rest and tiffin, I go round and see how the weeding and picking is done? then to the factory to weigh coffee, afterwards attend to office work, which sometimes carries me on till eleven o'clock at night."

"But I don't allow that *now*," said Nancy with a proprietary gesture.

"No," agreed Travers, "because this young lady wants a playfellow, and has no conception of the labour and anxieties, that belong to a coffee estate. Sometimes a planter will awake, to find what has been compared to a fall of snow,—the blossom in flower! It is a pretty sight; but for three days, he lives in a quaking agony for fear of rain—rain would spell the ruin of the whole crop. To insure a good setting of the bean or berry, we must have several days of sunshine."

"I suppose the picking is all done by hand?" said Mayne, who from his place could observe various black heads bobbing about among the coffee bushes.

"Yes, I get my labour from Mysore. I must take you down to the pulping-house, and let you see some of the process."

"I gather that coffee-planting is an uncertain business?"

"You may say so!" replied Travers. "We are liable to leaf disease, rain, and rot. However, a planter is a sanguine creature, and if he has a bad season, his cry is 'next year.'"

"Now Daddy, we won't have any more coffee till *after* dinner," announced Nancy authoritatively. "Captain Mayne has not been introduced to the best dogs. This"—pushing forward a large white bull terrier,—"is Sam. Uncle Sam, my property, and shadow."

"I say, what a splendid fellow!" exclaimed Mayne. "Come along and talk to me, Uncle. I love dogs—have you had him long?"

"Ever since he was born. Bessie, his mother, was brought from England as a puppy. She looked after me when I was small, and was so clever and wise. I am sorry to say she died before I came home,—but her son has adopted me."

"Well, Bessie lived to a ripe old age," said Travers; "she must have been thirteen—an extraordinarily intelligent, almost human creature. When the poor old lady felt that her end was approaching, she went round every one of her haunts to bid them farewell—down to 'The Corner,' up to 'Clouds Rest,' and even to the nearer sholahs and beats. Day after day she was to be seen hurrying along all by herself—a strange journey——"

"You have not talked to Togo yet," interposed Nancy, the irrepressible. "Father belongs to him, and sleeps in his room. Come here, and show yourself, my Togo! He is a shy, and eccentric person—nearly always carries a stone in his mouth—a trick inherited from his retriever ancestors."

The animal in question was a yellow and white, curly-haired, long-legged spaniel, with a jaunty tail carried high over his back, and a pair of beseeching dark eyes.

"What do you think of him?"

After a moment's hesitation Mayne replied:

"Well, I've no doubt Togo is a good sort—he reminds me of a variety of dogs I've seen!"

"Variety—you mean he is a mongrel?"

"I'd rather not commit myself. Perhaps he is a particular hill breed?"

"No, but one of the best of our pack," said his owner, "and if he seems all leg, he is really all heart. Come here, Togo,—'handsome is, that handsome does,' eh Togo?"

And Togo went over and laid his head on his master's knee, and turned a deeply reproachful gaze upon the stranger.

"I'm going down to the factory, if you'd care to come," said Travers. "I'll show you the lie of the land, and Nancy can concentrate on her tea-party."

Mayne accepted with alacrity, and in a few minutes, the two men, followed by the two dogs, were to be seen descending the hill.

"I knew a fellow of your name long ago," announced Travers; "I was one of the juniors, when he was in the sixth form at Harrow; a remarkably good-looking chap, Derek Mayne. We small fry worshipped him—he was Captain of the Eleven."

"It must have been my father; he was at Harrow, and his name was Derek Mayne—so is mine."

"Then in that case," said Travers, halting for a moment, and confronting his companion, "I am delighted to meet his son; although I lost sight of him for ages and ages, I remember your father just as well as if we had met but yesterday; such an active, cheery sort of chap, with a wonderful influence, and personality. I know he went into the Army, and died young."

"Yes, twenty-five years ago out here—cholera. I don't remember him at all—I wish I could."

"Once he came and spent a few days at Lambourne, my father's place, and I felt tremendously flattered, and proud. Everyone was taken with him, and such a cricketer! Those were the pleasant days before our grand smash. Are you an only child?"

"I am."

"What hard lines for your mother to have six thousand miles between you and her! *I* know what that means."

Mayne made no reply. He had good reason to believe, that distance was of no account, and his absence, more or less of a welcome relief.

"Yes, I know exactly how she feels," repeated good, simple-minded Travers; "when my little girl went away from me to England,—the whole world seemed changed, and dark."

His love of Nancy was the keynote of the man.

"Well, here is what we call a factory—not much like your idea of one, I'll swear,—and a bit of an eyesore into the bargain."

The factory was an ugly, solid brick building, with a flat zinc roof, and vast verandahs; in and out of which, the laden coolies swarmed like ants in an ant-heap. All seemed working at the highest pitch, and everything pointed to a big crop; here Travers was the acute, energetic and authoritative Manager; eyes and ears, hung upon his words, which happened to be in fluent Canarese.

At the appointed hour, Mayne,—whose kit had arrived,—presented himself in the drawing-room at Fairplains; looking very business-like, in his well-cut white flannels, and tennis shoes. Here host and hostess were already awaiting their guests.

The apartment was gloomy and old-fashioned—in spite of Miss Nancy's obvious attempts to work a change, with gay cushions, white curtains, and a wealth of flowers; these items entirely failed to overpower the depressing effect of a double suite of Black Bombay furniture—sofas, armchairs and tables; all heavily carved, and upholstered in shabby purple damask,—the original Fairplains furniture, brought from Bombay at vast expense, fifty years previously.

The walls were hung with a weird grey paper, covered with a pattern that recalled urns, and weeping willows; the ceiling was crossed by great beams, and the yellow keys of an aged piano, seemed to grin defiance at every innovation! Mrs. Travers and her daughter had been in turn defeated by the overhanging beams, and funereal furniture, and so the apartment of the early sixties, remained more or less deserted. Nancy generally received her friends in the verandah, or the cheerful, shabby "Den," common to her parent, and herself.

"Is not this room hideous?" she said, appealing to Mayne. "No one likes it. I think it's because when people die,—they are laid out here."

"Nancy!" protested her father, "you don't know what you are talking about! The fact is," turning to Mayne, "this room was once the glory of the old lady who first lived at Fairplains, and there was a sort of understanding that it was not to be transformed,—so here it is, as you see! We only use it on state occasions."

"Once in a blue moon," added Nancy. "The servants say it's haunted, and I believe the old lady comes here still. If any article happens to be moved, it's put back in its place, the same night—it really *is*; flowers die in a few hours, and I always feel as if this was a brooding, creepy sort of place—I don't like to be here alone after dark—I feel a sense of something terrifying in that far corner—! Dad, shall I take Captain Mayne down and show him the tennis ground? We are proud of *that*."

"All right, Nan, I'll do figurehead, and receive the company,—and pass them on to you. They will be here at any moment."

The four tennis courts had been, so to speak, scooped out of the hill, and lay open on one side to a sheer descent, enclosed with stout wire netting. A flight of steps connected the ground with the broad terrace in front of the bungalow.

"It's A1," remarked Mayne, "kunkur courts, I declare!"

"My mother had it made in the days when Daddy was rich," explained the girl, "but for years and years it was forgotten,—and overgrown with grass and brambles."

"And you restored it?"

"No indeed, Mr. Fletcher resurrected the poor old tennis ground—wasn't it good of him?"

"He plays himself, of course?"

"Oh no, he is quite old—much older than father. We have lived with him, since I came out."

"Were you long at home?"

"Eleven endless years. Daddy came over four times to see me; only for that, I believe I'd have died. Here are the Hicks!"—pointing to a party who were riding up the road in Indian file. "The stout lady on the white pony is Mrs. Hicks, or ''Icks'—she drops her aitches all over the place; once someone sent her a sheet of paper covered with them,—and she took it as a capital joke."

"Why not?" said Mayne. "After all, why make a fetish of *one* letter?"

"Yes, and some people who cling to their aitches, work the poor letter 'I' to death."

"That's rather sharp, and very true too, Miss Nancy."

"I believe I am sharp in seeing some things. Mrs. Hicks is blind as a bat, but immensely good-natured,—and so kind to animals."

"Do you call her kind to that unfortunate pony? She must weigh fourteen stone if she weighs an ounce!"

"Oh, he's a 'Shan,' and well up to weight. Anyhow, she is active—wait till you see her skipping about the tennis courts! Those two girls are her daughters, Fanny and Jessie—they keep her in great order."

"Do they indeed—but why?"

"Because of her love for bright colours, her giggling, and loud laugh, and the funny things she *will* say—before they can stop her!"

At this moment, the lady in question loomed large upon the top of the steps, and Nancy ran to meet her. A ruddy, dark-eyed matron, with a rollicking expression,—wearing a stiff white skirt, comfortable canvas shoes, and a flowing green sash.

"Well, Nance!" she called out, "'ow are you? This your friend?"—indicating Mayne with a nod.

"Yes; Captain Mayne—Mrs. Hicks."

Mayne bowed, with slightly exaggerated deference.

Mrs. Hicks nodded approvingly, and said:

"These are my two girls, Miss Fanny and Jessie—Captain Mayne," and she waved her bat towards two trim, lady-like young women. "They are first-class tennis players," she continued, "and you can't go wrong,—whichever you choose."

Mayne had not intended to make a selection, but the matter was taken out of his hands by Nancy.

"I'm playing with father; and Mrs. Hicks, I know you like to play with Andy Meach. Captain Mayne, you had better secure Jessie," and she gave him a little push.

Thus committed to a decisive move, he asked if Miss Jessie would honour him?

Her blushing acceptance was rudely cut short by her parent, who said:

"It's all very fine for you to make up sets, my good Nancy! but you know as well as I do, that as soon as our commander-in-chief arrives, she will upset the whole of our little bag of tricks, and make us play with whoever *she* chooses—and talk of an angel!"—lifting her eyes—"here comes the Honourable Mrs. Ffinch."

CHAPTER V
"FINCHIE"

The Honourable Mrs. Ffinch was a woman of forty; thin, dark, rather sallow, and not specially noticeable, until she spoke—then her face became transformed; the half-closed, greenish-grey eyes, lit up; the ugly wide mouth revealed beautiful teeth, and an enchanting smile. "Finchie" as her intimates called her, had been endowed with an attractive voice, inexhaustible vitality, and a big brain.

Even her enemies—and these were not a few—admitted her cleverness, and powers of fascination; whilst her friends deplored the lamentable fact that poor "Finchie's" great talents, had no suitable outlet within the circumscribed orbit of a planter's wife. She was gifted with the capabilities of a brilliant hostess, and could have held a *salon*, or seriously engaged in political and diplomatic affairs; having the gift of a strategic silence, wonderful success in extracting confidences, and the capacity for holding strings;—unfortunately her talents transcended her opportunities!

As the eldest girl of a well-born, but impecunious family, she had, so to speak, "taken the bush out of the gap," for her five sisters, sacrificed her Romance, and married Hector Ffinch; a prosperous tea-planter, whose stolid reserved character, found an irresistible attraction in vivacious Julia Lamerton,—who had the power of imposing her personality on all her surroundings.

After a short and undemonstrative courtship, a quiet wedding and handsome settlements, he carried off his bride to the East. India fell far beneath the lady's expectations; a vivid imagination had misled her; at "Clouds Rest" she found no gay, amusing cantonment, or gorgeous, and amazing entourage—merely a vast tea estate, a large, half-empty bungalow, and a tribe of brown retainers,—last, not least, a dull enough husband! Hector was as heavy and immovable as a block of granite; she, as mobile and restless, as a bit of quicksilver.

For a time, she secretly wept, and bitterly bewailed her fate. It was all so utterly different to what she had expected! Alas, for her plan of inviting her sisters one by one, and marrying them off with success and *éclat*! "Clouds Rest" was as hopeless (from a matrimonial point of view) as any dead-and-alive rural village.

However, she had one solid consolation—money; also, the still undimmed halo of "the bride"; so she exercised her gifts of oratory and persuasion, and pleaded most eloquently for the company of guests, for a motor, for quantities of new furniture, and a trip home,—at least once in three years. To all these requests, Hector lent a favourable ear; even his lethargic mind realized what the change of surroundings meant to a member of a large and talkative family, and any amount of lively society. The couple had now been married twelve years; and in spite of various visits to England, and many gay excursions to the plains, Julia Ffinch was beginning to weary of this comfortable exile; she could never be happy without a certain amount of excitement—excitement was as necessary to her well-being, as petrol to an engine.

She did a little racing (under the rose)—the telegraph peon's red turban looming along through the tea bushes, gave her appropriate thrills; she played Bridge for rather high stakes; but what afforded her the keenest enjoyment, was intruding into other people's lives; pulling strings, directing their affairs, and making her puppets dance right merrily! This, she considered to be a legitimate and delightful entertainment, and by dint of clever manipulation, contrived to make her immediate neighbours perform with praiseworthy success!

It was thanks to *her* offices, that a planter's wife at Tirraputty had left her home in a cloud of mystery; she had stage-managed the engagement between Blanche Meach, and a civilian; a notable match,—but then Blanche was very pretty. On the other hand, to her, was attributed the rupture of the affair between Fanny Hicks, and a young fellow in the Woods and Forests, and the dire disgrace of a German Missionary. Many and various matters in which Mrs. Ffinch had taken a part, afforded scope for interviews, letters, stormy scenes (at which she assisted), cables, telegrams, sudden entrances and exits. All of these, the clever operator of the puppet-play, most heartily enjoyed.

Mrs. Ffinch descended the steps with leisurely precision,—offering as she did so, an interesting display of brown silk stockings, and neat brown shoes.—She was immediately followed by her grey-haired, square-headed, and somewhat paunchy lord; and also a guest; a slim, well-groomed gentleman, with closely set black eyes, and a slightly vulpine nose. Some people thought Captain Calvert handsome; to others, he unpleasantly recalled a well-bred greyhound with an uncertain temper.

"Well, Nancy darling," Mrs. Ffinch began in her clear high voice, "so here we are at last! We had a smash—ran into a bullock bandy at a corner—the bandy, like the 'Coo,' got the worst of it!"

Her glance travelled to Mayne, and as her eyes rested on him, they brightened,—after the manner of a hunter who sees game afoot!

A tall, well set-up young fellow, with clear-cut features, candid dark eyes, and an air of distinction—*quite* a find!

"This is Captain Mayne," explained the hostess, "Captain Mayne—Mrs. Ffinch. He only arrived last evening," she added.

"Oh, really!" murmured the lady; then turning to address him, "I did not hear you were expected, and we always know our neighbours' affairs, as soon as they do themselves."

"*Sooner*," growled Dawson, who had joined the group, in a hideous green and yellow blazer.

"As a matter of fact," said Mayne, "I was not expected—but came."

"As an agreeable surprise, I am sure!" interrupted Mrs. Ffinch, with one of her radiant smiles. "I must hear all about it later. Nancy, if we are to finish before dark, there's not a second to lose. Do let us begin? I shall choose Captain Mayne, and you Nancy, had better take on Captain Calvert."

"Oh, but I'm booked to play with father!" she protested.

"Nonsense, child! how ridiculous you are! You and he can play all day to-morrow—*now* you must entertain your guests."

It happened precisely as predicted by Mrs. Hicks,—who made a valiant but useless attempt to retain the young man of her choice,—the Commander-in-chief took all arrangements upon herself. Mayne was secretly amused to see the tall thin figure in a panama hat, the centre of an eager and well-disciplined crowd—who presently scattered—each to their allotted post.

After winning a hardly contested set, Mrs. Ffinch retired to a seat, and called upon her partner to supply her with refreshments. At a long table in their vicinity, two white-clad servants dispensed iced drinks, and a tempting variety of cakes, and sandwiches. As Mrs. Ffinch sipped claret cup, she asked for details respecting Mayne's visit, and remarked as he concluded:

"So you fell from the skies into a crowd of strangers! Well, at any rate Laurence Travers can get you fine sport. You have come to the right shop for that!"

"Yes, but I am rather ashamed to take up his time; he is most awfully busy just now."

"That's true; he works like a horse for another man, and yet he would not put out a finger to save the estate, when it was his own. I suppose you have heard the tale?"

"Well—Dawson did say something about trouble, and absence——"

"Yes, the death of his wife broke Laurence Travers' heart, and the loss of the child nearly sent him off his head."

"He seems fairly sane now," remarked her listener.

"Yes, case of locking the stable door when the steed—or the estate—is gone. Laurence is much too emotional for a man; it was lucky for him that Fairplains was bought by Tom Fletcher, who was sent out here for his health. He is rich, entirely independent of coffee; such a good old fellow, who always looks kindly on the under dog!"

"And Travers was very much under?"

"In the depths," was the emphatic reply; "he was dragged into unknown liabilities by Doria, his manager—an absconding thief. Thanks to Tom Fletcher, he has been set on his legs again; but he only has his monthly screw—should anything happen to Laurence, that girl will be destitute."

"Well, we will hope for the best," said Mayne cheerfully. "Travers looks as active as if he were five and twenty—more than a match for young Byng," nodding towards the players. "I hope he may live long, and be always as happy as he is now!"

"Happy! that is just the word. Did you *ever* behold anything like the absolute adoration that exists between father and daughter? She is a dear child, but too elemental to be sophisticated, in spite of her eleven years at home. You see her *heart* was always out here. She is quite a unique flapper, and plays tennis like a boy. What a strong service—do look!"

Mayne looked as desired, and saw the light figure skimming about the court, and noted the remarkable contrast between her brown face and arms, and snow white linen frock; also the uncovered masses of rough reddish hair that now and then caught a gleam of gold.

"No beauty, poor darling, is she?" murmured Mrs. Ffinch.

"If she would only give her complexion a chance!"

"She won't. She is making up now for years of strict hat and glove wearing; and doesn't bother about her personal appearance; all she really cares for are—her father, and Sam the bull terrier. She is also rather devoted to *me*." A pause. "Well, Captain Mayne," and she laughed, "I'm waiting for you to say, 'I'm not surprised at *that*!'"

He coloured a little, laughed too, and said:

"Somehow I don't fancy such a compliment would go down up here."

"You are right! We are a simple, and primitive community. If you will dispose of my glass, I'll make you out a social A B C."

"All right," he agreed, as he resumed his seat.

"There is my husband, aged fifty-five, a hard-working enthusiast, who lives for coffee, and sales; sales, and coffee. Ted Dawson too—though he is a bit of a boor—is also an enthusiast, and will also be rich by the time he is fifty—unless he finds gold."

"Gold," repeated Mayne. "What—up here!"

"No, down nearer the plains—some believe there are great reefs and old workings swallowed up in the jungle. Learned people say that Herodotus wrote of how the Indians paid Darius tribute in gold; also that Malabar is *Ophir*! You know we are not far from there."

"I've just come up from the coast,—and there's no sign of gold—that I am prepared to swear."

"Dr. Hicks believes in the reefs, and he is a very shrewd little man. There you see the family. Mrs. Hicks has money; they say she was a publican's widow; he doctors us all gratis, has a son in a Bank in Madras, and the two girls, Fanny and Jessie. Jessie was extremely pretty at sixteen; then suddenly her nose began to grow! We were afraid it would never stop, but become a real proboscis—only for this feature, Jessie is a beauty. She would look lovely in a Yashmak—her eyes are so fine. Their mother is such an anxiety to those girls."

"It's usually the other way on!"

"Or rather it *was*—domestic affairs are upside down in these days. The girls cannot control their parent's free and easy manners, her love for bright colours, and dancing, and a good coarse story—a *man's* story! Do look at her now, leaping up and down like a great india-rubber ball! Isn't it depressing to watch such misdirected energy?"

After a moment's pause, she resumed: "There are two or three of the Meaches here. Their old tyrant usually keeps them at home, toiling for him, that he may gobble up all manner of delicacies, and live on the fat of this land! I'm speaking of Major Meach, who owns a large family, a small estate, and is our champion vampire; bleeds his descendants white, and terrorizes over them all, from his chair in the verandah—he always makes me think of a sick tiger."

"Your neighbours don't seem to be very attractive," remarked Mayne dryly.

"I am beginning with the least interesting—keeping some as a *bonne bouche*. Nancy, is what you see; refreshingly young, plastic, and impulsive. The Meach sisters are remarkably pretty; their poor mother is a dear martyred saint. The Pollards—those fair-haired boys and the pink girl—are nice young people, but unfortunately a good way off. Mrs. Pollard has a tongue! *she* cannot be too far! Fairplains is central and here we all meet. India provides its own amusements. How Captain Calvert is enjoying himself with Nancy! Her saucy answers delight him; he has a ridiculous fancy for very young girls, and—*parle du diable*—here he comes!"

"Hullo, Mayne," he said, mopping his face as he lounged up, "I believe we have met before—on board ship, eh?"

"Yes, the *Medina*, coming out last September."

"Fancy our forgathering on the hill top like this! Making any stay?"

"A few weeks—I've come for a shoot."

"Lucky chap! Well, I hope you'll have good sport. Can I get you anything, dear lady?" turning to Mrs. Ffinch with anxious solicitude.

"Yes, a match; I'm simply dying for a smoke."

As he bent over her, Mayne rose and relinquished his chair to Mrs. Hicks, who painfully out of breath, was clamouring for "a real big tumbler of hiced 'Ock cup."

The refreshment table was now besieged by a noisy intimate and animated crowd, making fixtures for tennis, picnics, or shoots; in short all manner of social meetings and amenities, and into the midst of them, Mrs. Ffinch glided, in order to contribute her veto, arguments, commands, or consent.

Presently the sudden Indian dusk began to fall, enshrouding the view; a cold blue haze was creeping nearer and nearer, and the congenial company prepared to disperse.

A great "Napier" car belonging to "Clouds Rest" lingered after the Hicks, Meaches, and Pollards had ridden away, and when the lamps were lighted, Mrs. Ffinch said:

"Captain Mayne, I do hope we shall often see you; when Laurence Travers is busy, come up to us. Nancy child, good-bye," embracing her with motherly affection; "I intend to steal your new friend—whenever he is bored here, send him to me," and with these words still trembling in the air, the great motor slid silently away.

"That was not very complimentary to *you*, was it?" said Mayne, turning to Nancy.

"Oh, she didn't intend it in that way," protested the girl. "She says a great deal she does not mean—so do I!" and she laughed. "There are no end of attractions at 'Clouds Rest'; a billiard table, an electric piano, the motor, and a 'mug' cook, and here we have so little to offer. No indeed—I'm *not* fishing! but when father has an extra heavy day, and you are idle, I do hope you will not worry about *us*—but just take Finchie at her word, and ride over to 'Clouds Rest.'"

CHAPTER VI
THE PANTHER'S FIRST VICTIM

The tennis party had dissolved, dinner was an agreeable memory, and Mayne with his new friends, sat out in the broad verandah, and gazed at a moon,—which, like a pale golden disc, hung midway in the dark blue sky.

The two men were smoking, Sam was circling uneasily round his unheeding mistress, when she suddenly said:

"Do tell me, Captain Mayne, what you think of Mrs. Ffinch—isn't she charming?"

"She seems to be awfully clever, and amusing, and full of go."

"Yes," said Travers, "she manages the whole community with the very best intentions. I can't help feeling a little sorry for her."

"Sorry, father!" exclaimed Nancy, "why *sorry*?"

"Well, you see, she has no children, no positive home interests; her wonderful talents and exertions, are squandered among strangers. Ffinch has made a fortune—some say *two*—and yet he won't stir. He is rooted in coffee; so poor woman, is she! If he only would take her to London, there backed up by his long purse, she would be in her natural element; an admirable organizer of important functions, bazaars, charity balls, and political receptions; dealing with affairs on a grand scale, instead of running our tuppenny-halfpenny concerns."

"But these, no doubt with success?" said Mayne.

"Well, yes, on the whole—there have been one or two lapses, but a sacrificial goat was always on the spot!"

"Father!" broke in Nancy, "how can you be so horrid? You are talking like an odious cynic. Finchie has done no end of wonderful things—patching up all the quarrels, and getting people into good posts. She is always right— if ever she wants a scapegoat—here am *I*!"

"Noble child!" Travers ejaculated, and he surveyed his daughter with laughing eyes.

"Captain Mayne," she resumed, "don't you think Captain Calvert good looking?"

"Um—no," then after a doubtful pause, "more the other thing,—since you ask me."

"Bad looking, I suppose you mean. How funny!"

"I understand," said Travers, "that Mephistophelian cast—it does appeal to women and children."

"You have got into the wrong side of your chair, Daddy. What dreadful things you are saying—talking of Finchie's scapegoats, and seeing a likeness to the old gentleman, in Captain Calvert."

"I must confess I am rather surprised to find him in this part of the world," said Mayne, "he is not a sportsman—but a Society man, who likes big functions, the theatre, and cards."

"Oh, it's pretty warm down below just now," replied Travers, "and the Ffinches do their guests uncommonly well. Calvert is a pleasant fellow, and comes over here sometimes for a game of tennis; he and Nancy are pals. Well," rising as he spoke, "to-morrow I must be up and about at five o'clock—so that you and I can shoot in the early afternoon. Nancy child, it is time for bed, and just look how Sam is yawning!"

"Why, Daddy, it's only half-past ten," she protested, but all the same she rose, and having bid Mayne good-night, and folded her father in an overpowering embrace, went away to her own room, attended by her sleepy shadow.

Time at Fairplains flew with what seemed to Mayne, amazing speed; the shooting surpassed his most sanguine expectations; his excursions to the low country had resulted in two fine tigers, and several pairs of noble horns. When Travers was unable to accompany him, Ted Dawson and Andy Meach had come to the front, and shown the stranger capital sport. Mayne found this simple life delightful; a novel perspective and atmosphere; instead of familiar barrack bugles, here he was awoke by the clanging of a gong, summoning the coolies to their labours.

With Mayne it was a case of a happy surrender to his environment; the delicious life-giving air, good wholesome food, and congenial society, all contributed to this condition. He enjoyed listening to playful family arguments and squabbles,—when weary, after a long day's tramp, he lounged at delicious ease, in a comfortable, if shabby old chair; there was generally something piquante and provoking in Nancy's conversation. He and she were now on the most friendly footing; he had given her elaborate instructions in the important art of making a tie; she mended his socks, replaced lost buttons, and had even cut his hair! Also he called her Nancy, and was a little disposed to lecture, and tease her, in big elder brother fashion.

Mayne, however, discovered that there were two distinct Nancies; one of the morning, the other of the afternoon. The earlier young lady was a serious person, with the heavy responsibility of a household upon her shoulders. From chotah hazri till mid-day, she was occupied, first with the cook—a bearded retainer, who had carried her in his arms. The two conferred with the deepest solemnity over menus, the bazaar accounts, and the contents of the store-rooms. Then she visited the poultry yard, and the garden, superintended and helped to fill and trim the lamps, and finally sat down to make or mend. Nancy was an expert with her needle, and frequently extended a kindly hand towards the rags and tatters of "The Corner"; altogether a grave, silent, industrious mistress of Fairplains.

The afternoon Nancy was her opposite; neither grave, nor silent, but an exuberantly irresponsible chattering chit, who broke into song as she went about, in a sweet rather childish voice, waltzed her reluctant parent up and down the verandah, played tennis, rode with boyish pluck and abandon, sat with dangling legs on the ends of tables, talked ridiculous nonsense to the dogs and ponies, and was rarely seen to open a book, or to write a letter.

Mayne, who had no sisters, or girl cousins, mentally adopted Nancy as something of both; but as Miss Travers, and a young lady, it never occurred to him to take her seriously.

The Fairplains guest had been hospitably entertained by all the neighbours; tennis parties at the Hicks', tiffin at "The Corner," and dinner at Clouds Rest—where he was in particular request,—a request that savoured of a command—for Mrs. Ffinch had discovered that she knew his people at home—and her invitations were both frequent, and imperious. Travers was far too busy to dine abroad, Nancy never deserted her parent, and on several occasions Mayne went alone to Clouds Rest to dine and sleep. This abode was more on the lines of an English country house; here were curtains, carpets, elegant modern furniture, and appointments; nothing shabby or ramshackle, in or about the premises, which was staffed with first-rate native servants, had a luxurious "go as you please" atmosphere, and kept late hours. Champagne and caviare, and other important importations were offered at dinner; after the best Havanas came Auction Bridge at high points.

Captain Calvert still lingered in these "Capuan" quarters. One morning, he and Mayne awaited their hostess in the verandah, where breakfast was served; she was an hour late, and Captain Calvert's sharp appetite had undoubtedly affected his temper. After one or two nasty speeches about "damned lazy women," and "rotten arrangements," his remarks became more personal, and he twitted his companion with his mad craze for shikar.

"Upon my soul, I believe you'd go anywhere, even among half-castes and natives, if they were to promise you an extra good bag."

"Perhaps I would—in fact, I'm sure I would," admitted Mayne. "By the way, apropos of natives and shooting—what about *your* shoot up North? I heard you talking to a Nawab coming out on the *Medina*, and you put in pretty strongly for an invite."

"Yes—did I?" drawled Calvert, lifting his thin black eyebrows, "I forget—I believe. I—er—wanted to have a look at the country."

"So it did not come off, eh?"

"No, as well as I remember, there was some hitch about dates. Talking of dates," he went on, with a significant glance, "are you putting in *all* your leave at Fairplains?"

"I hope so," was the bold rejoinder, "I shall be jolly sorry when it comes to my last week!"

"Ah! Well, yes, the little red-haired girl is not half bad fun,—brown as a coolie, but what delicious feet, and ankles! If she were to sit reversed, with her feet above the table—I see," catching Mayne's furious glance. "Well then, I'll give you another picture. Some day, Miss Nancy will be a handsome woman,—though she's more of a boy, and a tomboy now. She has odd flashes—that set one wondering, and I bet you, will give her husband a lot of surprises!"

"That'll do!—don't let us discuss her any further!" exclaimed Mayne impatiently.

"Hullo!" exclaimed Calvert with a loud laugh, "I apologize! Upon my soul I'd no idea——"

"There *is* no idea," interrupted Mayne. "Miss Travers and I are very good friends. She is one of the straightest and the best. So natural and simple."

"How nice for you!"

"I only wish she was my sister," persisted her champion.

"By Jove,—do you?" drawled Calvert. "Well, *I* don't!" and he expelled a cloud of smoke from his thin, well-cut nostrils. "I'm, as you see,—smoking like the Indians,—to appease hunger. Presently I shall take a reef in my belt. I say," after a pause, "look at old Ffinch riding along the hillside. *He* breakfasted hours ago! I can't imagine why he does not chuck all this? Everyone knows he is quite too grossly prosperous—and she, with her talents, and her energy, is thrown away out here."

"Yes," agreed Mayne, "she's awfully clever, and go-ahead."

"A lot of what Americans call, 'Get up and go!' about her," said Calvert. "Wonderful driving force,—and what a woman to talk! She'd make a fine figure of a Sunday in Hyde Park; or taking a hand in some big revolution. Yes"—slowly closing his eyes—"I can *see* her in the tumbril," he concluded, with morose vindictiveness.

"I say, what amazing pictures you have in your mind's eye," said Mayne—who was not imaginative, "a cinematograph isn't in it!"

"Oh, here she comes at last!" said Calvert, tossing away his cheroot, and rising, he added with his most courtly air, "Welcome, welcome, dear lady—as the sun upon a darkened world."

Immediately after breakfast, Mayne ordered the cob, and rode away in spite of Mrs. Ffinch's urgent appeals for him to remain, and "spend a nice long day." He felt that at present, he could not endure any more of Calvert's society. What a poisonous tongue,—what a shameless climber; and there was such calculation and method in his schemes. He, by his own confession, made a point of cultivating the right people—chiefly through their womenkind—and cherished well-founded hopes of a comfortable, and prominent post on someone's staff.

He insinuated that he (Mayne) was sponging on the Travers', he read the accusation in the fellow's eyes—(Calvert himself was just the sort to cheat at croquet, and sponge on old ladies).—With regard to his host, he felt blameless. Travers treated him as the son of his old school-fellow; he and Nancy made him one of themselves, and allowed him to share in their interests, jokes, and even secrets. *He* knew all about the new habit, that was on its way from England for Nancy's birthday. Here his reflections were put an end to by the sight to Fairplains plantation, the motley pack, and Nancy herself.

That same night after the household had retired, and the premises were supposed to be wrapped in sleep (though some of the servants were gambling in their go-downs) Mayne was aroused by a wild piercing scream. He jumped out of bed, and as he hurried on some clothes, saw a bare-footed white figure, lamp in hand, flash down the verandah shrieking:

"Sam! Sam! A panther has taken him! Daddy—Daddy—hurry!"

Mayne snatched his gun, and rushed out; the light was very faint, but as he ran up the path, he was aware of a choking noise, and a something large bounding along not far ahead. He followed the sound, in among the rocks and bushes, and then suddenly lost it. By this time, the whole place was swarming with men armed with sticks and lanterns, Nancy in a blue garment, and her father half dressed, heading an excited crowd. Alas! the tragic truth had to be faced—Sam was *gone*! taken from the door of his mistress's room, and carried off in his sleep, by one of those treacherous devils.

With bobbing lanterns, crashing sticks, and loud harsh shouts, the whole of the rocks were most thoroughly beaten, but without result; of dog or panther there was not a trace. After an hour's exhaustive search, Mayne returned to the bungalow—his lamp had gone out. Here in the verandah he distinguished a sobbing figure; Nancy, alone and in uncontrollable grief. Between her sobs she moaned:

"Oh, my poor darling Sam! Oh, the cruelty—oh, Daddy, what shall I do—what shall I do?" and she suddenly flung herself upon Mayne, and sobbed out in the tone of a child asking for consolation, "Daddy, Daddy, what *shall* I do?"

They were the same height, and in the dark, she had mistaken him for her father,—who was still pursuing a hopeless search among the rocks,—but the situation was not the less embarrassing,—especially as the girl clung to her supposed parent, with both arms clasped tightly round his neck, and her face buried in his coat. Suddenly she realized her mistake, and with a violent jerk, drew herself away.

"Why, you're not Daddy!" she gasped out, breathlessly, "I know by the feel of your coat. It's Captain Mayne—I've been—hugging."

"It's all right, Nancy," taking her hands in his. "Poor little girl! I'm just as sorry for you, as ever I can be, and I'll never rest, till I bring you in the skin of the brute that has killed Sam. Here is your father now," and Mayne tactfully withdrew, and abandoned the pair to their grief,—Nancy's the wildest, and most poignant, that he had ever witnessed.

The following day, Francis the butler, mysteriously imparted to Mayne the news, that Sam's collar, and one paw had been found.

"But say not one word to the Missy. We bury in dogs' graveyard; the beast is a big female with young cubs, therefore is she overbold. That dog Sam," and his black eyes looked moist, "I also loved him, too much."

CHAPTER VII
EIGHTEEN ON TUESDAY

For two days after the loss of Sam, Nancy remained inconsolable; she could neither eat nor rest, her face looked small, her tragic eyes sunken and dim; also she wept for hours,—utterly indifferent to consolation, or chocolates. "The Corner" after the day's work, ascended to sympathize, Mrs. Ffinch descended with a similar kind intention, and expressed shocked concern; but her kissing, endearments, and honeyed words, were a waste of time and breath.

"I shall never get over it, Finchie, never!" moaned the girl, "and I won't rest till the panther has been killed, and *skinned*. Daddy has offered a reward of thirty rupees,—but so far it is no use."

"Take her out riding—*make* her go," commanded Mrs. Ffinch, "she can't sit here all day nursing her grief. Try what you can do, Captain Mayne, take her up to the Meaches, Nellie has returned home, and Major Meach always amuses Nancy."

"I don't think anything would amuse her now," he answered.

"Look at Togo," burst out Nancy, "*he* knows. All yesterday he lay with his face to the wall—here in the verandah—and he has not touched a morsel since it happened. Oh, my poor Sam!" The name was almost a cry.

"If you and Togo starve yourselves, my dear, what good will that do poor Sam?" inquired the practical visitor, "I'm sure he would not like you to die too. You really must cheer up, for your father's sake. I am awfully sorry myself; as the son of our dear old Dan, Sam was a sort of nephew. We will all give him a great funeral——"

She stopped abruptly as it flashed into her mind that there were no remains. Ultimately her powers of persuasion, proved effectual, and Nancy reluctantly agreed to give her pony some exercise, and not to indulge her emotions in such frantic ungovernable native fashion. Travers was as usual busy among his coolies, and Mayne and Nancy set off alone, and rode over to the Meaches, precisely as Mrs. Ffinch had ordained.

It was a cheerful breezy trip; sometimes the road lay in hollows, winding round a valley, and between blackberry bushes, wattles, ash trees, and wild roses, recalling an English lane; or again, over grassy uplands, with a delightful breeze, driving white clouds overhead.

By and by, Nancy recovered her self-control, and her tongue,—a member that was never long mislaid.

The Meach family lived eight miles from Fairplains, on a poor worn out, and out of the way estate; Major Meach, having spent all he possessed, invested his wife's little fortune in this, so to speak "refuge," and here she and her offspring slaved and struggled, in order to provide their old man of the sea, with everything he demanded in the way of attention, and comfort.

Part of the estate was let to a native, part was worked by Andy, whilst Mrs. Meach and her three pretty daughters kept cows and poultry, and sold eggs and butter among their neighbours. Blanche, the beauty,—thanks to Mrs. Ffinch,—was satisfactorily married; Tom, the youngest son, slaved in an office, and sent all he could spare to his harassed mother who struggled to keep house, and maintain a presentable family, on one hundred rupees a month.

The Misses Meach emerged into the verandah when they heard the glad sound of voices, accompanied by the clatter of hoofs, and Gladys and Nellie joyfully hailed Nancy, who instantly in a strangled voice, claimed their sympathy for her irreparable loss.

"The dear faithful fellow!—how dreadful!" said Nellie. "I remember one time, you went home by the old road, he missed you, and came back here, and lay all night by the chair you had been sitting on."

"Bah! what's a dog!" snarled Major Meach, a preposterously fat man, who now appeared, and with a curt salute to Mayne, sank with heavy violence into a creaking wicker chair. "Lots to be had! We can give you half a dozen—greedy, good-for-nothing brutes!"

Mrs. Meach, a worn, thin woman, with remarkably red hands, and a still pretty face, who had been ordering tea, now came forward to welcome her guests. Poor lady! her life had been, and was, a tragedy. Once a beauty, she was thought to have made a fine match when she married Captain Meach of the Light Lancers,—a man with a nice fortune. The nice fortune, he squandered on himself; and poor Amy Meach, after knocking about the world from garrison town to cantonment, saving, pinching, rearing a family, and keeping up appearances, was now the drudge, and servant, of her selfish and unwieldy tyrant.

Her hope, comfort, and joy, was in her children; possibly some day, she may be in a position to sit down and be served by other people, to read a novel, or even to take a morning in bed!

Everything at Panora seemed cheap and faded,—except the fat helpless old Major, and his three pretty girls. He insisted on keeping up "his position," as he called it; the shabby, timid-looking servants, wore in their turbans, the badge of a regiment that had been only too thankful to get rid of their master!

He, who was a notorious slacker, now posed as a former martinet, and present authority, and his faithful family believed in the fable. The truth was, that but for Mrs. Meach, who was popular, and for whom everyone was sorry, he would not have been "let down," so to speak, without a nasty jar.

The Tyrant liked to fasten on Mayne,—who occasionally escorted Nancy, when she came to see her friends,—and to question him sharply on Army matters, and utter high boastings of "my old regiment—Cavalry—I never could stand being a mud-crusher!" and as he knew that Mayne was an Infantry officer, this remark was, to say the least, tactless.

When they all sat at tea, he talked with his mouth full, helped himself to hot cakes—two at a time—bragged, snubbed his family, laid down the law, and made rude personal remarks. With regard to his daughter Nellie, he said:

"We sent Nellie down to try her luck in Bangalore; but there was no market, no buyers—and here she is, back on our hands like a bad penny."

Poor Nellie blushed till there were tears in her eyes.

"I'll give her to anyone with a pound of tea—ha! ha! ha!"

"If you were *my* father, and made such rude speeches," said Nancy fiercely, "I'd be very glad to give *you* away, with a whole plantation!"

"There you go, spitfire!" he exclaimed.—He rather liked Nancy, because she boldly opposed him.—"You've been spoiled, my good girl; if your father had given you some *sound* thrashings, you would not be so cocksey—and such a bad example to other young women."

"I think," said Mayne, rising, "it is time for us to make a start," and he eyed the old bully, with a menacing stare.

"Oh, ho!" and he chuckled. "Nancy is used to me—aren't you, red poll? *You* don't mind!"

"I'll overlook the outrage this time, but as an apology, I must have Gladys and Nellie to spend the day on Monday."

"Can't be done—no ponies!"

"Then I'll borrow the Clouds Rest car."

"Will you! You've cheek enough for anything! If you can get the car, you shall have the girls, and the Missus thrown in—there's an offer for you!"

Mayne, who felt a touch of sincere pity for poor Mrs. Meach and her browbeaten daughters, experienced a sense of profound relief when the farewells were over, and he and Nancy rode away.

"Look in again soon, young fellow!" shouted Major Meach. "Nancy, tell your father to send me up a bag of his number one coffee—it can come in the car."

"I don't know about that bag of coffee," said Mayne; "but old Meach won't see *me* again."

"Isn't he a horror?"

"I'm awfully sorry for his daughters; when he told the fair one to 'shut up,' I felt inclined to shy a plate at him!"

"And he is such an ungrateful old monster! Only for the way those girls work, and go without things, there would be no cigars, no Europe hams, tinned stores, or whisky and soda. He *must* have everything he wants, or he yells, and storms like a madman. I've told him one or two plain truths about his selfishness."

"Have you? I must say you are fairly plucky."

"Nicky Byng admires Nellie, but it's no good; all the same, if I *do* get the car, I'll let him know."

"Fancy trying your hand at match-making,—a child like *you*!" and Mayne turned in his saddle, and surveyed his companion, with a broad smile.

"Of course, I know it's no use. Finchie throws buckets of cold water on the affair; she hopes to marry Nellie off, the same as Blanche Sandilands. Blanche has a splendid car, lives in a big house on the Adyar, and entertains half Madras. All the same, I think Nellie likes Nicky."

"Then why mind Mrs. Ffinch, and her cold water?"

"We all mind her; she is so far-sighted, and clever—all but Ned, he thinks her too meddlesome, and anyway, she *did* talk Jessie Hicks out of accepting him."

"Do you suppose, that Mrs. Ffinch could talk you out of accepting anyone?"

"How can you be so silly! Anyway, there will be no occasion, for I don't intend to marry."

"Bosh! Wait till you are older, and then we shall see what we shall see."

"I'm quite old enough to know my own mind."

"Not you!"

"Don't be rude. Do you know, that I shall be eighteen on Tuesday?"

"I know that you are trying to pull my leg, miss! You are not an hour over sixteen—if so much. I should put you down at fourteen if I were asked."

"Well, if you won't believe me, you can see the certificate of birth and baptism.—I was born at Fairplains."

"But, Nancy," suddenly pulling up his cob, "I've always understood you were a mere child—if you really *are* eighteen—I—I feel completely *bouleversé*; in other words, shattered; for I've been treating you as a little girl, and all the time, you are a young lady! I declare, I'm so upset, I shall tumble off the cob!"

"Don't tumble yet; stick on, and I'll explain. Daddy likes me to look a mere child, and can't endure the idea of my growing up. So I always wear simple frocks, and short skirts—it was only the other day, I put my hair up."

"Did you wear a pig-tail?"

"Yes, of course I did—it was a beauty, too."

"And I know I'd have pulled it! that's one temptation removed! Well, let me here and now apologize for my many enormities. I'm most frightfully sorry; I wish you were only sixteen."

"You may go on just as if I were. They all do."

"Thank you, Nancy. And so Mrs. Ffinch is law-maker, the local dictator, and match-maker?"

"Yes. She is immensely proud of the Meach affair; but not so proud of Fred Pollard's match. She married him off to a girl who was most unsuitable—so much so, that Fred fled to Ceylon, and the Pollards are not very good friends with Finchie! She does not wish Ted to marry Jessie Hicks; for then Nicky would have to move out of The Corner, and he might take it into his head, to run away with Nellie—and she has magnificent plans for her."

"Wheels within wheels," exclaimed Mayne. "It strikes me all the same, that these young people are not desperately in love; if they were, they'd never take all this so tamely, or so to speak, lying down."

"Well you see, they are all very busy one way or another, and have no time. When they *do* meet at tennis, Finchie mixes the sets, and sorts them out, as you saw!"

"Yes, I saw; but I must confess I did not notice the usual interesting signs of mutual attachment."

"No? What are the signs?"

"I don't know much about it, but sitting in one another's pockets, holding one another's hands, and obviously wishing us all at Jericho."

"Yes. Haven't you been in love yourself? You *must*—you are getting on!"

"Getting on, you rude child! Why, I'm only seven and twenty. As to being in love—no, never what you may call, seriously."

"Seriously?"

"That is to say unable to eat, or sleep—living solely to see *her*—or if not her—the postman, who carries her priceless letters."

"Ah, you jeer at love! Perhaps it may pay you out one day."

"Perhaps! And what about you, Nancy? Has no smart young tennis champion awakened your interest?"

She burst into a peal of laughter—her first laugh for four whole days.

"No, I've never been in love—or ever will; I haven't a tiny scrap to spare from Daddy; and here he comes to meet us—with poor lonely Togo."

"Well, Nance," he called out, "I've just fixed up a splendid treat for your birthday."

"What is it? Oh, tell me quickly—quickly!"

"We are going down to Holikul for three days for a shoot. There is a big native holiday that draws off our coolies, and I've invited the Corner boys; you shall undertake the commissariat, and play the queen of the party."

"How delightful, Daddy!" cried Nancy; then as she glanced at Mayne, "Oh, poor Captain Mayne!—your jaw has dropped four cubic inches; but I do assure you, it will be all right—when I'm out on a beat, and sit up in a machan, I'm so deadly, deadly, quiet, that you might hear a fly sneeze!"

CHAPTER VIII
THE PANTHER'S SECOND VICTIM

The expedition down to the Holikul jungle, proved a triumphant success, not only in the matter of sport, but of well-chosen and congenial company; Nancy, far from being an encumbrance, largely contributed to the comfort of the party.

The little camp was surprisingly well found; ice never failed, a tablecloth and brilliant tropical flowers, gave a touch of civilization to the alfresco meals, and after a long arduous beat among sweltering undergrowth, it was agreeable and refreshing, to sit out in the starlight, whilst Nancy and Nicky Byng sang solos and duets, the servants squatted round at a respectful distance, and Togo kept solitary ward.

Nancy proved to be well versed in forest lore. What she had picked up as a small child, when accompanying her father on various shooting expeditions, had never faded from a mind which held all impressions with tenacity. She knew the names of strange trees, and gorgeous flowering shrubs, and could relate, stirring legends and fabulous tales of the mysterious white tiger.

In her own line, Miss Travers proved as successful a hostess, as her great example at Clouds Rest, and in spite of her ingenuous girlhood,—had a way of mothering, and managing, the entire circle. There was not a spark of coquetry in her composition. She chatted to Ted and Nicky, precisely as if she were their pal and comrade, and it was evident to Mayne, that the "Corner boys," no less than Travers himself, worshipped the sole of this wood elf's small brown shoe!

Her birthday was an auspicious occasion. The house-servants, and head shikari, offered bouquets and wreaths; "The Corner" presented a tennis bat, and Mayne had surreptitiously placed a little parcel upon Nancy's plate. As she opened the blue velvet case, and beheld its contents, she gave a scream of delighted surprise.

"Oh, Daddy, how dare you? you wicked man!" she cried; "it's far too beautiful for me. I've always longed for a wristlet watch,—but never a gold one like *this*—why, it's prettier than Finchie's," and she rose to embrace him.

"Here is the wicked man," he protested, pointing to Mayne; "my present has not arrived, but I expect it is waiting for you up at Fairplains."

"Captain Mayne," she exclaimed, with dancing eyes, "how ever so much too kind of you! I declare I'd like to kiss you. May I, Daddy?" glancing at him interrogatively.

Mayne looked at him expectantly, and stood up, prepared to accept this astonishing favour.

"My dear child," said Travers, "you are eighteen to-day, and must not go thrusting your kisses on young men."

"But I never did before," she protested.

"You should keep your first kiss for someone, who may come along one day!"

"Oh, Daddy," she murmured, blushing deeply through her tan, "now you have made me feel so shy, and uncomfortable. You all know," appealing to Ted and Nicky, "that I only wanted to do something, just to show Captain Mayne, how delighted I was—and am."

"You can do that in another way, Nancy," he replied, resuming his seat. "Call me by my Christian name—the same as these fellows."

"Derek—yes—and it's much prettier than Ted, or Nicky."

"So now, Mayne," said Nicky, "you are paid off handsomely, and at *our* expense."

It was a merry, not to say noisy breakfast party; Nancy with two long white wreaths round her neck (in a third she had invested her father), the wristlet watch on her mahogany wrist, was in the wildest spirits.

"I woke this morning very early," she said; "almost before the birds, not because I was expecting presents in my stocking,—like at Christmas time, but because I was going to be eighteen, and I seemed to hear the bamboos— you all know how they whisper—murmuring to one another, 'Eighteen, eighteen, eighteen!'"

"Eighteen, will have to take to gloves and corsets," said Nicky, as he fumbled for his pipe.

"Fancy mentioning such an article in the free-as-air jungle," protested Nancy; "and anyway, my waist is only twenty inches."

"Nancy, spare us these particulars," protested her father. "One would think you were among a pack of women."

"Never mind him, Nancy," said Byng. "Tell him it's too late to start to keep you in bounds—and as for waists—Ted's is fifty."

"Daddy, I do wonder what you have got for me," she asked abruptly. "Won't you tell me?"

"I know," said Mayne; "it's awfully nice, you'll like it better than anything—and it's coming all the way from London."

"Then it must have cost a heap of money," she exclaimed. "Oh, Daddy!"

"Oh, Nancy," he echoed, "it's time we made a start; the shikaris are hanging about, so don't let us waste any more time," and he rose, and broke up the party.

Those three days in the Holikul jungles were a delightful, and flawless memory, to all concerned. How rarely can mortals say this! Sunburnt and weary, the Fairplains party returned to the shelter of a roof, and a daily delivery of letters, and parcels. The habit had arrived—moreover, it fitted.

Two evenings later, Travers and Mayne, Nancy and the head shikari, had been for a short, perfunctory beat, round the base of the hill on which the bungalow was situated. They were homeward bound, the bag, a mere peacock. Mayne and his host were a little in advance of Nancy, and last came the shikari, carrying the peacock, and Travers' gun.

"This day week," said Mayne, "I shall be on my way——"

As he was speaking, they turned an abrupt corner, and there, within forty yards, on a slab of rock, lay a sleek panther, and her two fat cubs! As she sprang erect, Mayne ran forward, and fired. But slightly wounded, she instantly leapt at him, and with such headlong ferocity, and impetus, that the weight of her body knocked him down, and sent his gun flying. Without a second's hesitation, Travers, armed with only a stick, rushed to where the savage brute was worrying her prostrate victim, and with all his might, hit her a smashing blow across the nose. Turning on him, with a furious snarl, she seized him by the forearm, but before she could do more, Tipoo ran up, and shot her through the head. She fell back, and after a few kicks, and one convulsive quiver, rolled over stone dead.

The whole scene had taken place within less than the space of two minutes. Nancy at first had stood by, a horrified, and paralysed spectator, but when the panther attacked her father,—she ran forward, and struck at it frantically, with her stick.

And now to take stock of the casualties! Mayne, thanks to a heavy shooting coat, had merely a few bruises, and scratches—nothing to speak of,—in short a miraculous escape. Travers also, had got off with a scratch on his neck, and a bite on his forearm. The latter might have been worse,—but his coat had also saved him.

"Sam's leopard—and you nearly got him!" he said to Mayne. "You fired a bit too soon, my boy."

"I believe I did—I was so keen to get the brute before she bolted,—I'm most awfully sorry."

"Oh, it's all right," replied Travers. "I'm well used to these scraps—she's a fine size."

"Never mind the panther, Dad," interposed Nancy, "but come along at once and have your arm dressed, and Captain Mayne too," and she ran on before them towards the bungalow, to collect, and prepare remedies.

Nancy had learned "First Aid," and was accustomed to doctor the household and coolies; she dressed the wounds, and scratches with prompt and skilful fingers, forbade all stimulants, and commanded her patients to rest till dinner-time. This was by no means the first time that Travers had been in a "hand to claw" combat, with a wild beast, but to Mayne, it was a novel experience, and he felt not a little shaken, and excited. It is not a pleasant sensation to have a heavy, evil-smelling wild animal, on the top of you, and murderous yellow fangs within six inches of your throat.

The following morning, the two patients described themselves as "quite fit." Travers with his arm in a sling, went about his everyday business, and Mayne commenced to make arrangements for his impending departure. That evening Travers appeared to be fatigued, his eyes were unusually bright, and Nancy's smiling face, wore an anxious expression.

"Dad, I'd like to send for Dr. Hicks, to have a look at your arm," she said, as they sat in the verandah after dinner.

"Certainly not, Nancy," he replied testily; "you have done everything that is necessary. I daresay I have brought a touch of fever from Holikul. That's all that ails me. The bite is nothing. Now look here, little girl, I won't have you worry."

As his tone was authoritative, Nancy, whatever she may have thought, said nothing further.

The next day Travers made a very early start, and did not return,—as was often the case,—in time for breakfast; and Nancy and Mayne were *tête-à-tête.*

"Father is so hardy and wiry, and so used to jungle accidents," she remarked, "he won't ever allow me to look after him properly. On Tuesday, only for him and his stick," she paused and glanced expressively at Mayne.

"Yes, by Jove! the panther would have had me! There's no doubt your father saved my life. That brute was making for my throat. I saw her yellow eyes glaring into mine, she had her claws dug into my shoulders, and, Lord, how her breath smelt! Yes, for once, I was face to face with death; and I'd be dead and buried *now*—only for that swinging stroke across her muzzle."

"The cubs made her savage," said Nancy. "Tipoo has shot them both—such well-fed, fat, little creatures. All the family skins are now being dried. Only for those cubs, the panther would never have faced you—they are such slinking, treacherous cowards."

"And only for your father, *I'd* not be sitting here."

"And how dreadful for your poor mother, if anything had happened to you! If I were to die, it would almost kill Daddy."

Mayne made no reply. Mentally, he was comparing his mother, with her father. Nancy looked as if she would still be flourishing at the end of half a century, but if anything were, as she expressed it, "to happen to her," it was quite possible, that Travers would go clean off his head.

Travers returned at tea-time; as he stumbled into the verandah, and sank exhausted into a chair, he looked completely "done."

"Ah, I see you have been down to the lower ground," said Nancy. "Now that was really *too* bad of you,—when you have a touch of fever."

As she handed him his cup she added:

"Let me feel your hand—why, it's almost red-hot!"

"My dear child, don't make a fuss," he exclaimed irritably; "I'll take a dose of quinine, and lie down till dinner-time,—will that please you?"

Nancy said no more, but shut her lips tightly, and began to prepare his special buttered toast.

"I can't touch anything," he protested, "but I've an awful thirst on," and he swallowed greedily, one after the other, two large cups of tea.

"I'm afraid I must worry you, dear Daddy, and dress your arm," she urged. "I promise I'll be as quick as I can," and she led him away to his own room. Presently she returned, and said to Mayne, who was still sitting in the verandah: "I want you to ride over at once, and ask Dr. Hicks to drop in this evening,—quite casually, of course. I simply dare not tell Daddy I've sent for him; he always pooh-poohs doctors, and illnesses, and he won't allow me to take his temperature, nor will he go to bed. His arm has a queer, livid appearance, and is terribly swollen; I must say, I cannot help feeling rather nervous."

"Oh, all right," said Mayne, rising; "I'll be off at once, and I'll bring Hicks back with me,—dead or alive."

When Mayne arrived at Panora, Dr. Hicks happened to be out, and it was nine o'clock when the two men reached Fairplains. By this time Travers, who now admitted that he was "feeling a bit out of sorts," was obviously worse.

As they rode over, Mayne had given the doctor full particulars, about the panther affair,—including the bites, and scratches.

"There may be poison in them," said Dr. Hicks; "these old panthers eat garbage, and putrid carcases, and are nasty brutes to deal with; and if septic poison sets in, Travers is rather a bad subject, and it may go hard with him. However," he added philosophically, "there is no use meeting trouble half way, and whatever happens, we must keep a cheerful face before Nancy. There's a good, single-hearted child, if ever there was one, and if by any chance, she were to lose her father—mind you, I'm not saying there *is* a chance—I don't know what would become of her!"

CHAPTER IX
"GIVE NANCY TO ME!"

Having examined his patient, Dr. Hicks came out into the verandah in order to confer with Mayne. His face was alarmingly grave, and he spoke with his eyes anxiously fixed on the communicating doors,—and in a lowered voice.

"He's pretty bad; high fever, temperature 104; his arm is frightfully swelled—it's the bite. I am sending for a nurse and vaccine, also for my wife. She's uncommonly capable, and always comes well up to scratch on these occasions, and of course, we must have some woman here to look after Nancy—in case of"—he hesitated for a second, and added—"delirium and complications."

"You don't mean to say it's as serious as all that?" cried Mayne, aghast.

"I'm afraid it is; but I'll move heaven and earth to pull Travers through. We can spare anyone, sooner than the Earl,—as we call him."

"Can't I go some message, or be of some use? For God's sake give me a job," and Mayne paused, half choked. "You see, it was through saving *me*, that Travers is like this!"

"Oh, all right," agreed the doctor briskly, "then you can ride down to Tirraputty, and send off a couple of wires. It will take you about three hours to get there,—riding hard."

"What about Mrs. Ffinch's car? I can drive a motor."

"She's away in it herself!—gone for a week's tour. She took my girl Jessie, and Nellie Meach, and left no address. 'Expect me when you see me' style. Ah, here comes Nancy!" as the girl, now looking strangely worn, and haggard, came into the verandah.

"What are you two conspiring about?" she asked, with a startled expression.

"I'm only telling Mayne a piece of news. Mrs. Ffinch is away on a motor tour."

"Oh!"—evidently relieved—"is that all?"

"Word of honour, yes," the doctor lied with emphasis.

"Won't you stay and have something?" she urged.

"Oh, well, I don't mind. Just anything at all—a bit of cold meat, and a hunch of bread.—I'll ask for a shake-down, too."

"A shake-down!" staring at him with widely-opened eyes; "then you think——" and she paused, unable to utter another syllable, or articulate her heartsick uneasiness.

"I think you're a silly girl!" he said brusquely. "You know as well as I do, that I must dress your father's arm every three hours. You'd like him to have the very best attention, my dear, wouldn't you? It isn't everyone I'd do as much for. I can tell you,—losing my dinner, and sleeping out. I'm sending Mayne here to Tirraputty to wire for a nurse."

"A nurse! Certainly not!" protested Nancy with energy. "*I* am his nurse."

"Now, my good Nancy, if you are going to be silly and obstructive, and to stand in the way of what is necessary for your father, I'd like to know what I'm to do with you?"

"But a nurse—an utter stranger!"

"Yes, a professional, clear-headed, experienced woman, who has no emotions—to counteract her work."

"Father won't have her!!" declared the girl triumphantly.

"He will, if *you* ask him," rejoined the doctor. "My dear child, I had no idea you were so set upon your own way."

"Then I am to realize that father is—in *danger*?" she demanded, with trembling lips.

"Nothing of the sort," he replied, now lying boldly and well. "You are to realize that you must be a sensible girl, and instead of fighting against remedies, and the doctor, to help him with your last breath."

Nancy gazed at him steadily, and after a moment's silence, she said:

"All right, you need not ask *me* to do my best," and she returned to the sick-room.

At eight o'clock the following morning, when, stiff and weary, Mayne dismounted from his cob, he found that a dark cloud had settled down on Fairplains. In the verandah, he discovered an anxious gathering, talking together in low voices, and in groups. Here were Ted and Nicky, Tom Pollard, young Meach—and Mrs. Hicks. They each nodded a welcome, and the lady advanced, and said:

"I came over early; he is worse. The fever is septic," she added, and her round black eyes filled with tears.

"He is sleeping all right," announced Dr. Hicks, who joined them; "so is Nancy,—I put something in her tea. She was up all night, poor child, and is thoroughly worn out. The nurse will be here about eleven,—and another doctor."

"It's too awful!" stammered Mayne, who had grown ghastly white. "Do you know, Mrs. Hicks, that by rights, I should be in Travers' place?"

"Tut, tut, tut!" she protested, giving him a push; "you go and have a bath, and some breakfast."

"Tell me," appealing to her husband, "will he get over it? Is there no chance?"

"There may be a turn at sundown, please God."

"If not——?"

"These cases last about four days—that brute's claws were so many poison-bags."

Without another word, Dr. Hicks turned away.

At noon, the nurse and specialist, arrived together, and presently there ensued grave consultations, whisperings, and ominous shaking of heads.

On account of its superior size, and in spite of Nancy's frenzied entreaties, the patient was moved into the drawing-room,—the most spacious apartment in the bungalow, with a northern aspect.

Mayne did not venture to speak to Nancy, who looked as if she scarcely recognized him, when she flitted about like a wraith between the sick-room, and verandah. Kindly, vulgar Mrs. Hicks, at whom he used to laugh, was now his support and comfort. She brought him bulletins, insisted on his taking food, and appeared to keep the whole establishment together; interviewing callers, writing chits, dispatching messengers, concocting dainties, and altogether reversing Mayne's opinion of "silly Mrs. Hicks." For her part, she was sincerely sorry for this worn, haggard-looking young man, who seemed to dread the impending tragedy, almost as much as Travers' own daughter.

Once or twice Mayne had been permitted to stand in the door of the drawing-room, and there exchange a few words with the patient. Quite late that evening, when he was disconsolately pacing the avenue, Mrs. Hicks came out, and joined him.

"How has he been since sundown?" he inquired.

"Neither better nor worse. We have sent for Mr. Brownlow, the padre; he will be here early to-morrow evening. Anyway, he'd have had to come up for the funeral."

"The funeral! Oh, good Lord!" exclaimed Mayne in a choked voice, "surely you are not thinking of *that*?"

"Now don't *you* go and break down, my dear boy," said Mrs. Hicks, thumping him on the back; "we must all keep up; while there's life there's hope, and we have to put on a bold face before Nancy. I have contrived to get her to bed. *He* sent her. May God forgive me for all the lies I've told that poor child. If this ends badly, it'll break her heart. Poor dear! I can't think whatever is to become of her? She won't have a penny of her own in the wide world,—and there's no relations to speak of."

"What—no relations?" repeated Mayne incredulously.

"None that would come forward, anyhow. Her mother was an orphan, and Travers' people broke with him; first of all, because he married a governess, and lastly, because he lost his money. However, if Nancy has no belongings, she has lots of friends up here; we will all do what we can. Well now, I see Francis—he wants me," and she hastily abandoned her companion, leaving him to meditate upon her information.

Mayne went slowly down to the tennis ground; the tennis ground, entirely secluded, was a refuge, and here he could hold a long and uninterrupted conference with himself. Considering the affair from every point of view, he soon arrived at the conclusion, that *he* was solely responsible for Nancy's future. Why should these good, kind-hearted people offer her a shelter, when he, who was accountable for a tragedy, that cost her a parent and a home, made no effort to provide for her?

During one whole hour, he did a sort of meditative "sentry go" up and down the kunkur courts. Mrs. Hicks' illuminating remarks, had presented Nancy's situation, in its true light: the girl had no relations, no income, and would be entirely dependent on the charity of her kind-hearted neighbours; and he was answerable for the fact, that she would be left homeless, and penniless. If her father had not interfered when the panther attacked him, in another second, the brute would have torn his throat out—the blow, transferred her fury to Travers. But for Travers, he would now be lying in a new grave in the garden. The least he could do, was to provide a home for Travers' daughter—though nothing could make up to her, for the one she was about to lose. Had his mother been like the usual run of mothers, Nancy could have lived with her; unfortunately there were half a dozen "buts," and Lady Torquilstone abhorred girls.

There was one alternative;—vainly he thrust this from him; but it returned again, and yet again, to confront him inflexibly. Yes, he was powerless against the malignity of events, powerless to evade the inevitable. *He must marry Nancy.* It was the only thing to do! He would thankfully have given her half his income; but, it was not to be supposed, that she would accept his money; she might look upon it as the price of blood!

He liked Nancy, she was a really good sporting sort; straight as a die, a capital pal; but as a wife—he would not know what to make of her? She would be such an unlikely and unaccountable Mrs. Mayne. She looked a mere flapper too, in spite of her eighteen years, and was occasionally capable of the most startling behaviour. He recalled the kiss she had offered him on her birthday, and her various tomboy tricks. What would the regiment think of Nancy? and what would Nancy think of the regiment?

After many pacings to and fro, his mind became definitely resolved. There are moments in the lives of individuals, when their conduct has to be decided, not by material profit, but by instinctive loyalty to what is best in their nature; and although marriage was the last step Mayne had intended to take, nevertheless he determined to adventure the great plunge! Yes, his decision was unalterably fixed, there was actual relief in the sensation. He was turning about for the fiftieth time when he noticed a figure in the moonlight beckoning to him violently from the top of the steps. It was Mrs. Hicks, who screamed out:

"So you're down there, are you? I could not find you! Been looking for you all over the place. He has been asking for you, and the doctors say you may go in, and stay a quarter of an hour."

As Mayne entered the sick-room, he noticed even within the last few hours, a grave change in Travers: a change that was the unmistakable forerunner of the last change of all. The sick man's face looked drawn, his sunken eyes extraordinarily bright and restless,—with a sort of watching expression. There was also some strange element in the room: something that seemed to be waiting—the silence was pregnant, with significance.

"My dear fellow, I'm very glad to see you," Travers began, in a thin weak voice; "come and sit down. They are making out that I am in a bad way, and won't allow anyone near me, but Nancy, poor girl. I may pull through, and I hope I shall, for her sake; she's such a child to be left all alone to battle with the world."

"Not alone," said Mayne gravely, "as long as I am to the fore. By rights I should be lying there instead of you, and if the worst——" He could not go on.

"You are very good, my boy! Although I have only known you for six weeks, I am as fond of you as of an old friend,—and indeed you seem so. I've never saved money until lately. There will be enough for Nancy's passage, and perhaps my sister may take the child; she was a spoiled beauty, and is now, to all accounts, a hard, selfish woman. She and I have not spoken for twenty years. Still Nancy is her niece—her only near relative."

"Look here, sir," interrupted Mayne, "by rights I should be in your place,—it was all my fault. I was in too great a hurry. I blundered shockingly when I aimed, so deadly keen to shoot Sam's panther; but I only enraged her, and made her charge. You knew my father, and are good enough to say, you like me. I have five hundred a year, besides my pay—give Nancy into my care. Give Nancy—to *me*!"

Travers gazed at him steadily; the sunken dark eyes were interrogative.

"As my wife, of course," he continued nervously. "I swear to you, that I'll look upon her as a sacred trust, and do all I can to make her happy. As it is, we are capital friends; I believe she likes me—and I am awfully fond of her. We really know one another far better than most people who marry—having lived here together for the last six weeks. What do you say?"

"I am a bit surprised," replied Travers at last: "although the notion of my little Nance being married seems preposterous, you have lifted a heavy load off my mind, and God bless you." He put out a burning hand, which Mayne wrung. Then he added, "But I cannot allow you to talk as if I had sacrificed myself; it was all in the day's work, the fortune of war—and—I'll be with my other Nancy before long."

"May I speak to Nancy?" asked Mayne, after a short silence, "or shall I wait?"

"No, I never was a fellow to put off things. I'll see her as soon as possible,—and look here, Derek," and he gazed up at him appealingly, "would you think I was rushing you, if I asked you to have the marriage before I go? Then she will not be left so desolate, my poor little darling. She will have her natural protector. Do you mind? I know—it may seem a bit sudden."

"No," replied Mayne firmly. "I think it will be best. I'll make arrangements at once."

"All right, then I'll have a talk to Nancy by and by, and you shall hear what she says. Of course I know there's never been any sort of flirting, or love-making between you—she's just a child! but I'd leave her with a happy mind, if I knew that my little girl was in the care of a good, honest fellow, like yourself. It will be a queer coincidence if Derek Mayne's son is to be the husband of my daughter. The parson will be here to-morrow, and may find two jobs. Ah, Nurse, all right—I'll stop! No, I've not been doing myself any harm—very much the other way. Good-night, my boy."

CHAPTER X
MARRIAGE AND DEATH

Very early the next morning when Nancy came out of her father's room, she found Mrs. Hicks already in the verandah, wrapped in a flaming kimona, and sipping a cup of tea.

"Well, dear child?" she began, then paused, and looked at her interrogatively.

"Daddy has been talking to me," she announced in a dull voice, staring at Mrs. Hicks with a curious dazed expression, "and—he—he wishes me—to marry Captain Mayne."

"Lors!" exclaimed her companion, jumping to her feet. "Whatever for?"

"Because I'm so alone in the world, and have no home!" replied the girl, as if she was repeating a lesson.

"And what does the Captain say?"

"He wishes it too."

"And what do *you* say, Ducky?"

"Oh," with a frantic gesture of her hand, "is it any matter about *me*? Don't you know, that I would kill myself, that I would be cut in little pieces, if it would give any relief to Daddy,—and I am the one *thing* that seems to trouble him."

"Well, I won't say that it isn't a wise plan!" declared Mrs. Hicks, folding her fat arms in her kimona; "the Captain is a fine young fellow, and has everyone's good word,—even Mrs. Pollard, and you know how she takes a bit out of people. But still, if you don't really fancy him, dearie, I *wouldn't*. Marriage," now sitting down, "is a big affair, not to be settled at a moment's notice, like a game of tennis. This Mayne, they say, has high and mighty relations, and I don't believe there's ever been a word of love talk between you—much less a kiss."

Nancy made a movement of fierce repudiation.

"And from something Mrs. F. dropped," resumed Mrs. Hicks, "I know she has her plans for you—as well as others."

"Don't!" cried the girl. "Don't talk of plans, and schemes—it's this very second that counts. I shall do whatever pleases Daddy—and I'm going to speak to Captain Mayne now."

"Well, maybe it's all for the best! Anyhow, it'll be a wonderful ease to your poor father. God help you, my child!"

"They wish the marriage to take place to-morrow," said Nancy, and her lips twitched visibly as she added—"when Mr. Brownlow comes."

"Well I *never!*" ejaculated Mrs. Hicks, and her round ruddy face assumed an awestruck expression, "but there's sense in that too. If it was put off, and you were to go home, things might happen. Some young men are as slippery as eels. Mind you, I'm not saying one word against Mayne; he doesn't seem that sort—his mouth has a tight look. Still, one of you might be talked out of it—like my own Jessie."

During this oration, Nancy's face had become as rigid and set as that of a waxen mask, suddenly laying her hand on Mrs. Hicks' arm, she said:

"If father dies, I don't care *what* becomes of me! I only hope and pray, I may not live long. I'll do anything he asks for now,—fancy the horror that would haunt me,—if I were to say no, to his very last wishes!"

"Nancy, child, if you could only cry, it would be such a wonderful relief to your poor heart. Lors, here is Mayne coming! Maybe you'd better take him into the Den, and talk it out face to face."

"You know all about it, Nancy," he began, when she beckoned him to follow her into the little room, where both had spent such pleasant hours.

She nodded assent. Within the last three days the girl appeared to have undergone an extraordinary change; the childish air had vanished; her face was shrunken, and drawn, all life and spontaneity had departed. She wore a long white peignoir, which gave her height and dignity, and looked years older—in short, it was another personality.

"You know I'm awfully fond of you, Nance," continued Mayne, stooping to take a cold, limp hand, "and that I'll do my very best to make you happy."

"*Happy!*" and she dashed his hand aside, "as if I could *ever* be happy again!"

"You will, by and by," he went on steadily, unmoved by her outburst; "we shall settle down; you will get used to soldiering—and this awful time will be as a bad dream."

"Never," rejoined Nancy with emphasis. "Bad dreams are forgotten. Do you imagine, that I shall ever forget *this*?" and she stared at him with a pair of tearless, glittering eyes. Then there ensued a long, expressive, and uncomfortable pause, during which Togo trotted in, and gazed at the couple. They seemed so odd,—almost like two strangers: the girl sitting by the closed piano, the man with his hands in his pockets, standing with his back to the wall. After a moment's hesitation, and bewilderment, Togo trotted out.

"Well, Nancy, what do you think?" inquired Mayne at last.

"I'll do anything father wishes—anything to make him at ease. They say," and she choked, then continued in a hard, metallic voice, "he has only two days to live."

"I wish to God it had been me instead," burst out Mayne.

"So do I," agreed Nancy, with pitiless fervour, and something wild, and hostile, looked out of her eyes as she added, "and only for Daddy, it *would* have been you."

"That is true; he gave his life for mine."

"And," said the girl, rising as she spoke, "I am to give mine to you; well, since he wishes it, you may take it!"

Without another word or glance, she turned her back upon Mayne, and departed to her post in the sick-room.

During all this time, Mrs. Hicks, as her husband had boasted, came well to the fore. Apparently accustomed to sickness, and death, she was surprisingly energetic and practical, altogether a saner, more subdued, and silent, Mrs. Hicks.

The doctor's verdict had now gone forth, and the whole establishment was figuratively clothed in sackcloth and ashes. Neighbours from far and near crowded the verandah; melancholy and dejected, these awaited bulletins, and in some cases, farewell interview with their dying friend.

Nancy never appeared among the callers,—everything remained in the hands of Dr. and Mrs. Hicks. When a visitor entered the sick-room, she noiselessly slipped away, but at other times, Travers' dog, and Travers' daughter, were his chief companions.

The grim drawing-room had been completely altered to suit its present use. Most of the hateful black furniture was piled up behind the screen! A small camp bed, a long arm-chair, and a round table occupied the middle of the apartment. On the latter, a few books, photographs, and odds and ends—Travers' poor treasures—had been hastily collected.

The sick man was not in bed, but reclined in the long chair wrapped in his dressing-gown,—with death in his face, a stout heart in his breast,—the only cheerful inmate in Fairplains. His left arm and hand were terribly swollen. With his right he had written a few lines to his sister, and to Fletcher.—Short notes enclosed and addressed by Nancy.—Also he had made his will, and given her many directions, and much advice; to all of which the girl had listened with immovable composure—knowing that to break down would be terribly distressing to her father—who, with extraordinary fortitude, now calmly awaited the end.

The following morning Mr. Brownlow arrived, and was hospitably entertained by Mrs. Hicks. To his immense surprise, the wire which summoned him, had invited him not only to visit a sick friend, but to prepare for the solemnization of a marriage, and his amazement was not lessened, when informed that Travers' little Nancy was to be the bride!

A lengthy interview with the dying man was interrupted by Mrs. Hicks, who entered the drawing-room, bearing in either hand a large vase of white lilies—a signal for the wedding ceremony. Presently Mayne appeared in his Sunday suit, prayer-book in hand, followed by Dr. Hicks, Ted Dawson, and, by special desire, Francis, a Catholic. The last to arrive was Nancy wearing a fresh white linen frock. Then the doors were closed, and after a little confidential discussion, and whispering, the ceremony commenced.

The couple about to be married, took their places before Mr. Brownlow,—who used an old prie-dieu as desk.—Nancy stood as close as possible to her father, who, at the question, "Who giveth this woman to be married to this man?" in a firm, loud voice, answered, "I do."

Accordingly "Eleanora Nancy" was married (with her mother's wedding-ring) to "Derek Danvers Mayne." The bridegroom appeared grave and anxious, the bride looked like an automaton, going through a mechanical performance, for which she had been carefully wound up.

When the Service was ended, the certificate duly signed, and witnessed, there was a celebration of the Holy Communion, and the little gathering retired.

It was an ominous fact, that as soon as she found herself alone, the first thing that the bride did, was to tear off her wedding-ring, and lock it away. It had been decided by Mayne and Travers, that the marriage was to be kept secret, at least until after the funeral, and everything went on precisely as if it had not taken place.

With regard to the funeral, the presence of Mr. Brownlow awaiting the occasion for his services, seemed to Nancy, Mayne, and others, a most hideous and heartrending necessity: Laurence Travers was still in the land of the living, and here was his friend Brownlow, waiting on at Fairplains,— as all the world was aware,—in order to read the funeral service over his dead body!

Nancy and Mayne encountered one another in the sick-room and at meals,—for Mrs. Hicks was inflexible with regard to food. She scolded vigorously, in a subdued voice, when the girl refused to eat; demanding to know, what was the good of her starving herself, and of being laid up, and no use to anyone?

Nancy rarely opened her lips, the dread of her impending bereavement was beyond words. She had lost much of her deep tan colour, and looked pinched, and haggard; it was a young face, aged and racked with torture, yet so far, she had not shed one single tear. On the contrary, her eyes had a fixed glassy stare, like those of a wax doll.

"Feed her up, and keep her going!" was Dr. Hicks' counsel to the newly-wed bridegroom. "The girl is so unnaturally restrained, that I'm afraid of some sort of a bad collapse."

But whenever Mayne urged Nancy to rest, or to spare herself, he was met with an impatient shrug, or a brusque refusal; and realized the uncomfortable fact, that she rarely spoke to, or looked at him, of her own accord; but naturally every precious moment was devoted to her dying father.

Travers' slight recovery on the day of the wedding was followed that night by a grave relapse, turning to delirium, finally coma; and the following day, he passed away at sunset. The prayers for the dying offered by Mr. Brownlow were almost drowned in the clanging of the coolies' gong. Their task for the day was over—and Travers' life's work ended at the same hour.

That night the bungalow itself was silent as a tomb, but the peaceful repose was broken by the weird death wail in the go-downs and coolies' quarters.

The funeral was immense. People from great distances, hills and plains alike, flocked to pay the last tribute to an old friend.—Laurence Travers had been in Coffee for twenty-five years.

Among the most prominent mourners were Mr. and Mrs. Ffinch; she had only returned home that morning, and was shocked by the news which assailed her, almost before she had set foot in her house. Having been beyond the reach of letters, this was the first that she had heard, even of Travers' illness: and the sudden announcement of his death, was a stunning blow. Although tired, and inclined to be hysterical, she pulled herself together with a great effort in order to accompany her husband to Fairplains.

During the Burial Service many of the women wept. Nancy never shed a tear, but stood by the grave-side like a graven image in white stone. Afterwards, she fled away to her room, where she locked herself in; refusing admittance to all,—even deaf to the beseeching of her own dearest, and broken-hearted, "Finchie."

Truly these were really miserable days for Derek Mayne! who weighed down by the loss of a good friend, and his own share in the tragedy, had now added to his trouble, a wife who undoubtedly *hated* him! He read this fact in her dull, but still expressive eyes. She avoided him pointedly; even at the funeral, she had moved from his side in order to stand by Mrs. Ffinch; and once, when he had made an attempt to offer consolation and a caress, she had looked at him so fiercely; almost as if she could have struck him! Of course the miserable child was nearly off her head—and no wonder; but this was not an encouraging beginning for a life-long partnership!

His leave would be up in three days, and what then? The estate must be taken in hand at once: Ted and Nicky were working it at present, like the good fellows that they were, but a capable manager who could live on the spot, was in this, the busiest season, absolutely essential.

In the East, events march with amazing speed; as one man falls, another fills his place—and so the world rolls on. Almost everything at Fairplains, except such matters as books, guns, a few pieces of old china and silver, belonged, as Travers had once expressed it, "lock, stock and barrel" to Tom Fletcher; so the personal estate was easily wound up. The assets were small; but on the other hand—there were no debts.

Dr. Hicks had taken his departure, but his good, capable wife still remained in charge of Nancy, and the household. Mayne and she dined *tête-à-tête*; and somehow in her brusque matter-of-fact way, she cheered him: she talked of Nancy as "a darling; a girl with a heart of gold, who, when she had found her breath again, after such a terrible experience, would make him the best of wives, and was fit for any society."

"You only saw the jungle side," she explained, "but I can tell you, that Miss Nancy is accomplished; she can play the piano, and sing and dance as well as the best of your tip-toppers; she didn't waste her time at school, you bet! She cost Laurence Travers about two hundred a year, he never spared any expense upon his girl—we all know that."

When Mrs. Hicks had withdrawn—she was an early to bed lady—Mayne wandered about alone in the bright moonlight, thinking sorrowfully of the dead man.

Was it but a week ago, when they two, discussing a question of European politics, had paced this very path, and since then, his companion had set out for the undiscovered country? It seemed incredible.

By and by he went and stood by the newly made grave; something was lying across it, crushing all the beautiful wreaths and flowers. What was it? On nearer inspection it proved to be Togo; who recognized his disturber with a threatening growl.

From the grave Mayne returned to the bungalow, and sat for a long time alone in the empty verandah—what a change was here! The merry voices, and the laughing that filled it a week ago, already belonged to the past; every door stood wide, and a chill death-like stillness pervaded the premises. Even in the servants' quarters—what a singular absence of sound!

All at once a wholly inexplicable impulse impelled Mayne to enter the room where Travers had breathed his last; the corners looked mysteriously, and forbiddingly dark; but in the centre, where the moonlight streamed,—it was as light as day. The little iron cot had been neatly made up, in the long chair—Mayne started, the moon discovered a prone figure—Nancy! with her head buried among the cushions; and something in the absolute abandonment of her limp and lifeless attitude, brought to his mind the picture of a dead white bird.

He stole away, noiseless as a shadow, with these two scenes indelibly fixed upon his memory; Togo, keeping watch and ward over the grave, Nancy prostrate in the death chamber. Surely few men had ever awakened such profound grief, as Laurence Travers.

CHAPTER XI
MRS. FFINCH INTERVENES

The Honourable Mrs. Ffinch was not merely the happy possessor of an energetic mind, but of an elastic physique. As soon as she had recovered from the shock of Travers' death, heart and soul she set about arranging his affairs—naturally beginning with his orphan daughter!

Accordingly the afternoon after the funeral, the Clouds Rest car once more glided up to Fairplains. On this occasion the visitor was immediately admitted to see Nancy; who thanks to Mrs. Hicks' almost violent insistence, had rested and eaten a mid-day meal. The white and tearless girl submitted very patiently to her friend's caresses and condolence. At last Mrs. Ffinch released her, and sat down,—still holding her hand, as if she feared her escape,—began to talk to her most seriously.

"Well, my dear child, I've settled everything! your room at Clouds Rest is ready, the Dirzee is waiting to fit your mourning, and I have come to fetch you away,—for I don't intend to leave you another day with Mrs. Hicks."

"She has been so very, very kind," murmured Nancy, "I don't know what I should have done without her."

The visitor dismissed this statement, with an impatient gesture, as she resumed:

"And there's Captain Mayne! What is *he* waiting for?"

"I suppose he is waiting for *me*," was the unexpected reply.

Mrs. Ffinch's large thin-lipped mouth opened, but no words came forth, she merely gaped upon her young friend.

"We were married on Friday," calmly announced the bride.

"You were—*what*?" cried Mrs. Ffinch, hastily rising and towering over the speaker.

"Married—married in the drawing-room here. Father wished it."

"And *you*?" demanded her breathless inquisitor.

"Oh no."

Here, within a few hours, was the second shock which Mrs. Ffinch had sustained. To return to a hum-drum neighbourhood, after merely a week's absence, and to find awaiting her, not only a sudden death, but a sudden, amazing, and crazy marriage! Her head felt swimming; yet such was the lady's ruling passion and ardour for managing, that even this unparalleled situation, presented its compensations! With admirable persistence and patience, she succeeded in dragging some facts from her half-stunned and apathetic companion; and when all was made clear, she said:

"Fancy! of all people in the world—you and Derek Mayne! Such a hopelessly unsuitable couple to be chained together for life! *What* have you in common?"

Nancy shook her head. She was not in a frame of mind to furnish either reasons, or arguments.

"Nothing whatever," resumed Mrs. Ffinch, answering her own question. "Certainly not sport—you merely went shooting, so as to be with your Daddy: you know you hate killing things; you and Mayne agreed to sacrifice yourselves, just to give that poor fellow an easy mind. My dear, have you thought of the future?"

Nancy made no reply, her eyes were fastened on the corner of the room. Undoubtedly her thoughts were miles away from her companion.

"Has Captain Mayne any plans? Come, come, Nancy, don't look so dull, and dazed."

"I don't know."

"Don't know," repeated her friend, in a tone of exasperation. "My dear good child, do try and rouse yourself, and think."

"I think," said the girl, speaking very deliberately and as if talking was an immense effort, "that he is going away the day after to-morrow."

"And you too?"

"I suppose so," assented the bride, in a tone of stolid indifference.

"Good heavens—you 'suppose,' and you 'don't know.' Have you talked it over together?"

"No," was the whispered reply.

Mrs. Ffinch threw up her shapely hands with a gesture of despair.

"This private marriage has taken place simply because your father saved your husband's life."

"Don't call him my husband!" burst out Nancy, with a lightning flash of her former self.

"Well, dear, I won't, if you don't like it. Your poor Daddy has left you alone—and from what I hear—almost penniless."

These were hard words, and facts; but the Honourable Julia Ffinch never flinched from the plainest of plain-speaking.

"And Mayne naturally feels bound in honour to provide for you."

An expressive silence followed this bald statement.

"Dear me, how you do stare, child! You know, I'm fond of you, Nancy, darling, and I'm most frightfully upset about all this terrible trouble; but just at the moment, I want to put my own feelings *entirely* aside, and try and act for your benefit. I had no idea, that we were in the least likely to lose you, or that you were on the brink of such an *awful* leap in the dark. There's no time to be lost; now is the moment for action. I shall go and have a good square talk with Captain Mayne. I see him wandering about outside, looking for all the world as if he were a lost dog."

As Mrs. Ffinch stepped down from the verandah to accost him, her first words were:

"So you and Nancy are married!"

"Yes," he replied. "Don't you approve?"

"I am simply horrified," she answered, with deliberate emphasis. "Yes, I *am*."

"But why?" he asked. "It was quite a sound thing to do."

"Only for the circumstances of the case, neither of you would ever have dreamt of such a mad proceeding. Come, would you—honour bright?"

"Well, I don't suppose we should," he admitted reluctantly.

"Now look here, Captain Mayne," turning to pace beside him. "I must speak my mind. You don't care a pin for one another. Nancy is a mere child of freedom, a child still in many ways, and totally inexperienced; you spend your life in military harness. What will become of her as a regimental lady?"

Mayne coloured, and gave a short uneasy laugh.

"Oh, she'll be all right, I daresay."

"Why, only the other day you solemnly assured me, that you wouldn't marry for years—if ever. I remember you quoted Kipling, 'He travels fastest, who travels alone.'"

"That's true," he admitted, "but unexpected things happen. One never can tell. I daresay Nancy and I will worry along as well as other people."

"What a nice, cheerful way of looking at it," exclaimed Mrs. Ffinch.

"Well, of course we have made an awkward sort of start; and at present Nancy, who used to be my best friend, cannot endure me in her sight. I shall let her have everything her own way—anyhow for a time—for I can thoroughly understand her feelings. Only for *me*, her father might be here talking to you at this moment. However, I intend to do my big best. Perhaps once Nancy has left these surroundings, she may not take things so desperately hard. Our Colonel's wife is a rare good sort, and will mother her; and I'll bring along the old ayah, the pony, and the dog, so that she won't feel altogether too strange. I must go down the day after to-morrow; and there are lots of things to settle up before that."

"You will come over, and say good-bye to us, won't you? Hector would like to see you, to talk business. He is arranging for a temporary manager until he hears from Mr. Fletcher. He sent him a cable yesterday."

After a little conversation respecting the new manager, and the winding-up of the household, Mrs. Ffinch returned to Nancy, whom she found precisely as she had left her, sitting with clasped hands, and downcast eyes, staring hard at the floor.

"Come, come, my dear!" she protested briskly, "try and put away your grief for a few minutes, and listen to me,—for I'm going to talk to you, for your life-long good."

Nancy raised herself with an effort, and gazed at her adviser with a pair of large, lack-lustre, eyes.

"Nancy, I have come to the conclusion, that you and Captain Mayne can never be happy together. He is not one bit in love—I suppose you realize *that*. He married you simply to fulfil what he considered a duty,—the payment of an enormous debt! He belongs to a totally different class—County people. I know his uncle—and I know his mother—an odious, overbearing, cat! A super cat! I daresay you are just as well born, but you will find that between you, and his people, a great gulf is fixed. They will forget the true reason for the match, and declare that he has been 'run in.' He has assured me more than once that he had no intention of marrying; and is excessively anxious to get on in his profession. I remember him saying that his sword was is helpmate, and I know from my own experience, that an officer hampered by a wife with no fortune, no helpful connections, is *too* heavily weighted."

"Then what do you advise me to do?" murmured Nancy, almost inaudibly.

"Remain with me at Clouds Rest, and let him return to Cananore alone. Leave details to *me*; I can arrange everything,—I shall love doing it! Scarcely a soul knows of the ceremony, and we shall keep it dark. When once you are comfortably established with us, you shall write to Captain Mayne, and tell him that he is absolutely released."

"But will it not be breaking a promise to father?" and Nancy rose out of her chair, and stood before her adviser, a limp, and dejected figure—an almost unrecognizable Nancy!

"No, my dearest child; you know, as well as I do, that your Daddy's sole idea was for your *happiness*. This scrambled up 'shilling shocker' affair would be for your *misery*."

Mrs. Ffinch waxed eloquent. She warmed with her subject; excitement, and enthusiasm carried to her feet, and she stalked about the room, declaiming with both hands. On more than one occasion, she had made a marriage; here was a notable opportunity to break one! This idea, to do her justice, was not the sole cause of her energetic intervention. Nancy, more dead than alive, had apparently no interest in her future; and was willing to drift wherever a miserable fate would take her; but Julia Ffinch was not the woman to suffer a favourite puppet to be lost to her in such a fashion! Nancy should have another chance, recover her health, and spirits at Clouds Rest—and let Captain Mayne go his own way.

Mrs. Ffinch had mapped out Nancy's future with a bewildering thoroughness, and continued her exposition, and arguments with unabated zeal. As for Captain Mayne, he would thankfully snatch at such a chance of liberty; for never had she seen a young man so alarmingly altered, and depressed.

"If you and Captain Mayne stick to one another, it will be," she announced, "a deplorable calamity for both,—and his professional ruin. If either of you were in love, of course I would not say a word; but this is really *too* cold-blooded! Mayne married you to pay the price for his life—you married him—because your father was naturally anxious to see you provided for; there is the whole affair in a nutshell," extending two expressive hands, "and in my opinion, the kernel is rotten!

"If I had been at home, this preposterous ceremony would never have taken place. Thank goodness, it can be hushed up, and smothered here— among the coffee bushes. Should it ever try to come to life, the marriage must be annulled. As far as witnesses are concerned, there will be *no* difficulty. Doctor and Mrs. Hicks won't talk; and Mr. Brownlow is about to settle in Tasmania. You will come and live with me, and be my daughter," then with a cautious afterthought, "at any rate for the present. As for Captain Mayne, he will rejoin his regiment, and there won't be a whisper! He is coming over to-morrow to Clouds Rest. I'll have a serious interview with him, and tell him that he must really leave you with *me*. I know he will jump at the offer, and be only too thankful to go off alone. Then as soon as he has cleared out, you and I will put our heads together, and write him such a clear, decisive letter, and put the matter so effectively, that he will withdraw all claim."

Here Mrs. Ffinch paused, a little out of breath from this long oration, and surveyed her companion judicially.

"Now what do you say, Nancy? Take your choice? Will you come to *me*?—or go to *him*?"

"I hate him!" was the startling rejoinder.

"Ah, so I see you've made up your mind! Then the day after to-morrow, I'll fetch you; I shall tell your ayah to put your things together. I've given you the big room—so that you can have all your own particular belongings round you—and I've ordered lots of mourning paper. Well now, good-bye my own darling, don't think *too* much; don't let Mrs. Hicks worry you, and don't see more of *him* than you can help," and she nodded her head expressively.

Then Mrs. Ffinch went forth, and was ceremoniously conducted to her car by Captain Mayne, who, as he walked beside her, dropping a casual "yes" or "no," little dreamt of the scheme that was maturing in his companion's ever active brain.

CHAPTER XII
"EXIT NANCY"

It was after sundown, when Nancy's eloquent visitor had taken a prolonged farewell, and a reluctant departure. She was immediately succeeded by Mrs. Hicks, charged with cheerful talk, anxious interrogations and an enticing description of the forthcoming dinner; nevertheless, the girl declared that she felt dead tired, and would rather not appear, but have something sent in to her on a tray.

As soon as the servants' voices, and the clatter of plates, assured her that the meal was in active progress, Nancy slipped out, and stole down to the tennis ground, in order to breathe a little fresh air, and secure an uninterrupted think. The tennis ground was the most secluded resort about the premises,—being sunken in the hillside, and invisible from the bungalow. It was a pregnant coincidence, that the recently married couple had each sought the same sanctuary!

Nancy paced slowly to and fro; the agony of apprehension, and the tension of a desperate hope, had come to an end. She was turning over in her mind the various statements that Mrs. Ffinch had so frankly disclosed. One or two stark-naked facts boldly presented themselves. Fact number one: Captain Mayne had married her for no other reason, than to discharge a debt, and to give her his protection, and a home. This plain and odious truth, was unbearable. Once upon a time—indeed only a week ago—she had liked Captain Mayne so much; but now her feelings had undergone a sharp change, and all she felt for him, was shuddering aversion. Yesterday, when he had put his hand on her shoulder, she had felt inclined to scream! It was undeniable—proclaimed another stout fact—that she had assented to the marriage; but if it was ruinous to Captain Mayne, abhorrent to herself, and unfair to them both,—*why* hold to it?

Another glaring truth revealed, that she was absolutely homeless—unless she followed her fate to Cananore, or accepted what was neither more nor less than Mrs. Ffinch's charity! Surely there must be a third alternative? For the last eighteen months, she had held the purse-strings, and saved her Daddy many rupees, and after the servants' wages and other expenses were settled, there remained sufficient money to pay her passage home, and leave a margin of about twenty pounds.

She would go straight to her old school at Eastbourne: Mrs. Beccles—who had always been her friend—would no doubt allow her to remain there for a week or two, and assist her to find a situation as companion, or governess. She was determined not to be carried off to Clouds Rest; there, to become a pensioner, and non-paying guest. She was really fond of Finchie, who was immensely kind, and generous; but Finchie had more than once openly lamented, that "she so soon got tired of people!" What if she grew tired of her? As Nancy cast her thoughts back, she recalled the reigns of Blanche Meach; of Nicky Byng; of Jessie; and there was no denying the fact that at the moment, she herself was the official favourite. Even if she went to Clouds Rest for a few weeks,—it would be only to prolong the present agony, and defer a crisis.

To remain in the neighbourhood of Fairplains, where she and her father had been so supremely happy; with strangers occupying their rooms, riding their ponies, playing on this very tennis ground,—no, never! And then all the talk and commiseration, although so kindly meant, would drive her crazy! There was a loop-hole of escape overlooked by Mrs. Ffinch. She would go down to her old nurse, Jane Simpson, at Coimbatore, and start to-morrow night, leaving two letters, one for Captain Mayne, and one for Finchie. Finchie would be furious; she could almost see her face, after she had read and digested her leave-taking epistle! But, after all, she must live her own life, such as it was; and go her own way. What she did, or where she went, was of little matter to anyone. Nurse Jane would not worry her with plans, and questions—she understood; she always did; and later on, when she felt stronger, not so queer, and dazed, and the monsoon was over, she would go home—that is to say, to England.

As Nancy made up her mind to this plan, she beheld Togo coming slowly down the steps, and looking about cautiously. Catching sight of the object of his quest, he flew to her side.

"So you were afraid we were *all* gone, dear, were you?" and she lifted him,—a heavy armful,—sat down, and placed him on the bench beside her. Togo endeavoured to make frantic demonstrations of affection,—but was firmly restrained. His mistress held him fast with her arm round his neck, and there the two sat, and gazed on the moon-flooded plains,—an exquisite scene in silver. It all looked so still, so calm, and in a word, so heavenly. "Oh, Togo," she murmured. "The world is the same, but everything in it, is changed for you—and me."

Suddenly something in Nancy's throat seemed to give way, and she buried her face in Togo's woolly neck; the ice had melted, and for the first time, she wept,—but not for long. In a surprisingly short time, she choked back her sobs—and with a supreme effort recovered her composure, restrained her streaming tears, as she had done Togo's caresses,—and administering a kiss in the middle of his forehead, rose and returned to the bungalow,—stealing into her own quarters almost like a thief.

Manœuvring among the shadows, she had caught a glimpse of Mrs. Hicks and Captain Mayne smoking together on the verandah. What good friends they seemed to be! In her room she found awaiting her, a dainty little meal (now cold), and offered it to Togo. As a rule the dog had a healthy and unfastidious appetite, but to-night, he merely sniffed at the plate, and turned sorrowfully away. To avoid a scene of recrimination, and remonstrance, Nancy gulped down some cold soup, and ordered the ayah to remove the tray, "quick, quick, quick," and when Mrs. Hicks had gone to bed, to send Francis to speak to her.

Sounds in the still hill regions carry far, and the Clouds Rest "gurra" would be heard striking ten faint strokes, when Francis appeared in the doorway. Salaaming with grave dignity, he awaited Nancy's commands.

"Francis," she said, "you have known me as a baba, and have always been good to me."

"No, no," he protested, "Missy good to me."

"Yes, you have," she contradicted flatly, "and you know it, Francis— and I want you to help me now."

"Whatever the Missy says, that I do," and once more he salaamed with both hands.

"Well, I want you to do a good deal! You know that I was married by the Padre Sahib, because my father wished it, and I was thankful to please him, but it is not a good marriage; and I do not intend to leave here with the Captain Sahib on Wednesday, but will go down to Nurse Jane at Coimbatore instead—and you must manage it."

"Nurse Jane, Missy," he repeated, "but for why? That very, awfully foolish business. The Captain Sahib very nice gentleman. Master like him,— everyone too much like him."

"And I," pointing to herself, "do *not* like him! Francis, can you understand?" and she gazed at him steadily.

Francis made no answer, but looked down, and gravely contemplated his flexible brown toes.

"Listen to me," she continued, "to-morrow night, I am leaving Fairplains; you will get a bandy, and coolies, for the luggage, and the ayah; also I am taking Togo. If I return to England, he shall be in your keeping. At present, he and I, comfort one another. I will ride the grey pony down the ghât, and Tumbie syce can attend, and bring him back. Later, all my belongings are to be sent to Coimbatore. Do you bring them yourself. I shall have much to say to you—to-night it hurts me to talk."

"May I speak one word, Missy? Now you are married to this gentleman Captain,—suppose you run away, he making plenty bobbery; he not swearing or calling names, that gentleman I know. All the same, I think he is strong,—and there will be much trouble."

"It will be all right, Francis; you need not be afraid. I shall give you a letter for him, and he will be *glad* to let me go,—and never see me again."

Francis made a noise like "tch, tch, tch." "Oh, Missy, already have we got too much sorrow—will you thrust more upon us—and yourself——?"

"More—sorrow—we could not have," declared his reckless young mistress. "Now for my plans," she continued.

"I want you to send a coolie with a telegram to prepare Nurse Jane. I shall remain in this room to-morrow; sick—and I *am* sick—and I wish I was dead! At night, when all is still, I intend to ride away down to the railway station. Francis, it is for you to make all the bandobast. I know you will help me. Good-night," and he was dismissed.

By the first streak of dawn, the next morning, Nancy crept out to visit, for the last time, the newest grave. She was so early that no one beheld her, but the birds, and Togo.

During the long hours when Mrs. Hicks was busily engaged in counting glass, china, and cooking pots (for the inventory), or reposing on her beloved bed, Nancy and her ayah were occupied in making final, but secret arrangements. When these were completed, Nancy sat down and wrote two letters. The first was to Mrs. Ffinch,—and began:

Dear kind Finchie,

This is to say, that I am going my own way. Please do not be vexed. You will hear of me at my nurse's in Coimbatore. I feel somehow that I want her, as when I was a small kid, and had had a bad fall; later, I hope to go to England; for much as I adore the hills, I cannot endure them just now. Give my love to all my friends, and please *do* understand, that I am most grateful to you for your kind offer, to have me with you at Clouds Rest,—and forgive,

Your loving,
Nancy.

Having completed and addressed this, she sat for a long time with a sheet of note-paper before her, resting her head upon her hand, nibbling the penholder, and making up her mind how to frame a letter to Captain Mayne. At last she began, and wrote—rapidly, almost without a pause:

Dear Captain Mayne,

Before you read this, I shall have left Fairplains. I have been thinking hard the last two days, and am quite sure, that it is best for us to part *now*,—and never to meet again. Let us forget the dreadful ceremony of last Friday. You know, that we agreed to it, only to satisfy my dear father,—at least that was *my* intention,—so that he might be at ease in his mind, before he left me. On this point, our aim was accomplished; and there let the matter *end*. I feel certain, that you have no true wish, that I should live with you—'until death us do part.' Far from it. I am just a little hill girl, and not the least one of your sort. For my own part, the mere sight of you brings before me that horrible struggle with the panther, when Daddy interposed, and saved you. I *know* you are honourable, and a man of your word, and wish to give me— as payment—a home and your name; but I cannot accept one or other, for—to be honest—I shall *never* like you again, and if I were forced to live with you, I should loathe you.

It seems dreadful to write this down in black and white, but it is the truth; and surely the truth is best? I am so absolutely miserable that I wish I was dead: I could easily kill myself with an overdose of chlorodyne—we keep a large store on account of the coolies—and I would be buried in the garden beside *them*, and be no further trouble to anyone; but Daddy always said, 'Suicide was a coward's act,' and I shall struggle on somehow. Mrs. Ffinch, who, as you know, is immensely clever, had a long talk with me yesterday. She pointed out that you and I were entirely unsuited; that apart from the circumstances, we would have been almost the last people in the world to think of marrying one another; that you had told her the idea of marriage had never entered your mind, and it would be the *ruin* of your career. This can easily be prevented. No one, except the Hicks and Teddy Dawson, knows of the ceremony. The parson is about to settle in Tasmania;—they will *all* be dumb. Here in India, people so frequently separate, scatter, and forget that they had ever met. I shall do my utmost to forget you, and I hope you will let me drop out of your thoughts as completely as if you had never seen me; and should we meet—which I trust is unlikely—let it be as strangers. Do not be at all concerned about my future. I have sufficient money to pay for my passage, I have friends at home, and if the worst come to the worst, I can be a lady's help, or governess. At any rate, I shall be independent. I hope you will not think, that in taking this step, I am also breaking my promise to father. You know, that his *one* idea, as he lay dying, was for my happiness; and I shall be far happier—if I ever can be happy again—to feel, that I am free—also that you are free. I believe, that if I had followed my first intention of keeping to the letter of our contract, and accompanied you down to Cananore, we should have been the two most miserable people in the whole world.

Believe me,
Yours faithfully,
Nancy Travers.

This was a much longer and fuller epistle than Nancy had intended to send; but she was determined to make everything absolutely plain. Possibly it was a stupid letter, and no doubt she had repeated herself several times; also it was brusque, and rude. It might make Captain Mayne dislike her extremely. In that case; so much the *better*! If Mrs. Ffinch had written such a letter, how well it would have been expressed; how beautifully she would have taken off the raw edges, and made it almost a pleasure to read! Well, there it was; she would not look at it again, in case she might alter something, so she thrust it into an envelope, sealed it, and laid it beside her other despatch.

Mrs. Hicks was only too sympathetic with Nancy's severe headache. She paid several visits, imparting remedies, and outside intelligence. Captain Mayne had not yet returned from his round of farewell calls, but all his baggage had been packed by his "boy," everything was ready for a start the next afternoon, and he had ordered up a pair-horse tonga, for the use of the ayah, and herself.

"I shall remain here to see you off, Nancy, my dear," she announced, "and I've got hold of an old shoe that I intend to throw after you!"

"Dear Mrs. Hicks, you are always so kind," said the girl, "and I'll never forget what you have been to me, during this last awful week."

Afterwards Mrs. Hicks remembered, that in Nancy's kiss there was something soft and lingering—something in the nature of a farewell.

Nancy, having taken an emotional leave of Francis, handed him two letters to be immediately delivered, and prepared to depart at twelve o'clock that night. Under the auspices of a high full moon, she rode away from Fairplains, accompanied by Togo, and followed by her syce. The domestic servants were aware of her impending departure,—for is not everything known in the cookhouse, and go-down? When she came up the drive, they were all, so to speak, paraded—standing in one long line, to see the last of their little Missy. As she passed, she nodded to each individually, and when she had reached the corner, where the private track joined the great cart road, turned in her saddle, to look back on her home, and to wave a valediction to the crowd.

CHAPTER XIII
IN BLACK AND WHITE

Mayne, an early riser, was generally the first to appear at chotah hazri; and when, with an impressive gesture, Francis laid Nancy's letter on the table beside him, he instantly recognized the writing, and felt a premonition that there was something in the wind! With admirably concealed impatience, he waited until the servant had retired, to open this, the first communication from his wife. He read it standing; then he sat down with a sudden plunge, and went slowly over it again, whilst a curious, rather grim expression stole across his face. Nancy's strange attitude was here most fully, and frankly explained. Her look of cold dislike, her frigid silence, and pointed avoidance, were amply accounted for, by the fact that she hated the man, whom in her heart she accused of being the cause of her father's death. Her love for *him*, was so absolute and overwhelming, that it had changed her kindly liking for Mayne, into horror, and detestation, and she spurned what she termed his "payment." The information was before his eyes in clear black and white—the girl wrote a good, legible hand—she had shot her bolt and fled. So after all his anxious heart-searchings, stifled reluctance, and sincere good-will, Nancy had deserted him, and gone her own way, to live her own life!

His feelings were an extraordinary mixture; various and unusual sensations, in turn swept over him; anger, humiliation, astonishment—then finally, relief. It was a relief, to be free from the desperate embarrassment of being married to a girl, a mere playfellow, with whom he had never exchanged a word of love, nor for whom he had ever felt the smallest touch of passion; yet on the other hand, Nancy was his legal wife, and—in spite of her ignorant confidence, and offer of release—to the best of his belief, it was impossible to sever the bond between them. Also, he was in the position of being sole executor of her father's will, and scanty personal estate.

The actual fact of the marriage was known to few. He could now rejoin his regiment as a bachelor; and the distasteful vision, of presenting himself at Cananore, in company with a stony-faced, abjectly miserable bride, faded away into the background. He would still continue to live at the Mess, and if later, there were any awkward developments—"sufficient unto the day was the evil thereof!"

Mayne paused in his tramp to and fro, and was about to pour himself out a cup of tea, when he beheld the shiny, copper-coloured face of Teddy Dawson, appearing above the steps.

"So I hear you are off this afternoon," he began, "and I have just looked in to know if I can do anything to help? I was the first to welcome you, and I should like to be the last to speed you, from this part of the world."

"You have come at an opportune moment," said Mayne, holding out his hand; "the very fellow I particularly want to see. But first let me get you a cup of tea."

"All right, I don't mind," said Ted, tossing down his battered topee, and taking a seat at the table. "How is Nancy?"

"Nancy has gone."

"Gone! What the Dickens do you mean?—Nancy gone! Gone where?"

"As you were at the marriage, and are altogether behind the scenes, also my first friend here,—I think I may show you her letter," said Mayne, and he handed it across to his gaping *vis-à-vis*.

Dawson read it with irritating deliberation; going back over sentences, and frowning heavily as he did so. When he came to the end, he looked up and said:

"Nancy was always a queer child, and you will have to let her alone. You couldn't well follow her, and drag her back—could you?"

"I shall not move a finger," said Mayne, with deliberate emphasis.

"It's just like one of her tempers; she'll cool down all right."

"And where do I come in?" inquired Mayne. "She has made a pretty good fool of *me!*"

"Oh, you'll forgive her some day, for you're a real white man! I'm awfully fond of Nan; she is clean, through and through—couldn't lie if she tried; knows nothing whatever of love; or what's called 'sex,' and that sort of thing. Her heart and soul were given to her Daddy; and now that he is gone, the poor child feels that her life is smashed to bits."

"That's true," assented Mayne, "and I can understand her grief. I have made every allowance, and never intruded on her for a moment. I have not laid eyes on Nancy since the funeral; she has remained shut up in her own room. This," holding up the note, "is the first sign that she has recognized my existence, and it gives me my dismissal, or 'jawaub.'"

"Well, well," resumed Dawson, after an expressive pause (during which he disposed of a large cup of tea), "it's rather a facer, I'll allow. I believe I can trace the delicate hand of Mrs. Ffinch in it—she always has a finger in every one's pie—and hitherto she has looked upon Nancy as her own particular property. By the way, have you made any fresh plans?"

"Yes. I leave early this afternoon. Nancy's baggage will, of course, remain, and as not a word of this business is known to anyone, bar the Hicks, Mrs. Ffinch, and yourself, I shall rejoin my regiment, as if nothing had happened."

"And keep up the delusion?" said Ted, opening his large blue eyes; "that won't be easy."

"Why not? I don't intend to follow, or to trace Nancy: she can go her own way. Money affairs, I'll arrange with you. I shall make her an allowance, paid half-yearly to your bankers. Who are they?"

"Grindlay and Co., but you may spare yourself the trouble, for Nancy won't accept a penny—if *I* know her."

"I shall lodge it all the same," said Mayne, looking obstinate. "Two hundred and fifty pounds a year. I won't have her governessing, or any of that nonsense. The inventory here has been seen to by Mrs. Hicks, and the station-writer; I have wound up a few business matters, paid off the servants, and, excepting a couple of yearly cheques, I shall have no more to say to—Mrs. Mayne!"

"Is that so?"

"Certainly; it is Nancy who has left me,—and, as the natives say, 'one hand cannot clap.'"

"I must confess, I don't wonder you feel a bit hurt."

"Hurt!" repeated Mayne, with an angry laugh.

"I've a good idea where Nancy is. She has gone down to her old nurse in Coimbatore; an excellent woman, who married a chap in the Telegraphs. Nance could not be better fixed up, for the present; the girl feels like a mortally wounded animal, that wants to hide from its own sort. It would have been a terrible ordeal for a child like Nancy, with her hurt, so to speak, *raw*, to find herself launched amongst complete strangers, with no one to hold on to, but a fellow she had known for a few weeks. One of my coolies told me, that last night he had seen the ghost of a woman on a white horse riding down the ghât road. Of course, that was Nancy, making for the railway station."

"I'm fairly broad-minded," said Mayne, "and I can see the matter from your point of view; naturally, you hold a brief for Nancy. I remember the first time we met, you told me she was the apple of your eye!"

"Aye. And what queer things have happened, since we overtook you that day on your way here. Now I wonder, if I had turned you back, would it have made any difference?"

"No—I believe it was 'Kismet.' I wish to goodness, Kismet had left me alone. However, I shall give the girl a wide berth,—and her freedom."

"Oh, will you?" Dawson's tone implied doubt.

"Yes, I shall hold my tongue; none of my brother officers would dream of my having got married up on a coffee estate. Later, it may be a bit awkward. You see I am my uncle's heir." He paused for a moment, and fumbled with his tobacco pouch,—which, all unconscious, he was holding upside down. "However, I'll manage somehow—even if there *are* complications."

"And how about Nancy? When she has recovered from this blow, has gone to England and grown up, how will it be, if she comes across a fellow she takes to? If ever she falls in love, it will be the devil of a business. A case of all—or nothing. What will happen then, eh?"

"There's no good in looking so far ahead," declared Mayne, preparing to light his pipe. "Why meet trouble half way—one of us may die——"

"Who is talking of dying?" inquired Mrs. Hicks, suddenly launching herself into the verandah. "Boys, I've overslept myself most disgracefully! and I'm shockingly late; but I always *was* a lazybones,—and fond of my little bed. I've not even been in to see Nancy yet."

When it had been carefully explained to her, that there was no Nancy to see, her fat, florid face was a study.

"Well, this *is* a nice how-do-you-do!" she exclaimed. "If I hadn't been an old silly, I might have had my suspicions, from her being so quiet. Well, well, well! Fancy her running away! I didn't think she 'ad it in her."

"Oh, there's a lot in Nancy," declared her champion.

"She kissed me something extra last night," resumed Mrs. Hicks, "and I suppose it was for *good-bye*. Lors! what will people say!"

"Nothing," replied Mayne emphatically. "They don't know anything about *me*, and they will think it only natural that she should—as Dawson suspects—have gone to her old nurse."

"And so it's—you know what I mean—to be a dead letter, and hushed up?"

"Yes."

Mrs. Hicks gave a shrill, unladylike whistle.

"Well, I declare! All the servants are 'in the know,'—but that doesn't count; folks don't ever believe 'bazaar' talk, and of course Hicks and I will 'old our tongues—you bet."

"That will be very kind of you, Mrs. Hicks—but——"

"But," nodding her head expressively, "if either of you go and marry other people, it will be bigamy, eh?"

"I suppose so," replied Mayne. "There is one thing positively certain."

"What's that?"

"That I have been married for the first, and last, time."

"Well, there's no saying; queer things 'appen. I'm sure this day week, you never dreamt you'd be a married man to-day; and you and Nancy are married, just as tight as 'Icks and me. You've got the certificate?"

"I have, and I do not intend to shirk all my responsibilities. I shall make Nancy an allowance; but I'll never see her again."

"Many's the woman that will be thankful to be married on *those* terms," chuckled Mrs. Hicks, now lighting up.

The good lady was enjoying a thorough holiday, and being as free and easy, and talkative as she pleased; far removed from the irritating criticisms of her daughters. She and her would-be son-in-law were pals! It was Jessie, influenced by Mrs. Ffinch—and Dr. Hicks—ambitious for his daughter— who were the real obstacles to the alliance.

"I'll run down to Coimbatore," she announced, "and see the child. Hicks doesn't like the look of her, and I'll just tell her what I think of her, for giving me the slip, the sly little toad! I suppose you don't send her no message?" suddenly turning to Mayne.

"Well, yes, perhaps I'd better. I'll go and write a line now, no time like the present," and he rose and went towards the den.

Mrs. Hicks' eyes followed him steadily. Then she burst out:

"Nancy has been a fool!—fine, upstanding young fellows like him aren't to be found on every coffee-bush, that I can tell you."

"Maybe it'll come all right yet," said Dawson soothingly.

"Maybe not. She has given him a nasty whack, and I think myself he has a pride. My old boy will fetch me to-day, and everything here is now settled, and cleared up, and the Travers' belongings are packed and ready for the road. I believe the new acting-manager comes to-morrow. My, what a change!" she added gloomily; "and all in one little week."

"Yes, and somehow I can't realize it," said Dawson. "As I sit here, I half expect to see Travers riding up from the Factory on his brown pony, and Nancy flying along this verandah, like a gale of wind."

"Aye, that's true," assented Mrs. Hicks, and she heaved a great sigh; "we have all had good times here, and the Travers' can never be replaced," and again she sighed heavily.

Meanwhile Mayne was writing rapidly on the estate note-paper:

Dear Nancy,

I have received your letter, and accept the situation, all shall be as you wish. I am sorry to find that you dislike me so inveterately, and decline what you describe as 'Payment'— but it cannot be helped. Let me assure you, that I have no intention of coming into your life, and the marriage, as far as I am concerned, shall be as though it had never taken place. I have arranged to make you a yearly allowance (£250) which will be paid to our mutual friend, Ted Dawson. The estate and personal affairs have been satisfactorily settled.

Yours faithfully,
Derek Danvers Mayne.

When he handed this note to Mrs. Hicks, she turned it over, looked at the superscription, and remarked:

"I see you've addressed it to 'Miss Travers.'"

"Well, why not?" he protested; "I feel sure Nancy would not have opened it, had it been addressed to 'Mrs. Mayne.'"

Early that same afternoon Mayne rode down the ghât,—in what a different frame of mind, to the blithe expectations with which he had gaily ascended the same road! Near the foot of the hills he encountered a syce, who salaamed to him profoundly! Could there be anything ironical in that salute? The man was leading a remarkably hot grey pony; the pony was carrying a side-saddle.—An episode was closed.

CHAPTER XIV
"NANCY SITS WITH SORROW"

Nancy, the ayah, Togo and the luggage, arrived at Coimbatore station without any incident, much less a half-expected "hue and cry." Here Mrs. Simpson awaited them with her roomy bullock cart, drawn by a pair of huge Nellore bullocks, and carried the little party to her large and comfortable bungalow on the outskirts of the town. She was delighted to welcome her nursling,—to whom she had always been devoted.—She made her eat, and insisted upon putting her to bed, and treating her precisely as if she were still a small child!

When Nancy was at rest, in her spacious white cot, Jane Simpson sat by her side, and listened with tearful sympathy to details of the illness and death of her former master; for all this, she had been prepared, but the unexpected news of Nancy's marriage, reduced her to a condition of stunned, and horrified silence.

Jane Simpson was by nature excessively prim, a little narrow-minded, strictly conventional, but a most worthy person. Her house, her person, and especially her hands, were beautifully kept. When she had deposited Nancy at school in Eastbourne, she subsequently turned her attention to professional nursing, and after several years' experience, had attracted the attention of one of her patients, married him, and returned to India,—a country she abused for its slack unpractical ways, but nevertheless liked it all the same. Bob Simpson's pay was liberal, and although they had no family, Jane was a very busy and contented woman.

From her point of view, everything should be foreseen, cut and dried, punctual to a second, and absolutely proper and correct. This sudden marriage of her little girl to an acquaintance no better than a stranger, figuratively swept her off her feet! However, like a prudent woman, she *said* little. Nancy was looking desperately ill, a different creature from the buoyant Nancy of Fairplains: so silent, haggard, and lifeless. What further information Mrs. Simpson required was eagerly supplied by the ayah, who though not actually present, had witnessed the marriage ceremony in the drawing-room,—through an obliging crack in the door.

"Mayne Sahib and the Missy, standing before the Padre, both looking *too* sorry. Mayne, he very nice gentleman. His butler telling, a good sahib, and no evil liver,—everyone liking. He money got, too. Yesterday giving me twenty rupees," and the ayah's black eyes glistened greedily.

"Do you think he will come down here after Miss Nancy?" anxiously inquired Mrs. Simpson.

"How I telling, Memsahib?" throwing up her small brown hands, "but for what good? My Missy plenty sick, soon, soon, very sick—and maybe die.—Ah ye yoh!" and she wrung her hands.

Part of this augury came true. The dreaded reaction set in, Nancy had a bad attack of fever, and was seriously ill. She was lucky to find herself in Jane Simpson's care, and with the help of a good doctor, and the best of nursing, at the end of three weeks, she had recovered; but rose from her bed a shattered wreck, wasted to a shadow, with a small wan white face, from which all trace of sunburn and tan had now completely disappeared.

During the fever, Mrs. Simpson kept all visitors steadily at bay. Training as a professional nurse, had invested her with an inflexible attitude, and even Mrs. Ffinch, who had motored down on two occasions, could not succeed in interviewing the invalid; but when Nancy was convalescent, the position was stormed.

Mrs. Ffinch brought her neighbour, Mrs. Hicks, with her in the car, and during most of the journey, the two ladies wrangled, for they held diametrically opposite views with respect to the protégée they were about to visit. Mrs. Hicks declared "that it would be a great pity there should be a complete breach between Nancy and Captain Mayne." She was sentimental, and soft-hearted in her way,—fond of the girl, and well disposed towards the man.

"By and by, if they're *let alone*, believe you me, they'll make friends! After all, Mayne is a fairly good match. I am told he has five hundred a year, and expectations from an uncle."

"Yes," broke in Mrs. Ffinch, who was not soft-hearted, and whose own love affair had been strangled. "You can imagine the uncle's delight—*I* know the old man—when he hears that his nephew and heir, has picked up a little nobody off an Indian coffee estate!"

"I don't think that's a very nice, or kind, way to speak of Nancy," gobbled Mrs. Hicks, swelling with indignation.

"My dear, good Mrs. Hicks, don't be angry; it's not *my* idea, I do assure you; only one that would undoubtedly present itself to this rich old man! I propose to shelter Nancy under my own wing. I shall be going home next spring, and as soon as she has recovered from her grief, I shall take her about, and give her a good time—and——"

"And marry her off," broke in Mrs. Hicks, with challenging insolence. "Match-making with you is just a play; all excitement and amusement. However, you can't marry Nancy, for you know as well as I do, she has a husband already!"

"Nothing of the sort," rejoined the other, "any claim that Captain Mayne would put forward could easily be refuted. He won't do it though, and I suppose if he chose, he could sue Nancy for desertion."

Argument waxed fast and furious, and Mrs. Ffinch had much the best of the conflict. She kept her temper admirably, whilst her opponent was in a red-hot towering rage. On such occasions she completely cast all fear, and awe of the "Dictator," to the winds, and told her various, plain, and unpleasant truths. On the present occasion, she said:

"You know very well, that if *you* had been here and had a hand in this marriage of Nancy's, you would have *made* her stick to it through thick and thin—but as it was all got up in a hurry, and, so to speak, behind your back, you'll do all you can to smash it!"

Mrs. Ffinch's reply was an icy and dignified silence. The proper and suitable punishment for her companion would have been to open the door of the car, request her to descend, and allow her to walk the remainder of the distance down to Coimbatore.

For a long time, neither matron spoke; and the motor skimmed rapidly down the winding road, passing many familiar land-marks. The cold fit was now on Mrs. Hicks. She had let herself go, and said too much, and there wasn't the smallest doubt that her companion—from what she knew of her—would hold a truce for the present, but in some way or another "have it in for her" on a future occasion!

As they sped along the flat plains, in the direction of Coimbatore, Mrs. Ffinch broke the silence.

"I propose to take Nancy back with me this evening; her room is ready, and most of her mourning has been finished, so, dear Mrs. Hicks, on our return journey, I'm sure you won't mind sitting in front with the chauffeur, and I will take the poor child in beside me."

In her own opinion she was carrying out the part of a benevolent friend—she was saving Nancy from a loveless union, and the misery of being dragged round the world, by a man who did not want her.

The two well-meaning visitors were greatly shocked when they beheld their young protégée. She looked so dull, and vacant, almost like another creature! Her attitude resembled that of a wounded creature, cowering, and withdrawing, from those who wished to do her good. She resisted all Mrs. Ffinch's importunities and persuasions to accompany her to Clouds Rest. This, was the one subject on which the girl seemed to have a fixed opinion; nothing would induce her to return to the hills. Otherwise, whether she was to remain at Coimbatore, or go to England, to live, or to die,—was apparently a matter of complete indifference.

Whilst Mrs. Ffinch was holding a whispered conference with Jane Simpson, Mrs. Hicks seized the opportunity to give Nancy the note from Mayne. The girl turned it over listlessly.

"It is his answer to yours," explained Mrs. Hicks. "He wrote it right away, and gave it to me. I thought it better to wait until I could bring it down myself."

"I suppose so, thank you," she said as she opened it, glanced over it, and then tore it into four pieces. "*That's* done," she said, looking at Mrs. Hicks, with unexpected animation.

"Well, I'm not so sure!" rejoined the matron, "and I'm not of the same mind as Mrs. Ffinch. We quarrelled about the business the whole way down. Indeed, I think myself, she had half a mind to put me out on the side of the road! I'm afraid I let my temper get the better of me, and said lots of things I'm sorry for now. I expect Mrs. Ffinch is bitterly disappointed that you won't go back with her, Nancy. I shouldn't be surprised if she carried her point yet, and you know we'd all be only too glad to have you among us. Hush! here she comes!"

As the time passed, Nancy's grief and misery, instead of abating seemed to increase. She was no longer an invalid, but helped Nurse Jane about the house, knitted, sewed, and walked out daily. Her attitude was one of an unnatural passivity. Grief had burnt into her very soul, and her inner being was absorbed with one obsession: the memory of her father. Apparently his image filled her thoughts to the exclusion of all else. This much, Nurse Jane gathered, during their infrequent conversations—for Nancy now was almost dumb. As for Mayne, the girl appeared to have forgotten his existence! She was completely prostrated by the loss of her parent, and gradually sinking into an apathetic condition of mind and body, from which at all cost, she must be redeemed.

As Bob Simpson's cheery good humour, and Jane's authoritative efforts, had not the smallest effect upon this white-faced silent inmate, Mrs. Ffinch and Mrs. Hicks and Ted Dawson were summoned,—and held, so to speak, a committee upon the case. They decided that the girl must have a complete change, otherwise, it would be impossible for her to regain her normal balance! Mrs. Ffinch relinquished her efforts to induce Nancy to live with her, had obtained her aunt's address, and sent her one of her most diplomatic letters—to which there had been a cool, but polite reply.

Mrs. Jenkins had also written to her niece, offering to receive her, and to give her an asylum until she could make other arrangements. Nancy, who had been two months at Coimbatore, was a wan, hollow-eyed spectre of herself: it was evident, that in her present environment she would never recover her mental poise. In the day-time she sat and walked, and talked like some dull automatic figure—entirely indifferent to her surroundings. As Mrs. Ffinch gravely considered her—she mentally concluded that, "that way madness lies!" and Mrs. Simpson's friends, who had known the gay and happy Miss Nancy Travers, assured one another, there was no doubt at all, but that the broken-hearted girl was either dying, or going out of her mind!

"She must be sent away at *once!*" such was Mrs. Ffinch's mandate, after a protracted interview with Nurse Jane. "There is her aunt's invitation—she has the money for her passage, her mourning is ready, and, as it happens, most providentially, Mrs. Sandilands is going home by the *Patna*. They can travel together. I shall wire to Cook, make all arrangements, secure a separate cabin for Nancy, and this day week, she will find herself at sea!"

CHAPTER XV
A FRIEND IN NEED

Thanks to Mrs. Ffinch's promise and her prompt exertions, within a week's time Nancy found herself in the Madras roads, on board the P. & O. steamer *Patna*, bound for London. The *Patna* was a full boat, carrying a mixed multitude of cheerful passengers. Among these was Blanche Sandilands (née Meach), a remarkably pretty woman in exuberant spirits,— embarking on her first trip to England in the character of a rich, popular, much admired young matron. Her cabin was crammed with flowers and books, friends to bid her good-bye were assembled in flattering numbers, and among these, she anxiously looked about for her charge.

Yes, there was that invaluable Mrs. Ffinch,—and could it be Nancy Travers? Nancy, so altered as to be almost unrecognizable. The bright school-girl, she remembered, as just out from England, brimming over with happiness, and gaiety, was now a wan white creature in deep mourning, with sad abstracted eyes. Thank goodness, they were not sharing the same cabin, or she would certainly be flooded out with tears! What, she asked herself, could she do with her? Mrs. Sandilands had been looking forward to such a ripping time on the voyage: the Bruffs, and the Colvilles, Captain Yates and Mr. Orme, were on board, but there would not be much fun for *her*, if all day long she was tied to such a wet blanket as this poor child—who appeared to be actually stupefied with grief.

To her immense relief, the lively lady soon discovered that Nancy Travers would be no encumbrance. It was true that she sat beside her at meals (nobly representing the traditional death's head), but otherwise effaced herself, seeming to prefer solitude, and her own company, sitting aloof with a book, or disappearing for hours into her nook of a cabin in the stern.

Mrs. Sandilands lent her novels, offered her chocolates, and little toilet luxuries, kissed her perfunctorily night and morning, and left her to herself,—assuring her friends, that such was the truest kindness, and went her own light-hearted way to play deck games, and Bridge; or to embark on such amusing and harmless flirtations, as are expected of the prettiest woman on the ship.

At Colombo the passengers went bodily ashore, and enjoyed the few gay hours at the Galle Face Hotel, explored the bazaars, or darted off in rickshaws to inspect the Cinnamon gardens. With their return at dinner time, they brought a horde of new comers,—tourists, planters, and their belongings.

Among the crowd, one figure was conspicuously prominent, and proceeded at once to dominate the ship.

"Yet after all, what was Mrs. De Wolfe?" asked a girl plaintively, "but an ugly, rude, old woman?"

The lady appeared to know several of the passengers, and to be a sea friend of the captain's; for a special place had been reserved at his table, also she enjoyed a large double cabin, and was attended by a hard-featured, but dignified maid.

In appearance, Mrs. De Wolfe looked formidable enough! Tall and bony, with a long, wrinkled face, a commanding hooked nose (a family feature descending through generations), sharp black eyes, heavily marked brows, and a tightly closed mouth, which, when open, displayed two gleaming rows of expensively fitted teeth. Her hands exhibited knotted veins, and surprisingly large knuckles, but the lady's most distinctive endowment was a far-reaching, masculine voice. Her style of dress was tailor-made, and suitable, her only jewellery, a thin wedding ring.

What was her claim to the almost subservient homage which she received? She was suffered to break into the most interesting conversation; her remarks were listened to with profound respect, and she was waited on with slavish assiduity. Perhaps the answer was, that the old lady had influence, a strong personality, a sharp tongue, and great possessions. She was a masterful, independent individual, who did what she liked, went where she fancied, and said what she pleased! Nancy shrank from her instinctively, and when on deck, kept well out of her orbit, and beyond the range of those piercing eyes.

One evening, as she sat pretending to read, she was startled by a deep voice speaking over her shoulder. It said:

"What's the matter with you? Why don't you go and play about? You look like a sick chicken!"

As Nancy gazed straight up into the old wrinkled face, her lips twitched, but she made no reply. Mrs. De Wolfe, who evidently expected an answer, waited for a moment, still staring fixedly. It was something like the children's game of "Who will laugh first?" Then with an indignant "Humph!" she moved away.

The *Patna*, four days out from Colombo, had experienced fairly fine weather, and real tropical heat. Nancy slept in the top berth of her tiny cubby hole, with the port wide open, and was dreaming a delightful dream, when it suddenly turned to a sense of horrible reality and *drowning*. She was roused by a wandering green wave, which, having discovered an inviting porthole, flowed in torrents over her prostrate form, and completely swamped the cabin. As soon as she had recovered her breath, and the shock, she endeavoured to close the port. It proved much too stiff. Then she sprang down into the water on the floor, snatched at her dressing-gown, and opening the door, screamed for a steward. A man in the next cabin had evidently met with the same catastrophe, and was in a similar plight. He and Nancy faced one another in the passage, a dripping, shivering pair! Very soon a bedroom steward appeared on the scene, there was loud talking, splashing, mopping. In the midst of this, a door opened, and a gruff voice demanded:

"What's all this noise about?"

Then the face of Mrs. De Wolfe appeared. She wore a large lace-frilled nightcap, "and looked for all the world," as the young man subsequently described, "like the wolf in Red Riding Hood."

"There's been a sea into these two cabins, ma'am," explained the steward, "and this 'ere lady and gentleman has been washed out!"

The old woman now came forth, and surveyed them impartially; the smart clean-shaven man in pink pyjamas, and a blanket; the girl in a blue dressing-gown, with two long plaits of hair dripping down her back, and instantly recognized the "Ghost," Nancy's nickname on the boat.

"You come along in here," she commanded, stretching out her bony hand, and taking her by the wrist. "Steward, send my maid at once," and the cabin door closed on the pair—the wolf, and the lamb!

"You shall have dry things immediately," said Mrs. De Wolfe, "and Haynes shall make you up a bed on the sofa here."

"Thank you, ma'am, you are very kind," chattered Nancy, whose teeth were like a pair of castanets.

"Take a towel and dry your hair, Haynes will be here in a moment."

Almost as her mistress spoke, Haynes made her appearance in a trim red flannel dressing-gown, and took the matter in hand with quiet promptitude. Nancy soon found herself invested in a beautiful silk and lace nightgown, which she regarded with unspeakable awe.

"It's quite all right, chicken," declared the old lady who had returned to her berth, "I wear plain upper garments, and keep the show for what I call my 'Undies.' It fits you to a T. Better sleep with the towel round your head. How on earth do you manage to hide all that hair!"

"Less talking!" growled a voice from the neighbouring cabin.

"Haynes, you'll bring two teas at half-past seven," continued Mrs. De Wolfe, totally unmoved by this command, "and now you may turn out the light, and go."

In the ensuing darkness, Nancy was able to reflect at leisure upon her novel position. She was actually sleeping in the cabin—and the nightgown— of the woman she most feared and avoided of all the passengers on board the *Patna*. Yet in spite of her overpowering personality, she had proved to be a good Samaritan, and not so alarming after all; consoled by this conviction, Nancy dozed off.

In the morning, Haynes—a celebrated Treasure—brought Nancy a cup of delicious "private" tea, and when she had drunk it, and thanked her hostess for a night's lodging, she slipped on her dressing-gown, and fled into her own quarters—once more habitable.

The little episode of the "wash-out" had no immediate results beyond the exhibition of two mattresses, and several blankets hung out to dry, and Nancy's acquaintance with Mrs. De Wolfe went no further. She shrank more and more into solitude and silence, and gave way to the gnawing misery and loneliness of her heart—plunged in the agony of a terrible loss, she was left to struggle in it quite alone.

One morning Mrs. De Wolfe encountered her face to face, at the top of the companion ladder, nodded brusquely, and stared. The girl's face subsequently haunted her. Oh, what a picture of real grief,—and nothing but grief! Impressed by this vision, she proceeded to make inquiries respecting the solitary young woman in mourning. Mrs. Sandilands (a notable chatterbox) volubly related the tale of tragedy, dwelt on Nancy's adoration for her father, their ideally happy life, his death,—and her altered fortune.

"Nancy has no one belonging to her, except a disagreeable aunt," she said, "a half-sister, who has been at daggers drawn with Mr. Travers for twenty years; however she has offered what she calls 'an asylum' to the girl, until she can find some job."

Mrs. De Wolfe nodded and grunted; she also marked, learned and inwardly digested this information.

A grand fancy ball was got up on board the *Patna*, in order to inaugurate her entrance into the Red Sea; the preparations, arrangements and expedients, afforded almost as much enjoyment as the dance itself. Such were its attractions, that Mrs. De Wolfe's special Bridge table was ruthlessly dissolved. One of the keenest players was appearing as Neptune, another as Mephistopheles, a stout, middle-aged lady as Ophelia. Mrs. De Wolfe made no change in her plain rich evening toilet—though more than one malicious tongue had suggested that "she might get herself up as the Witch of Endor."

Tired of looking on at the whirling crowd, she went on deck, and having descried a solitary figure leaning over the side, approached it stealthily and, so to speak, pounced!

"No, don't go away, little sick chick!" she said, laying her bony grasp on Nancy's arm. "Come over here, and talk to me," and Nancy was carried away a helpless prisoner, to where two deck-chairs happened to be placed close together. "You're not looking on?"

Nancy shook her head.

"No, I'm told you have had great trouble—and I'm very sorry for you."

"Thank you," said the girl stiffly.

"Come now, do you think it is right to give way to it like this? keeping apart from your fellow creatures, and fretting yourself to death?"

"I cannot help it."

"You could, if you tried."

"Oh, you don't know——" and Nancy caught her breath.

"Pardon me, I do know! Your chaperone told me all about it. I'm sure if your father could see you,—and we have no proof otherwise,—it would hurt him terribly to witness such hopeless, useless, misery."

"My father was the same himself," declared Nancy, "after my mother died, and I was sent to England."

"I know; your friend, Mrs. Sandilands, an exhaustive talker, assured me, he was so heart-broken, that he allowed his affairs to what is called 'go to the dogs.' Did he not regret *that*?"

"Yes, he did—but I have no affairs."

"You have your life to lead, my dear. Come, do not play the coward, but brace yourself for the race that is before you."

"Oh, I can't," she muttered; "if I could only *die*!"

"What nonsense," protested the old lady, "I've no patience with this silly sort of talk."

For a moment there was no answer, and the silence was filled with the blare of the band, and a rousing Two-step.

"Because perhaps you don't know what trouble is," murmured Nancy at last.

"Don't I? I am not disposed to talk of my private affairs with strangers—but for once, I will." A harsh tragedy looked out of her old eyes, as she added: "Listen. You possibly see me a gruff, selfish, overbearing old woman, with not a thought in the world beyond her dinner, and a rubber of Bridge. Nevertheless, I have indeed known anguish—the wounds throb still. My husband left me, when we were young and happy; my eldest boy was killed at Magersfontein, my youngest, died of typhoid in India,—all alone; and here am I, all alone,—with nothing awaiting me but the grave." She paused, for a moment. "Now you have, I trust, a long useful life, and many happy hours before you. Why, you cannot be more than eighteen."

"I was eighteen three months ago."

"And eighteen wishes to die! Mrs. Sandilands tells me you are going to live with an aunt in London. May I hear her name?"

"Yes, it is Mrs. Jenkins. She has a house in Queen's Gate."

"Strange, I think I've heard of her. She is a widow like myself,—very comfortably off. Her chief interest in life, is her health, a *malade imaginaire*. Do you know anything of nursing?"

"Not much, I am afraid."

"Well, then, my dear, I am well experienced—and I am going to prescribe for you. You are to come along with me, and look on at the ball; and then we will go and have a bit of supper. Yes, I *insist*!" There was no gainsaying this old lady.

When Mrs. De Wolfe and her young friend parted that night in their mutual passage, she said:

"I intend to take you in hand, Miss Nancy Travers. I shall not allow you to sit idle in the market-place, eating your heart out. To-morrow I'll give you some knitting, and teach you to play Piquet and Patience. You can look upon me as your deputy chaperone."

As deputy chaperone, she took entire charge of Nancy—who felt powerless to resist—the girl interested her surprisingly. When she forgot herself, she could talk, she could sew, she could even smile! By the time the *Patna* was in the Canal, Nancy was better. The sea-air revived her; her new acquaintance acted as a tonic, kept her incessantly occupied, promenaded the deck with her, told her stories, gave her sound advice, and from being a mere crumpled heap of hopeless misery lifted her once more to a foothold in life.

It had been discovered that the "Ghost," as she was called, was an excellent pianist, and consequently much in request to accompany song or violin. This demand brought her into communication with other young people—which was good for Nancy.

Mrs. Sandilands was amazed at the acquaintance which had been struck up between two such incongruous characters as Mrs. De Wolfe, and the Travers girl. What had they in common? However it came about, the old woman had effected a wonderful change, and as it were restored the Ghost to life, and the material world. She now went to and fro and mixed with other people, and no longer spent hours shut up in her little cabin.

When the *Patna* was in the Channel, Mrs. De Wolfe said to her protégée:

"Do not forget to give me your address, my dear, and I will come and see you."

"That will be very kind."

"I stay in London occasionally, but my home is in the country,—also in the wide world—for I travel a great deal. Excuse my plain speaking, my dear, but have you no income at all? I understand that your father was a Travers of Lambourne, and I believe they went through every penny they possessed?"

"I have twenty pounds a year," replied Nancy, "and I have had a good education; but I'm afraid I look too young to be a governess. If the worst comes to the worst, I might go into a shop. I think I'd rather like that— millinery, or a ladies' outfitting—a sort of place where there are no men."

"Are you afraid of them?"

"Oh no," and she laughed.

"No love affairs yet, I should imagine," said Mrs. De Wolfe, with customary bluntness.

"No love affairs," repeated Nancy, but she coloured vividly.

"Ah! then there *is* someone?" remarked her astute questioner.

"Yes, there was someone; someone I don't like; but it had nothing to do with a love affair—and I pray that we may never meet again."

"I'm afraid that will be no use, my dear—we all meet the very people we don't want to see!"

"Well, I shall always want to see *you*!" said Nancy impulsively.

"I'm glad of that, my child, for the number of people who never wish to see me again, is fairly large. I hate cruelty, and snobbery; I speak out my mind rather freely, as I tramp through life. Well, my little chick, I've given you a lift on the road, haven't I?"

"You have indeed; I can't tell you all you have done for me, roused me from a stupor, that was creeping over me,—and helped me to make a fresh start. I can never thank you enough, never!"

"I don't want thanks. Give me deeds. You must write to me, Nancy. My bankers, Coutts, will always find me, and if I don't answer, never mind; I'm a shocking correspondent, my pen never saves my tongue. I'll come and see you when I pass through Town, and I hope I'll find you doing well. Be amenable to your father's sister: a rich, self-centred, elderly woman. Accept hard knocks—they will brace you—later on, you may find your life in pleasant places. I'd like to take you with me to Scotland, but I am under orders to visit old friends, who fix one's date of arrival, train, and room, with a firmness there is no withstanding, and I dare not be a deserter."

Nancy's were not the only thanks received by this social missionary. Pretty Mrs. Sandilands overwhelmed her with effusive gratitude, and flattering speeches.

"You took the girl off my hands, dear kindest lady, and have turned her into a new creature! I cannot imagine how you did it!"

"A little sympathy, and fellow-feeling, was all that was required."

Mrs. Sandilands coloured guiltily, and then replied:

"Nancy is like her father, you see—she takes everything so terribly, so foolishly, to heart."

"But what a good thing it is, that she happens to have a heart to take things to! Such folk are not common objects of the sea or shore in these days."

"Perhaps because people don't wear their hearts on their sleeves," retorted Mrs. Sandilands sharply. At this moment, her companion was summoned to receive a Marconigram, and she found herself unexpectedly abandoned with all the honours of the last word!

Later that same day, the *Patna* was berthed in the London Docks, and her horde of passengers scattered afar, every man and woman to their own; in most cases to forget within a few hours, those who had been their daily associates for the last four weeks.

CHAPTER XVI
AUNT ARABELLA

Mrs. Arabella Jenkins (née Travers), a stout little widow of sixty-four, occupied a large and lugubrious mansion in Queen's Gate, S.W. She was also the mistress of five thousand a year, eight servants—not including a permanent "char"—and one dog. Her mother, a pretty Scotch girl, had been of "no family," according to various disappointed dowagers—"just someone Charles Travers had picked up when shooting on a moor, and by no means a suitable châtelaine for Lambourne."

However, the poor despised lady reigned but a few short years, and was succeeded, after a heartless interval, by a dashing damsel of undeniable birth,—the mother of Laurence Travers, and his two brothers,—who ably assisted her reckless husband to squander the remains of a famous estate.

At nineteen, Arabella Travers was a beauty of the Dresden china type: a fair, fluffy little creature, with sunny hair and an exquisite pink and white complexion. Possibly she was shrewd enough to foresee how family affairs were drifting, for at the age of one and twenty, she accepted a rich elderly suitor from the City, and exchanged a cheery country life for a somewhat gloomy establishment in town.

There had never been much in common between Arabella, her smart stepmother, and riotous, high-spirited brothers. The Travers boys laughed at, and mimicked old Sammy Jenkins, and old Sam openly abused their mad folly, and extravagance, and rarely invited them under his roof.

However, he made Arabella an adoring and indulgent husband, spoiled and petted her most injudiciously, and permitted her to believe, that there was no one in the whole world as important or as beautiful as herself! Having entirely uprooted all that was best in her character, he died, leaving his widow every shilling he possessed,—to the wrathful indignation of his anticipating kindred.

A long impending crash promptly followed the death of Charles Travers. The estate was sold for the benefit of creditors, Mrs. Travers retired to Bournemouth, and there died within a year. Her three sons scattered over the world; one went to India, another to Australia, a third to South Africa.

In a short time, the family were extinct, all but prosperous Arabella, and handsome Laurence,—who, having made a fair start in coffee, returned home for a few months' holiday.

As he was a most presentable relative, his stepsister saw a good deal of him, proudly exhibited him at tea-parties, and dinners, and exerted herself to find him a suitable—that is to say—a well-dowered wife. In one direction, she had even made overtures on his behalf, but before her plans had time to materialize, Laurence returned to the East, and married a wretched, penniless little governess! If he had been guided by his wise relative, he could have married a rich, rather plain young woman, who had been greatly attracted by his personality, and have enjoyed the easy life of a country gentleman, and revived something of the Travers prestige; instead of which, there he was, grilling out in India, grubbing away at a coffee estate.

Figuratively his sister washed her little fat hands of him; there had been a brief interchange of disagreeable letters—such as appear to be the copyright of near relatives—subsequently succeeded by a death-like silence.

Mrs. Jenkins ceased to trouble herself further with respect to her brother—"impossible," she declared, "to help those who refused to help themselves"—but vague scraps of information had reached her indirectly. She heard of the birth of a child, the death of his wife, and his financial collapse.

Sunken in selfishness, and egoism, Arabella Jenkins had almost forgotten her brother Laurence, when a twenty years' silence was broken; a letter written by an unsteady hand, announced his impending departure from this world, and appealed to a childless woman to give his little girl a home. Later, she had seen the announcement of his death in the *Times*.—It had been duly advertised by the ever thoughtful Mrs. Ffinch.

So Laurence was gone—and only forty-seven!—and now there was his orphan. What was she to do about her? As dear Mrs. Taylor truly said, "at her time of life, and in her state of health, it was monstrous to suppose, that she should be saddled with an encumbrance." Of course she must receive the girl for a few weeks, and possibly some of her many friends, such as Lady Constance Howler, or Mrs. Fitzallen Jones, might find her a situation. As for being permanently troubled with this responsibility, the idea was simply too utterly ridiculous.

The early beauty of Arabella Travers had not lasted—save in the lady's own opinion. Bright hair and a rose-leaf skin, belong to the days of one's youth. Mrs. Jenkins was now a stout, short-necked, squat little body, with a pair of arrogant blue eyes, and an assertive nose. Happy in the delusion that she did not look a day over thirty, she dressed the age at great expense, and in the most villainous taste.

Her house was warm, dark, and stuffy; very thick red carpets led the way from hall to drawing-room. Here again was a red carpet, heavy crimson curtains, and solid furniture of the most debased Victorian type, of which the crowning atrocity was a large distorted ottoman in the middle of the room. The walls were covered with chromes, and mirrors in ponderous frames: a life-sized portrait of the mistress of the house hung opposite the fireplace, and seemed determined to challenge attention; it had been painted more than thirty years previously, and portrayed a slim young lady, with rosy cheeks, snow-white neck and arms,—and a voluminous blue dress. On her satin lap reposed a small King Charles,—which same animal, beautifully stuffed, and sheltered in a glass case, confronted visitors on the first landing, and struck terror into the hearts of his own species.

The portrait, the ottoman, and a grand piano, were the chief features of the apartment, which also contained a good many "occasional" chairs, and tables, various gaudy cushions, and lamp-shades (the spoils of bazaars), and a large collection of small rubbish. Mrs. Jenkins was not what is called "house-proud," and had made no alterations in what had been her bridal home,—merely contributing the cheap little souvenirs she had picked up on the Continent; such as Swiss carvings, Italian delf, marble letter-weights, and paper fans. Her interest was mainly centred in herself,—and the condition of her health; fortunately she was as strong as the proverbial horse, and endowed with a hardy Scotch constitution, otherwise she must have succumbed to the extraordinary variety of medicines she sampled, and the different "cures" she underwent. The lady took too little exercise, and too much nourishment. Even when she was supposed to be completely prostrate, heavily laden trays were welcomed by an astonishing appetite, which disposed of their dishes with healthy voracity, and provoked much ribald jeering among her retinue below stairs. The assimilating of prescriptions in the shape of drops or tabloids, were with Mrs. Jenkins, a confirmed habit and joy,—and took the place of cigarettes,—so soothing to other women.

Doctors who attended Mrs. Jenkins, were legion in number— occasionally two or three, unknown to one another, prescribed for the same case. According to her statement, she had been threatened with almost every known complaint: arthritis, appendicitis, angina pectoris, seemed to dog her steps, and yet her recuperative vitality was incredible.

One week prone in bed with nurses in attendance, and straw laid down in the street: long ere the straw was removed, the invalid might have been seen making a hearty lunch at "Prince's" or doing a matinée at the Haymarket. Indeed, it was on record, that a bewildered caller had found the knocker at No. 900 muffled, and on inquiring for the sufferer with almost bated breath, was informed that she was at Ranelagh!

Arabella Jenkins endeavoured to make the most of two worlds: the gay, hustling, social world, and the invalid sphere,—bounded by doctors, friendly inquiries, flowers, and commiseration. Nothing made Mrs. Jenkins more indignant—indeed furious—than any doubt of the bona fides of her ailments.

She posed as an extraordinarily plucky woman, who bore her sufferings, after the manner of the Spartan boy and fox; and those doctors who refused to see eye to eye with her, or to take part in a medical farce, were inscribed in her black books as not merely incapable, but the deadliest of enemies. For all her masterful, despotic ways and heavy purse, Mrs. Jenkins was more or less in the hands of her eight servants, her old friends, and her numerous parasites.

She held a court of elderly women; ladies in waiting (for favours) attended her, flattered her, and sung her praises,—particularly in her own presence. These, she rewarded with dinners, presents, drives, her cast-off gowns, and her confidence. They had all expressed deep sympathy over the impending invasion of this girl; for it was no secret that "dearest Arabella did not care for young people." Intensely jealous of each other's influence, they combined in a solid phalanx, against an intrusive outsider.

Two of Mrs. Jenkins' chief friends were sitting with her one afternoon late in June. One had presented flowers, the other had propped her up with cushions, and brought her a footstool—almost as if she was recovering from one of her notable heart attacks. In reality, she was awaiting the arrival of Miss Nancy Travers,—and Miss Nancy Travers was late!

Mrs. Taylor, chief counsellor, and parasite, was a widow with a masculine cast of face, a dark red complexion, and beetling black brows; being tall and massive, Mrs. Jenkins' dresses required a vast amount of letting out and letting down, before she could assume them. She lived in a little flat in Earl's Court, and was dependent on dearest Arabella,—whom she had known as a girl, a fact which made her position as mistress of the robes impregnable,—for many an excellent meal, a serviceable cast-off costume, and her summer holidays. In return for these benefits, she offered continual incense in the shape of flattery, and much engrossing gossip— having a wide, and illegitimate knowledge of other people's affairs.

The other lady, Miss Dolling, was well and fashionably dressed—no genteel mendicant this! but she was unfortunately plain: a long nose, no chin, and fat flabby cheeks, largely discounted her string of valuable pearls, and French toilette. Bessie Dolling, the original wife selected for Laurence Travers, was as yet an unappropriated blessing: after twenty years, she still hoarded Laurence's photograph, hugged his memory, and firmly believed that if he had not been caught by an adventuress, he would have returned to claim her. This fiction was a sustaining consolation to the poor lady, did no one any harm, and need not be begrudged.

The three friends were grouped round the open window overlooking Queen's Gate; Galpin the butler had just removed the tea-things, and departed with the tea-cloth neatly tucked under his arm. He was a stout, clean-shaven man, with a considerable meridian, and a stern mouth. N.B.— His mistress was not a little afraid of him.

"I wonder what she will be like?" said Miss Dolling suddenly.

"My dear Bessie, that is the tenth time you have made the same remark," peevishly protested Mrs. Taylor. "We shall know in a few minutes."

"She will be exactly like her father," announced Mrs. Jenkins as if stating a fact; "a dark Travers, with black hair, and well-cut features, especially the Travers' nose," and as she spoke, she put up her hand and stroked her own organ, which was short, thick, and first cousin to a *nez retroussé*.

"I shall send her to her room almost at once. These interviews are so dreadfully trying for my poor heart."

"Yes, dear friend," purred Mrs. Taylor, "and we will take care, that she does not talk to you about the panther, or how her father was killed."

"Not killed at the time," contradicted Miss Dolling; "he died days afterwards."

"It was the panther's doing all the same," argued Mrs. Taylor, "and to think of Laurence Travers making *no* provision for his girl,—I call it downright wicked, leaving her entirely dependent on his dear, good, golden-hearted sister."

At this moment, there was a sound of violent commotion, and deafening barking on the stairs. The Pom who left the room in close attendance on cream, and savoury sandwiches, had undoubtedly encountered a stranger. Miss Dolling looked hastily out of the window and said:

"Yes—she has arrived! a four-wheeler, and several large boxes."

Further information was postponed, as the door opened, and Galpin announced "Miss Travers." Enter, a thin, woebegone girl, with reddish hair: dressed in a crumpled black muslin, and carrying a waterproof on her arm.

Half way to the window, she paused for a moment, endeavouring to discover which of these three women might be her aunt? Was it the big one with the shiny red face, the thin one with the tortoise-shell pince-nez,—that gave her such an owl-like expression,—or the little fat one in pale blue chiffon? Evidently the latter, for she struggled out of her arm-chair, and offered a podgy hand blazing with diamonds.

"How do you do—*no!*" drawing back. "No, no, please don't kiss me!—I'm dreadfully afraid of microbes. My health, as you know, is so uncertain, and I have to be very cautious. We have been expecting you for the last half hour. What has kept you?"

"I believe the train was late," replied Nancy in a meek voice. Could this little cross fat woman, be Daddy's sister?

"Oh, was it? Have you paid the cab?"

"Yes."

"How much did he charge from Charing Cross?" demanded Mrs. Taylor,—an authority on fares.

"Four and sixpence."

"What!" The word was almost a shout.

"But I had luggage."

"Oh, yes, and your big boxes had better be kept below," said her aunt; "I am so afraid of my poor walls being damaged. You can sit down, Nancy. These are my friends, Mrs. Taylor, and Miss Dolling."

The ladies shook hands in silence. After a moment Miss Dolling said:

"Had you a good passage?"

"Yes, thank you."

Meanwhile her aunt was surveying Nancy with a look of puzzled disappointment.

"So you are *not* a Travers after all," she remarked. "How odd, and unexpected."

"No, I believe I am a Blake."

"A Blake," repeated Mrs. Jenkins, "I never heard of the people," and she knitted her light eyebrows as she reflected that possibly "Blake" had been the maiden name of the adventuress? "I daresay you would like to take your things off?"

"Yes, if you please, I should."

"Then will you ring the bell? It is close to the chimney-piece—on the far side."

When Galpin awaited orders in the doorway, Mrs. Jenkins said:

"Tell Baker to come and show Miss Travers to her room."

Baker promptly appeared, took the new arrival, so to speak, in tow, convoyed her to the fifth floor, and into a somewhat shabby apartment, next to her own bower.

As soon as Nancy had left the drawing-room, the three ladies closed in together comfortably, in order to discuss the new arrival with unreserved enjoyment. The ultimate finding of the conference proved unfavourable.

"The girl was not a Travers; her manners were awkward, and she was quite hopelessly plain!"

CHAPTER XVII
AS POOR RELATION

Nancy soon fell into the routine of the household, and led an active, useful life at 900, Queen's Gate. Undoubtedly it was good for her, that she had no leisure, nor any opportunity for reflection and solitude, save when in bed. Then she was so thoroughly tired, that she fell asleep almost as soon as her head was on the pillow. After all, the daily régime of this elderly establishment, was not so irksome to a girl who had been for years, accustomed to the strict discipline of a boarding school.

Within a week, the new arrival had learnt her aunt's chief ailments and requirements, taken a sharp impression of her character, and was not a little amazed at her own capabilities in measuring drops, picking up stitches, and writing notes. She also read aloud, and went endless messages. Many a tiresome errand did she save Baker, and the cook; many a toilsome journey did she make up those long flights of stairs: the excuse for such constant perambulation, being, "that she was *young*!"

At first, her visit had been spoken of as "temporary," Mrs. Taylor and Miss Dolling being actively engaged in searching for a suitable post for the interloper. The former, was particularly anxious to be rid of this too useful, and obedient relative,—who accomplished her tasks without complaint or murmur. The truth was, that Nancy had not forgotten Mrs. De Wolfe's wise counsel, and inwardly soothed her *amour propre* by saying to herself, "Aunt Arabella is Daddy's sister, and I must try to please her; though lots of the things I have to do, are hateful,—and Mrs. Taylor is more detestable than everything put together!"

Her most unwelcome task, was that of exercising the Pom twice daily on a lead—a job that really belonged to Baker. He was a little animal with an odious character,—and not a gentleman; quarrelsome, and insulting to other dogs, shamelessly greedy and inquisitive, and with a bark, that was almost worse than a bite!

Meanwhile Nancy plodded along, buoyed up by hope and letters,— hope that "Finchie" would be home in the spring, and find her a nice situation—with payment. Here, naturally, she received no salary; her wealthy aunt was in some ways surprisingly stingy; a miser with respect to stamps, and extraordinarily mean in the matter of coal, electric light, cab fares, and newspapers. As for the electric light, they often sat in semi-darkness, and yet Mrs. Jenkins thought nothing of paying from twenty to thirty guineas for a gown, or a shilling for a plover's egg!

Nancy's happiest moments were when the Indian mail arrived, and brought her long despatches from "Finchie," from Francis, from the Hicks family, and Teddy Dawson. The latter had once enclosed in a letter what is known as a "fat" cheque, amounting to sixty-three pounds and some odd shillings, which had been paid into Ted's account on her behalf by Mayne. This cheque was promptly returned, and Nancy scribbled at white heat, "I will not touch this money; please do not offer it again, or ever mention Captain Mayne; all *that* is a dreadful dream, which I am doing my best to *forget*."

Letters from India were not the only ones addressed to Miss Travers from the outer world. She had received a short note from Mrs. De Wolfe, and several ill-spelt scrawls, indited by Mr. Fletcher's valet. He was now living in a sanatorium in Switzerland, a confirmed invalid; indeed the valet, who was a Scotchman, informed Nancy that his master was "far through." Mr. Fletcher wished to hear how his little Nancy was faring? if she had need of money, and if her aunt kept her well supplied? otherwise she knew where to come for it. *He* would be her banker. But poor as she was, Nancy preferred to be independent. A portion of her savings, still remained intact.

She sent frequent letters to her old friend, gratefully declining his offer—telling him everything about herself, that she thought might interest or please him,—carefully omitting all disagreeables; she also added scraps of news, gleaned from her Indian correspondence; in short, Nancy had the art of composing cheery epistles, which were deeply appreciated by a sick, and solitary exile.

In August, Mrs. Jenkins journeyed to Harrogate, bearing Nancy and Baker in her train. The lady much preferred Scarborough, and cast many wistful thoughts in that direction, but then Baker had a married sister living at Harrogate, so there it was—or rather, there *she* was!

Mrs. Jenkins stayed for several weeks at a fashionable hotel, consulted a new doctor, sat about the gardens, sipped the waters, and compared gossip and symptoms with her friends. During the latter part of the visit, she allowed Nancy to spend a short time with Mrs. Briscoe at Eastbourne, whilst Mrs. Taylor, who had been languishing in her poky little flat, stepped nimbly into her shoes.

Nine hundred, Queen's Gate, was reopened at the end of September. The charwoman's parties came to an end, and the carriage horses no longer took the coachman's friends to Hampton Court, Kew, or "the pictures." Everything gradually settled into the usual routine, as far as Nancy was concerned; exercising the Pom, changing the library books, shopping at the Stores, and attending upon her relative.

One afternoon, as laden with parcels, she re-entered the house, Galpin handed her a card, on which was inscribed, "Mrs. De Wolfe, Newenham Court. So very sorry to miss you." The card was presently followed by a note, inviting Nancy to lunch with Mrs. De Wolfe at her hotel, but this, alas! she was compelled to decline, as the date fixed, happened to be her aunt's weekly "day," and she was on duty with the teapot.

A second note from Mrs. De Wolfe, repeated her disappointment at not seeing her young friend, especially as she was about to leave London, in order to spend the winter in the West Indies. Her disappointment was as nothing to Nancy's, for in her case, it was increased by despondency.

Ever since her arrival, under her aunt's roof, Mrs. Taylor had been ceaselessly endeavouring to remove her elsewhere. She had sought out, and suggested several situations, but these on examination had not proved to be satisfactory. One, was as an apprentice in a ladies' blouse and hat shop—to assist in the showroom and workroom, hours eight to six, dinner provided— no remuneration, but then "it was such a good opening," that Mrs. Taylor was enthusiastic. Another "opportunity," of which Nancy refused to avail herself, was as typist to a rising young dentist—and to give some assistance with the patients!

"But I'm afraid of dentists, and I cannot type!" protested Nancy. "If Aunt Arabella wishes, I can find a situation. Mrs. Briscoe will arrange for me—she has offered to do so."

Greatly to her friend's dismay, Mrs. Jenkins was not at present disposed to part with her useful slave, and sternly commanded Henrietta to postpone the search.

Autumn passed without any particular change; Nancy developed into a sort of extra lady's-maid, companion, secretary, and butt; Mrs. Jenkins saw a good deal of company: when her health permitted she was at home on "Tuesdays," and received many visitors,—as her teas were proverbially well provided—fruit and ices, were not unknown. These Tuesday afternoons, entailed weary hours for her niece, who stood pouring out, handing cakes, and generally assisting Galpin.

Mrs. Jenkins also gave occasional solemn dinners. These banquets were usually attended by various elderly men of her acquaintance, as she had a notable cook, and a famous bin of superior old port. At such festivities, Nancy was not expected to appear; her mourning was too deep. It was for this reason also, that Nancy was never invited to accompany her relative to any place of amusement. Mrs. Jenkins declared, that she could not possibly go into society for a full twelve-month. Her idea on the subject of mourning, was strict, and old-fashioned—mourning by the year,—crêpe by the yard. When the banquets took place, Nancy wrote out the menus, and name cards, arranged the flowers, and Bridge tables, and then thankfully retreated to the breakfast-room with a novel, and the Pom.

Sometimes she felt that this life was almost too difficult! Mrs. Taylor's poisonous influence told heavily against her; her enemy was so often with her in the Gate; she lunched or dined two or three times a week,—and having a genuine appetite for small doles, carried away fresh eggs, extra flowers, half-cut cakes, a box of scented soap, and similar useful largesse! After her visits, Nancy always found her aunt more than usually snappy, and ill to please; yet on the other hand, Mrs. Jenkins had what her niece mentally called "her good days." On these, she would talk glibly enough about her brother Laurence; his mad pranks, his high spirits, his good looks, extraordinary love for animals, and general popularity with old and young.

It also seemed to the girl—who was gifted with a vivid imagination—that now and then, in her aunt's conversation, she caught a faint echo of familiar expressions, and that she saw at long intervals on the face of her despotic relative, a glimmer of her father's smile! For these somewhat far-fetched, and flimsy reasons, Nancy still clung to her post. After all, Aunt Arabella, with her funny ways, was her only *near* relative. She was Daddy's sister too, they had been brought up in the very same nursery, and had shared the same home.

The talks of "old times" at Lambourne, were considerably discounted by Mrs. Jenkins' rosy and prosy reminiscences of her own personal triumphs. On this subject, she could expatiate for hours,—content with a silent audience, or an occasional ejaculation.

"I daresay, my dear," she remarked to her niece, "that your father often told you, that I was the beauty of Blankshire, and how people would stand upon the road to look at me, and push and fight each other, to travel in the same railway carriage. The County ball was actually postponed, until I had returned home. After I was married, when I had a box at the theatre, it was most unpleasant the way the audience stared—every opera-glass levelled at poor me—and people waited in the vestibule, to see me pass out. Once when we were dining at a foreign restaurant, the prince of a royal house, sent round to inquire my name? Your uncle was furious, and I am sure it was the prince who sent me every morning, a most beautiful bouquet of flowers!"

She also related at considerable length, how several great artists had humbly implored permission to paint her portrait, but had been rudely snubbed by dearest Samuel: who had never allowed her picture to be on public exhibition.

Nancy listened with attentive interest to these tales of triumph, and faithfully believed in them. It may have been due to this artless confidence and appropriate deference, that she and her aunt were perceptibly drawing closer to one another; Nancy would receive an occasional kiss, a little patting of her hand, or even a word of praise, and thanks.

Alas, shortly before Christmas, a slump in Mrs. Taylor's dividends and a severe financial crisis, figuratively cast that lady at the feet of her wealthy school-fellow. Dearest Henrietta was received with open arms, offered the best spare bedroom, the second best, and most comfortable arm-chair, and soon settled down with remarkable ease into the position of an established resident.

Not long after this acquisition to the family circle, Mrs. Jenkins' manner to her niece underwent a change; she became querulous and fault-finding, and her "good days" were rare. Once, when the girl had ventured to speak of her old home, her friends, the far-away blue hills, and the coffee estate, Mrs. Taylor had coughed significantly, and her aunt had said:

"There, that will do, Nancy, that will do! I don't want to hear anything about those people; I am not interested."

As there were visitors present, Nancy was overwhelmed, and put to open shame by such a resounding slap in the face. Perhaps, after all, it was excellent discipline; Nancy the impulsive, was rapidly mastering the noble art of self-effacement and self-control. Her sorest trial was experienced of an evening, when Bridge was played, and Miss Dolling made a fourth. The scoldings administered to Nancy—especially when playing with Mrs. Taylor—made her so nervous that her mistakes were flagrant. She had actually been known to trump her partner's best card; more than once, she had been driven from the table in disgrace, and the rubber had ended in "cut throat."

Only for Mrs. Taylor (whose dislike amounted to personal enmity), Nancy believed that her aunt would have given her a small share of her heart; and for her own part, she made a great effort to storm her affections;

but her attempts were invariably foiled by the sinister influence of Mrs. Taylor, who had marked "darling Arabella" for her own! She had reason to believe that her name was in "the will"—and naturally the fewer legatees the better!

Arabella was so weak and impressionable, she might take it into her head to make this niece her heiress! The girl was apparently good-tempered, and willing—but in reality, cunning, and deceitful. Arabella was of full habit; an apoplectic seizure might carry her off in a few hours, and she (Henrietta Taylor) was bound to be on her guard, and to take the situation firmly in hand. With this virtuous intention, she made stinging speeches, transformed harmless remarks, accused Nancy of untruth, and impertinence, and did her utmost to figuratively crush her out of existence like a black beetle, and create a wide breach between aunt and niece. Mrs. Taylor was particularly careful never to leave the pair alone; a *tête-à-tête* was always a serious danger to be avoided: precisely as if Mrs. Jenkins was a lovely young heiress—and Nancy, some unprincipled and discountenanced suitor! If by chance, she entered a room and there discovered the girl established with her relative, she looked so alarmingly black and lowering, that Nancy received an impression, that she had been caught in the act of stealing something that was the property of Aunt Arabella's old friend!

On the other hand, when Nancy found the couple together, her appearance was the signal for an abrupt and significant silence,—undoubtedly she and her short-comings, had been the topic of conversation.

In spite of this, Nancy had an instinctive impression that her aunt was a little afraid of her towering, black-browed inmate; once, when she made her a trifling and inexpensive present, she added:

"Don't show it to Henrietta," and on several occasions, she had whispered, "Not a word of *this*, to Mrs. T.!"

Mrs. Taylor was now enjoying what might be called "the time of her life." Of an afternoon, she accompanied her friend in the comfortable landau, behind a pair of fat brown horses,—royally arrayed in a superior, if secondhand, ermine stole, and muff. She was carried to theatres, lectures, concerts, and At homes: was suffered to make the first pounce upon new novels, enjoy breakfast in bed at pleasure,—and glasses of port at discreet intervals. Moreover, she had been endowed with several imposing costumes; and yet she was not happy! for Nancy Travers represented "Mordecai the Jew," in Queen's Gate,—and until she was dislodged, her enemy could know no peace.

It was ten months since Nancy had arrived from India, ten months of suppressed grief, hard work, and complete isolation. She had recovered her health,—thanks to incessant occupation, early hours, and good plain food. "The girl was picking up," as her aunt expressed it, and once or twice, she had actually been moved to remark, that in Nancy's now flawless skin, she saw something of "the family complexion!" (meaning her own). In spite of "the family complexion," Nancy was not treated as a relative, but an employée; her status in the establishment was that of a superior "tweenie"; as time went on, there were no longer any references to "old days at Lambourne," no affectionate pattings or strokings, no confidences, or small gifts—much less a condescending kiss.

Mrs. Taylor made as much mischief as lay in her power, and fomented and instigated "rows." She never gave her adversary credit for one good trait, but held up all her short-comings, in the domestic limelight. Late at night, when established at her ease in her friend's bedroom, she "talked over" the iniquities of the day with unctuous eloquence.

She (the chief parasite) loudly bewailed her poor darling Arabella's fate, in being compelled to support a thankless hanger-on! Pointed out, that Nancy was secretive, that she wrote too many letters, wasting her time and stamps; that she was cruel to the Pom, and flirted with the new doctor—even going so far as to lie in wait for him in the hall! Every one of these indictments was a deliberate and inexcusable falsehood; and perhaps Mrs. Jenkins, at the back of her mind, reminded herself that Henrietta "exaggerated"; but at last, after many vigorous efforts, Henrietta succeeded in rousing her effectually. One night, as soon as she had settled herself for the usual talk, she began abruptly:

"I do believe that girl has been complaining to Mrs. Devine, telling her that she is miserable here,—at least, that is what *I* inferred, from what Mrs. Devine said to me to-day. She was quite sniffy and stand-off, and refused a cup of tea."

"What did she say?" demanded Mrs. Jenkins fiercely.

"She said, that it was noticed how Miss Travers always went about alone; quite a well-known figure in Kensington Gardens, a tall girl in mourning, taking a Pom for exercise. That she was never to be seen with her aunt in the carriage, or at any place of amusement."

"Why, of course not!" burst out Mrs. Jenkins; "her year of mourning is not nearly up. What else?" she demanded dramatically.

"That she appeared to have no young friends."

"Is it likely, my good Henrietta, that I would allow my house to be overrun and turned upside down by a pack of young people, simply to amuse a girl who has to look to *me*, for her daily bread? I never cared for Mrs. Devine, but I had intended to invite her to my next large dinner-party. Now I shall cross her name off the list—she shall eat no more dinners or luncheons, *here*!"

"I should hope not!" said Mrs. Taylor emphatically, "for Mrs. Murray told me privately, how Mrs. Devine had remarked to her, that the girl was treated more like a servant, than a relative: said she was shabbily dressed, neglected, and snubbed, and that if Miss Travers had a spark of spirit, she would find another situation—and clear out!"

This conversation proved extremely agitating to Mrs. Jenkins. It came as a revelation; a shattering mental avalanche: that anyone among her acquaintance should dare to find fault with *her*! The extraordinary influence of Mrs. Taylor, was entirely due to her unfailing supply of the most honeyed flattery! Misguided Arabella, was invariably told the things she wished to hear, and lived under the impression, that she was beyond the reach of criticism; everything she did was right; she had felt complacently assured that her neighbours and friends unanimously applauded her, for her benevolence in giving a home to her orphan niece!

The recent exciting and unexpected information, brought on a sharp attack of nervous palpitation.—Whenever Mrs. Jenkins was annoyed, she immediately complained of "palpitation."—Mrs. Taylor had swift recourse to the usual remedy, a bottle of drops—and as she handed the wine-glass to her patroness, she said impressively:

"Darling Arabella, you *know*, you will never have any comfort or peace, until you get rid of that girl. She is accomplished, I understand, and now she is nineteen, and looks years older than when she arrived, surely her friend Mrs. Briscoe can find her a situation as governess?"

"No, no," protested Mrs. Jenkins, "I won't have that—Nancy is useful; clever with her fingers, active on her feet; the Pom is fond of her, and you know how few people *he* likes! Baker, too, though terribly against Nancy at first, thinks her a nice young lady. Of course, I need not tell you, that I never bargained for a girl in the house; and I daresay I should be happier without her, but if I were to allow Nancy to go away, and take a situation—just think of the *talk*!"

"It would be much better to have one big talk,—and get it over," declared Mrs. Taylor philosophically, "better to clear the air, than to have perpetual whispering. Some people are never happy, unless they are picking holes in such as you—whose shoes they are not fit to clean. And now, dearest Arabella, I cannot bear to see you worried,—as you know. If you could only make up your mind to let Nancy take a situation, we should all be so *much* more comfortable. Remember she is not actually your own niece; only your stepbrother's daughter. Do, *do*, think it over—good-night, my own—darling!"

"Good-night, Henrietta, and be sure you turn out the electric light on your landing. Last week, you left it on all night, and just think of how *that* will add to my quarterly bill!"

CHAPTER XVIII
A RESCUE

The winter had been long and dreary, and held no bright gleams for Nancy, who was sensible of a continuous atmosphere of suppression and oppression! It was now the capricious month of April, and in sympathy with its showers, she secretly shed many tears. Mrs. Jenkins had arrived at the definite decision, that her niece was "unsatisfactory"! This expression had been specially coined by Mrs. Taylor, who put it into daily currency. It was true that now and then the girl had absented herself for an hour or two in the afternoon, taking prolonged walks round the Park, or Kensington Gardens,—attended exclusively by the Pom.—She wasted time in the Victoria and Albert Museum, the Natural History Museum, and had even penetrated to the National Gallery!

Also, she had found her tongue, and ventured to talk to and make acquaintance with the elderly crowd assembled every Tuesday. More than all, she had become careless! She had broken a pet vase, value three francs, and—incredible enormity!—lost a library book—dropped it into the street from the top of a motor-'bus. Her last misdeed was of such gravity, that she had been formally summoned to the drawing-room, there to appear before her judges, and be sharply reprimanded. As Mrs. Jenkins, Miss Dolling, and Mrs. Taylor awaited the culprit, the latter said:

"My dear, you can see for yourself, how that girl is growing worse and worse, and becoming more unsatisfactory every day."

(It should be here explained, that Miss Dolling took a lenient view of Nancy's delinquencies, and was on occasion her ineffectual champion. She had even offered to take her to places of amusement—these invitations never came to Nancy's ears—for Miss Dolling cherished a mild, sentimental regard, for the daughter of her one and only love,—whose photograph, enshrined in silver, she treasured as a sacred relic).

Nancy's latest misdeed was of far-reaching consequence. Detailed to fetch her aunt's best transformation from the hairdressers' (where recently it had been renovated), she had left it in the Tube; abandoned it to the heartless jeers of railway officials, and the publicity of the Lost Property

Office! The truth was, that Nancy had that morning heard of the death of Mr. Fletcher, and her thoughts were sad, and far away, as she travelled to South Kensington.—This valuable work of hair art, had cost no less than twelve guineas,—and what was poor Mrs. Jenkins to wear that evening at dinner?

The scolding had been so bitter, and impassioned, that Nancy's humility had at last given way, and as, with heightened colour and shining eyes, she seemed inclined to protest and expostulate, the enemy brought heavier guns to bear.

"Is it true?" demanded Mrs. Jenkins, sitting Buddha-like, with folded arms, "that you write to young men?"

"Yes," replied Nancy, "I do."

"She couldn't deny it!" broke in Mrs. Taylor; "I've seen the letters myself, lying upon the hall table."

"And you smoke cigarettes up in your own room," she added.

"Yes, occasionally," admitted the sinner.

"And waste the electric light, reading in bed," resumed Mrs. Jenkins, raising her voice with each accusation. "Mrs. Taylor saw the light under your door after eleven o'clock at night!"

"I do read in bed,—I've no time to read in the day," answered the girl defiantly.

"Keep your temper, miss!—that is not the way to speak to *me*," shouted her aunt, in an angry voice.

"No indeed, darling," chimed in Mrs. Taylor, "and after all you have done for her—taken her in, when she was a penniless orphan, and— —"

"Yes," interrupted Mrs. Jenkins, "and I hear you have gone behind my back, and complained to Mrs. Devine,—oh, you abominable, ungrateful, double-faced minx!"

"To Mrs. Devine?" repeated Nancy. "I have never spoken to her in my life!"

"I don't believe you!" declared the accuser, her face alarmingly aflame; at this sharp crisis, the door was pushed open, and Galpin announced:

"Mrs. De Wolfe."

Mrs. De Wolfe, handsomely dressed, and completely self-possessed, walked forward to where Nancy stood before her accusers, and said in her masculine bass:

"Oh, my dear Nancy, I'm delighted to find you in at last! Pray introduce me to your aunt?" and she glanced at Mrs. Taylor,—who was still heaving with virtuous indignation.

The atmosphere was heavily charged with electricity, and for a moment Nancy was speechless. Then, hastily recovering herself:

"This is my aunt, Mrs. Jenkins. Aunt Arabella, here is Mrs. De Wolfe, with whom I travelled home in the *Patna*."

The shock of such an unexpected interruption had suddenly sobered Mrs. Jenkins: for a moment, she had been threatened with palpitation,—but thrust the temptation aside. Recently, she had heard Mrs. De Wolfe referred to as a woman of wealth and social importance; she therefore made an effort to recover her poise, and accord her a gracious reception. After a somewhat breathless and incoherent conversation with her hostess, Mrs. De Wolfe turned to Nancy.

"Have you been here ever since you came home?"

"Yes," she replied, and then boldly added: "I have not taken a situation yet; but I intend to see about one immediately," and she looked straight at her aunt, who encountered her gaze with sullen hostility.

This unexpected reinforcement by Mrs. De Wolfe had given Nancy a species of ephemeral, or "Dutch" courage.

"Oh, are you, my dear? But before you arrange anything definite, I hope you will come and pay me a little visit. I am staying for a couple of weeks at Brown's Hotel, in Dover Street, and shall be glad to have your company at once."

The eyes of Mrs. Jenkins and Mrs. Taylor met; their expression was significant.

"You are very kind," replied the former, now addressing her visitor, "but my niece is not leaving me—as far as *I* am aware—but I shall be pleased to spare her to you, for a few days."

"Thank you very much," replied Mrs. De Wolfe. "Then if you will allow me, I will call for her to-morrow."

At this moment other visitors were announced, and Nancy's ally rose and took leave. As she pressed the girl's hand she murmured:

"Had you not better come down with me to the hall,—and see that I don't carry off the umbrellas?"

On the landing, she halted opposite the stuffed dog, and said:

"My poor dear child! The door was ajar, and I heard every word about the cigarettes, the electric light, the reading in bed, the penniless orphan, and Mrs. Devine. What people! As for the big, dark woman, with the red face, positively she frightened me!—she is like a Gorgon!"

"I was getting on all right until just before Christmas when Mrs. Taylor arrived," replied Nancy; "she is dreadfully poor; she hates me, and thinks I am an interloper, and a fortune-hunter. Ever since she came into the house, Aunt Arabella is completely changed."

"I intend that you shall be completely changed," declared Mrs. De Wolfe. "Oh, I must go! I see the man is waiting at the door. I'll call for you to-morrow before twelve o'clock,—and I think you had better bring most of your luggage."

A visit to Mrs. De Wolfe proved a change indeed. Nancy felt another creature, living in another atmosphere, and another city. Oh, the blessed relief, from hearing the ponderous tread of Mrs. Taylor, Galpin's pompous announcements, and the Pom's maddening bark!

She and her hostess shopped in the mornings, motored in the afternoons, and at night, went to concerts, lectures, and the theatre. Within a few days, it had been decided, that Nancy was to be Mrs. De Wolfe's companion for the present,—and to receive sixty pounds a year, on which to dress. Already the girl had felt the stimulating effects of a new and fashionable outfit!

"Without flattering myself, I think I may say, that you will be happier with *me*, than with Mrs. Jenkins," observed her benefactress; "though I am by no means an angel! Every character has its odd corners, its limits, and its secrets. You are too young to harbour any secrets yet—whilst I have dozens!"

She also added, that later, should anything more satisfactory turn up, Nancy was not to consider herself bound in any way; and so the arrangement, or engagement, was concluded—an engagement which existed for little more than a week.

One afternoon, Nancy, who had just returned from the Park, was informed, that someone who had brought a message, particularly wanted to see her, and she was a good deal surprised, when the door of the sitting-room was opened, and no less a person than Galpin emerged from the passage. He was surprised, too,—as he subsequently confessed, when he imparted particulars of his visit to the lady's maid.

"There was Miss Travers, looking like another girl! her hair all fluffed out, wearing a great big hat covered with feathers—quite the fashionable young lady. I declare to you, Miss Baker, I hardly knew her!"

Galpin, who carried a packet of letters in his hand, peered cautiously round the room, made a stiff little bow, coughed, and said:

"Mrs. Jenkins sent me over special with these letters for you, Miss. She said, there was one that looked like a business matter, and is anxious to know what it is all about? She thinks, as you have been doing secretary work for her—that maybe there's a mistake in the name—as it's from a firm of lawyers. I was to bring back the letter, Miss, and to give Mrs. Jenkins' love, and to tell you how the Pom misses you."

Nancy received and hastily examined the letters. The Indian Mail was in. There was a thick one from Finchie, a thin one from Nellie Meach, and a postcard from Francis, on which was inscribed, "The dog Togo is too well." Besides these, one was in a blue envelope, on the flap of which was printed, the name of a legal firm. She sat down to open this,—in order to at once satisfy her aunt; whilst Galpin waited, hat in hand, with an air of respectful curiosity.

As Nancy glanced over the neatly-written lines, she faintly grasped an almost incredible fact. Mr. Fletcher's will had recently been read; he had endowed her with Fairplains, and an income of two thousand a year! This was the substance of what she gathered, through a maze of legal expressions. For a moment, she imagined that she must be dreaming. Then she slowly went over the pages, and noted, that the firm requested an immediate interview, and that one of their clerks would wait upon her at an hour, and date, to be hereafter fixed.

For a moment or two she sat motionless, endeavouring to collect her faculties; then, with considerably heightened colour, she raised her head, and looked up at Galpin,—who almost conveyed the impression that he was in attendance at table, and waiting to remove her plate!

"Please tell Aunt Arabella, that the letter was really for me, and contains good news. I will write to her to-night."

"Very well, Miss. Is that all—ahem—*no* particulars?" Galpin's tone expressed extreme disappointment.

"No particulars," rising as she spoke; "good afternoon, Galpin, I think you can find your way down," and she indicated the door.

As soon as this had closed behind Galpin's broad back, Nancy, letter in hand, rushed into Mrs. De Wolfe's bedroom. The old lady, who had only recently come in, was changing her boots, assisted by the invaluable Haynes.

"I've just had this," announced the girl breathlessly. "Aunt Arabella sent it over by Galpin; she wanted so much to know what it was all about? Do look at it—and tell me if you think it's *real*?"

Mrs. De Wolfe hastily dismissed her maid, and with one boot on, and one boot off, assumed her glasses and deliberately studied the letter; then she looked up at Nancy, and said·

"An heiress, I declare! My dear, I congratulate you. I *am* glad."

"Do you think it's true? I can hardly believe it! Oh, I feel I'd like to run about, and tell the whole hotel of my wonderful good fortune. It's not the money so much,—but Fairplains—how splendid of Mr. Fletcher, and oh, if father were only alive!"

"Fairplains. Yes, it was your father's once, now it is yours; you were born there, and love it; but a solid income is a satisfactory fact. Well, now you are independent, and can engage a companion—or a chaperone."

"I want to stay with you!"

"But what will Mrs. Jenkins say?" and Mrs. De Wolfe laughed. "How I should like to see her face, when she hears that you are no longer 'a penniless orphan!'"

When Mrs. Jenkins received the news, she was so startled, and upset, that she felt compelled to ring for Baker to bring her some special heart drops; and yet she was gratified in a way. To have a niece who was an heiress, increased—if that were possible—her sense of her own importance. Mrs. Taylor was also gratified. There would now be no question of the return of Nancy to Queen's Gate; no fear of her inheriting Mrs. Jenkins' substantial fortune; she would without further exertions, have the house, and the, so to speak, "field" to herself.

When the heiress arrived to pay her formal visit to Queen's Gate, she found her aunt in her most agreeable temper. Nancy might almost have been a titled acquaintance, so effusive was her welcome! After a few preliminaries, she said:

"Well, Nancy, so you've come in for a coffee estate, and a large sum of money! That is nice for you."

"I suppose there's no fear of the will being disputed?" said Mrs. Taylor—ever ready with disagreeable suggestions.

"I think not," replied the heiress. "I remember Mr. Fletcher telling us, that he was the last of his family."

"You won't know what to do with all your money," declared Mrs. Jenkins with a complacent smile. "Of course you will return *here*."

"Return!" repeated the girl blankly.

"Why, certainly, you must live with *me*; it is your natural home. It would be most extraordinary if you did not! What would people say? I am your only near relative. You will be putting off your mourning, and I shall take you out this season,—and perhaps give a dance for you. You shall have a room on the next floor,—and I daresay you can keep a maid."

Mrs. Taylor's face clouded over as she listened to these luxurious arrangements. How close Arabella had been; the sly old thing had never dropped a word of these plans, during their nightly conferences.

"Thank you, Aunt Arabella," replied Nancy, "but I am going to travel with Mrs. De Wolfe. We shall probably be abroad for a year. I have never been on the Continent; and I think we shall start as soon as the lawyers have finished with my affairs."

"That is a monstrous idea; I shall not give my consent," declared her aunt with a very pink face. "Mrs. De Wolfe is a complete stranger. Ten days, or a fortnight, is all very well, but you cannot go about the world with a woman who is nothing to you beyond being a fellow passenger. It would be most unseemly. Remember that you are not of age yet,—and have no right to do just as you please."

"I see no objection," murmured Nancy.

"You see *me*," announced Mrs. Jenkins with emphasis, "*I* am the objection. You cannot deny, that I stand to you in the place of a parent—that I have received you,—and adopted you"—here she paused to sneeze.

"I was not aware that you had adopted me, Aunt Arabella; and I think I had better say at once, that I should be sorry to have any disagreement with you, but I cannot admit that you have any right to control me. Mrs. De Wolfe and I, are starting for Italy in a few days, and this visit is not merely to tell you about my plans,—but to say good-bye."

"My dear, I think Nancy is *very* wise," proclaimed Mrs. Taylor, advancing unexpectedly to her rescue. "You know, that she has seen nothing of the world as yet; and she is so young; the tour will complete her education. Mrs. De Wolfe is a friend of the dear Foresters, and the aunt of Lady Bincaster, *quite* all that she ought to be! Judging by my own feelings, I am sure that Nancy would not care to go into company yet; and anyway, the state of your health could never stand the strain of playing chaperone, and keeping late hours. Now *could* it?" laying her heavy hand upon her friend's fat arm. "Of course we all know, that you are always only *too* ready to sacrifice yourself for others; but your friends could never permit you to undertake, what would be practically, a sort of prolonged suicide!"

"Well, I suppose there is something in what you say," admitted Mrs. Jenkins, after a moment's reflection, reluctantly releasing the vision of a wealthy niece on show—and so to speak, bearing her own train.

Indeed, such was the effect of Mrs. Taylor's soothing, and cooling remarks, that by degrees, her old school-fellow recovered her temper and complacency. She talked about the Continent, of her triumphal progress through various cities, and related the tale of a tragic experience in the Tyrol, where it had been whispered "that a gallant young Austrian officer had precipitated himself from a mountain peak, solely on her account!"

After half an hour's discourse,—chiefly reminiscent,—Mrs. Jenkins had talked herself into a condition of the utmost good humour, and with the promises of letters, and many picture postcards, the visitor was permitted to take leave.

As Nancy departed, she noticed Baker peering at her over the banisters, and nodded to her affably, as she descended the stairs,—on which she had made many weary journeys—also it seemed to her, that Galpin the pompous, held the hall door extra wide, and was impressively benignant, as she passed forth.

CHAPTER XIX
"A MYSTERY ABOUT MAYNE——"

More than two years had elapsed since Derek Mayne left Fairplains. Almost immediately afterwards, his regiment had been removed from Cananore, to the distant cantonment of Bareilly,—a station which instead of lying on the damp seaboard of the Malabar Coast, was situated in the heart of a sugar cane district, with the white Himalayas glimmering on its horizon. Here, in hard work, and strenuous play, parades, manœuvres, inspections, cricket, polo, and fishing in the Sardar, time passed only too rapidly; thanks to new surroundings, new friends, and incessant occupation, the memory of Nancy became a little blurred.

Mayne recalled her existence, when he dispatched his half-yearly cheque to Teddy Dawson; for although his friend had assured him, that the money would lie untouched, nevertheless he persisted in lodging the amount at Grindlays. Teddy had volunteered the news, that Nancy was now living in London, with her father's sister; but of this information, Mayne vouchsafed no notice, and correspondence, save for the bi-annual cheque, had completely lapsed. The yearly sum of two hundred and fifty pounds,—which was half of his private income,—left Mayne somewhat pinched in his finances. To keep a couple of ponies, to go on fishing, and shooting trips, required a certain number of rupees; and occasionally Captain Mayne found considerable difficulty in making both ends meet! His brother officers wondered why the deuce Mayne was now so economical? and what he had done with his money?

An incredible story had leaked out through Mayne's Madras servant—who had accompanied him to the Hills; it whispered, that when there, he had got into some sort of entanglement with a girl! This tale was frankly discussed, and believed, in the Gorrah bazaar at Cananore, but had never risen in any substantial form to higher circles,—such as the club or mess; and yet all the time, though nothing was said, there was a vague uneasy feeling, that Mayne was keeping back some incident or experience, connected with his six week's leave on that coffee plantation. It was noticed, how, although he had apparently enjoyed extraordinarily good sport, he was strangely reserved with regard to his hill friends; rarely referred to his expedition, and sat dumb when other fellows less successful, loudly bragged of their "shikar."

Also it had been remarked, that when he returned from the Neilgherries, he had appeared to be extraordinarily depressed, and that Mayne always such a cheery fellow, with lots to say for himself, hadn't a word to throw to the traditional dog. Former enthusiastic letters received by his friends, describing his delightful quarters, his first-class sport, were subsequently discounted, by a mysterious, and significant silence. One surprising fact, had been much discussed; Mayne was just the ordinary young man, and not in the least eccentric, and yet when his trophies were unpacked, displayed and praised (two magnificent tiger and three panther skins, all in first-class condition), as the largest panther skin was unrolled, he seemed strangely put out, and gave a hasty order to his bearer. Later, but four skins were exhibited, and when the fifth was inquired for, the bearer promptly answered that "the Sahib had given orders, that it was to be taken away and *burnt!*"

In a small Mofussil station such as Cananore, topics of conversation are but scanty. There was a good deal of talk and conjecture, respecting this same panther. Why had Mayne ordered such a prize to be destroyed? Why could he not have given it to someone—if he had a particular down upon the animal?—the Colonel's wife would have been proud to accept its skin.

No satisfactory answer to this was obtained at the time, but later, it became known that Mayne's friend, the coffee planter, had died, as the result of an encounter with a panther; it was conceded that possibly *that* was the reason of Mayne's agitation, and the order for the destruction of an unusually fine trophy.

Skin or no skin, there was some mystery connected with Mayne's visit to the Neilgherries. Since then, he had been obviously short of money, and given to unwonted economy. He drank cheap claret, refused himself a new rifle, and another polo pony. A hard player like Mayne, found it difficult to manage with less than three. Whatever the trouble was, he did not avoid society; he was popular with women; his good looks and good manners, made him a general favourite. He went to dances and picnics, was conspicuous in gymkhanas, and every afternoon, when nothing was "on," he played rackets or tennis at the club. Once or twice, when a particularly active girl happened to be his tennis partner, he recalled Nancy,—not one of the lot could approach her as far as play was concerned. Who would have believed that her thin brown arm and wrist, was capable of such smashing strokes, and disastrous service?

Mayne had now been three years in India, and never exhibited any intention of taking leave home. Apparently he preferred an excursion into Thibet, or Cashmere. At the back of his mind, he had a conviction, that as long as he remained in the country, he was safe from any awkward developments that might result from the ceremony which had taken place in the drawing-room at Fairplains.

Yet at the same time, he had an impression that some day, like murder, it would all come out,—and there would be a holy row! Meantime he thrust the hateful prospect into the lumber room of his brain; the poignant memories of the last week of Travers' life had now become a little dim. Supposing he had held back, and not suffered himself to be moved by an exceptionally tragic situation: by Mrs. Hicks' observations, and carried away by an almost irresistible impulse? he could have guaranteed an acceptable income to Nancy, which would have left them both free!

Now, they were bound together by that deadly certificate in his despatch box, on which were inscribed the names of Eleanora Nancy Travers, spinster, and Derek Danvers Mayne, bachelor. Nothing but death could release them. Occasionally plunged in contemplation, he would let his mind work; endeavouring to trace some way out of this desperate situation. His thoughts would travel to and fro, as in a maze,—vainly seeking some safe, and honourable exit. Sometimes, during these moods of reflection, his companion for the moment, would wonder at Mayne's abstraction? Once or twice, he had been offered "a penny for his thoughts," but had invariably dismissed the offer with a laugh.

Finally summing up the affair, he assured himself that some day or other—perhaps in twenty years—the whole business must be disclosed. Supposing Nancy wanted to marry someone?—supposing he were to meet *the* girl, and fall in love with her? what a complication that would be! After all, the present was calm and peaceful, he could discern no clouds on the horizon, and soothed his uneasiness, with the well-worn sedative,— "Sufficient unto the day is the evil thereof."

Such were Mayne's sentiments, when he received a cable from home, informing him that his uncle had met with a serious accident, and begging him to return at once. As there could be but one answer to such an appeal, Mayne instead of taking his intended sixty days' shooting leave into Garwalb, immediately applied for three months to England—on "urgent private affairs."

CHAPTER XX
NEW SCENES AND NEW FRIENDS

Nancy and her chaperone spent a year on the Continent, visiting several capitals, and various scenes familiar to Mrs. De Wolfe. Not a few foreign hostelries knew and respected the dominating personality, and heavy purse, of this hawk-eyed "bird of passage."

Nancy was now twenty. Like a flower she had expanded in the sun of happiness, and developed into a strikingly beautiful girl. The mahogany tint had given place to a matchless complexion: her figure no longer boyish and angular, was slender and graceful, her dress was dainty, and she carried herself admirably. After a long and complete eclipse, Nancy's vitality and vivacity had returned with undiminished vigour: the girl was never tired, idle, bored, or—silent; the mere fact of her presence, seemed to neutralize weariness and depression. Yet the death of her father was a never forgotten grief; he stood apart, as the one impressive, and beloved figure connected with her life in India. Memories of Finchie, the "Corner boys," and the Hicks', had become a little faint; as for the acquaintance of a mere six weeks, she had thrust him entirely out of her mind. At first, like some pernicious and persistent insect, he had returned again and again; but for many months she had been free from this hateful visitation.

Possibly when a young woman determines to evict from her thoughts a disagreeable lodger—such banishment is complete. Nancy had assured a quaking heart, that the ceremony of her marriage might be dismissed to the limbo of a bad dream. It had been carried out solely to comfort and relieve the anxiety of her dying father; but as a binding contract, Finchie had positively declared, that it could be easily annulled.

It was more than two years since Nancy had heard of Captain Mayne, "out of sight, is out of mind," especially as her mind was full to overflowing of new scenes, new interests, and new friends.

During their wanderings, Mrs. De Wolfe had encountered various neighbours, acquaintances, and connections. Her circle was world wide. At the Hôtel National, Lucerne, she came across the Miller family,—who lived within a motor drive of her home in Moonshire.

Truly, it was a strange and startling tale that Lady Miller poured into the ear of her neighbour, when she had carried her off to her own apartment, and could there talk without restraint! It appeared that the four Miss Millers, had combined to break loose, had cast off all obedience, and so to speak, flung the fourth commandment to the winds! Headed by Wilhelmina—the eldest—they revolted against home life, and clamoured to be taken abroad, in order to see something of what they called, "the world." "Wilhelmina," continued Lady Miller, "has an iron will and enormous influence over her father. It took her a whole fortnight to gain her point, at the end Lucas yielded, and, my dear old friend, I know you will pity us, for 'here we are!'"

Yes, Wilhelmina's triumph had been remorseless, and complete!

Glancing round the luxurious bedroom, whose windows commanded a fine view of the lake, Mrs. De Wolfe was not disposed to offer much sympathy to the lachrymose lady.

"Of course I don't approve of the present ordinance," she said: "Parents obey your children, but possibly a little change may be no harm for any of you. Your girls are grown up. Why! Billy must be six and twenty! The twins are a charming couple, and so far, have been born to blush unseen! Millfield Place *is* rather isolated, and surely you would not wish to have four old maids on your hands,—now *would* you?"

"*I'm* no husband-hunter," declared Lady Miller with considerable warmth, "and if girls are to be married, they'll *be* married."

"Well, that depends on circumstances! I remember an Irish servant who gave, as her reason for leaving an excellent, but dull situation, that 'she was out of the way of Providence.' I think there is the same drawback to Millfield."

Millfield Place was situated in a remote part of Moonshire, and in the days of Charles II., it had been the nucleus of many a robust and rollicking festivity: but time works changes, the Place was now generally referred to, as the "Back of Beyond." It was six miles from the nearest railway station: on the mere outer fringe of County Society, and to many of the rustics in Millfield village, the word "pictures" or "telephone" carried no meaning! Here years had passed swiftly—as they generally do, when spent in an uneventful, and monotonous round.

The four Miss Millers were endowed with an unusual amount of good looks, and intelligence; Wilhelmina, the eldest and heiress, was small, active, clever and outspoken: with a heart that knew no fear, and full of devotion to her sisters. Minna and Brenda (twins) were tall, vivacious and very fair to see. Amy, the youngest, aged twenty, had a wonderful mop of dark red hair, a pair of twinkling sea-green eyes, and uncontrollable spirits; she was still addressed as "Baby!"

For some years, the sisters had contented themselves with tennis, the sewing club, village entertainments, and the rearing of prize poultry; and then Wilhelmina, when her twenty-sixth birthday struck, began seriously to consider the situation. As alone she paced the long terrace, she held a solemn debate with herself, and this was the burden of her meditations: "Here we are embedded in the country, and growing into fossils. We haven't even a motor—because mother loathes them! We never see a soul, except the same old set, the Rector and Mrs. Puddock, Doctor and Mrs. Frost, father's elderly shooting friends; and once in a blue moon, the Hillsides, or Mrs. De Wolfe. Other girls go about, and visit new places, make new acquaintances, and have a good time; and we are young but once! I shall urge the Pater to transport us all to the Continent, for one whole year. If he resists, and won't listen to reason, I shall just tell him, we will leave home; the twins to go on the Stage,—front row,—Baby, to an A B C shop, and I to be a stewardess; I know I should love the sea,—which by the way, I have never seen!"

When Wilhelmina cautiously opened the subject to her mother, that lethargic matron was almost as startled as if a bomb had exploded on the hearth-rug! When she had recovered her senses (momentarily paralysed), with unusual animation, she expressed indignant horror at the mere suggestion of such a move. She pointed out to Billy that she and her sisters were extraordinarily fortunate; they had carriages, maids, saddle-horses; and every possible indulgence; the newest library books, a handsome dress allowance; what more did they want? Besides, how could such a pack of girls go dragging about the Continent! Certainly she would be no party to the crazy undertaking. Of course if they had been *boys*, it might have been different!

"Yes!" retorted Billy, "boys always get everything they want, and girls go to the wall."

"Well, boys or girls, nothing will induce *me* to leave my comfortable home," declared Lady Miller. "Paris, Switzerland, Egypt!" slightly raising her voice, "why, Wilhelmina, you must be mad! You know perfectly well, that I've not been even to London, for more than two years."

Lady Miller, a pretty, plaintive, fragile-looking woman, had been a celebrated beauty in her day,—but was now disposed to rest on such laurels, as remained. She relinquished visiting, and entertaining—beyond a small tennis party, or a few neighbours to tea,—pleading the state of her health; which, as it happened, was excellent; but the poor woman suffered from the dire and mortal malady of inertia; which is known to attack victims who live remote, and idle. The disease had grown from bad to worse, and Lady Miller had now abandoned herself to an existence of self-indulgent indolence. She was contented with her comfortable sofa, her embroidery, novels, patience cards, visits from newsmongering matrons,—and on fine days, an inspection of her celebrated rock garden! Wilhelmina had relieved her mother of all housekeeping worries: she managed the school, the village,—and her father.

The younger girls were amusing, chattering creatures: fond of racing through the rooms, banging doors, and bringing in dogs, but remarkably pretty—especially Brenda, who at times, was almost startlingly lovely! Once or twice, Lady Miller had murmured to her husband "that she wished Brenda's rich godmother would invite her to pay her a visit in London,"—and her husband had accorded an indifferent assent—*he* did not wish to part with *any* of his girls.

Sir Lucas Miller was an active, fussy, little gentleman of fifty-five, whose time was absorbed by tenants, shooting, the county club, and the Bench! Little did he suspect, how soon the pleasant current of his days was to be diverted. One evening after dinner,—a particularly good dinner,—the bold, adventurous, and *cunning* Wilhelmina, accompanied him to the smoking-room, and as he enjoyed a Havana, calmly proceeded to lay her plans before him.

Everything had been most carefully considered: the whole itinerary minutely sketched; reasons for the expedition were confidently advanced, and dilated on, and when at last, Wilhelmina had ceased to speak, she discovered that her communication had left her father speechless! For quite a surprising interval, he remained silent,—Sir Lucas was thinking things over! He liked to see his pretty, lively girls flitting about the house and tennis courts, but it had never once dawned on him, that they craved either change, or other diversions. "Why, they had the Hunt Ball in January,—weather permitting,—the cricket week in July,—also weather permitting!"

In his opinion, they were remarkably well off; and as Billy, his favourite, had carefully unfolded her schemes, he could scarcely believe his own ears.

"Close the house for twelve months! take you all abroad!" he cried at last. "What a monstrous idea. How about the estate, and the shooting?"

"You have an excellent agent, Dad, I've often heard you say so,—and now you may as well give him something to do. You know you're one of the people who keep a dog,—and bark yourself!"

"Rubbish! rubbish! preposterous nonsense!"

"I know you won't mind, dear, if I speak a little plainly. Looking at it from our point of view, do you think you are quite playing the game? You and the Mater have had your good times! You talk of Ascot, Scotland, and Paris; of dances and balls, operas, and races. Now *we* should like to be in a position, to enjoy the same experiences. We are very ready to be amused: or even employed; but there is not enough work here for the four of us. Are we always to content ourselves with visiting old women, rearing Buff Orpingtons, and finding our chief excitement in scraps of village news! Why, it was only yesterday, that Baby ran the whole way home, to tell us that the Postman's parrot was dead! *I* can jog along all right, I'm not in my first youth, and I never was pretty; and being the eldest, I can find plenty of occupation, and interest of sorts; but, dear Daddy, *do* consider the three girls; please think of what I've said," and Wilhelmina patted her parent encouragingly on the shoulder, and walked out of the room.

In the end, after some remarkably stormy scenes, Billy prevailed; for Billy, as her mother complained, "could twist her father round her little finger." Then what Brenda termed, the "great Exodus of the Millers" actually took place, and poor Lady Miller found herself with her husband, four daughters, two maids and a mountain of luggage, carried off to Paris; and from Paris they journeyed to Lucerne.

At Lucerne, to his audible consternation, Sir Lucas was thrust into the too prominent post of chaperon—his wife having declared that her health was not equal to society. Nevertheless, she took a certain amount of comfort in a sofa, her lace work, and patience cards,—although the rock-garden, was far, far away!

At first, Sir Lucas instinctively shrank from following five grown-up women into a dining-room, or restaurant; but most of his party were so handsome as to draw all eyes, and in this fact, he found considerable compensation; also, when he beheld other men doing similar duty, he became more resigned; and by and by actually began to enjoy this amazing, and absolute change! He and his girls played golf on the Sonnenberg, and made excursions, whilst her ladyship and maid, sat in the shade, listening to the band, or ventured on a little shopping, purchasing Swiss embroidery, and Italian tortoise-shell.

In spite of their already large party, the Miller girls good-naturedly invited Nancy to join them. She and Billy became immediate allies, and on the Sonnenberg links, laid the foundation of a lasting friendship.

"We are such a squad of women," she said to Nancy, "but it had to be all, or none; people get used to us, and find we are quite rural, and harmless. I think Mr. Holford, and Major Berners are becoming accustomed to Minna and Brenda, and I'm not the least surprised. At home, we thought little of their good looks! They were just nice, cheery, accomplished, girls. Minna has a lovely voice; but here, they stand out as beauties, and the Pater looks as proud as a peacock with two tails! They are the prettiest girls in Lucerne, bar yourself!"

"Oh, what nonsense!" Nancy protested, but Billy signed to her that she was about to make a drive, and thereby closed the argument!

At the Grand Hotel, Locarno, Mrs. De Wolfe again encountered neighbours; Lord and Lady Hillside, their son, and daughter; these were not merely neighbours, but connections,—and not only connections, but friends! It turned out, that Lord Hillside and Mrs. Ffinch were brother and sister, and on the strength of her intimacy with a relative, Nancy was welcomed by the family.

Lady Hillside had been an heiress: her fortune had paid off heavy mortgages on the estate, and repaired the dilapidated castle. So flourishing now were the Hillside concerns, that Theodore Lamerton, the heir, a young man in the Guards, was looked upon as a desirable parti. His mother, was a little woman with a yellow, haggard face, in which burned a pair of jet black eyes,—eyes of the reformer and fanatic.

Lady Hillside was feverishly energetic, and full of philanthropic plans: her name was well known on Boards, and Committees, and she cherished a secret passion for being, what is called "Chair." Her interests abroad, were so wide, and so various, that she could spare but little time for her own family;—in fact, she was something of an aristocratic Mrs. Jellaby. Her correspondence was enormous; she kept two secretaries, but rarely looked into her housekeeper's accounts—or answered what might be termed "a domestic letter."

Recently her health had broken down from overwork, and a specialist had ordered her abroad, with strict injunctions, as to absolute rest. Rest was impossible to a woman of her temperament! It was true that she now left correspondence in abeyance, but she was actively engaged in making a wonderful collection of seals and rings,—which enterprise carried her far, and wide.

Lord Hillside, a handsome, bearded individual, a great authority on Egyptology, lived much to himself, and took his walks apart. With his chiselled aquiline features and well-trimmed beard, he might almost have passed for an Egyptian Tetrarch himself. Next to Egyptology—and Rameses the Second, his chief interest in life was his daughter Josephine Speyde, a widow of eight and twenty. "Josie," as she was called, had not inherited the family good looks, but had been endowed with some of her father's brains, and more of her mother's inexhaustible energy,—which in her case, took the form of a tireless pursuit of amusement. In appearance she was thin, and hipless; her complexion was sallow; a pair of magnificent black eyes illuminated a long, but expressive countenance. Such was her art in dress, and deportment, that she actually persuaded her world, that she was as handsome as she was amusing, and otherwise attractive. Married at twenty to a distant cousin, the alliance had proved unfortunate, and as Josie herself confessed, "they had found one another out too *soon*." She was restless, capricious, and extravagant: Victor Speyde was dissipated, ill-tempered, and jealous.

The relatives put their heads together, and predicted "*trouble*," but the death of Captain Speyde in a motor accident, relieved their apprehensions, and liberated his wife. As a widow, with an independent income, she returned to live with her parents,—a changed young woman, who had seen the seamy side of life; she rode hard, smoked incessantly, and had the reputation for a keen appetite for adventure, and stories, more or less risky! Mrs. Speyde belonged to a smart Bridge Club, possessed a car, and a latch-key—and claimed all the prerogatives of a self-chaperoning widow,—whilst enjoying as she described, "a really topping time."

Possibly because they were such a complete contrast in appearance and character, Mrs. Speyde took a violent fancy to Nancy Travers, called her by her christian name the second time they met, graciously instructed her in a new style of hairdressing, offered her the name of a *very* private dressmaker, and imparted amusing information respecting the affairs,—love and otherwise,—of her very dearest friends.

Not the least among Josie's accomplishments, was her art of story-telling; she drew little word-pictures with audacious and dramatic effect, and her voice, if slightly guttural, immediately claimed an audience. Nancy wept and screamed with laughter, as she found herself unexpectedly in the company of Lady Miller,—and all her invalid airs; not to speak of several of the inmates of the Grand Hotel; and Josie's own aunt, Julia Ffinch, was also taken off to the life!

Nancy was dazzled, flattered, and enslaved. Josie Speyde was so clever, so gay, and entertaining: she read aloud scraps of delightful letters,—chiefly from men in foreign parts,—related stirring little episodes in her own past, and more or less opened the girl's grey-blue eyes, to their very widest extent.

CHAPTER XXI
ON COMO

Mrs. De Wolfe rarely remained long in one place; she assured her friends that she must have gipsy blood in her veins, and offered this idea as a sufficient excuse for her unexpected, and erratic movements. Weary of Locarno, she adjourned to familiar quarters at Cadenabbia, and as soon as she was comfortably installed in her favourite sitting-room, proceeded as usual, to scan the lists of visitors at the various hotels in the neighbourhood.

"I see the Gordons are over at Bellaggio," she remarked. "The Mackenzies are back at the Villa d'Este, the Wynnes are in this very hotel; and oh! what a piece of luck!—Dudley Villars is here too," and as she made this announcement, Mrs. De Wolfe turned an unusually beaming face upon her companion.

In answer to Nancy's glance of interrogation, she explained: "He is the son of my greatest friend; I held him at the font, tied his sashes, heard his prayers, and if I am not greatly mistaken, smacked him soundly.—I am very fond of Dudley."

"Do you think the smackings give him a certain claim?"

"No, indeed, poor fellow; he makes a stronger appeal than that!"

"And is he really a poor fellow?"

"On the contrary, he is rich; but his life has been spoiled, he has no fixed home; Shandmere is let. Years ago he made an unfortunate marriage: after a few months of cat-and-dog life, he and his wife parted, he has no near relatives, or ties, and spends his time rambling about the world."

"One of the idle rich?"

"Idle rich yourself! Dudley is always intensely occupied; in pursuit of new schemes, the development of a voice, or some literary undertaking. He is a charming fellow, so popular, and remarkably handsome!"

"I'm simply dying to see him," exclaimed Nancy.

"Do not die just yet; I'll send him a little note, and ask him to look me up as soon as he returns. I thought he was in Greece, but Italy always draws him. His grandmother was an Italian, one of an ancient Roman family, and from her, he has inherited his graceful manners, and taste for art. She has also bequeathed him her olive skin, and matchless dark eyes."

"I don't believe I can possibly wait until he calls," said Nancy. "I think I shall go down, and hang about the hall."

"Oh, you may laugh, my dear, but you won't make such an acquaintance as Dudley, in a month of Sundays. He is one of my boys—although he *is* getting on for forty—and a particular favourite."

"So I see."

"And not without good reason; Dudley is so attentive and thoughtful, to an old woman. His tender solicitude is quite touching! For instance, he *never* forgets my birthday; he knows my tastes in flowers, and books, and people; remembers my likes and dislikes, the little remedies I use,—and how I hate sugar, and adore asparagus. Besides all this, I am his godmother, and since his dear mother is gone, I think he is a little inclined to look to *me*."

"I hope he will not be furiously jealous, and insist on turning me adrift," said Nancy.

"On the contrary, my dear, you will become friends,—great friends, and in one way, he will complete your education. He knows Italy, 'au bout des ongles,' and every yard of these lakes. He will widen your literary horizon, take you out sketching—he really *is* an artist. It is marvellous how, in a few strokes, he can place a scene or a face before you. And not only does he sketch, but write; his books are praised in the Press, his poems, called masterpieces. Strictly between ourselves, I buy his books,—but I cannot read them. His poetry is rather, rather ..." she paused, momentarily at a loss for a word.

"Improper!" suggested Nancy, raising her brows.

"No, you evil-minded girl! or if there is anything of the sort, it is too deeply hidden for *me*. His writing is vague, and—er, what I may call nebulous! There are rhapsodies about colour, sunset, perfume, and eyes. It all seems to me a sort of hotch-potch, but I keep my opinion to myself, and when anyone asks me what I think of Dudley Villars' last? I throw up my hands and say 'it's amazing.'"

"Does he do nothing but write amazing poems, paint, and travel?"

"Oh, yes, he goes into society. You will see him in London next season. He is what I may call in 'fierce demand' for balls. Women intrigue and squabble, to get him to their houses. He knows all the right people, and dances like.... Give me a simile."

"A moonbeam."

"Thank you. It is considered a very high distinction to be his partner. I've been told that girls, whom he has overlooked, have actually been seen with tears streaming down their faces."

"Poor idiots!" and Nancy laughed heartily, and heartlessly. "So much for Dudley Villars. Now please tell me something about his wife?" "I've never seen her; she lives in Florida, I believe, and it is an old, old story,—they parted many years ago, and possibly people over here do not suppose that she exists! I happen to know, because I sent her a wedding present. It is a most unsatisfactory state of affairs, I must say."

"I wonder they don't get a divorce? Isn't there some place in America, where it can be managed,—just while you wait at the railway station?"

"You mean in Dakota? Well, it's not quite so rapid as all that, and my dear child how gliby you talk of divorce! What can you possibly know about it?"

"I have seen and known divorced people. Don't you remember the pretty American at Locarno? She had been divorced twice, and was going to marry that Swedish baron! I believe one of her former husbands happened to be passing through, and left a card, and a bouquet!"

"Pray who told you all this?"

"Josie Speyde!"

"Oh, Josie," and Mrs. De Wolfe made a gesture of angry impatience.

"Well, she said the lady was really charming: they made great friends, and played poker together,—she gave Josie lessons."

"That reminds me," said Mrs. De Wolfe, looking round, "I see Hardy has brought down the card box; we shall just have time for a game of piquet, before we dress for dinner."

The two ladies had scarcely settled down to piquet, when the door was flung wide, and a sonorous voice, announced, "Sir Dudley Villars!"

CHAPTER XXII
"SIR DUDLEY VILLARS"

The meeting between Sir Dudley, and his godmother, was warmly affectionate. Nancy gazed in amazement, as she beheld him kiss the old lady foreign fashion, on either wrinkled cheek. After one or two ejaculations, and explanations, he was presented to her, and wonderful to relate, neither fell short of her lofty expectations, nor her chaperon's glowing description. Sir Dudley was slightly built; admirably turned out; he had clear-cut features, wavy dark hair,—the front locks picturesquely powdered with white;—his smile was almost an embrace; whilst his eyes, which were dark, were the very saddest, and most arresting, that Nancy had ever encountered.

But these tragic, heart-broken eyes, had no connection, with their owner's real disposition, and feelings; they were merely a notable family endowment, and had been for generations, a valuable asset in the fortunes of the noble Casserini. It was whispered, that these same eyes, had won vast estates, a ducal palace, and even,—but this is in your ear,—a cardinal's hat! In the present instance, the eyes were allied to an agreeable voice, a cultivated taste, and a captivating personality. Indeed one enthusiastic friend, had been heard to speak of Villars, as "a delicious fellow!" Delicious or otherwise, he was not to the taste of various married men, and one or two nervous chaperons. These, viewed him with no favour; but rather, as a shepherd beholds a strange, and suspicious dog!

The visitor and Mrs. De Wolfe immediately embarked on an animated conversation, an eager exchange of plans, and news, and Nancy, after listening for some time to the sayings and doings of complete strangers, made an excuse about dressing in good time, and left the friends to enjoy a *tête-à-tête*. No sooner had the door closed upon her, than Sir Dudley said:

"My dear Auntie Wolfe, where did you get hold of such a beautiful young lamb? Is she the new companion you mentioned?"

The old lady nodded a complacent assent.

"You never were much given to companions, were you? I only recollect two; unprepossessing elderly females. What an amazing change!"

"Yes, I couldn't stand either of those elderly females; one had such decided views, and argued every question, — from the proper way to boil an egg, to the age of the world. The other, had a maddening sniff, and read all my letters. Still, an old woman cannot live entirely alone. There are wet days, and long evenings! I want someone to read to me, and play piquet. Nancy is pretty good for a beginner, but not like you, — a foeman worthy of my steel!"

"Nancy! What a nice simple name," said Sir Dudley. "Miss Nancy has lovely eyes; I admire their clear, crystal gaze of childlike innocence. Do tell me *all* about her?"

In a few short but pithy sentences, Sir Dudley was made acquainted with the history of Miss Travers, — that is to say, as known to her chaperon.

"An orphan with tons of money, no undesirable relations, and a truthful, affectionate, nature; dear Auntie Wolfe, allow me to offer you my warmest congratulations! And how long do you suppose this delightful alliance will last?"

"To the end of my days, if I could have my wish," was the prompt reply. "The child is my right hand, and simply radiates happiness; however, some odious man is sure to snatch her from me, and carry her off as *his* companion for life!"

"Yes," he assented, nodding his head, "I'm afraid your partnership is doomed! A beauty, an heiress, and launched by Mrs. De Wolfe—your chance of keeping her, is not worth the traditional button! But how you will enjoy yourself in the meanwhile! You who are always so interested in love affairs, and happy marriages."

"Well I give you my solemn promise, that I shall be in no hurry to marry off Nancy."

"Has she had any love affairs, do you think?"

"No, indeed. Why, my dear Dudley, you've only to look at the girl's face, to see that she has yet to experience the heart's awakening."

"*Dio mio*, and what a delightful task for some too lucky fellow!"

"Now look here, Dudley," and Mrs. De Wolfe suddenly sat erect, and tapped his sleeve with her pince-nez. "No experiments if *you* please, — no philandering. I'm not in the way of seeing the gay, and gallant aspect of your character; you turn the good and steady side to my old eyes, — but I have *ears*, and I have heard tales."

"No doubt you have, dearest Auntie Wolfe, but you know you should never believe anything you hear, and only the half of what you see. I grant you, I have amused myself, *pour passer le temps*, but only with hardened, and accomplished flirts, who know how to play the game; never with girls,—and I thought you barred girls yourself?"

"Yes, I do, the usual run, who giggle, and whisper, and have silly secrets, and make faces at me behind my back. Now Nancy hasn't a secret in the whole world; if she had, she couldn't keep it! Her life is an open book, 'who runs may read.' A coffee plantation, an English school, once more a coffee plantation; her father's death, a year's slavery to an abominably selfish aunt; from this aunt she came to me—and there's her history!"

"How old is she?"

"Past twenty, and in some ways, absurdly young for her age."

"And I am thirty-eight, and absurdly old for my years, so I think you had better appoint me deputy-chaperon. Well now, I must be off to dress! May I look in again after dinner?"

"To be sure," assented Mrs. De Wolfe, "come in and out, whenever you please, just as you always do, and arrange to sit with us in the restaurant. Don't let *Nancy* make any difference!"

"All right, then, I won't! I've got a capital motor-boat; I'll take you both on the lake, all day, and every day, and anywhere you like."

Sir Dudley Villars promptly installed himself as one of Mrs. De Wolfe's party, whilst Antonio, his valet, enacted the part of *cavaliere-servente*, to the two lady's-maids. He sat with them at meals, entered their sitting-room, when so disposed—which was often; played piquet, sang tender and emotional love songs in a melting tenor, to Nancy's accompaniment, and was even suffered to smoke! He was evidently attached to his godmother, and full of *petits soins* on her behalf. His manner to her was charming; that of a cheery, sometimes teasing, and yet always devoted son! He went her errands, carried her wraps, brought her flowers, books, and papers; also occasionally, his letters from mutual friends; made a capital sketch of her for Nancy, a sketch of Nancy for his godmother, and altogether lived up to his reputation.

Mrs. Wynne, her daughter Flora, her fiancé—a young diplomatist on leave from Rome—joined forces with Mrs. De Wolfe. A party of six, just filled the motor-boat, and were admirably paired—two matrons, two lovers, Nancy and her new friend. Sometimes the younger people, went up and spent a long afternoon on the links above Menaggio; but as a rule the days were devoted to picnics and excursions, about the lake. Mrs. De Wolfe was anxious that Nancy should see all her old favourite "beauty spots," and proved an active, and indefatigable chaperon, but a long tiring day at Grave-dona, was too much for her seventy-four years. Returning amid the late mists, she caught a severe chill, and was confined to her room for one whole week; and as the Wynnes had betaken themselves to Bellaggio, Nancy and Sir Dudley were abandoned to a *tête-à-tête*!

The invalid would not suffer her young companion to sit what she called "stuffing,—in a sick-room," and drove her forth to enjoy the exquisite autumn weather; to walk, to boat, and to sketch,—and so it came to pass, that Nancy and Sir Dudley—a rather striking pair—went about together, to play golf, to visit old villas and lovely gardens, or to climb the hills to well-known holy shrines,—also to flit around the lake in the motor-boat; now to Como, now to Varenna,—in short, wherever their fancy carried them!

Nancy had found old friends in Menaggio; the two Clovers (her schoolfellows), and their belongings,—which included their parents and an elder brother. They were eager for her company; she played golf with them on several occasions, but somehow most of the shining hours were claimed by Dudley Villars,—who pronounced the Clover family to be "bourgeois," and the son,—who exhibited a fervid interest in Miss Travers, "as a blundering lout, with a calf-like smile, and dull to the verge of idiocy."

Dudley, to do him justice, was a delightful companion; so entertaining, so thoughtful, always ready to fall in with the slightest whim; and he did things so well! To Nancy his painting was a revelation and a delight, his voice was sympathetic, and he told her many entrancing tales, of his wanderings in the far-away East, and then his good looks,—what a haunting face!

Sir Dudley's manner to his charming companion, had been partly that of a kindly teacher, and comrade; tinged with an infusion of chivalrous reverence.

Oh, how different to Teddy and Nicky, who never hurried to open a door, or stand up, when she entered the room. Once or twice Nancy had asked herself, if she was not growing to like this charming friend, *too* well? After all; he was no relation. Simple Nancy! And she could not forget, that when he had gone to Milan for two or three days, she had missed him even more than his godmother; and once or twice, when, looking up suddenly, she had met his eyes, she found herself blushing to her hair.

That he liked and admired her,—Nancy felt instinctively, and a chilly little inward voice asked, if she was going to what is called "fall in love?" She dismissed the idea with horror. Sir Dudley was married, and had a wife living; she too was married, and had a husband, somewhere—incredible as it seemed, even to her own thoughts. One night, she took herself solemnly to task—sitting at her bedroom window, looking down at the stars, reflected in the lake, she held an inquiry. Dudley had often given her flowers; he had lately assumed an attitude of exclusive protection and possession; once it had seemed to her,—though it might have been imagination,—that he had pressed her hand, as she alighted from the motor-boat. There must be no more of *that*. What would her father have thought of his Nancy, if she gave her heart to a married man?

Mrs. De Wolfe had recovered from her chill, and resumed her responsibilities, but she no longer went on expeditions and picnics,—contenting herself with going across to Bellaggio, to call on friends, or to prowl about among the antiquity shops; whilst her companion sketched in the villa gardens, or endeavoured to immortalize the tall cypresses, above San Giovanni.

With the exception of one or two eloquent glances, and an involuntary hand-pressure, Dudley's manner to his godmother's beautiful companion, was admirably guarded. With the fear of his old friend's displeasure before his eyes, it had been a case of what he mentally termed "paws off," but how could any man under eighty years of age, withstand such an exquisite creature? So simple and transparently innocent; so warm-hearted and intelligent, and beyond and above all, what a lovely vision of glorious youth! It was this, that enthralled the *blasé* dilettante.

He had played the part of genial comrade,—for he knew instinctively the sort of girl he had to deal with; how easy to alienate, and scare! She had been informed that he was married, and her Irish spirit and Irish chastity, were inscribed upon her exquisite lips. He and Nancy had many talks, and interesting discussions, as they took their daily stroll along the romantic thoroughfare, which leads from Cadenabbia through and beyond Tremezzo. Mrs. De Wolfe frequently accompanied them, and then, when half way, a half-hearted chaperon, sat down on a low wall to rest, and there await their return.

Nancy, who always enjoyed the sound of her own voice, and an appreciative listener, was neither shy, nor self-conscious; at a very early period of their acquaintance, and with consummate ease, the subtle man of the world, had made himself master of her simple history. He enjoyed listening to her vivid descriptions of the Indian hills, and to confidences as fresh, and pure as the dew of the dawn. He heard all about her school-days, her father's money troubles, and his splendid character. She spoke of the Corner boys, and Sir Dudley's old friend, Mrs. Ffinch. Once and once only had she touched on the tragedy of her bereavement,—when with averted face, and broken voice, she related particulars of Travers' death.

"And what became of the fellow who missed the panther?" inquired Villars, after a pause.

"I don't know; he is somewhere in India," she replied, almost under her breath.

"Well, I suppose, he was ashamed to show his face." But to this remark there was no reply.

Late one afternoon, Sir Dudley and his pupil,—having finished a sketch of the Baptistery, at Lenno, crossed over in the boat to the Villa Arconati,— which stands on its promontory half surrounded by water, and embowered in shade. Here the pair sat on the edge of a low wall, overlooking the lake, and carried on a lively discussion,—of which Mrs. Ffinch was the subject. Nancy did gallant battle for her friend, and patroness, and spoke with enthusiasm of her generosity and kindness of heart.

"Of course I am not denying old Julia a few good qualities; I've known her since I was a kid,"—and Sir Dudley unkindly added—"she's four or five years older than I am.—I remember her in the nursery, a big, overbearing girl, *very* stingy with jam. In those days the Hillsides were terribly hard up, and had a large family. Ju Lamerton was a sensible young woman, with no romantic nonsense about her, and she made room for her sisters, by marrying the biggest bore in the whole of India."

"Well, at any rate, they seem quite happy."

"*Seem*," repeated Sir Dudley; "that's her cleverness; she manages him. She manages everyone! She married off Emma and Mabel, and last time she came home, got a lout of a brother, into a capital sinecure." Then turning to look at Nancy, he added—"I wonder she didn't try her hand on *you*,—but I suppose you were too young?"

Nancy felt herself colouring up to the roots of her hair, and carried off the suggestion with a rather embarrassed laugh.

"I expect you had all the young planters on their knees, young as you were? Come now, own up, strictly between ourselves! How many scalps did you bring home?"

"Not one," she answered, with decision, "we were just good friends, like you and I,—nothing more."

"I am delighted we are good friends," murmured Villars; and after this sentence, there fell a strange and dreamy silence. The surrounding scene was exquisite, the beauty of Italy's lake land, tinged with a kind of roseate romance. Above them to the left, towered hills, clothed with olive and chestnut woods; at their feet gently lapped the jade-green water of the lake. The glow of a wonderful sunset touched the quiet landscape, and the only sound that recalled one to a workaday world, was the chime of the Angelus, stealing across from San Giovanni.

The stillness and solitude, had a compelling effect upon Villars; turning to Nancy, he said abruptly, "I must speak! Here is the hour, and the place! I want to tell you, that I have not had such a happy time, as this last five weeks—for many a long, long year. Nancy, may I call you Nancy?—everyone does, and Miss Travers sounds so formal! I may, may I not?"—as Nancy made no reply, but nervously twisted a rose between her fingers. He moved an inch or two nearer, and in a low, seductive voice continued: "There is no one to object,—is there?"

"No one," she answered, raising her head, and meeting his burning dark eyes, with a flash of pride. He gazed at her critically and in silence. What a darling she was! From the very first he had been enthralled by her high spirits, *entrain*, and beauty; here, he assured himself, was the perfect treasure for which he had vainly sought; and in many and far lands. He had made this discovery on former occasions,—but the prize had eluded him, or proved a bitter disappointment. Close beside him, twirling a red rose in her taper fingers, sat his one, and only love.

If that devil Cassandra, would but divorce him, here was her successor,—the future Lady Villars! But Cassandra, the most obstinate and malignant of her sex, was adamant; hitherto, his appeals, prayers, threats, and flagrant indiscretions had failed to move her. This was her revenge; she refused to release him!

Something in this long and unusual silence, filled the girl with a sense of vague uneasiness: and this uneasiness was not dispelled, when her companion broke the long pause, with the startling question: "May I kiss you, darling?" His voice was very humble and pleading, but there was a smouldering fire, in his melancholy dark eyes.

"Certainly not," she answered sharply.

"But why?" urged Villars, moving still nearer, "since we are such friends?"

"Because I should hate it," she declared decisively.

"*Une jeunesse sans amour, est comme un matin sans soleil,*" he quoted. "I suppose no man has ever touched those perfect lips?"

Nancy tossed the rose away, but made no reply: she was feeling excessively uncomfortable.

"So you know nothing about it, darling little girl?" he went on. "No one has ever yet drawn your soul through in one long kiss! Listen to *me*, Nancy," and he made an effort to take her hand. "Won't you make room for a very lonely fellow in your heart? You *would*, if you only knew how miserable his life has been."

Nancy slipped down off the low wall, and stood erect, surveying her companion with a heightened colour, and irrepressible tears glistening in her eyes. She had received a tremendous shock, and felt a horrible impression of degradation, and insecurity.

"Sir Dudley, please don't talk to me in this way. I," and she gulped down an inclination to burst into tears, "I—I don't like it!"

Then with a desperate snatch at her ebbing self-possession, she added: "Will you be so kind as to signal for the boat?"

"Horrified! frightened! affronted! easy to see *she's* new to the situation," he said to himself. "I must go slow, *chi va sano—va lontano.* I've been a bit of an ass, but the sunset and the Angelus were too much for me."

"You know I wouldn't offend you for the whole world," he murmured, as in strained self-consciousness they awaited the boat. "Only forgive me for this once! One never can tell. Most girls like admiration, and kisses—I see you are different."

Nancy made no reply, but picked up her red Lugano umbrella, and got into the boat, without a word.

"She has taken the little scene seriously," he said to himself, as he looked at her set profile, and it was now his turn to be uneasy, and alarmed! Supposing she were to go and lodge a long complaint with Aunty De Wolfe? He must make his peace before they returned to the hotel. Accordingly on their way there, with all the eloquence, cleverness, and guile of a well-experienced diplomatist in emotion, he pleaded with his companion, for forgiveness; his misery and regrets appeared to be so acute, that they touched her sensitive feelings, and cooled her indignation. How *could* she withstand, the tears that stood in his wonderful eyes?

Notwithstanding this patched up peace, Mrs. De Wolfe might have noticed a certain constraint, between her young companions that evening, and there was no singing,—but as it happened, the mind of their chaperon was occupied with a recent interview, and the old lady was happily unconscious of any cloud.

CHAPTER XXIII
A WARNING

Among Mrs. De Wolfe's friends at Bellaggio, was a certain lady, known to her intimates as "Sally Horne," a well endowed, unencumbered widow of sixty; her daughter was married to an Indian official, her son was quartered in Cairo,—and her London house was let! She and her maid were staying at the "Victoria," where she had many acquaintances, and vainly endeavoured to inveigle Mrs. De Wolfe to cross the water, and establish herself in her company,—but Mrs. De Wolfe declining the lure of Bridge, preferred to remain where she was!

The afternoon that Nancy and Sir Dudley set out to sketch the Baptistery, Mrs. Horne came over to see her friend. The old lady was sitting in the little garden by the lake, and recognizing her visitor on the boat, hastened to meet, and welcome her.

"Would you like to go inside, Sally?" she asked, "or shall we have tea out here?"

"I've had tea, thank you," said Mrs. Horne, "but by all means let us sit outside. Where's your girl?" she inquired, looking round, and her air was inquisitorial.

"Gone up to Lenno to finish a sketch."

"With Sir Dudley?"

Mrs. De Wolfe nodded a careless assent. After a moment's hesitation this bold visitor announced: "I have something disagreeable to say to you, Elizabeth."

"You needn't tell me that!" rejoined her companion, with a grim smile, "I saw it in your face, before you came off the boat."

"I wonder if I shall make you very angry!"

"*Try*," said Mrs. De Wolfe; the word was a challenge, "I've not been in a good wholesome rage for ages."

"Well, it's about Nancy, and Sir Dudley Villars.—People are talking."

"Bah!" ejaculated Mrs. De Wolfe, "let them talk!"

"But do please listen, my dear! I am fond of Nancy, and I can't bear to hear it said, that she is being compromised."

"Compromised," shouted Mrs. De Wolfe. "What nonsense! What infamous scandal."

"Yes, it's all over my hotel, and only this morning, as we sat in the garden, Lady MacBullet, said she was sorry for Miss Travers; such a pretty young creature, and she understood an orphan, making herself so cheap and conspicuous, with a man of the character of Dudley Villars. They were on the lake together all day,—and the hotel was full of stories."

"Only cat women's gossip,—I know the style! I'm sure the men don't talk of Dudley's character! Men are not gossips!"

"Oh! and why not; what about men's clubs?"

"Well, I've never heard a *man*, say anything against Dudley."

"No, because he is straight enough with *them*, I believe;—both rich and generous. For women, he has a different code! Elizabeth, I know you are devoted to Dudley Villars,—and although an old grandmother, I am not altogether insensible to his fascinations, *myself*! When he chooses, he can be irresistible, so do pray imagine the spell he can cast over an impressionable young girl like Nancy?"

"*No* spell has been cast," protested her friend, sharply, "and really I'm surprised at you, Sally, taking the trouble to come over here, and tell me your hotel was talking scandal. Dudley Villars is my godson, I have absolute confidence in him you may be sure, or I would never have suffered him to be the continual companion of Nancy."

"Well, at least I meant well," said Mrs. Horne, stiffly, "and my good intention must be its own reward. I like Nancy, otherwise I wouldn't have bothered." Then rising, "I see the Tremezzo boat coming in, and I will go back in her!"

"No indeed, Sally," pulling her down, "you will do nothing of the sort. I'm an ungrateful, ungracious old harridan, and I'm sincerely obliged to you for your interest in Nancy. I confess, that I have never seen anything but the best side of Dudley; I believe, and I feel in my bones,—that he has behaved most honourably, with regard to the girl; not one indiscreet word has he spoken! *That* I can guarantee; and she is not susceptible! Every scrap of love in her heart was absorbed by her father, and since his death, I do not think she has much to spare for anyone. Dudley and Nancy are good friends, and no more. I've allowed them a little extra liberty, to go sketching and boating, not knowing that *every* eye was fixed upon them! I have already told you, I trust Dudley, and as for the girl, before she ever saw him, I informed her that he was a married man."

"Sometimes that makes no difference," remarked her companion.

"Oh! my dear Sally, I'm afraid you are getting infected; let me again assure you, that Dudley's friendship with Nancy, is entirely platonic!"

"Then, my dear Elizabeth, it's something entirely new for Dudley Villars," and Mrs. Horne, imparted to a reluctant ear, a brief account of one or two affairs of which he was the hero.

"I suppose you haven't heard that the Bellamys are separated on his account, and Daisy Bellamy has gone home to her mother?"

"*I've* never believed that Dudley was responsible for that business! still I'm afraid, Sally, that I've been a little slack as a chaperon; so I'll put an end to the talk, by taking the girl on to Florence."

"A very wise move, my dear, and I sincerely hope it will not be a case of 'locking the stable door, when the steed is stolen.'"

"No indeed! *my* palfrey is safe. Nancy is heartwhole. I am getting rather tired of the lake, and am such a well-known old tramp, that when I bundle off at a couple of days' notice, it never excites remark."

"Do you think that Dudley Villars will make his way there too?"

"No," rejoined his champion with decision, "for although it is a perfectly harmless friendship, I draw the line at followers."

After the boat had carried her visitor away, Mrs. De Wolfe remained for a long time buried in profound meditation; then she rose, went into the hotel, despatched a prepaid wire to Florence, and give notice of her intending departure.

The next morning as the little party were at *déjeuner*, Mrs. De Wolfe received a telegram. Having read it, she laid it aside and said: "Well that's all right, we have got our rooms! Nancy, prepare to march on Florence, the day after to-morrow!"

"You are not serious!" exclaimed Sir Dudley, setting down an untasted glass.

"Perfectly serious, I wonder that I was not away long before this! My campaigns, like Napoleon's, are rapidly organized."

"But *you* have no campaign."

"No! but what about Nancy?"

"Beginning with this forced march, Auntie Wolfe, I wonder you can exchange this lovely clear air, for the gloomy streets of Florence."

Mrs. De Wolfe laughed, and said: "I am tired of looking out on water; in my hotel, which is not on the Lung' Arno, I can lie at my ease in a comfortable bed, and stare at the Duomo; think of that!"

Dudley realized how foolish it was to argue with Auntie Wolfe at present, but when Nancy had departed to give instructions to her maid, and the old lady was alone, he said:

"Why are you going off so suddenly?"

An unwelcome idea flashed into his brain. Could Nancy have confided in her chaperon?

"To a plain question, I'll give you a plain answer, my dear boy. There are two kinds of discretion: one voluntary; the other enforced. I find that people have begun to notice that you and my little girl are very much together, and although it is a most innocent friendship, still it does not do for Nancy to be talked about, so we will remove ourselves."

"What an infernal shame," exclaimed her godson, looking surprisingly vexed. "The venomous tongues of some devils wouldn't leave an angel alone."

"And you, my dear Dudley, are by all accounts, far from being an angel!—I have heard some sad tales."

"Which of course you don't believe! Have you ever known me to play the fool with any of your friends?" He paused for a reply. As none was forthcoming he continued, "I cannot tell you what a happy time I have put in here. You know I always feel so much at home with you, dear Auntie Wolfe!" and he stooped and kissed her on her cheek. Then, straightening himself, he said, as if struck by a bright idea: "I've not been in Florence for a couple of years,—I believe I'll run down there next week."

"*No*, Dudley," protested his godmother, raising her thin old hand, "*that* I positively forbid. You will see us in town,—and later at the Court, but abroad, no more! It is so easy to be conspicuous in a small do-nothing circle, and I'm sure you are quite as sensitive about Nancy's reputation—though that is too big a word—as I am myself."

During the remaining two days, Dudley's manner to Nancy was perfect, and entirely of the kindly elder brother type. He gave her sketches of their favourite spots, supplied her with books for the journey, and went all the way to Como, to put the ladies and their parcels into the train, himself. Then returned down the lake alone, in a condition of most abject misery. For days he walked and boated in the neighbourhood of Cadenabbia; a melancholy object of picturesque dejection. Those who witnessed and marked this change, said to one another, "Dudley Villars has been badly hit this time; serves him jolly well right!" He wrote cheerful (and exchangeable) letters to both ladies, giving them to understand, that he was excessively gay, and well occupied.

But do what he would, he could not get Nancy out of his head; however he consoled himself with the belief, that time and persistence would be his staunch allies. And how he longed to see her! Sometimes this longing overpowered him, and he nearly drove Antonio crazy by his conflicting, and capricious orders. Twice, he arranged to go to Florence, twice, he changed his mind; at last, he positively took his departure. Was not Florence free to all the world?—Auntie Wolfe's attitude implied that she had it on lease,—and even if he only saw Nancy in a church, a picture gallery, or the street,—that would be something!

On his arrival in the city of flowers, he boldly drove direct to Mrs. De Wolfe's hotel; and here he had the mortification of learning, that "the Signora and the Signorina, had left that morning for Palermo!"

From Sicily, the ever wandering Mrs. De Wolfe, took ship for Egypt, where she put up at the Savoy Hotel, Cairo; here she discovered her friend, Mrs. Horne, already established, and heard that all the Miller party were at the Mena House.

"Six months' travelling had wrought a surprising change in her family," as Billy explained to her friend Nancy,—to whom she paid an immediate visit.

"I declare we are so altered, you will hardly recognize any of our party,—except myself. There is the Pater, he has cut off his little side whiskers, and wears up-to-date collars, and looks years younger; he plays golf, is very keen about excursions, and actually dances at our hotel balls! He has met crowds of old friends, and has come out of his shell in a most remarkable manner. Then mother has floated to the surface. She now goes about with us; dresses very smartly, has taken madly to Bridge, and can ride a donkey with the best. I think it was Minna's engagement that aroused her from her torpor. She was so immensely interested in a love affair at first hand! Minna is making a splendid match, and we *all* love Major Brently; he has become our brother, and what he calls, 'wheels us into line'; and is awfully good to us. Mother having, to use a sporting expression 'tasted blood,' has now great hopes of Brenda; and many people consider Baby, our beauty! The fact is, what with this inspiring climate, heaps of new friends, a whirl of excitement and amusement, our existence has been quickened, and we don't know ourselves, we are so happy!"

"Then your exodus has been a wonderful success! What a triumph for *you*, Billy? No one now dare call you 'Silly Billy!'"

"Yes, it has turned out all right, and even if nothing particular had occurred,—like Minna's engagement,—we would have had enough to think and talk about, for years. As it is, we have souvenirs to fill a room, and thousands of picture postcards; have enlarged our ideas, and made many friends,—even mother has her pals."

"You like Egypt, I can see," said Nancy.

"I just love it, the sand, the delicious desert air, the cloudless blue sky, and then Cairo itself. You and I must go about together, Nancy. I've been here six weeks, and am getting quite clever at finding my way, and making bargains. I can even talk a little Arabic. I have collected ever so many presents for the people at home."

"I am sure you have," said Nancy; "how I wish that I had people at home, I could take presents to."

"Oh! that will all come in time, my dear. Do tell me, have you come across any interesting young men?"

"Yes, several; good dancers and tennis players, but not otherwise specially engaging."

"You don't appear to have lost your heart?"

"No, I don't believe I've *that* sort of heart to lose."

"It remains to be seen. When I've married off my three sisters—I'll see about settling you."

"Thank you, Billy."

"And talking of settling, I wonder how father and the Mum will content themselves at home, after this gay and giddy whirl about the world?"

"They won't settle; they will be continually on the move. I warn you, that you have started an avalanche."

"A good thing I did! better than being an iceberg all one's days. By the way, I hear you have done some exquisite water-colours of Como; do show them to me."

"Oh! how good!" she exclaimed, after Nancy had displayed her treasures,—artfully keeping the best to the last—

"Nancy, these are quite top-hole,—who taught you?"

"I had a good master at school, but a friend of Mrs. De Wolfe's, who was at Cadenabbia, gave me lessons. We went out sketching together, almost every day."

"With a chaperon, of course?"

Nancy shook her head.

"Who was he; had he a name?"

"Certainly he had! Sir Dudley Villars."

"Oh! Some call him 'Prince Charming,' others, 'a Deadly villain.' He is not very young,—but so handsome, isn't he? and a merciless lady-killer."

"Well, here am I, alive and well, so you see he has spared *me*," said Nancy, who had almost forgotten a certain conversation which had taken place on the low wall, by the Villa Aconati.

Cairo is said to be the most typical Eastern city in the world, and it appealed very strongly to Nancy Travers. The palm trees, the dark faces of a gesticulating voluble throng, the dense blue sky, the warm and golden sun, in some ways recalled India. In February Cairo is socially at its gayest. Nancy and her chaperon were in flattering request.

However, it was not society, but this land of tombs, temples and a river, that engrossed her interest, and fired her warm imagination. One afternoon, towards the end of her stay, as Mrs. De Wolfe and Nancy drove out to the Mena House, behind a dashing pair of long-tailed Arabs, as they sped along Ismail's road, the old lady discussed her plans.

"I must give you a bit of the season, Nancy, and you shall be presented at a May Court."

"Oh! no, no, please no!"

"Well, you know, you will have to make your curtsey to your sovereign, some time! Shall we say on your marriage?"

Nancy made no immediate reply, but the cheek nearest to her friend, was unusually pink—Why? She appeared to be engrossed in watching a long string of clumsy, heavily-laden camels. Nothing to blush at there!

"After June, we will go down to the Court," resumed Mrs. De Wolfe; "it is such a dear old place, you will love it."

"How can you desert it, as you do?"

"That is what my neighbours ask, but I don't mind their remonstrances, I yield to the *Wanderlust*. The Court is too large for one old woman, and though I am attached to it,—it holds agonizing memories, and I cannot endure it, unless it is packed,—so to speak,—to the roof, when my guests and their doings monopolize my attention, and distract my thoughts from the long illness, and death of my dear husband, the parting with my two sons,—who never came back to me. One was killed at Magersfontein, the other died of typhoid in India. The Court is full of reminders, of Freddy, and Hugh. Their bedrooms, with their personal belongings, are precisely as they left them, with their pictures, books, birds' eggs, and butterflies. The gardens they worked in, are still kept up, and planted with their favourite flowers; their old pony, Barkis, only died two years ago, at an immense age. I often ask myself, why the lives of those two promising young men should be cut short? and a useless old woman, their mother, still cumbers the ground?"

To this question Nancy—who had a large lump in her throat—could make no reply, and there fell a long silence.

"I wonder what you see in me, my dear?" began Mrs. De Wolfe suddenly. "My life is now behind me, you are young and stand upon its threshold,—a radiant, and expectant figure."

"Radiant! I'm afraid not; you are too partial, and as for expectations— they are strictly moderate."

"That at least is something. On the *Patna*, they were positively nil. Poor forlorn child, I took pity upon you, as I would on a drowning kitten!"

"You did," assented the girl, with laughing eyes, "and here I am on your hands, a full-grown young cat!"

"Claws and all complete, a most formidable responsibility! Well, I threw you a plank and brought you to land,—some of these days I may float you off again, upon the sea of matrimony."

"No, no, dear Auntie Wolf," laying her hand on hers, "I'm very happy as I am,—please don't dream of such a thing."

"Well, if I do not,—others will. Ah, there are Sir Lucas and Major Horne, waiting for us," she added, as they turned into the garden, and dashed up the entrance of Mena House. "I wonder if the Millers have secured their cabins in our steamer?"

"I think so, and you will find Major Horne will be of the party,—I have a presentiment, that he hopes to marry Billy."

CHAPTER XXIV
A LITTLE DINNER FOR THREE

The end of April found Mrs. De Wolfe and her protégée in London, installed in a fine suite at the Hyde Park Hotel. The position suited the old lady, as here she was surrounded by connections and friends. There was her sister-in-law in Park Lane, her niece in Belgrave Square, the Hillsides within a stone's throw, and the Millers in Pont Street. She and her young companion were soon sought out, and overwhelmed with invitations, and Nancy lived in a whirl of agreeable engagements.

First an early ride in the Park, then the morning shopping; luncheon parties, receptions, dinners, and above all, dances! Spare moments were devoted to "fittings," and hurried visits to girl friends.—These various claims, literally devoured the long summer days.—Nancy was very gay and happy in this new life, a conspicuous figure in her immediate circle! admired in private, stared at in public, and favoured with yet another gift besides beauty, and youth. Wherever she went, she appeared to bring sunshine; and those who knew her, revelled in her endowment. Among her chief partners and cavaliers were, Sir Dudley Villars, Major Cathcart—now enjoying a nice soft staff appointment—Toby Lamerton, Lord Lanark, and various others too numerous to mention.

Soon after her arrival in London, Nancy had reported herself in Queen's Gate, and waited upon her aunt,—unsupported by her good friend, Mrs. De Wolfe. Mrs. Jenkins' little blue eyes opened to their widest extent, when they beheld her niece, no longer a shrinking and humble satellite, but a self-possessed, well-dressed, and independent damsel.

As her envious glance wandered over an elegant toilet, she realized that this "bird of paradise" would be entirely out of place, in her own ordinary "Hen Run." It was evident that the girl had a good maid, and a good conceit of herself; she resolved to secure Nancy for a visit,—which would include at least, two state dinners,—in order that her own friends should have an opportunity of beholding a niece whose success and striking appearance, would add to her own importance.

Mrs. Taylor and Miss Dolling happened to be both in attendance,—the one as faded and sentimental, the other aggressive, and glum—as of old. At the end of twenty minutes' conversation,—chiefly questions and answers,— Miss Dolling rose, and said, "I'll just go and fetch the Pom, I'm sure he'd love to see Nancy."

"And I'm sure he wouldn't recognize her *now*," said Mrs. Taylor, with significance, and for once Mrs. Taylor happened to be right. The Pom merely sniffed indifferently at Nancy's smart gown, and then rudely retired into his comfortable padded basket.

"And how is the Coffee?" inquired Mrs. Jenkins, in a condescending manner.

"Oh, doing well. One of my old friends has taken over the management; and gold has been found on the estate."

"Gold? well I never!" ejaculated Miss Dolling. "Fancy owning a gold mine!"

"It's a reef, I believe," explained Nancy, "and has been taken over by a company."

"So you're *quite* a millionaire," remarked her aunt, rather sourly. "And what are your plans for the summer?"

"We are going down to Mrs. De Wolfe's place, Newenham Court—later on."

"Oh, so she *has* a place; I always understood, that she lived in hotels and steamers, and had no home?"

"She found it so lonely, living all by herself."

"Then why not have a companion?" demanded Mrs. Taylor, "goodness knows they are cheap enough!"

"She has a companion now,—she has *me*," declared Nancy with a smile.

"Oh, *you*!" with an impatient sniff, "you won't last her long; young women with money, are soon snapped up. You'll marry within six months."

"I assure you, I shall *not*."

"Ah, that is how girls always talk," broke in Miss Dolling, "I used to say the very same things myself; you have yet to meet your fate," and she heaved a heavy sigh, as with her head on one side, she dreamily contemplated Nancy,—the daughter of her one, and only love!

Before the visitor took leave, she was invited, nay, almost commanded, to come and stay at Queen's Gate. This invitation she firmly, but very civilly declined. Mrs. De Wolfe could not possibly spare her.

"Well," said Mrs. Jenkins, looking alarmingly pink and angry, "I do think your own aunt has a claim before *strangers*; I shall expect you to give me at least a week."

But the niece of her own aunt proved to be adamant, and submitted a long, and imposing list of her engagements. She, however, consented to appear at a dinner-party,—the date of which Mrs. Jenkins, diary in hand, fixed so far ahead, that excuse or evasion, was out of the question.

One Sunday afternoon Nancy, and a party of friends, betook themselves to the Park, chaperoned by Mrs. De Wolfe and Lord Hillside. The usual rendezvous near Stanhope Gate, was crowded, and the promenade bordering the grass, so thronged that progress was difficult. Nancy and Tony Lamerton lagged somewhat in the rear of their companions, and during a block in the seething mass, she descried a face she hadn't seen for more than two years: the beaming visage of Teddy Dawson, wearing a wide smile upon his half-open mouth. Oh, how funny he looked! His coat sleeves and trousers, inches too short; an old-fashioned tall hat crammed on the back of his head, otherwise the same blue-eyed old Teddy. Nancy instantly extended a delicately gloved hand, but instead of grasping it (as expected), he failed to recognize a friend in this smart young lady, and became the colour of a boiled beetroot.

"There must be some mistake," he said to himself, "*he* had no acquaintance with this dazzling creature, who had so to speak, summoned him to halt,"—but when Nancy smiled at his overpowering embarrassment, and he looked into her eyes, he exclaimed, "Great Christmas, can it be *Nancy*?"

"Why not?" she demanded. "Of course it's Nancy."

The pair were unaffectedly glad to meet, and exchanged very cordial greetings.

"When did you arrive?" she asked. "Yesterday?"

"Now, how in the world did you guess?"

"By your wardrobe; Jessie will have to take you in hand."

"Oh, so you've heard!" he replied, with a conscious grin. "My coming home was a bit sudden; but at the very last moment I got a passage in the same boat, with Jess, and her mother. Where are you stopping?"

"At present, we are *both* stopping the public thoroughfare,—but you will find me at the Hyde Park Hotel. I've no end of things to hear, and to say to you. Will you and Jessie come and dine to-morrow night at eight?"

"I can't answer for Jess,—I believe she has no frocks yet, but I'll come all right."

"Don't be late," and with a parting nod, she drifted on.

"I say! that's a rum-looking chap," said Tony. "Did you ever see such boots?—like coal boxes, and what a hat! no gloves, hands the size of a ham,—where on earth did you get hold of him?"

"In India, he was our nearest neighbour; I've known him since I was in socks. He is one of the best; something quite extra! You mustn't judge him by his clothes! If you had put in ten years on a coffee estate, perhaps you wouldn't be so *very* smart yourself!"

"Perhaps not! Well, I hope when Jessie has got her frocks, she will do something for him, poor chap! His coat would be a find for the wardrobe of our regimental theatre. Is *he* a specimen of the men you met out in India?"

"He is a specimen of a successful planter, a first-rate sportsman, and a real friend. He was like a kind elder brother, when I was in frightful trouble. Well!" in a totally different voice—"there are Mrs. De Wolfe and Sir Dudley beckoning—I do hope, they have kept us chairs!"

"Mr. Edward Dawson," as announced in Mrs. De Wolfe's sitting-room, arrived to dine, alone, bringing a long epistle from Jessie, who was staying in West Kensington, with some of her mother's relatives. Teddy had invested in a new black tie and a pair of shiny shoes, and looked quite passable when presented to Mrs. De Wolfe,—who gave him a cordial reception. She knew all about him,—and had even read his letters!

The two ladies, who were "going on" to a ball, were in full dress; Nancy so transformed and lovely, that Teddie could scarcely take his eyes from her. His surprise and bewilderment were such, that several times, he entirely forgot what he was going to say, and blundered about, with spoons and helpings, as if he had never dined in company before! He and Nancy had much to discuss, and he spoke freely and openly before the "old lady," as he mentally called her.

"I must confess, I wonder how you got round Finchie?" said Nancy.

"Oh, you mean about Jess? You see she was away up in Cashmere, and the mice played about! She declares that Jessie's mad,—and that I'm a savage and belong to the Stone Age; but Jessie stood up for me and said, 'At any rate, he is a rock of sense.' Rather smart, eh?"

"Yes," agreed Mrs. De Wolfe.

"And then the General, that's my father," he explained to the old lady, "has come forward nobly, and is going shares in the rent of Fairplains; he and I, will be your tenants, Nance."

"Yes, and I shall go out and stay with Jessie and you, for such ages,— that you'll be obliged to leave home!"

"And what about the gold?" inquired Mrs. De Wolfe.

"I believe it's paying hand over fist. Nancy, you will remember Nicky always swore that there was gold in those old workings. I thought it a fairy tale, but when some engineer chaps came sniffing round for reefs, Nicky put them on, and went down with them himself. The gold was all right, and he has stuffed several thousands a year, into your pocket. Mind you don't forget *that*!"

"You may be sure I won't.—And so he is staying on at the Corner?"

Teddy nodded.

"Alone?" Her tone was significant.

"I don't think so! Perhaps you can guess the name of the new partner? By the way," lowering his voice, as he noted that Mrs. De Wolfe was absorbed in the menu, "what about that chap?" ... name indistinct, to the sharp-eared chaperon. "Do you ever hear anything of him?"

"Never!" was the emphatic reply.

Mrs. De Wolfe waited to hear more, and continued to stare steadily at the word "asparagus." "He pays in the money for you to the day; it is lying in my name at Grindlays—about six hundred pounds."

The anxious matron felt immensely relieved; of course the money, had to do with *coffee*. She laid down the card, and glanced over at Nancy,—never had she seen her with so high a colour; and yet it was not a warm evening, and the girl hadn't touched anything stronger than barley water. Nancy, too, had violently assailed her with her foot. Why? She was not aware that she had made a social blunder, or *faux pas*; and how the girl chattered! Undoubtedly these tidings and reminiscences, and "Plain tales from the hills," had excited her, and made her rather odd and unlike herself!

CHAPTER XXV
THE MEDITATIONS OF DEREK MAYNE

The cable dispatched to Mayne, had been so urgent and alarming, that he half expected to hear bad news when the mail steamer called at Port Said,—however, neither cable nor letter awaited him. Arriving in London early one May morning, he drove up to his mother's house in Charles Street,—intending to ask for news and a meal. The door was opened by a somewhat dishevelled footman, who informed him that "her ladyship was out of town."

"But was I not expected?" inquired the caller, glancing at his luggage-laden taxi, "I am Captain Mayne."

"Oh yes, sir, you were *expected*, but her ladyship said as 'ow you couldn't possibly be here before Monday, and she and his lordship has gone down to Brighton for the week-end."

This was but a tepid welcome after an absence of some years; however, there was nothing for Mayne to do, but re-enter the cab and have himself driven to his club. Here, he encountered various old friends, lunched, paid a hasty visit to his tailor, bought an umbrella, and took the afternoon express to Campfield, the nearest station to Maynesfort.

Maynesfort was a venerable, but well preserved Jacobean house (with artfully hidden Georgian patches), and stood amidst delightful and rural surroundings. On the south side, lay a prim Dutch garden, beyond that, an undulating heavily wooded park,—both overlooked by the windows of a once famous library. This library was now the chief reception room; ever since the death of Mrs. Mayne, the drawing-rooms had been closed!

Here, the master of the house received his guests and tenants, here he smoked, gossiped and read the newspapers—*The Times*, *The Field*, *Country Life*, and with special avidity, the local Rag,—but he never opened a book,— although encompassed by thousands of neglected volumes.—He was not, as he boastfully declared, "a reading man." "Jorrocks" was his favourite hero; his, was an outdoor temperament; hunting, shooting, gardening, and farming were all to his taste; and the house was merely a sort of refuge, where he ate, and slept; four weeks' incarceration indoors, was to him an unexampled experience. On a lounge in the library, surrounded by a volume of tobacco smoke, and attended by a buxom nurse, the invalid was found by his nephew and heir.

Richard Mayne, J.P. and D.L., was a remarkably active little man, some years over seventy; he had keen dark eyes, flexible brows, a firm, clean shaven mouth, and a pleasant smile. The arrival of his nephew, afforded him real and unqualified pleasure, and he greeted him with outstretched hands, and a full resonant voice—by no means the feeble squeak of an invalid.—"Got your wire this morning, sent the car, glad to see you, my boy—very glad!"

"And how are you, Uncle Dick? you look fairly fit. Going on all right, eh, nurse!" glancing at his companion.

"Yes, Mr. Mayne has made a remarkable recovery," she rejoined, "I expect in a few weeks, he will be quite out of my hands," and she rose and retired, leaving the uncle and nephew to themselves.

"It's the healthy outdoor life, eh, 'um, 'um, that's what has stood to me—but I tell you, when that brute rolled on me, I thought it was a case for the undertaker!

"Yes," assented his nephew, "from that cable, I was afraid you were in a bad way, Uncle Dick, and I'm awfully glad to find you so well."

"We wrote to Port Said to tell you I was going on all right,—but I daresay we missed the mail. You are looking uncommonly fit, not a bit yellow or tucked up! India has taken no toll off *you*: good stations, good sport, 'um, 'um?"

After such a long absence from home, there was much for Mayne to hear, and for his uncle to impart; the old gentleman was a fluent talker, and enchanted to get hold of a listener, to whom all his news was absolutely fresh. He was ten times more anxious to relate, than to listen, and unfolded a heavy budget,—without displaying any curiosity as to what the traveller might have to offer in exchange?

First, there were the full details of his accident,—including the weather, the condition of the ground, the character, and pedigree of the horse; then came "the case," the doctors, the specialist, and a warm eulogium of his nurses. After this, the county news; succeeded by estate and domestic intelligence; who had come, and who had gone, how the pheasants had done; how the great fig tree was dead,—also the hen swan, and the old woman at the west lodge.

Mayne found the place but little changed—everything in the same apple-pie order. Maynesfort was his uncle's hobby, he loved the old place with an absorbing passion,—and to tell the truth found her a very extravagant mistress! A series of reckless predecessors, had dissipated and gambled away the property, till but about a thousand acres remained; and although the owner lived, so to speak, rent free, there was much to maintain; the ancient house like its kind, was in constant want of repair; the drains, the roof, the chimneys, called for outlay, and supervision; the gardens, greenhouses, and avenues, had to be kept up,—as Maynesfort had a reputation to support, and there were no nice fat farms, to bring in a steady revenue.

The late Mrs. Mayne, had been a woman of fortune, and her money had assisted to maintain Maynesfort, as a sort of show place.—Its mullioned windows and heavy chimney stacks, were a great feature on the local post cards.

As the long May days went by, the heir of Maynesfort found time to hang heavily on his hands,—although he successfully concealed the fact. There was no shooting, except a few pigeon of an evening; naturally there was no hunting, he was not a fisherman; most of the neighbours were in London for the season, and the Parsonage was in quarantine with scarlet fever. Mayne rode about the lanes on an elderly cob, strolled through the park and gardens, played cricket with the village team,—but still the days were long and empty.

He read the papers to his uncle, played dominoes and backgammon, and even "cut-throat" Bridge with him and the nurse. He smoked many pipes, and listened to many stories: descriptions of the season's good runs, and best days' shooting.

Strange to say, the old gentleman exhibited but little or no interest in Indian sport,—nor wished to hear, in what way his nephew had passed the last four years? It was sufficient for him to know that he was there, sitting opposite to him, looking a little older,—but both hale, and hearty.

Richard Mayne was a man of one idea at a time,—but that idea, excluded all others, and would occasionally hold the fort of his mind for months. His present obsession, was, that Mayne should, could, and must, marry,—and that without delay. At first his nephew had put the suggestion aside with a joke, and a laugh; but he soon realized that indifference and frivolity raised his uncle's ire; the flexible eyebrows went up and down, or met, alarmingly; the "'um, 'um, 'ums" came thick, and fast,—he resigned himself to the situation, and suffered the old gentleman to talk and talk, and even to arrange a formal, and imaginary parade of all the available spinsters in the county!

"You see, my dear boy," he urged, "that time, when I was lying on my back, and they were not quite sure, if I was internally injured, I could not help thinking of this dear old place,—and its new master."

"What nonsense, Uncle Dick," protested Mayne, "you will be master here for years, and years."

"No, no," waving away the idea, "if I'd snuffed out, you would have had to come back, and take over my shoes, and sit here all alone; no mistress for the house; so I made up my mind, that if I recovered, I'd take right good care to see you *married*; married to some nice girl with money; family not so important, you have enough family for both! Now tell me, Derek, is there any young woman, you have a fancy for?"

"No, not one."

"Well, then, my dear boy, you must look round, now you are at home, and find a pretty girl, with a pretty fortune, that will keep the old place on its legs,—otherwise it might have to be *let*, and if that came to pass, I believe I'd come out of the family vault! You know your aunt's money goes back to her own people; the property itself is not worth much. There is the grazing, and the woods, and Jones sells some of the garden stuff, but the men's wages and coal and coke, run into hundreds a year; our gambling ancestors staked farms and livings, and fishing rights on the length of a straw, or the activity of a snail, and I tell you, my blood boils when I think of them!"

"To marry, to look out for a nice girl with money," was the "motive," which, like the ever recurring air in an opera, ran through all Mr. Mayne's jokes, reminiscences, and solemn exhortations to his nephew; the subject became intolerable; his good nature and patience were wearing a little thin, and it was an immense relief to escape into the park of an afternoon, whilst the invalid dozed, there to wander about, accompanied by two happy brown spaniels.

To find himself thrown entirely upon his own society, was a rare experience for Derek Mayne; opportunities to meditate, and hold counsel with his subconscious self, were invariably passed over and neglected; his impulse was for action, to be up and doing, not thinking, or mooning; but for once he found his thoughts arrested, and intensely occupied, by his uncle's "idea," for once, he approached a subject, with which he had hitherto refused to grapple,—and a swarm of thoughts, not hitherto entertained, suddenly invaded his brain.

It was his nature to face things—but there was one stern fact, he had always thrust aside. "Nancy!—their marriage! What was to be the end of that coil?" Was he to go through life alone?—to live in that place in the hollow, with no companionship, and no affection,—save what was offered by the dogs? He might, he believed,—though he had never looked into the subject,—obtain a divorce for desertion; but the idea was repugnant,—such an action impossible!

He thought of Travers, who had given his life for him,—his anxiety about the future of his little girl; the subsequent relief, and gratitude he had read in those dying eyes; how could he drag "the little girl" into the blaze and publicity of "a case in the courts"; oh, it was altogether a deadly business, and yet, where had he gone wrong? Possibly, when he had suffered a mere chit of eighteen, to take command of the situation; on the other hand, he recalled with a guilty qualm, his sense of profound relief, and satisfaction, when he discovered that she had cut the knot, severed their bonds, and fled!

The haunting vision of a miserable, white-faced, blighted, flapper, accompanying him back to Cannanore, had undoubtedly had its terrors; his colonel did not encourage matrimony,—it spoiled the mess,—and all his little world would marvel at his choice! He wondered what Nancy was like now? and what were her surroundings? Possibly she lived in some third rate suburban circle, was prominent in the local tennis club, wore home-made frocks, adored (platonically) some preacher or actor, and led her old aunt by the nose. Only for the secret tie, which held him, he might have been married long ere this. There was that lively little girl up at Murree. What marvellous red hair, how she danced and chattered; and she had liked him too,—but he had never gone beyond the flirting stage, or dropped into serious love-making; the memory of Fairplains constrained him.

A pretty face, had always appealed to Mayne, and certainly Nancy was no beauty,—possibly by now, she had improved in appearance,—when her complexion was no longer exposed to the sun, and her hair was properly dressed, she might pass in a crowd; she would always be quick witted, quick footed, and quick tempered. After much serious reflection, and many pipes, he came to the conclusion, that now he was at home, it was his business to find out something about *Mrs. Mayne*. The name made him pause, and laugh aloud,—to the great bewilderment of the two spaniels.—He need not necessarily seek an interview, no, far from it; but he might as well make cautious inquiries, and discover where she lived? and what she was doing?

Mrs. Ffinch was the right woman to lend him a helping hand, and as she was expected home within the next few weeks, he would ask her to look up Nancy, without bringing him into the question. Here was a field for her particular activities; it was just the sort of commission she would eagerly undertake, and thoroughly enjoy.

At the end of a fortnight, Mayne prepared to take his departure for London; not without a half expected, and feared, opposition on the part of his uncle; but to his surprise and joy, the old gentleman received his hint of a move, without demur,—for he assured himself, that Derek was about to act on his advice, and "look about him," and the sooner he commenced his quest, the better. It was true that he had given no definite promise; he had said but little; just lounged, and smoked, and stared at the carpet, or out of the window; however, it was a well known, and well proved adage, that "silence gives consent."

It was with a blissful sense of escape, that Mayne found himself seated in the car, and once more bound for Campfield station. The sensation was unusual,—for it was the first time, that he had ever felt glad to leave Maynesfort, and he was secretly ashamed of his joyful relief. The old man, accustomed to a life of constant outdoor activity, was putting in a dull time,—and it had enlivened his empty hours, to build castles in the air,— instead of model cottages,—and reckon upon the future of his successor's wife, yes—and children! The nurseries had not been occupied for nearly fifty years; but as the car skimmed round the last bend in the avenue, and the tall chimney stacks sank out of sight, Mayne, as he lighted his cigar, sternly assured himself, that as far as *he* was concerned,—Maynesfort would never have a mistress.

CHAPTER XXVI
THE MEETING

The new arrival in Charles Street soon discovered that he had by no means bettered his position, on the contrary, appeared to have gone out of the frying-pan, into the fire! Four years had wrought surprising changes in the ménage: Lord Torquilstone had become "more so," as Mayne mentally expressed it; his moustache was blacker, his coat more padded, his temper more irascible, than formerly. He belonged to a type of club man happily becoming extinct,—loud, aggressive in argument, quarrelsome, gouty, and greedy. He and her ladyship did not now hit it off,—and saw as little of one another as their mutual ingenuity could contrive. She, never appeared before one o'clock; he, lunched, and frequently dined, at his club,—unless they happened to have a few guests, or were engaged to present themselves, at some particular function.

Mayne noticed a woeful alteration in his mother; she looked faded, and worn, there were deep lines about her mouth, her voice was querulous, and her attitude the pose of one enduring "the bitter winter of her discontent!" In her cold, unemotional way, she was glad to welcome Derek, a handsome, creditable fellow and like his father; but in character much stronger, and more self-assertive.

He seemed to be thoroughly capable of shaping his own life, had excellent manners, plenty to say for himself, and judging by the number of his letters, with regimental, and other crests, was claimed by hosts of friends! In honour of his return, Lord Torquilstone dined at home, and abused the dinner; and he and his wife passed the young man under the harrow of a searching examination, with respect to his life, during the last four years. Mayne found it useless to protest, "But Mater, you had my letters."

"Yes, my dear boy,—they were rather dull. Not your fault I know, I always hated India,—the deadly paradise of the middle class. It's just what was *not* in your letters, that I want to hear about."

"Oh well, if you mean manœuvres, camps of exercise——"

"Don't be so silly," she interrupted impatiently.

"Your mother wants to hear about those lively grass widows up in Simla," broke in his lordship; "come now, own up!" and he chuckled diabolically.

"I have nothing to own. Never had any use for the frisky matron, at home, or abroad."

"Oh, Derek," protested his mother, "what about Josie Speyde?"

"Yes, what about *her*?" leaning back, with his hands in his pockets.

"You were one of her boys, I know!"

"She taught me to dance,—I'll say that for her."

"She taught you to flirt too."

"Don't expect the fellow wanted much teaching!" broke in Lord Torquilstone. "Any nice little girls out in India?"

"Oh yes, lots."

"I hope you didn't leave your heart, behind, Derek? I warn you that as daughter-in-law, I refuse to receive an Indian spin."

"Oh, there's no fear of that," replied Derek, lighting a cigarette, and tossing the match into the fireplace.

"I suppose you know your uncle is very anxious that you should marry."

"I suppose I do know! I suppose he has it on the brain, I've heard of nothing else,—he has driven me to the verge of idiocy."

"You were twenty-nine last April; time to be looking about, Derek. I know some charming girls; I do hope you will let *me* have a say?"

"Oh, my dear mother, you are welcome to as many says as you like, but I haven't the smallest intention of marrying."

"That's the way you young fellows talk," declared Lord Torquilstone, setting down an empty glass, "and then before you know where you are, you're *caught*," and he glanced at his wife with deadly significance.

"I'd like to see the girl, who could put salt on my tail," rejoined his stepson with extravagant confidence.

"Well now, Mater," glancing at his watch and rising as he spoke, "if you'll excuse me, I'm going out."

"Going out!" she repeated blankly, "*where* are you going?"

"To look on at a boxing match; I have promised to join a couple of fellows at the Sports Club."

"A boxing match, how horrible—disgusting!"

"Well, I admit that it's not exactly a pretty sight sometimes; but I like to see an active muscular fellow, that knows how to use his fists; I do a little in that line myself. I won't be in till all hours,—so I'll take a latch-key."

Before her ladyship could offer any further objection, he had kissed her on her powdered cheek, nodded to his stepfather, and departed.

"Quite his own master!" remarked his mother, as she heard the whistle for a taxi, "and I had promised to take him to the Rutherfords' 'at home!' Last night he was at the Opera,—it's almost impossible to get hold of him."

"You'll find some young woman will get hold of him," snarled Lord Torquilstone. "I hope she'll be, er! er! respectable. It's just those young fellows home on leave—that the worst of women pounce on."

Upon this subject, arose an immediate argument, Lady Torquilstone declaring, that "no man with good blood in his veins, would be likely to marry out of his class." Her husband held the opposite view, and backed his opinion, with an imposing string of names. The argument waxed louder, and presently developed into a personal quarrel, and (unmindful of the grey parrot's warning cry, of "Hullo! Hullo! Police! Police!") they continued exchanging nasty thrusts, until a footman brought in the ten o'clock post, and her ladyship having collected her letters, left the smoking-room, fortified with the consciousness, that the last word, had been *hers*.

It was the day of a very "Big" race at Sandown, the weather was perfection, and half society, and all the racing world poured out of London in a long succession of specials.

Captain Mayne and a brother officer, had secured the last two seats in a smoking carriage; the train was just about to start, when the door was wrenched open, and a tall young man, leapt in, and hauled a girl after him. A stout individual by the window, rose, and offered the lady his place, and he and her companion, stood,—blocking up the compartment. "By Jove, that was a near squeak," exclaimed the young man, breathless, but triumphant. Mayne recognized him as an acquaintance—the Honourable Tony Lamerton.

"Yes!" panted his companion, "what a race! I wonder what has become of the others?"

"Left behind, I'll bet. I'll swear her ladyship could never leg it down the platform, as you did!"

"Then pray, what am I to do for a chaperon?" and the girl laughed.

There was something in the voice and laugh, that sounded oddly familiar to Mayne, and suddenly leaning forward, he looked round the substantial figure, which was planted directly in front of him. The first glance, gave an impression of a remarkably pretty girl; then with a shock, it dawned upon him, that the pretty girl was *Nancy*! A Nancy altered almost beyond recognition: beauty the crown of her youth!

It seemed to Mayne that nothing remained of the original flapper, but her merry blue eyes, and sweet, high-pitched voice. Her face was rounded, her complexion—if real,—was dazzling. She was dressed with surpassing elegance, in a gauzy white gown, touched with green; a large hat wreathed with green feathers, half concealed masses of reddish brown hair, a string of splendid pearls encircled her throat, and in her little white gloved hand, she held a gold bag, and a card of the races. Undoubtedly her aunt was a woman of wealth, and did not spare it upon her niece.

The niece was so engaged in laughing and chattering with Tony Lamerton, that Mayne had ample time to collect his wits, and make a prolonged and critical inspection. Nancy carried herself, with an air of graceful confidence, and the manner of one who was aware of her own value; and yet the face wore the same eager, almost childish expression; and a look of innocent mockery danced in the eyes that were raised to Tony Lamerton. Here was a beauty! an assured, and fashionable young woman; she and Tony appeared to be on the best of terms, and he noticed that the Guardsman's attention, was entirely absorbed by his lovely charge.

As the train cleared the suburbs, a clear young voice, said, "How dreadfully hot it is!! may we not have the other window down?" and as the stout gentleman instantly moved to obey her request, Nancy became suddenly aware of Derek Mayne! He was seated in the far corner, and hitherto concealed behind a bulky screen.

His grave dark eyes, encountered her startled glance, with the most penetrating composure. Yes, it certainly *was* Captain Mayne,—but little changed, beyond the transformation effected by London clothes, a tall hat and a buttonhole. How different to the rough Shikari garb, in which she had been accustomed to see him! When their eyes met in recognition, Nancy was sensible of an overwhelming shock; she gave little outward sign, beyond a quick indrawing of her breath, but her heart had made such a violent plunge, that it seemed about to leap out of her mouth!

Here within three yards of her, was the last man in the world, she expected, or wished to see. A man, she had almost succeeded in turning out of her mind, and to whom for weeks she never cast a thought. The discovery left her nerveless; every morsel of colour deserted her face and lips. The last time they met, was when they had stood beside her father's grave: that was exactly two years and four months ago, and although she had instantly averted her eyes, he was still before them; vividly different to her somewhat faded mental picture—that of a worried restless young man, smoking endless cigarettes, as he paced the terrace at Fairplains.

During this little scene, Tony and the stout gentleman had taken it in turn to struggle with an obstinate window sash, and as the former turned about, his eyes fell upon an old acquaintance. In a voice of hearty welcome, he exclaimed,

"Hullo! Mayne, when did you get back?"

"Three weeks ago."

"And never came near us,—how is that?"

"I've been down at Maynesfort."

"Oh yes, to see the old man! Getting on all right, isn't he? and now you're doing a bit of town, eh?—What are you backing for the big race?"

As Mayne discussed the favourites and weights, he noticed that Nancy had recovered her composure and colour; her self-possession was marvellous; but then he was not aware, that she had been through a rigorous training in a stern school, and had learnt to successfully repress her feelings and emotions. For the moment, she appeared to be engrossed in the study of her race card; but unless Mayne was greatly mistaken, it was not altogether the oscillation of the express, which caused that pretty little hand, to shake quite perceptibly!

CHAPTER XXVII
OLD FRIENDS AND STRANGE NEWS

By some unexplained miracle it turned out that Nancy's chaperon—Lady Jane Wynne—had actually caught the train, and Mayne overheard the party volubly congratulating one another, as they moved out of the station. And so that slim girl in white, carrying a green sunshade, was Mrs. Mayne! Among all that great crowd, there was no one to approach her in looks and distinction. If people were to know the truth, how widely he would be envied!

His uncle clamoured for him to take a wife, and there she was, strolling up the path in front of him—supported on either hand by an assiduous escort. Supposing he were to claim her? Here was a very different individual to the poor little girl in India, who was distracted with grief, and misery. There was something amazingly attractive about this new, and radiant Nancy. His inspection in the railway carriage, had shown him, an undeniably *happy* face!

Meanwhile the object of his reflections,—for all her assumed animation—felt shattered, by her recent experience, and talked the wildest nonsense to her companions, as she made her way to the stand. Here numerous acquaintances accosted, and surrounded her and her party. To-day, Miss Travers' gaiety was feverish, her colour unusually high, and her laugh almost hysterical. Soon after the second race, she complained of a headache, and sought a seat on the way to the paddock, where, attended by Sir Dudley Villars, she sheltered behind her sunshade.

Sir Dudley was not a racing man; cards, he could understand; but betting, and backing horses, he looked upon as childish! Races, were all right, as institutions—where you met your friends, had a fair lunch, inspected the newest beauties, and heard the latest gossip. To sit by Nancy Travers, studying her exquisite complexion, listening to her somewhat disjointed chatter, was a thousand times more agreeable, than being precariously perched on the top of a stand, following with a field-glass, the speedy movements, of a little bunch of thoroughbreds!

During a lull, before one of the big events, a seemingly endless procession passed backwards and forwards between the paddock, and the stand. Sir Dudley pointed out various celebrities to Nancy,—adding in each case some pithy, or cynical remark. She did not wish to be noticed and accosted, and kept her parasol well before her face, but the hat of her companion seemed to be scarcely ever on his head; his acquaintance appeared to be as the sands of the sea!

"There's the Duchess of Doncaster,—I see she is bringing out her second girl,—hard luck on Lady Alfreda. There's Claverhouse of the Blues, and the little American widow; I wonder if *that* will come off?"

These and other remarks were received by his partner, with nods and monosyllables. Her thoughts were elsewhere; her mind was in a tumult of fear, and bewilderment. Supposing Derek Mayne were to come forward, and claim her; what was to be her attitude? What would Mrs. De Wolfe think?—yes, and all her girl friends,—who talked to her so frankly, of their love affairs; Nora Wynne, Brenda Miller, and various others,—for she looked and was, a born confidante, and sympathizer,—what would be their feelings, when they were informed, that their simple Nancy had actually a *husband* in the background? Her reflections were interrupted by her companion suddenly asking, "I hope you had a good day?"

"'A good day?'" she repeated to herself. It was one of the *worst*, she had ever known! But she smiled faintly, and replied, "Oh, yes,—I've won! Tony Lamerton has given me tips. I put ten shillings on 'Dear Me.'"

"So I see that fellow Mayne is home again," remarked Sir Dudley; "strolling about with his old love,—Josie Speyde. She is looking remarkably well to-day,—those daring colours, suit her bold, black style."

Nancy raised her sunshade a couple of inches, and peeped out cautiously. There they were! promenading slowly together, Josie talking and gesticulating with unusual animation, and Mayne?—she surveyed him critically,—yes, he was remarkably good-looking; well set-up, well-dressed, and could hold his own, even with her present companion!

"Do you know him?" she faltered.

"Who? Oh, Mayne?—yes. Not very well, he's in my club, and we just pass the time of day. Not a bad-looking chap; one of the rough-and-ready sort: goes in for polo, boxing, and soldiering. He's afflicted with the most appalling stepfather, Torquilstone,—I actually had to leave the High Light Club, as I simply couldn't stand him; he seemed to *live* in the smoking-room, and never gave us a day off! I hear that Mayne's people are keen to get him married, and that Lady Torquilstone is looking about for a suitable daughter-in-law,—no penniless beauty need apply."

It did not strike Sir Dudley that he had said anything particularly humorous, yet Nancy had burst into rather a wild, and unexpected laugh. How odd, and jerky she was to-day! headaches affected people in different ways: as he looked at her shining eyes, and brilliant colour, he leant towards her, and said in his most seductive manner:

"If you will be a good little girl, you won't sit here in the sun, but allow me to take you straight home; and go and lie down, and have ice on your head."

"Ice!" she repeated; "you have put it *into* my head! I'm dying for one, and here comes Tony; I promised I'd let him take me to their tent. I'll be quite all right to-morrow; we were such a frightful squash in our carriage coming down, that I was nearly suffocated with the heat,"—then rising as she spoke, "Here I am, Tony! I'm coming; did I *really* win five pounds!"—as he handed her a note. "Well, I'll give it to the Dog's Home."

Sir Dudley, who felt himself injured, and deserted, relinquished his pretty companion with what grace he could assume, and swept off his hat in his very best style. As he looked after the couple, he said to himself, "'Dogs' Home!' Much better return it to that bumptious young puppy,—who by all accounts is uncommonly hard up!"

Mayne, man-like, was not nearly so overwhelmed by their recent encounter as Nancy. He was still able to make bets, talk sanely to friends, and to follow the racing, with the keenest interest (although running through his thoughts, and keeping well ahead of the horses, was Mrs. Mayne). His present idea, was to make a move; a quiet cautious move, and try to find out, how the land lay? He had not failed to notice Nancy's numerous admirers; more than once, he had focussed her through his glasses, and though she played the "Ostrich," he was perfectly aware of the identity of the girl, who was sitting on the lawn, with that tame cat, Dudley Villars!—A tame, but *not* domestic cat! he knew something about him; and what he knew, was not to his advantage. A song-singing, insidious, unscrupulous, rascal,—and no fit companion for any innocent girl.

The sight of Villars, and his proprietary attitude, had awakened Mayne's jealousy, and materialized his intentions; he must see, and that without delay, how he could approach Nancy? Possibly some friendly third person, would assist him? It would be, he was aware,—a most delicate enterprise, yet "nothing venture, nothing have!"

As Mayne and a friend, were leaving the paddock, they almost ran into Teddy Dawson, Mrs. Hicks, and Jessie; he halted at once. This amazing encounter, was as unexpected, as it was providential! Here, as it were spirited from the ends of the earth,—were two of the witnesses to his marriage! and Dawson his best man, would stand by him now, as formerly.

The greetings of the little party were exceedingly cordial. Mrs. Hicks, Jessie and Ted were unaffectedly delighted to see Mayne. Teddy was now presentable, and "more,"—as his fiancée said,—"like a human being!" Mrs. Hicks radiantly happy, and attired in a bright green gown, with a pink silk frill round her neck,—recalled to Mayne, the common parroquet of India!

To secure a word with Teddy, Mayne presented his brother officer to the two ladies, and drawing him aside, said in an undertone:

"Guess *who's* here?"

"Yes, I know; I've seen her," replied Teddy; "isn't she ripping? Takes the whole cake, eh? Have you met?"

"We came down in the same carriage just now; she cut me dead!"

"Oh well, I expect she was a bit taken aback——"

"Look here, Dawson, I want to see you,—I *must* see you! I know your time is not your own,—but fix an early date to dine,—or something!—My club is the 'Rag.'"

"And mine's the 'Oriental.'"

"I say, you two," interposed Mrs. Hicks, laying a yellow claw, on Mayne's arm, "I won't have this! When two men get so confidential, I know they're after no good! Oh, I'm up to all your little games!" and she poked Mayne sharply with her fan. "If you are fixing a dinner, you must both dine with *me*! I know of such a nice, risky little restaurant, in Soho, where they do you 'A 1' for half a crown; and we'll all go on to a music-hall afterwards. Now, you come along, and get me a cup of tea," taking possession of Mayne; "I suppose you have tickets?" and still holding him fast, she led him captive towards the refreshment room. "I'm awfully glad you're home at *last*," she remarked, with significant emphasis.

"Thank you," said Mayne,—meeting the amused eye of a friend, who stared hard at the lady on his arm.

"It's on account of Nancy," she continued, confidentially; "have you *seen* her?"

"Yes; to-day."

"Now, who would have thought, she'd bloom out into such a beauty! But her mother was rarely pretty,—and you saw the Earl for yourself. Jessie and me lunched with Nancy, and the old lady yesterday; the old lady has a voice comes out of her boots, and Nancy is just the same as ever!"

"Is she?"

"Come now; don't you be so stiff, and stand off; it isn't every man who has a beauty, and a real nice girl for a wife. And then there's all the *money*!" and she nodded her head complacently.

"Money? What money?" he asked.

"Oh, Lord! haven't you heard? Why, she's got *tons* of it."

Mayne stared at his companion interrogatively.

"Just squeeze me in there, and get me a cup of tea,—two lumps! and *then* I'll tell you all about it in a jiffy!"

With a teacup in her hand, Mrs. Hicks resumed: "Do you *mean* to say, that you never heard, that Mr. Fletcher left Fairplains to Nancy?"

"No. Did he really?"

"Yes, and a couple of thousand a year, as well."

After a long pause, he asked, "How long ago?"

"About eighteen months. She was living with an aunt,—a real terror, by all accounts, and having a mighty poor time, and then she came in for this legacy. An old lady who had a fancy for Nancy, took her in hand, and they have been knocking about the Continent for quite a time. Now they are staying at the Hyde Park Hotel. The old lady, who has no family, is just wrapped up in Nancy. She's one of the 'ordering-about sort,' and has a man's nose, and deep voice. Her name is De Wolfe!"

"De Wolfe!" repeated her listener, in amazement. "Are you quite sure?"

"Yes, I'm both sure, and certain,—how could anyone forget such an outlandish name as that?"

"I know Mrs. De Wolfe well," said Mayne, "she and I come from the same part of the world."

"I am glad to hear it, and you can take over Nancy. It is not fair or respectable, that she should be going about as Miss Travers, turning all the men's heads,—when you and I know, that she's a married woman!"

Mayne made no reply, but accepted an empty teacup in silence, and Mrs. Hicks continued: "Of course, you will leave the service, and take a fine country place; for there's not only the Fletcher money, but the gold mine.

I see! you've not heard of that, I suppose! They are working a big reef on Fairplains,—you know the place near Chuttibutti?"

"I've heard nothing whatever about Fairplains, since I last saw you," said Mayne, after a considerable pause, during which an agreeable day-dream, had been completely dispelled.

"You've only yourself to thank for that!" said Mrs. Hicks, shaking the crumbs from her green plumage. "You went away to the north of India, and dropped the whole lot of us, like so many 'ot potatoes. Those old workings have turned out very valuable,—Hicks always believed in them.—They say, they are bringing Nancy in about eight thousand a year, and will be worth more, as time goes on! What do you think of that?"—and she poked him facetiously with her pocket-fan. "Why, I declare, to look at you, one would say you'd lost a fortune! Come, come! buck up!"

"Mother!" interrupted Jessie breathlessly, "I've been looking for you everywhere; we are going to try, and catch the next train. You know we are dining in town, and doing a play,—so *do*, do make haste! Captain Mayne, you'll come, and see us, won't you?"

"Why, of course he will," replied her mother; "he and I have no end to say to one another,"—then turning to him, "Our address—have you a pencil, and I'll write it out on a bit of the race-card,—Torkington House, Baron's Court, quite in the wilds; but you're used to that! It was in the wilds that we met, ha! ha!"

"Oh, *do* come, mother!" cried Jessie, and seizing her by the arm, she dragged her parent almost forcibly away, but Teddy hung back for a second,—and said, "I'll telephone to your club, and fix a meeting!"—then he ran.

A change had come o'er the spirit of Mayne's dream; a bolt had descended from the blue! If Nancy had ten thousand a year, or thereabouts, how, he asked himself, could he come forward, and claim her? He had suddenly lost all interest in the meeting,—he had also mislaid his companion, and strolled over, and leant on the rails; not as others, watching an exciting race, but digesting Mrs. Hicks' unwelcome information. Her news, had altered the whole of his plans. Plans hastily made; and as hastily shattered.

Suddenly a heavy hand smote him on the back, and turning about he beheld Major Cathcart, looking remarkably spruce, and cheerful. "Glad to see you, old man," he began. "All the world seems to have turned up here to-day; and what a rare good meeting! I have pulled off a nice little haul." Then, after an expressive pause.... "*You've* had a bad time, I'm afraid!"

"Oh, no," replied Mayne, standing erect, and facing the speaker, "*I've* done pretty well, too."

"I say," now indicating a flowing tide of departures,—"if you are going by this train, we may as well toddle down together, and discuss old times."

Mayne nodded assent, and turned to accompany him.

"Where are you staying?" inquired Cathcart.

"With my mother, in Charles Street."

"And what leave have they given you?"

"All I asked for—three months."

"Of course you'll get an extension! Do you know that there has been quite a gathering of the hill tribes here to-day? I spotted Mrs. Hicks,—by George, what a sight! she ought to be in the Zoo, among the cockatoos. Her eldest girl, and Teddy Dawson, were with her, and then there's you and me,—and last but not least, Miss Nancy Travers! There's a transformation! She's a tremendous success, I can tell you. Men actually biting, and scratching one another, to get hold of her at dances, and so on. She's deuced ornamental, and well gilded too! and has slipped into the rôle of heiress, and beauty,—as easily as an old glove. You'd never believe she is the same girl as our little red-haired flapper! Have you come across her?"

"Not ... er ... to speak to."

"Well, all in good time; you and she used to be rather chummy, and by Jove, she could play tennis a bit! Mrs. De Wolfe, her chaperon, is a crafty old woman, and knows all the best people. She will do her best to fix a coronet, on that girl's head. I hear Lord Lanark is in the last stage of idiocy. I must confess I am rather surprised, that Mrs. De Wolfe allows Miss Nancy to be seen about with that fellow Villars. I am told, that he was always one of the little family party, on Como; painting, boating and caterwauling and all that sort of thing! He got the girl a good deal talked about,—but that's his little way!"

"Mayne never had much to say for himself," thought his companion, "now he did not seem to have a word, to throw at the traditional dog; but appeared to be totally dumb, and an absolutely uninterested listener. Well, there were crowds of other fellows, with whom he could improve the shining half-hour, to town," so with a "See you later on," Cathcart shook off this deadly wet-blanket, and hailed a passing acquaintance.

CHAPTER XXVIII
"ADVICE GRATIS"

For once, Mrs. De Wolfe was hopelessly puzzled; something had happened the day of the races at Sandown; for ever since that date, Nancy was a changed creature; her amazing spirits appeared to have evaporated; she no longer entered into plans, with the same keen enthusiasm, but was restless, nervous, and given to surprising fits of silence. Her anxious chaperon dated this phase, from the afternoon when she had confided her charge into the hands of Jane Wynne; yet Jane Wynne could throw no light on the matter—although her aunt had approached her with the most careful, and subtle questions. The girl did not bet, she had no quarrel with anyone, nor had she lost any treasured bit of jewellery,—something had gone much deeper than *that*. What was it?

Nancy described in somewhat laborious detail, the crowd, the heat,— which had given her a headache,—she had met masses of people she knew, including the Hicks, and Teddy; the Millers were there in great force, including Lady Miller in a wonderful French frock; but the glare was dreadful, and she had not enjoyed herself one bit. "How I wish I had stayed at home, with you, and sat out in the cool under the trees," she concluded, as she had bent over her old friend, and kissed her between her somewhat bushy eyebrows.

Subsequently, Mrs. De Wolfe (who was credited with eyes in the back of her head) noted, that when they were in the park, at a polo match, or a dance, Nancy seemed to be looking about her nervously, as if in quest of someone: some individual whom she was half afraid to see! Her talk and her manner suffered; she had become preoccupied, absent minded, and silent.—It was a puzzle.—Meanwhile, her young friend was going through a crisis of feeling, almost too terrible to support.

For a whole fortnight, Nancy never caught sight of Mayne, and then she encountered him riding in the park one morning early. He was with a lady. They passed within a few yards of one another; but made no sign. She had felt half inclined to bow, but her impulse had arrived too late.

Mayne had waited in due form upon the Hicks, sent a handsome present to the bride-elect, and invited Teddy to dine with him at his club; but Teddy preferred a *tête-à-tête* luncheon—his evenings were sacred to Jessie.

"I'm awfully glad you were able to come," said Mayne, as he ushered his friend into the stately dining-room of his club. "I couldn't get half a word with you the other day, and I wanted to have a *bukh*."

"Oh, it's all right,—Jessie let me off this morning; she is up to her neck, shopping! You see, we are to be married in ten days, and want to do our honeymoon at home, before I get back to the coffee. We intend to live at Fairplains, which belongs to Nancy,—as you know."

"Yes! Mrs. Hicks told me. I hadn't heard a word."

"Well, how could you? when you never wrote to any of us. Nancy was a jolly sight better, she used to send me screeds, when she lived with her aunt, and did Companion, and Tweenie, and Scapegoat. However, that's all over now; as she and Mrs. De Wolfe will live together: they are going down to her country place, after July. I dined with them the other night, and I have heard all their plans."

"Mrs. De Wolfe lives in our part of the world; she and my uncle are old friends, so Nancy and I, will find ourselves in the same boat, meeting every day, sitting next to one another at dinner; in fact, I see nothing for it, but to chuck the rest of my leave, and go back to India."

"Don't be a fool, Mayne! Why on earth should you do that?"

"Knowing what you know,—need you ask? How can I go about, and associate, with a girl——" He paused expressively.

"You can make it up."

"No! I did my best, and Nancy made a fool of me."

"Yes, but the poor child was out of her mind with grief; the whole tragedy got upon her nerves; to tell you the truth, she grew so strange, that they thought she was really going off her chump, and bundled her home,— where I believe some real hard knocks and shocks, brought her to her senses. She has a face you can't forget; awfully pretty, isn't she?"

"She is," assented the other.

"Look here, Mayne, if you will take *my* advice,—you will sit tight—and brazen it out!"

"But my dear fellow, how can I brazen out, what is a dead secret?"

"Everyone will know some day,—and there will be a most tremendous rumpus. Nancy is famous for her good looks, she has a whole string of admirers,—Finchie's nephew is making great running, and——"

"He may run till he is black in the face," interrupted Mayne, "he can't marry her."

"Aren't you rather a manger dog; you don't care about the girl yourself,—some day she may lose her heart to a fellow, and *then* what is to happen?"

"I'm afraid, I have not been quite candid with you, Teddy old man! although I have only seen this new Nancy twice; I find, that I *do* care for her. In old days I admired her character, and liked her as a pal, otherwise she only struck me as a sunburnt, talkative, tomboy. Now, added to her good points, she has become beautiful, and attractive; and if she hadn't a penny, I'd have come forward, have asked you to be my ambassador, and endeavoured to make friends. On these lines, I believe matters would have worked out all right, in *time*. Travers liked me, and I'd score there; but to find that Nancy is not only a beauty, but also a great heiress, is a bit too much to face. I couldn't stand a wife with heaps of money, and mines! I'd be buried in gold and grandeur, and lose my own identity—such as it is! I only wish I saw a clear and honourable road, out of the whole diabolical business!"

"That is to say, if the mine were to burst up, and the coffee to go smash. I suppose," added Dawson, after a moment's reflection, "there was no flaw in that hurried-up ceremony?"

"None! I made particular inquiries at the time. The parson had the Bishop's licence all right; they sent an express, and routed his lordship out of bed in the middle of the night. Without this licence, a marriage is no more valid, as a binding ceremony,—than taking a woman down to dinner."

"So there's no loop-hole in *that* direction," said his companion. "If Finchie were at home, I bet you anything you like, she'd clear a path somehow. Shove you and your queer wedding into limbo, and marry Nancy and her money, to her nephew, Tony Lamerton!"

"Yes, perhaps she'd have a good try, but she couldn't bring it off all the same."

"You're coming to see me turned off on Wednesday week, eh,—you really *must* support me, and Nancy is to be one of the bridesmaids."

"Is she? well don't put me down for best man,—I'm not eligible, but I'll afford you my presence, and moral support. Is it to be a big affair?"

"I'm afraid so! lots of Mrs. Hicks' old friends, every planter in London, and most of our fellow passengers; we've had some thumping presents. Nancy has given us a car, a piano, and a fine canteen. She takes the deepest interest in our affairs, and is with Jessie to-day. We are sending some new furniture out to Fairplains."

"Well, I must confess, I rather liked the old sticks. There was one lame chair in the verandah, the most comfortable I ever sat in,—just took you nicely in the back, and didn't poke your head into your chest."

"It shall be preserved, and kept ready for *you* whenever you come for a shoot."

"I'll never shoot again at Fairplains,—or set foot on Nancy's estate."

"What a stiff-necked beggar you are! and yet I think it is quite on the cards,—that you may never return to India."

"Yes, I see your meaning, why swither out there, when I have a rich wife in England? As it happens, I bar a rich wife, and never intend to claim her."

"Supposing she were to take it into her head to claim *you*? What then?"

Mayne stared at his guest for a moment, and then burst into a loud and hearty laugh. "Sooner than that, from what I know of Nancy, she would take a header off Waterloo Bridge."

"Well," replied Teddy, looking at his watch, "I must be off. Jessie is the soul of punctuality,—and I have to be, what the Americans call, 'on time.'"

"I score over you in one way, Teddy," said his friend, "I was never on duty; I had no long engagement,—at the outside, it wasn't more than thirty-six hours!"

CHAPTER XXIX
"THE SWORD OF DAMOCLES"

During these sunny summer days, although Nancy looked remarkably gay and pretty, and went what is called "everywhere," she was secretly miserable,—but bravely concealed her sufferings and kept her anxieties to herself. For more than two years, she had lived in a sort of fool's paradise, or as if she had been in a dream. Now, she had been awakened with a shock, and like a newly-aroused sleeper, began to look about her, and realized a changed world. She had never supposed that Derek Mayne would re-enter her life: he was in India,—that land of vague and indefinite banishments,—and she was in England.

How could they ever meet? Then she had his promise: his letter, treasured in her jewel-case. Nevertheless, here he was in London, actually within a few streets, and he had it in his power to ruin and upset the whole of her life; he could if he chose. She recalled his expression of cool scrutiny, and aloofness, as he looked at her across the railway carriage: his glance was direct, dominating, and almost stern.

Although the future horizon was vague and misty, recently life had gone smoothly for Nancy; she had been gliding along, as it were on a wide placid river; now all at once she seemed to be approaching unknown falls, and to hear the roar of the rapids! In her short life, she had known days, and days of intense mental anguish,—the agony of bereavement. This present pain was neither so sharp, or so poignant, but of an unceasing aching, and gnawing description.

She slept badly; she had little appetite for food, or amusement; each succeeding day she expected the sword to fall! Every time she and her chaperon re-entered their suite, her first impulse was to rush to the table, where cards and letters awaited them, and these she turned over, and examined with a throbbing heart. Would Derek Mayne call, and seek an interview with Mrs. De Wolfe? Would he claim her? He might try,—but she would resist,—or would he merely inform people that she was his lawful wife, and leave her, so to speak, to face the music!

By an amazing coincidence, two of the witnesses to her marriage were in London: Teddy and Mrs. Hicks; and she lived in quaking fear that *they* would open the subject! Much to her relief, it had never been approached. At present, Teddy and his future mother-in-law were far too much engrossed in their own more interesting affairs.

Lady Belmont's long expected and belated ball, eventually took place at the "Ritz"; and more than fulfilled the most exigent anticipations. Many of the best people, the pretty girls, and the smart young men were present. Nancy and her chaperon,—who, surprising to relate, delighted in a ball,—were early arrivals. Nancy loved dancing, danced beautifully, and was much improved since Dudley Villars had been her constant partner. She looked very lovely, and a little out of breath as she came up to Mrs. De Wolfe at the end of a long waltz, and found the old lady talking with unusual animation to some man,—who, when he turned about, she saw to her consternation, was Captain Mayne!

"Nancy," said her chaperon, "I want you to give a dance to an old friend of mine; one of my boys, Captain Mayne!—Derek, this is my young friend, Miss Travers."

Captain Mayne bowed, and said, "Miss Travers and I have met before. May I?" looking at her steadily, "have the honour of a waltz?"

Nancy, who had paled rather suddenly, glanced down at her crammed programme, and murmured, "Number twelve," and with a bow, he backed away into the crowd.

Nancy's card had been filled ever since she had appeared in the ball-room; nevertheless, she mentally threw over Lord Lanark—whose name was scribbled before number twelve waltz, "Destiny." She must speak to Captain Mayne, and learn the worst! what he intended to do? or not to do? and face this horrible ordeal.

Waiting and uncertainty had become unbearable; and yet the dread of the approaching interview, filled her with terror. For a moment she was seized by an overwhelming reluctance. All the fears of the last weeks, had now become real, and verified. She was fired by a wild desire, to feign illness, and rush home; but soon overcame this preposterous temptation. It was imperative to stand to her promise, and to listen to what her partner had to say—nothing agreeable, that was certain—she had glanced into his face, and there read an expression of cool and absolute indifference.

However, now they had been formally made known to one another, and were liable to meet, she must learn the rules of the game in which she was expected to take part! There it was, the first part of "Destiny!" and here he came; edging his way towards her through the crowd. She accepted his arm in dead silence, and in another moment they were launched among the whirling throng. Mayne danced extremely well,—steering his course with remarkable skill. (Nancy had noticed him waltzing with Josie; their steps suited admirably; graceful, lissom Josie, moving with a sort of foreign swing and abandon, murmuring into his ear all the time they floated round,—unquestionably they were *old* friends). He was not perhaps so accomplished a performer as Sir Dudley, but he held his partner with greater respect, and did not use an Oriental perfume on his sleek dark hair.

They exchanged one or two formal remarks about the floor, and the band, danced until the music ceased, and people began to pour out of the ball-room; then Mayne led his companion to a secluded little settee, and took a chair close by. Here was the supreme moment! He looked at Nancy narrowly: how young, fresh, and slim,—and yet how woefully white, and scared!—he could actually see a little pulse throbbing in her throat, her hands were tightly locked in her lap. Yes! brutal thought, he was getting a little of his own back! At last he said:

"Well!"

Nancy raised her frightened eyes, glanced at him quickly, and looked down; and there ensued an expressive silence, more eloquent than words. The pause was broken by Mayne, who quietly quoted:

"Gentlemen of the French Guard,—fire first!"

"I suppose you mean that *I* am to speak," said Nancy in a low voice.

He nodded shortly.

"But I don't know what to say."

Nevertheless she realized that she was fencing with her future life.

"Oh, of course I don't expect you to say you are *glad* to see me," and he gave an abrupt laugh.

Nancy made no reply,—but her lower lip quivered.

"May I offer you my congratulations?" he continued. "I hear you are now a great heiress; a goldmine! and Fairplains."

"Fairplains, yes! Oh, if only Daddy had been alive!"

"Yes, I know," he assented promptly, "please don't *spare* me! If I hadn't missed the panther——"

"I'm not quite so malicious as you imagine," she interrupted, "and you need not be so bitter—for you know as well as I do, how Daddy adored Fairplains."

"Pray accept my apologies," he said coolly, "I was not aware that you had modified your opinions. I wished to speak to you,—and here is my golden opportunity! You see, by most shocking bad luck, we happen to find ourselves in the same set! Your chaperon, Mrs. De Wolfe, belongs to my part of the world; she knew me in pinafores, so I am afraid we shall often knock up against one another."

"I suppose so," asserted Nancy, without raising her eyes.

"We may even find ourselves staying in the same house, and this would be a bit awkward; for if we were dead cuts, it might excite remark! However, this preposterous position, won't last long; I shall be returning to India." He paused for a moment and then added, with a smile, "Ah! I see you look relieved!"

"Do I? I did not know,—I rather wish I was going back too!"

"What, tired of the gay world already?"

To this she made no answer.

"Well, Nancy, you and I are in a queer fix, if ever there was one! God knows I meant to do the square thing," he went on gravely, "but I made a most awful hash of the whole business!"

"I believe you *did* mean well," she murmured, speaking with evident effort, "and I behaved—ungratefully; but I was crazy with grief. Everything was so awfully sudden, and, and——" she hesitated.

"And you couldn't bear the sight of me," he interjected, "and I accepted the situation. You made everything fairly plain in your letter,—didn't you?"—Another immense pause.

Nancy wondered how long this hateful scene was to continue—it seemed to have lasted for hours. Then in a meditative tone Mayne began:

"Now I wonder, if I had followed you to your hiding-place, and dragged you off to Cananore, how would that have answered?"

"It would have made me hate, and abhor you, as long as I lived," she rejoined with startling vehemence.

"Oh! and do you hate, and abhor, me now?"

She raised her eyes, and considered him gravely; but made no reply— she did not wish to be his wife, but in her secret heart, she knew she would be glad to be friends. Something in his voice, and his honest eyes, recalled old days, and the many happy hours, they two had spent together. Then he was so manly, and good-looking; also she began to feel, that she was not really afraid of him.

"What I wished to say to you," he continued, "is this: that, owing to the pressure of circumstances, we must meet, and pretend to be friends."

"Or be friends, and pretend?" she corrected timidly.

"What an explosion, if the truth ever leaked out! Think of your friends and relations; my friends and my regiment. However, you may rely upon me to keep my promise,—and to hold my tongue." After a moment's silence, he added: "How do you hit it off with Mrs. De Wolfe?"

"Extremely well,—I am very fond of her."

"Somehow I shouldn't have thought that she was your sort!—I've seen you going about, with her godson, that fellow Villars."

"Yes, he noticed you that day at Sandown, and he was speaking about you," replied Nancy, who had somewhat recovered her colour, and her courage.

"That was kind of him,—I am flattered. What did he say, anything libellous?"

"Oh no indeed; he only told me, that your uncle, is very anxious for you to marry."

"Well that's a true bill,—he *is*!"

"But *can* you?"

"What a funny question. No, not unless I wish to be run in for bigamy,—a Mrs. Mayne already exists."

"You mean me?"

"Yes, who else?" slowly turning his head to look at her. The question was sarcastically enforced.

After a short silence she murmured: "And is there *no* way out?"

"I imagine there is; but you see, I've not had much to do with matrimonial intricacies,—I believe, I could divorce you—for desertion!"

"Oh!" putting her hands up to cover her face, "and it would be in all the papers!"

"It would; and probably headed, 'Great military scandal,' and illustrated with our portraits."

"And what *would* Mrs. De Wolfe say?"

"Mrs. De Wolfe can stand a good deal,—she's had some pretty bad shocks in her time; and is a regular old brick; and you would achieve notoriety!—Then on the other hand, *I* might give you reason to divorce *me*," and he looked at Nancy with keen significance.

Nancy blushed to the roots of her hair: her very ears were red.

"But make your mind easy," he continued, "I am not going to wade through mud,—even to break our chain."

"And is there *no* way out of it?" she repeated with a sort of sob.

"I'm afraid not. With every good intention, your father and I made a serious mistake. It is not so easy, to order the lives of other people,—each must go his own road. You have no wish to walk in mine; or I in yours. I don't want you as a wife,—official or otherwise,—and I have excellent reason to know, that you have no desire to play the rôle of Mrs. Mayne."

His tone and expression, made Nancy wince—and yet this announcement was a profound relief. She glanced at him, as he sat in a favourite attitude, nursing his foot,—a very neat foot, and well turned ankle, in black silk hose.—She remembered how her father had chaffed him, and he said, "When I was at school I hurt my foot rather badly at rugger, and nursed it on my knee to keep it out of harm's way,—the trick has grown on me, I do it unconsciously."

"May I look at this?" he said, leaning forward and picking her programme off her lap.

"I'm not sure that it isn't one of my prerogatives. Hullo! so you threw over Lanark, and gave *me* his dance; I hope he won't shoot me? eh! Villars, Villars, Villars,—*toujours* Villars, *why* so much Villars?"

"Oh, because I know him rather well."

"I bet you *don't*."

"I see you don't like him."

"No: a fellow who can't play cricket, either physically or morally, who can't box, or shoot; just a good-looking blighter, with a glib tongue, and a face of brass."

"At any rate, he is clever, and accomplished; he sings and plays the violin, paints better than many professionals,—he dances like a dream."

"So *you* seem to think!"

"But *everyone* thinks it! I've been told, that girls have actually wept, because he ignored them at a ball."

"More fools they! shall *I* ever see the proud day, when a girl howls, because I haven't asked her to dance? Look here, Nancy," and his voice took a certain peremptoriness, "don't have anything to do with that chap Villars,—he is *not* a safe acquaintance!"

Nancy made no reply, and apparently assuming that silence gave consent, he continued—"I see our old friend Cathcart here, no doubt repairing his shattered nerves, after a spasm of work! He appears to be in great force. You have not favoured him,—how is that?"

"He didn't ask me for a dance."

"What!" staring at her. "Oh, so you've had a row!"

"Not exactly a row," and she hesitated.

"Exactly what? come, own up, we are not likely to have another interview, for some time."

"Well then if you *must* know,—he asked me to marry him!"

"To marry him!" echoed her companion, now no longer nursing his foot, and sitting erect.

"And was very angry indeed, when I said no, in fact he has cut me dead ever since."

For some time Mayne was silent, at last he said:

"Asked you to marry him; by Jove, that was too funny! I think I must propose to some girl,—so as to make us quits; though it might be rather awkward, if she happened to say 'yes'! However, of course I could easily jilt her!" Then in quite another tone, "No doubt you encouraged his hopes?"

"I did nothing of the kind," she answered hotly, "I've always disliked him."

"Ah! Well on one point we agree; I don't love him either. There's your programme; I wonder if you are aware, that we have sat out two whole dances? Time has flown,—hasn't it? Look here, one word before we part. We are bound to meet at home,—I mean in Moonshire. Mrs. De Wolfe and my uncle are tremendous chums, old lovers and that sort of thing, and I daresay she will wonder, that since we knew one another in India,—why you have kept me so *dark*? You must play up! You'd better say,—we had a quarrel."

"Very well," assented the girl.

"And don't let her run away with the idea,—that it was a *lovers'* quarrel," he added, rising as he spoke.

To this, Nancy made no reply, and they returned to the ball-room in absolute silence. The moment she appeared, she was instantly claimed by Sir Dudley Villars, who upbraided her with having "cut his dance." Meanwhile Mayne walked off in search of his own partner.

How pretty Nancy was; indeed lovely! How her colour went and came, and how her little under lip, had trembled. Perhaps he had been a bit rough on her! The old outspoken, spirited, Nancy he remembered, was gone! At first, she had seemed as frightened as a newly caught bird. But, after all, why should he not bully her a little? considering that he was her lawful lord, and master; and that his share, so far, had been the kicks,—whilst she, had collared all the half-pence!

CHAPTER XXX
CRITICAL MOMENTS FOR NANCY

Captain Mayne's remark with regard to no further interview, proved correct; he and Nancy merely encountered one another as very slight acquaintances, who have friends in common. She noticed him riding in the Park with Josie,—they never joined her, but merely cantered by with a cheery salute. At a polo match at Ranelagh, where Mayne had played and distinguished himself, she looked on, whilst friends gathered round to congratulate him, and she saw Josie go up and pat the damp neck of his considerably blown pony. That same day, at the polo match, his mother, Lady Torquilstone, was pointed out to her by Mrs. De Wolfe; a tall, supremely well dressed, well preserved, arrogant woman, who looked as if the whole of Ranelagh was her private property, and most of the crowd, insufferable intruders.

"So that was her mother-in-law!" said Nancy to herself. Her mother-in-law's husband, was a dapper, prancing sort of little man, with fierce eyebrows, and a hard stare.

As Mrs. De Wolfe and her companion were motoring back to town, they passed Captain Mayne, who waved to them from the coach.

"It's most extraordinary," said the old lady, "that since he has come home, I've seen so little of Derek. Long ago when with his uncle, he was in and out of my place like a dog in a fair! Now he has merely left a formal card, and although I have twice asked him to dinner, he has been engaged. *My* conscience is clear, I have not offended him in any way, and I can't bear to be dropped by my young friends, to say nothing of old ones. By the way, Nancy," glancing at her companion, "perhaps you are the guilty party. Did he by any chance make love to you?"

"Oh, no; no indeed," replied Nancy, with reassuring emphasis.

"Well of course in those days, you must have been a little girl in short skirts, with your hair down your back, and I'm quite sure that Derek Mayne would never look at a flapper."

Although Nancy and Captain Mayne maintained a cautious distance, they were brought in spite of themselves into close contact at the Hicks—Dawson, wedding. The ceremony was a grand affair; everything was done in a lavish, if somewhat showy way. Nancy was not a bridesmaid, for Mrs. Hicks had intervened, and helped her out, with a series of the most extraordinary excuses,—these being accepted by Jessie, with a somewhat indifferent grace.

The church, which was rather small, was handsomely decorated, and crammed to the doors. With respect to the guests, Mrs. Hicks had figuratively "gone forth to the highways and hedges, and compelled them to come in." Old planter friends; recent fellow-passengers, and even the inmates of her "family hotel." Mrs. De Wolfe and Nancy were among early arrivals at the church, and the latter drew many admiring eyes; her gown and hat were white; she looked bridal herself! white suited her wonderful complexion, and reddish-brown hair. Almost at the last moment, and when the bridesmaids were actually assembled in the porch, Captain Mayne,—very smart in frock-coat, and lavender gloves,—came strolling up the aisle, glancing from side to side, in search of an empty space! Mrs. De Wolfe's quick eye caught his. She made a little signal, he crushed into her pew, and took a seat between Nancy, and the door.

The organ pealed, the choir leading the procession, advanced slowly up the aisle. Jessie, carrying herself with dignified self-possession, looked unusually well,—indeed quite at her best. Not so, the waiting bridegroom; for if his new coat was creaseless, his countenance was painfully distorted. He appeared to be pitiably nervous, and was struggling with a (happily groundless) fear, that he had lost the ring! Jessie was staunchly supported by her mother, rustling in a brilliant blue costume,—destined to open the eyes of the Meaches, and other neighbours. Meanwhile Nancy, whose attention had been riveted on Jessie, became suddenly alive to the appalling consciousness, that the last time she listened to these prayers, and adjurations, they had been addressed to herself,—and the man who stood beside her! She felt overwhelmed by the shock of this poignant memory; how mean and cruel of fate to drag them together in such a heartless fashion; each sentence now felt like a separate stab.

At Fairplains, the service had fallen on more or less deaf ears; here, she was acutely alive to every syllable. Did her companion remember? She stole a swift glance at Mayne; he was looking straight before him, and his profile was absolutely impassive. Such were the close quarters in the pew, that their elbows were almost touching: could he feel how she was trembling? When it came to the words, *"forsaking all other, keeping only to him, as long as ye both shall live,"* Nancy, in spite of a determined effort at self-control, felt herself shaking from head to foot. The position was to the last degree embarrassing, and painful; compelled to listen to the celebration of Holy Matrimony, side by side with the man to whom she had been married,—and from whom she had run away! was an ordeal almost too terrible to be endured. Her face seemed to be on fire, her lips were twitching convulsively, as she kept her head down, and supported herself by the front of the pew.

Oh! what a relief, when they knelt, and she could more or less hide herself; but she was so unstrung and agitated that she let fall her prayer-book and her bag! Mayne picked them both up, and as he gravely restored them, he glanced at her heightened colour, and averted eyes. It seemed positively cruel to scrutinize her,—his bride of two and a half years! for in spite of his apparent composure he had not failed to realize the extraordinary situation, and Nancy's miserable confusion.

Strange to say, Mrs. De Wolfe was totally unaware of the little drama beside her; her attention had been closely engaged in viewing with much amusement the extraordinary collection of people that Mrs. Hicks' cards of invitation had assembled.—The end of the service found Nancy calmer; bodily release was at hand; but her mind had been grasped by a penetrating thought. She had made a vow more than two years ago; a vow to this man beside her, a vow she had deliberately broken. Would God punish her? It was the first time she had been invaded by this idea.—She glanced instinctively at her companion. Apparently he had not given the situation a moment's thought; and was carefully extracting from its haven of refuge, a beautiful, glossy new hat. And now the bride and bridegroom came pacing down the aisle, and Teddy, who had completely recovered his poise, halted as he passed, and said "You two," glancing from Mayne to Nancy, "must come out, and sign."

There was nothing else for it! Mayne at once stepped forth, Nancy followed him, and they fell into line behind the bridesmaids, and not a few who saw them, thought, "What a strikingly good-looking couple!"

They entirely eclipsed the real pair. Such a crowd in the vestry, such kissing and chattering!—Mrs. Hicks' voice, high above every other, Jessie radiant, with veil thrown back, kissed Nancy,—and Mayne kissed *her*!

When it was his turn to sign the register, he wrote, "Derek D. Mayne, Captain," then passed the pen to Nancy. For a moment she hesitated; she felt his eyes fixed upon her, and with a sudden and inexplicable impulse, and a very shaky hand, she scrawled, "Nancy Mayne": it was almost illegible; an inkstained spider could have done as well, if not better. She happened to be the last to sign, and no one looked over the register, except Mrs. Hicks,—who saw to everything;—little escaped that sharp-eyed matron, who instantly recognizing this unexpected signature, glanced quickly from the page to Mayne, and gave him a bold, and unmistakable wink.

The reception, which took place at a neighbouring hotel, was very crowded, very noisy, and very lively,—precisely what was to be expected from anything in which Mrs. Hicks had a hand! The presents on show, were well worthy of exhibition,—the refreshments were first-rate, the band not too blatant, and the champagne unexceptional. It was agreed by their many friends, that the Hicks' had spared no expense, and given the marriage "Tasmasha" in great style.

The crowd, crush, heat, and striving to be gay, natural, and like herself, left Nancy to return to her temporary home, figuratively in the condition of some half-dead, battered flower!

The memory of the ceremony, held her in a vice-like grip; as for signing the register,—*what* had possessed her? Was it a compelling look in Mayne's eyes, or was it a spasmodic effort of conscience? In the crush, at the reception, although she did not actually come across Mayne, she had seen him more than once. He had assisted to tie a shoe at the back of the motor which was to bear the happy couple away, and was active and prominent among the mob that threw rice. There had been neither slipper, nor rice, at *their* wedding!

Soon after this eventful occasion, one morning in the Row, Mrs. Speyde rode up to Nancy, and said to her escort, "Do you go away, Tony,—I want to have a talk with Nancy."

"No fear!" was the brotherly reply.

"But you really *must*," she persisted. "I particularly want to tell Nancy a secret,—though Mrs. De Wolfe says she can't keep one,—and that her face always gives her away."

"One of your good stories, I suppose; well, *I* may as well hear it too!"

"No, no," protested Nancy, with a nervous laugh, "I never listen to Josie's stories,—one, was more than enough!"

Mrs. Speyde knew from long experience, that her brother could be stubborn when it suited him, so she said, "Well, don't ask me to oblige you, dear Tony, next time you are in a hole, or otherwise." Then turning to Nancy, "I'll come in early this evening and talk, whilst you are dressing," and with a nod, she wheeled her horse about, and rode away.

At half-past seven, as Nancy, seated before her glass, was taking down her masses of hair, there was a sharp knock at the door, which the maid opened, and Mrs. Speyde sailed in. A shimmering cloak covered her smart French gown, and a diamond bandeau sparkled in her black hair. As she advanced, she discarded the mantle, and displayed a smart, and very *décolleté* red gown.

"I've got 'em all on to-night!" she announced. Then, as the maid disappeared, she sat down, crossed her knees, and took out a cigarette. "A cigarette makes me talk," she added. "This is a Doucet frock, Nancy, what do you think of it? My maid says the body has no back!"

"Nor much front either," said Nancy, as she inspected her friend; "indeed I call it an *a*ffront," and she laughed.

"How dare you?"

"Oh, I'm so thin, it's all right! Now on you,—it might be——" and she hesitated.

"Impossible!" declared Nancy.

"Dear, beautiful young creature, what a lovely neck! However, I didn't dress an hour earlier, and rush over here, to discuss necks, and bodies; I've come to break it to you gently, that I'm thinking of settling down at last."

"You mean getting married?"

"Yes. Giving up little suppers in Soho, racing, and gambling,—and turning over a new leaf."

"And who is to be the happiest of men?"

"I should think you might easily guess."

"Not so easily,—you have such crowds of men friends. Is it Colonel Deloraine?"

"Is it my grandfather!" she scoffed. "No! a thousand times no! Well, I won't keep you on tenterhooks,—it's Derek Mayne! You know him." A slight pause, and a quick glance. "I say! Nancy, why do you look so funny, and surprised?—I'm not poaching on *your* preserves, I know!"

"I'm not looking funny or surprised," she managed to protest, and Josie was too much wrapped up in her subject, too anxious to talk, to notice that she was more or less confused.

"He is such a dear fellow, straight as a die! one of the living best; not very emotional, you know,—keeps his feelings to himself, hates spooning, and all that sort of thing! Remember long ago, when I kissed him under the mistletoe,—he didn't like it a little bit!"

"Did he not?" said Nancy, who was carefully collecting hairpins. "I'm rather surprised at that."

"I'm dining and doing a theatre with him to-night.—I expect he has got another man and girl,—he is so frightfully proper. Well, my dear, the whole thing will suit me down to the ground; I shall love to go to India, just to see the Land of Regrets, and later on, we'll settle ourselves comfortably in our own county."

"Yes, er ... er ... will you?"

"Why of course,—at Maynesfort—our ancestral home. What fun I shall have turning out the garrets! I believe they are full of lovely old things, hustled away by the late Mrs. Mayne, who was a Victorian lady, and loved crewel-work antimacassars, chromo-lithographs; bead mats, and wax flowers!"

"Is anything settled?" inquired Nancy, with her eyes fixed upon her hairpins.

"Not yet, the fact is there is a little bit of a hitch,—and I believe you are just the one person who can help me,—and that's why I'm here! Oh yes, my dear, although you look so calmly indifferent, and can only throw me a casual yes or no; you knew Derek in India! Tell me honestly, Nancy,—did you ever hear a story about him and a *girl*? No, don't get so red, I'm not going to tell you one of *mine*, I want to know one of *his*! The uncle seems to have an idea, that Derek got himself into a mess—a nasty scrape—with some woman in India,—black, for choice,—but I'm sure that wouldn't be Derek's form. The old man is anxious; he has talked to me,—I may tell you that he adores me, for I amuse him and flirt with him.—Derek was out there for four years, and I need not assure you, one can manage to get through a good deal of mischief, in *that* time.—I've done my level best to pump Derek, but it was no go; I had better luck with one of his pals, Major Sanders, who is in the same regiment.—I screwed it out of *him*, that he believes there *is* something,—although he cannot name the lady. For the last couple of years, Derek has been short of money; he doesn't join in things as he used to do, and he sold two ripping polo ponies. Major Sanders thinks there may be some horrible creature, who claws half his income, as blackmail!"

Nancy, who had been brushing her hair, now swept a quantity over her face, which was burning. *She* was the horrible creature who twice a year, received, but rejected, the half of Captain Mayne's income.

"Tell me, Nance, did *you* ever hear anything?—what was he like, in those days?"

"Much the same as now," she murmured, through her veil of shining locks.

"More cheery and go-ahead?"

"Oh yes,—I think perhaps he was."

"I feel I knew Derek, and I'm certain, there's something on his mind,—some *secret*; but whatever it is, cart-horses would not drag it from him! He knows Aunt Julia, of course. If only she were at home, she would throw a search-light on the mystery. I never met such a woman for getting to the bottom of a business; but she won't be back till September! Tell me, Nancy, did Derek Mayne know any girls, when you met him?"

"Oh yes; he knew three or four planters' daughters."

"Did he flirt with them?"

"No, never, that I saw: he only cared for sport, and tennis."

"Well, I have reason to know that Derek likes *me*; we've been pals since we were children, and if only this little mystery was cleared up, I'd be perfectly happy! After all, there may be nothing in it,—what do you say?"

Nancy threw back her flowing hair, and looked up at Josie, who had risen, and was standing beside her,—one hand on her slim hip—the other fingering a cigarette. "I say ..." she paused ... and then, taking her courage in both hands, "I say, that from what I know of Captain Mayne,—I don't think he will ever marry!"

"What preposterous nonsense!" exclaimed her visitor. "I know it's not envy on your part, my child, for you don't like one another,—as anyone can see with half an eye. He will marry: in fact he must marry, and soon. His uncle is getting rampageous, and declares, that if Derek hangs back,—he will take a wife himself. Derek and I, will get on splendidly together," announced Josie, now walking about the room, "he is so steady, and I'm just exactly the opposite!—I won't be sorry to have a home of my own,—for I'm dead tired of my present existence; a sort of life, the American summed up as, 'One damned thing after another!'—Ah, here comes your maid with your frock; oh, my dear, what a dream!—so I'll clear out and leave you, to put on your rouge.—Joking apart, darling, you do look white; you've not been up to the mark just lately, I expect you want a tonic."

"Oh no," said Nancy, rising. "Of course going about from morning till night, and dancing from night till morning, *is* rather fagging, but I'm all right."

"Well, my sweet lamb, all *I* can say is, that you *look* all wrong; however, I suppose you know best. Mind you keep my little secret."

She halted on her way to the door, and looked back with eyes of expressive significance, then, satisfied with a nod, she swept out.

CHAPTER XXXI
NEWENHAM COURT

Newenham was a real eighteenth-century village, chiefly composed of red brick flat-faced houses,—some shyly withdrawn from the road, behind prim little gardens, others standing boldly upon the street. There was a dumpy, contented-looking old church, an ivy-clad parsonage, and an ancient inn, formerly a noted posting-house; now resuscitated, after nearly a century of neglect, as a halting-place and garage. The Court was situated in a land of heavy trees, green slopes and great peace; its back entrance opened directly into the village, but from an opposite direction a long and imposing avenue, with gates guarded by a pair of fierce stone wolves, wound up to the hall door.

The Court was a mixture of the Georgian and Victorian period, without any claim to architectural beauty; but it had the dignity of mellow age, and solid prosperity. The entrance faced north, and looked upon wide grass slopes, crowned by heavy plantations. In the interior was a vast hall, popular as a lounge and general sitting-room. Here people sat, read, had tea, played Bridge and had liberty to smoke. A spacious drawing-room, library, dining and billiard-rooms opened to right and left.

Almost every window in the Court commanded a view, and most of the sitting-rooms had French windows opening to the ground. Upstairs the passages were narrow, and rambling, with very low ceilings, and unexpected steps,—but the adjoining bedrooms dwelt long in the affectionate memory of many guests. These were furnished to suit the period, with large four-posters, and small looking-glasses, but were supplied with modern mattresses, comfortable armchairs, and the latest thing in Jacobean chintz! Here were writing-tables, well supplied,—including stamps,—fresh flowers, the newest books, and in season, the most cheerful fires.

Mrs. De Wolfe escorted her young friend all over the premises; she saw not only the kitchen, the still-room, the Justice's room, but the two apartments once occupied by the old lady's sons,—and now closed. Their mother displayed their books, and toys, of childhood,—as well as the trophies, and treasures of later years. The south side of the Court, overlooked a well-timbered park, and winding river; immediately in front, lay smooth green lawns, bounded right and left, by long herbaceous borders, and rose-covered pergolas. Somehow this unusual display gave the impression that an army corps of flowers, had escaped from the grim walled garden,—which lay half concealed beyond the shrubberies—and encamped in the grounds; immediately below the lawns were tennis courts; these were pointed out to Nancy by her hostess, as one of the chief features of the place.

"It is not for its gardens,—which as you see, are quite unique,—having boldly come out of bounds, and run into the park,—nor yet, for some very remarkable old furniture, nor even for its good dinners, that the Court is celebrated," said its mistress. "It is famed, for having the best tennis courts on this side of the county! My two boys were wonderful players,—Hughie was a champion, and in their day, the great tennis week took place *here*. There was always an immense gathering, we provided lunch and refreshments in big tents,—and the house was packed to the garret! When I am at home, I still endeavour to keep up Newenham Tennis week. I needn't tell you, that I never played tennis myself,—*my* game was croquet, in the good old days when croquet hoops were a generous size; but I still like to keep the tennis going,—indeed I don't suppose my neighbours would allow me to drop it; they consider it hard case, that it is not an annual fixture; but when I *am* here, I do my best to hold the meeting in all its glory. It is true, that, as it has been hinted to me, 'I now do very little for the county in the way of entertaining,' so I feel bound to put my best foot forward, once in a way. I fill the house with tennis-playing neighbours, I invite the residents for miles, I engage a band that I board in the village,—two extra cooks, tents, waiters, and supply all the delicacies of the season, and I offer, last not least, prizes that are worth while. There is tennis, more or less all day, the young people dance in the racquet court at night, others play Bridge, or billiards; oh, what a week it is! You will see, that I shall not be at home, more than a few days,—before letters come pouring in, to inquire the date of the Newenham Tennis Tournament?"

"It must be an immense undertaking for you," said Nancy, "but personally I think it will be great fun! I will help you, write out the invitations, and do the flowers, and any odd jobs you can find for me."

"Thank you, my dear, I'm sure you will be useful, but I generally get a man, to arrange dates, events, handicaps and so on, and more or less to run the show. I give him *carte blanche*; you shall be deputy hostess, and I will sit in my arm-chair,—and take all the credit! Four years ago, Derek Mayne was my helper,—I don't know who I shall have this time; perhaps Dudley Villars? he is not much of a tennis player, nor what I call practical, but he knows how to lay out money, and to make things go smoothly."

"And when do you think, you will have this tournament?"

"In about a fortnight,—or three weeks. First of all, I must go round, and look up my friends; and as soon as I have put the house in order, and reported myself to my people in the village, and had the Rectory people up to dinner, you and I will sally forth, and pay a round of calls."

Nancy had been given a delightful bedroom; it faced due south, her windows commanded the park, the shining river, a far-away distant blur of hills, immediately below lay the velvet lawns, and wide grassy walks, under rose-shaded pergolas. The whole place, seemed to be enveloped in an atmosphere of peace and good-will. "Only for one thing," she said to herself, "how very *very* happy I should be here!"

The afternoon when Nancy and her friend set forth in a new motor to pay a round of visits, the old lady said, "My first, must be to Richard Mayne; my old friend met with an accident a couple of months ago, and has been laid up ever since. I believe he is a shocking patient, impossible to keep indoors."

As they sped noiselessly along, she continued to talk about him. "He has been a widower for fifteen years,—his wife was always a delicate creature. She had a good deal of money,—which as they have no family, goes back to her relations. The Maynes,—the real name was Delamaine, but a Puritan ancestor chopped it up—the Maynes, have always been spendthrifts, and compelled to marry money! The property, has dwindled down to about a thousand acres, thanks to Mayne's ancestors' rage for gambling. It is said, that when they could find no other method, they used to race *worms* upon a deal table! The table is still exhibited at Maynesfort, and I have an idea, that the old gentleman is quite proud of it. If it were my property,—it would have been burnt long ago."

Maynesfort was ten miles from Newenham,—a distance soon covered by Mrs. De Wolfe's new "Rolls-Royce." As they turned into the gates, she said to Nancy, "You see it is a fine old place, and well kept up. It's a sort of estate, which having a great deal of wood, and vast gardens, and no fat farms, more or less eats its head off! Derek Mayne is bound to marry money, and I must say this,—that whoever he does marry, will be a lucky girl!"

Old Mr. Mayne, supported by a nurse, received the two ladies in the library: he was able to rise and hobble towards them, leaning upon a stick,— and offered his friend a most affectionate welcome.

"Well Elizabeth!" he said, "I'm delighted to see you, it's a good sight for old eyes," shaking her by the hand. "This time, I hope, you have come home to stay."

"Oh, I make no rash promises," she answered with a laugh. "Now, Richard, please sit down—and don't do company manners for us. This is my young friend, Miss Travers," she added, presenting Nancy.

"Oh yes, Miss Travers,—I have heard of you before. Was it not to you, that my old friend Fletcher left his property?"

"Yes," she answered, "a most unexpected legacy."

"Your father was his manager, I understand?"

"He was, but Fairplains originally belonged to him."

"Oh!" exclaimed the old gentleman with a look of blank surprise.

"And I'm afraid, he lost it through *me*."

"My dear young lady, surely you are not serious!"

"Yes, as I was delicate, I had to be sent to England, when I was a small child, and he was constantly coming over to see me, leaving a manager to look after the estate, the manager robbed him, and ran away with the money, leaving no end of debts, and difficulties for father."

"Well, I am glad it has gone back to *you*," said Mr. Mayne politely. "By the way, you knew my nephew Derek, I believe he stayed at Fairplains?"

"Yes,—for a short time."

"A nice fellow, isn't he, and a capital *shot*?"

Nancy hesitated for a moment, and then replied: "I—suppose he is."

"Ah! I see he is not your sort.—He never was much of a ladies' man, was he?" looking over at Mrs. De Wolfe, who had been conferring with the old gentleman's nurse. "I expect, we shall have him down in a week or two for the cricket and tennis."

Old Mr. Mayne then proceeded to talk about himself,—he gave full particulars of his accident, how the horse, had slipped up and rolled upon him, and then galloped home: the terrible consternation there had been when Rufus had appeared in the stable yard—without his master; next he discussed his doctor, the London specialist, and finally dropped into the local gossip.

During the latter part of this séance, Nancy had been sent out in charge of the nurse, to see the picture gallery and the gardens, and she received an impression of age, refinement, and large outlay. Certainly Maynesfort was a beautiful old place, and she did not wonder that its present owner was so pathetically anxious, that it should remain in the family,—and never endure the degradation of being let!

This visit to old Mr. Mayne proved to be the first of a long series. The Hillsides were at home, also the Millers, in fact most of Mrs. De Wolfe's friends, had shifted their quarters from London or Cowes, into the nice cool green country. No, not cool, for the weather in August proved to be unusually warm, the grass was burnt to a yellow brown; Mrs. De Wolfe's gardeners were kept incessantly occupied with hose, and water can: at times, there was scarcely a breath of air, and the great trees stood solid in the heat haze. After sundown, Nancy would run out to the garden, and gather fruit for dessert—apricots in mellow perfection, off the hot brick wall; she would also go round, and inspect the village cattle trough, and see that their own dogs, had water in their bowls, and cheer up Bob, a gasping brown spaniel.

In a month's time, she had contrived to make herself thoroughly at home amid her new surroundings, had been presented to the village, and parsonage, and made friends with most of the old women, and children in Newenham, also with the village dogs,—and indeed the post-office dog, a mongrel, like Togo, exhibited an ardent desire to attach himself to the "new young lady," as she was generally called. As August advanced, Mr. Mayne, attended by nurse, and valet, was convalescing at the seaside, his nephew was shooting in Scotland, but the remainder of the neighbours were at home, making the most of the very shining hours, at picnics, cricket matches, and little impromptu dances. The Hillsides were particularly gay, and entertained a large house party.

Although a certain amount of state was maintained, such as big stepping horses, and powdered men-servants, the *ménage* at the castle, was never taken very seriously; her ladyship was frequently in trouble with servants; household matters rarely ran smoothly, meals were unpunctual and indifferent,—it was a young people's house; and the friends of Josie and Tony, as long as they could have freedom, and dancing, and smoking and jokes, were not super-critical.

It was whispered that Lady Hillside was so intensely engrossed in works of philanthropy, that she sometimes forgot she had invited guests, and when they were ushered in by a bewildered butler, she would blandly inquire "where they were staying?" or she would order a dinner for twenty-four, and find that she had a party of eight, and when the party were seated, what frightful gaps at the table!

What was even more serious, she would invite two dozen of her confiding neighbours, and order the cook-housekeeper to provide for six. Then what awful waits ensued, whilst the distracted staff in the kitchen, scrambled together an impromptu meal, and the men-servants elongated the dinner table. Such an erratic mistress, drove her retinue almost crazy.

Good and efficient servants took their departure, with the result, that elderly guests who visited the castle,—rarely repeated the experiment.

The last week of August, was fixed upon for the tennis tournament, and for a long time previously, Mrs. De Wolfe and Nancy had been engaged in making preparations. There would be a number of guests staying in the house. Talking over the list, Mrs. De Wolfe announced:

"I shall get Dudley to do master of the ceremonies, and ask Roger De Wolfe,—he is my heir, such a dear good stupid fellow,—to help to manage the scoring, handicapping, and judging.

"There will be Tony and Josie, two Miller girls, Major Horne and his mother, young Wynne of the Blues, Cobden Gray, our great tennis player, Miss Strong the lady champion, old Sir Hubert Hamilton, to sit about and walk with *me*, and of course Derek Mayne,—he must be back from Scotland by this time."

"But why do you ask him to stay in the house?" inquired Nancy.

"Because it will save his going backwards and forwards to Maynesfort twice a day. The old man is very stingy of petrol; everyone has their pet economy: his is petrol,—and mine is string. I'm fond of Derek,—though he has given me the cold shoulder,—still I intend to have him here. Of course, I know *you* do not like him, but as a Roland for my Oliver, I shall invite one of your friends,—what do you say to Mrs. Hicks?"

"Mrs. Hicks?"

"Yes! why not? I fancy she is at a loose end just now. She told me she had never stayed much in the country,—at least it will be a novelty."

"And so will *she*! It is very good of you to think of her, and I'm sure she would love to come; the neighbours may think her a bit odd, and loud,—and I shall take it upon myself to tone down some of her costumes; but she has the best heart in the world: I shall never forget her kindness to me,—when my father was dying; and in one way, she will find herself in her element here, she is a wonderfully strong tennis player."

"You don't mean to tell me, that she *plays*?"

"I should rather think she did!—and I venture to say, will carry off one of your beautiful and valuable trophies. Where shall we put her?"

"In the blue bedroom next to you, so that you can talk old times to your hearts' content. Shall I write, or will you?"

"Oh, I think the invitation should go from the lady of the house."

"Very well, my dear, I will ask her to come a couple of days before the crowd, and I'll send off a note by this very post."

A letter from Mrs. Hicks, Newenham Court, Moonshire, to B. Hicks, Esq., M.D., Panora, near Khotagheri, Nilgiris, India:

My dear Hubby,

Won't you open your eyes to see where *I* am? I arrived a week ago, to stay with Nancy's friend, Mrs. De Wolfe, and am now living among the very highest company, and on the fat of the land! This is a lovely old place, something like what you read of in novels—with a great park, and lots of stiff-looking servants, and palms in the sitting rooms, and wonderful table silver. Here up in my room, every time I come into it, I find a fresh can of hot water standing in the basin—but I believe there are six housemaids—and such scented soap, and bath salts, and a big four-post bed, as soft as whipped cream. A great tennis tournament is being held all this week; so far I have done pretty well, in the 'ladies' doubles,' and this house is as full as if it were a fashionable hotel. Most of the people are strangers to me, except as tennis and Bridge partners, Finchie's niece and nephew are here, the Hon. Mrs. Speyde,—a black-eyed, flighty-looking widow,—and the Honourable Tony Lamerton, her brother: not a bad sort, and a good tennis player, but with a laugh to split your head! There is Major Horne, I came home with him on board ship last time but one,—terribly sea-sick he was too! and of all people in the world, who do you think, but *Captain Mayne*! His uncle lives in these parts.

Isn't it strange that he and Nancy should be staying in the same house, and talking politely to one another, as if they were bare acquaintances that had only lately met, for the first time? I suppose they have to pretend, as they are keeping their past very *dark*; and I believe they are both as obstinate as a pair of commissariat mules. I noticed that he sat next her at dinner last night, and they scarcely spoke, and they have played in the same sets at tennis. I also notice that he plays as a 'bachelor' against the married men. All the time, I'm the only one here, or in England, who happens to know, that he and Nancy are married; and when he addresses her as 'Miss Travers,' it's all I can do to hold my tongue. At tennis, I think they sometimes forget their feud, for I have heard him shout, 'Yours, Nancy,' and I have seen the two of them laughing together,—but elsewhere, as far as their manners to one another are concerned, they might have come out of a refrigerator!

I must say, it's an awful pity that such a handsome young couple cannot make it up. I think Nancy should come forward,—being the one in the wrong. She is a real darling, and such a beauty that you'd never know her, and so nice and affectionate to a dowdy old girl like *me*. I wish she and Mayne would make it up. I'd try my hand, only you say I always make a botch of such affairs, blurt out secrets, and give the show away. Well, well! perhaps something may happen to put things right.

Old Mrs. De Wolfe is wrapped up in Nancy, she might be her own granddaughter; the girl goes about the place, as if she had lived here for years; she is well liked too,—indeed *too* much liked by some! There's a dark foreign fellow, who is always trying to be her shadow, and who dances with her of an evening, but as far as I can see, I don't think Mayne minds—he has his own fish to fry!

By the time this is in your hands, Jess and Teddy will have arrived, and given you my news, and your new socks, and jerseys. I'm sending you some postcards of this place; but they give a very poor idea of its style. Many a time, I shall dream of it, I know, when I am back with you in old Panora. You and I fancy our roses; well, you should see those *here*; the Pergolas just smothered in them, and the rosery a sight for angels; as for the apricots on the south wall, my mouth waters, when I think of them!

Mrs. De Wolfe herself, in spite of all her engagements, has been mighty kind and friendly to me, and made me feel quite at *home*. When you look at the postcard of this place, and think of me, you will laugh at the idea. I play Bridge with her; my word! she is first class. Sees mistakes—but never scolds—not like *you*! Once she took me round the big garden all by myself. At the time, I felt it a tremendous honour, but on second thoughts, I believe she wanted to get something out of me about Nancy. She did her big best to pump me about Mayne,—and the reason of their coolness, but for once I was on my guard, and left her just as wise as ever! I'm afraid I told one or two small lies, but that under the circumstances, couldn't be helped. I'd give fifty rupees, cash down, to see her face, when she hears the *truth*. I'll write from London by next mail.

Your affectionate wife,
Susan Hicks.

CHAPTER XXXII
MRS. HICKS IMPARTS A SECRET

The letter from Mrs. Hicks to her "hubby" gave a fairly good sketch of events at the Court. There had been tennis, boating, Bridge, dancing, a certain amount of strolling about the lawns and turf walks, and sitting in rustic arbours, with congenial companions. Mrs. Hicks had played well, and vigorously in the married ladies against single, and it seemed to Mayne like good old days, when she served her cleverly placed balls, and shouted her triumphs.

On her arrival at the Court, Nancy, her neighbour, had taken her under her wing, inspected her wardrobe, subdued its too vivid colours with lace and chiffon, altered the style of her friend's hats with her own clever fingers, and made useful suggestions with regard to coiffure. Also, she gave her the names and characteristics of expected guests, and did her utmost to make her comfortable, and put her at her ease,—and Mrs. Hicks was not ungrateful. As she stood patiently, whilst the girl pinned and arranged a fichu upon her portly form, she said, "I declare to you, Nancy, you've done more to fix me up, and show me the ropes in two days, than my own girls in two years. Of course they are busy with their love affairs,—and you have none,—and it's your own fault. There isn't a young man I know, that can hold a candle to Mayne, as to looks and manners. He took the shine out of them all, at Jessie's wedding. *Why* can't you make it up?"

"It takes two to do that," said Nancy, as she took a pin out of her mouth.

"Ah, I suppose the letter you sent him choked him off? It's funny you and he being in the same set, and him coming to stay in this very house."

"Yes: too funny to be pleasant."

"Lots of girls like him; I saw that at Jessie's wedding, and when I was down at Burlingham,—and there's one lady, unless I am greatly mistaken, likes him uncommon,—that Mrs. Speyde, a niece of Finchie's. She is always running after him, I am told. Maybe they'll run away together, some day! Why, Nancy child, I declare you look quite vexed! You're not jealous, are you?"

"Of course not,"—now giving the fichu a twitch,—"what a ridiculous idea."

"Well, if he would only throw a book at you, before a witness,—and then run away with someone, it would make matters so nice and simple."

"Simple, yes, but not exactly nice."—After a moment's hesitation, and a fresh pin, "I always thought you liked him, Mrs. Hicks."

"So I do, but it's you, I'm *really* fond of; it's for *your* good I'm thinking. Don't I remember you a little darling in your nurse's arms? as for him, I only knew him for a matter of a few weeks. If you would put your pride in your pocket, all might yet be well: that is to say, *if* you liked him. Do you Nancy? Come now, own up?"

Nancy made no reply for some moments; at last she said, "I like him better than I did; there, now your fichu is all right, and looks very nice; you must wear it this evening,—but mind you don't put it on wrong side out! Now I must run and dress," and imprinting a kiss on Mrs. Hicks' hard and healthy cheek, she hurried out of the room.

A few days later, Nancy had reason to repeat Mrs. Hicks' question, was she jealous? Strange to say, the idea did not now appear to be so supremely ridiculous. Within the last week, she'd been a little startled at the discovery of emotions, the existence of which took her by surprise! She found, that it gave her a painful sensation to see Josie and Captain Mayne, on such excellent and intimate terms. They sat and talked, motored, and danced together—almost as if they were an engaged couple. She endeavoured to console herself with the fact, that it was Josie who was playing the part of enchantress: she had a wonderful power of appropriating the interest of a man.

It was a by no means unusual sight, to behold the fascinating Mrs. Speyde, encompassed by a little crowd of admirers;—whilst other and far prettier women were overlooked, and neglected. Of late she had an instinct that relations between herself and Josie were changed; and that Josie no longer liked her. More than once, she had caught her black eyes fixed upon her with a steady and vindictive glare; in her remarks there was a belittling and malicious note—and she had felt herself laughed at, and so to speak "baited," for the entertainment of the company,—yes, no later than that very day at breakfast! Josie was a splendid mimic, and if her manner was rather boisterous, no one could tell a story with more vivacity and point. Her usual plan was to relate the joint adventure of herself, and victim,—describing it with grotesque exaggeration, and gesture, and making her unfortunate butt, look contemptibly foolish, and ridiculous. Expostulation was useless,—after all, the story was *not* told behind the subject's back, but boldly face to face, with audacious effrontery, and Nancy's feeble explanations, were drowned in shouts of laughter. The merest incident was sufficient excuse, on which to hang a tale, and Josie's victims never had the wit or spirits, to carry the war into the enemy's quarter,—and the tyrant scored.

Although Captain Mayne and Nancy saw but little of one another indoors, they had been drawn to play together in the "Ladies' and gentlemen's doubles." This had excited the jealousy of Mrs. Speyde, and although she intrigued and manœuvred, nothing she did or said, could alter the detestable fact. Nancy knew by instinct, that her late friend hated to see her and Captain Mayne together,—even if it were only for a few minutes; when they barely exchanged a word!

The weather was perfect, though still rather warm; and the scene in the grounds and around the tennis courts, had been described in the local paper, as "brilliant." No such successful tournament had taken place for years; the sun had shone, and the world and his wife had flocked to Newenham from far and near, and there been entertained, with first-class tennis, excellent refreshments, and any amount of grapeseed!

It had been a particularly strenuous day for Nancy, who had not only played in two hard fought competitions, but in acting deputy hostess, among the very mixed multitude in the tents; seeing that ices and cup were unfailing, and in distributing little civilities among the crowd,—with Sir Dudley as her attendant. When the last game had been contested, and the last straggling group had dispersed, she strolled towards the river, accompanied by Mrs. Hicks, who pounced upon her bodily, and said, "Come you here, you little Nancy girl! I never get a word with you these times," taking her arm, and with a significant glance at Sir Dudley, she added, "turn about is fair play; he has had more than his share," she continued, as he moved off.

"My goodness! how the time flies, I've been here five days, and they have gone like greased lightning. Let us go and sit on the bench by the boat-house, and see if there is a bit of air from the river!"

"You played in your very best form to-day," said Nancy. "Your service was splendid; I felt immensely proud of you."

"Thank you, my dear, the same to you!" she rejoined, seating herself with a sigh of satisfaction. "Who's them two over in the boat? I'm getting a bit short-sighted?"

"Mrs. Speyde, and Captain Mayne."

"They don't seem to be rowing?"

"No, just drifting,—and talking."

"Drifting! so they are,—well! well! well! Look here, Nancy girl, I've got something to say to you. There's no one in the boat-house, is there?" peering round.

"No one,—and is it really such a secret?" and she laughed.

"You shall judge for yourself! The last three days I have kept my eyes open."

"Are they *ever* shut?"

"Now don't interrupt me, with your stupid jokes," protested her companion, with a touch of impatience. "I've seen, that you and him, for all your stand-off airs,—like one another right well."

"What makes you think so?"

"The use of my senses. I've noticed you smiling and jabbering together just like old times,—although you were only talking tennis; and I believe you're a bit jealous,—always a *very* healthy sign. Now, my dear child, take an old friend's advice, and don't make *the* mistake of your life! Good fortune, and a providential chance, have brought you and Mayne here together. Are you going to let him drift away?"

"But why do you talk as if *I* were the one to act and come forward?"

"Because you are! Now listen to me," seizing her hand in a firm grip, "it is for you to make the advance; you gave him the go-by; it was certainly an amazing act for a girl of your age. Now I think you have come to your senses; but he is frightened of your money. Yes!" she continued with emphasis, "he as good as told Teddy, and I dug it out of *him*,—that had you not been an *heiress*, he would have been willing to make it up!"

"He said that,—did he?" said Nancy with a quick catch in her breath.

"So Teddy informed me, and I have always found him to speak the truth. He told me, as a dead, dead, secret,—and mind you let it go no further, for if Teddy knew, he'd *eat* me,—although I *am* his mother-in-law! Seeing how things are, and being really fond of you, Nancy, I thought I'd not allow love to pass out of your life, without doing my best to interfere, and stop it."

Nancy's colour was high, her heart beat unusually fast; here, indeed, was a wonderful piece of information. So it was not altogether her unpardonable flight,—but the money, that stood between them. She sat for a long time in dead silence, with her eyes fixed upon the river. At last she murmured, "I don't see how I could possibly do it."

"You'll find it easy enough, once you and he are face to face; you will never have a chance *here*; never a moment together, unless when playing tennis: that gay lady in the boat, now lighting her cigarette on his, takes right good care of that!"

"But I thought you were so near-sighted?" said Nancy, with a faint smile.

"Only when it's convenient: and I thought perhaps you might not notice the pair. Well, here is that long-legged young Tony and Miss Miller, coming to fetch you," said Mrs. Hicks, rising as she spoke. "Think over what I have told you, my dear child, and don't let matters slide! I'll just go in, and get a bit of a rest before dinner,—my poor old joints, ay, but they do ache!"

CHAPTER XXXIII
AN INTERRUPTED INTERVIEW

The last set had been played, tennis prizes been distributed amid much clapping and applause, performers and spectators had dispersed, the great tennis week was over!

Nancy, who felt mentally and bodily fatigued, contrived to escape from her friends, to enjoy a short rest, and breathing time, before the evening gaieties set in; and by devious and cunning short cuts, made her way to a favourite seat, at the end of the least frequented Pergola. Here for once, she found herself out of the public eye,—the only eyes that rested upon her, were those of her companion, Bob, the brown spaniel,—nephew to the dogs at Maynesfort. Bob detested tennis, and had followed his mistress under the fond delusion that she was about to take him for a nice run by the river; alas! no, she threw herself down on a hard rustic bench, and heaved a long sigh. Poor disappointed Bob was in complete sympathy with this frame of mind, and inclined to sigh too.

All day long, Nancy had borne the fierce light, that beats on a pretty popular girl,—the most prominent figure in a society gathering; as deputy hostess, tennis competitor, adviser, referee, arbitress in little half-playful disputes, with an eye to the guests in the refreshment tents, and in perpetual demand, here, there, and everywhere.

Mrs. De Wolfe had abdicated and taken her ease, and an attitude of serene detachment, seated among her contemporaries, and intimates; all little anxieties and worries, were handed over to her vice-reine, and although she had the gift of social grace, youth, and energy, Nancy found the sceptre as heavy as lead! Here was Mrs. Harper looking alarmingly red and explosive, because no one had escorted her to tea, and there was Lizzie Stevens on the verge of tears, because the umpire had given her two faults; Mrs. Fitzhammond had lost a dear old silver brooch, she had had since she was a school-girl, and was unpleasantly querulous, injured, and fussy; whilst Sutton the butler had informed poor Nancy in a hollow whisper, that "the ice was running out!"

Well, it was all over at last! and had been a surprising success; but the deputy hostess felt completely exhausted, as she took off her hat, and closed her eyes. The previous night, she had lain awake for many hours, meditating on Mrs. Hicks' unexpected revelation. It seemed to her, that she was approaching a crisis in her life: looking into her own heart, she saw Derek Mayne; yes, Derek, and no one else. Far removed from the tragedy of former associations, in another hemisphere, and among other surroundings, she realized his personal attraction, his upright character, unfailing good humour,—and for a man,—surprising unselfishness!

She had noticed his thoughtful attention to his uncle; his pleasant ways to children, and to nobodies,—it was he, who had relieved her of Mrs. Harper, and carried off that swelling matron, to enjoy ices, and conversation (whilst Dudley Villars lay prone on the grass, at the feet of the county's duchess, entertaining her with scraps of highly-spiced scandal!). She recalled to mind, what a favourite he had been with her father; how he had given her to him when on his deathbed; later how fiercely she had thrust him aside, and fled. Yes! there was no doubt, that *she* was the offender; and it was for her, to venture the first advance—an advance bristling with difficulties and dangers. If she made an overture and was repulsed—how—how, could she ever hold up her head again? on the other hand, if she made no sign, and he went away, it would be something whispered,—for—*ever*.

During the last few days she and Derek had been on easier terms; naturally the tournament had thrown them together; more than once, he had addressed her as "Nancy," and more than once, she had surprised him surveying her with an expression of keen attention, and something else— "What?" What it was she could not analyse; interest, yes, perhaps interest; at any rate, the glance was neither cynical nor scornful! Possibly it might mean, that he wished to speak to her, that—oh no, never by word or look, had he intimated that he looked for any change in their relations; if she was to say, or do anything that would count; if she was to venture to break the ice, and her heart quailed at the mere idea of such an undertaking,—it must be *soon*. On Saturday, he was leaving the Court, and from what she could gather, shortly returning to India; so it was a case of now, or never! How could she begin?—she had not the gracious art of approaching the unapproachable. As she sat meditating, and by no means fancy free, the thumping of Bob's tail announced his welcome to someone; and opening her eyes, she beheld the subject of her thoughts, rapidly approaching along the turf walk. Was she asleep? or was his appearance the result of some strange telepathy?

How good-looking he was! a lover to gladden the eyes of any girl. His flannels set off an admirable well-knit figure—the touch of scarlet in his blazer, was eminently becoming to his dark hair and eyes; in one hand he swung a bat, and was apparently pressed for time.

"Well, what is it?" he inquired, as he came within earshot.

"I'm sure I don't know!" she answered, now sitting erect.

"But Mrs. Hicks told me to hurry here at once—she said you wished to speak to me."

"She must have been dreaming!"

"On the contrary, she looked particularly wide awake, and would take no refusal,—we are just getting up a match." Nevertheless, he lingered.

"I should have thought you'd had enough of tennis for to-day," remarked Nancy.

"Yes, I daresay. You are in great form, you and I, are the proud winners of the ladies' and gentlemen's doubles. I say——" he paused abruptly.

"What do you say?" she asked.

"Well,—it's about that fellow Villars;—you will remember, I begged you to drop him; and I find him here installed as Tame cat: in fact a sort of Puss in Boots,—running the whole show!"

"That's true," admitted Nancy, "but Sir Dudley was *l'ami de la maison* long before Mrs. De Wolfe knew me,—and surely you can scarcely expect her to turn out her old friends on *my* account,—besides, he is her godson."

"So you think that sanctifies him?" shifting his bat under his arm.

"No, certainly not; but I do honestly believe, you are prejudiced and that Sir Dudley is not any worse than his neighbours; he is religious in his way too, always down to family prayers,—of course, attendance is optional,—whilst *you* appear with the hot dishes! He reads the Scriptures beautifully,—I've never heard the twelfth chapter of Ecclesiastes read with such expression."

"If you would only take my word for it, the Song of Solomon is a thousand times more in his line—all about my beloved, and roses, and lilies."

"Do you know, that he has a *wife*?" said Nancy expressively.

"No, has he? Unhappy woman! but I *do* happen to know, that he has run away with another man's wife! Certainly, it was years ago,—if he made any scandal with mine"—he paused and looked full into her eyes, "by Jove I would kill him,—and I should *like* to kill him!"

Nancy burst into a peal of laughter. "How melodramatic you are! and how you do abhor him!"

"May I ask, if he is aware, that you have a husband?" Although his manner chaffed her—his voice had a ring of earnestness.

"What an absurd question; of course not! There isn't a soul in this country, who's in the secret—except Mrs. Hicks."

"I say," he exclaimed, "we are a fine couple of impostors! You may be amused to hear, that my uncle has taken an immense fancy to you."

"How nice of him."

"And between ourselves, he thinks you would be an ideal niece-in-law. The Maynes are poor, the place swallows up money, and the reigning proprietor is obliged to get hold of a consort with coin."

A thought instantly darted into Nancy's mind; here was her opportunity! and as if in obedience to some irresistible force, she rose, with a hammering heart,—looking, did she but know it, enchantingly pretty.—A little pale perhaps, but stirred by some inward emotion, her lovely face was unusually expressive. One or two rose leaves had fallen on her uncovered hair, and the light between the branches overhead, sent the shadows of leaves, to dance gaily upon her white skirt.

"A wife with coin," repeated Nancy, speaking with a desperate effort, and fixing her eyes upon the ground, "well! you did that yourself."

"Quite unintentionally, I assure you," was the emphatic reply; "the girl I married, was as poor as a church mouse! Nothing would tempt *me* to marry for money."

"I suppose," began Nancy—and she hesitated.

"You suppose what?" he asked sharply.

"That if ... if ..." she stammered—for the tone of his voice had been discouraging, and made her, if possible—more nervous. "If you could forgive me,—do you think.... Oh, how *can* I put it?..." and her voice shook, "that *I* could tempt you? Oh no, I don't mean *that*,—only I don't want all that money; no one knows better than you do, that I never was accustomed to riches, and—and I should be only too thankful, to give it to you."

Mayne stared at her amazed! She was no longer pale.

"Nancy!" he exclaimed, "I remember how in old days you talked the wildest nonsense, I don't suppose for a moment, that you know or mean, one single word of what you are saying."

"Yes, I do," she rejoined tremulously, "but I can promise you this," — her lips quivered — and she added with difficulty, "I will never say it again," she paused, struggling between pride, and emotion.

"Oh, my dear Nancy, if I could only believe you — don't you know — —"

"So here you are, Derek!" exclaimed a high, authoritative treble, and through a breach in the Pergola, Mrs. Speyde appeared, waving an imperative tennis bat. "Have you forgotten, that we are *all* waiting to make up a match?" She glanced sharply from him to Nancy. His face wore a strained expression, as for the girl, she was the colour of a crimson rambler!

"Ah," with a little malicious laugh, "I see you have been talking *secrets*. Yes, Miss Nancy, I always suspected that you knew a good deal more about this gentleman than you pretended. Well, for the present, you must leave the cat *in* the bag. Derek," laying an arresting hand on his arm, "you've *got* to come!"

Mayne drew back, but before anything further happened, Nancy had picked up her hat, and vanished through an opening that led into the old walled garden.

That same evening, Nancy selected her most becoming frock, and took particular pains with her hair — for she entertained high hopes, that Mayne would seek her out, and endeavour to resume the conversation so cruelly interrupted by Josie Speyde. At dinner, she saw nothing of him, — as he happened to be on the same side of the table; later, as he held the door for the ladies to pass forth, it seemed to her, that he gave her a glance of particular significance; but strange to say, he did not come into the drawing-room with the other men.

About an hour later, when she was singing a duet with Sir Dudley, she noticed him standing near the door. It struck her, that he looked pale and rather stern, — as if he had been annoyed, or disappointed; he made no effort whatever to speak to her for the remainder of the evening; and she retired for the night, with an acute sense of hopelessness, and depression.

CHAPTER XXXIV
STRANDED!

The following morning the guests who still remained at the Court, made up a party to attend a race meeting at Knapshot. Knapshot was thirty miles away, and could be reached by rail,—as the Court was but a short distance from a mean, and undeserving little station. However, most of the party decided to go by motor; Mrs. De Wolfe, Mrs. Horne, Sir Dudley and Nancy in the comfortable roomy Daimler, with Roger De Wolfe sitting by the chauffeur, Major Horne, Billy Miller, Josie and Captain Mayne, followed in the new Rolls-Royce. Several preferred to travel by rail, and Mrs. Hicks remained at home, to rest her weary bones, and repose upon her well-earned laurels.

The races, though not particularly notable, offered good sport; the lunch was excellent, the ladies had their fortunes told, and did a little betting. Mrs. De Wolfe and Mrs. Horne elected to return by train early in the afternoon, as there was a dinner-party at the Court that night—the last function of the week, moreover, the old ladies found motoring rather hot, and dusty; and escorted by Roger, left the rest of the party to follow, enjoining on all, that on no account were they to be late.

"We will go back just as we came!" said Josie, "we played games all the way, and don't want to break up our happy little set!"

This arrangement left Sir Dudley and Nancy to share the Daimler *tête-à-tête*, and she offered a seat to Billy, who, however (naturally), preferred to travel in company with Major Horne!

"We will take different roads," declared Josie, who seemed to have assumed command of the whole party, "and race, and see which car gets home first? The Charlton road is the shortest: but it's out of repair, the other by Langford is a couple of miles longer—but good going all the way. Shall we toss, Dudley?—come, be sporting, and have something on!"

They tossed accordingly, Mrs. Speyde won the long route—and booked a bet of five pounds.

With a good deal of laughing, and joking, the competitors started together, but within a quarter of a mile, the cars had separated, the Rolls-Royce to take a high road, more or less bordering the railway, the Daimler to plunge into what seemed to be the very heart and soul of the country. It was a light and lovely September evening, and they sped along with noiseless ease,—considering the ruts.

"This is a ripping good car!" remarked Sir Dudley, "and Josie's five pounds is already in my pocket,—I suppose your chauffeur knows the way?"

"Oh yes," replied Nancy, "Saxton belongs to this part of the country, he has been with Mrs. De Wolfe for years."

The couple discussed the races, the fortune-teller, and other matters, but neither appeared to be in a talkative mood. It was delightful flying along these quiet, grass-bordered roads, and lanes, breathing the soft delicious air, watching the homing birds, and the solemn rise of a splendid harvest moon. Suddenly Sir Dudley said:

"I thought Mayne's leave was up, and that he was sick of this country, but I heard him tell a fellow at the races, that he was going to apply for an extension."

"Is he?" murmured Nancy, and a bright colour invaded her face. "Was this the outcome of their interrupted interview?"

"Yes, and the sooner he goes the better! Josie Speyde is carrying on one of her most outrageous flirtations. Lord! what a number of them I've seen! If I didn't know her so well, I would swear that this time, she was in earnest. There was Chapman, Fotheringay, Montague——"

"Oh! Sir Dudley, it really isn't fair, to tell tales of your own cousin."

"Josie wouldn't mind, on the contrary, she's proud of her scalps. She's a queer woman, in her way—a freak! Here we are, on a by-road I see. I suppose it's all right?" then as the car slowed down, and drew up beside a picturesque old cottage, he added, "but what is he stopping for?"

"I expect to get water for the car," replied Nancy. "What a dear place"—looking in through the open door—"there's such a darling oak chest in the passage!"

"Yes, I know your craze,—and I think I see some china on a dresser further on! Do you wish to go in?"

"Only just for a second,—it looks the sort of cottage where one can pick up the most priceless treasures!" Before she finished the sentence, Nancy was already in the passage. A stout, grey-haired woman with a bulky figure and a pleasant face, appeared, wiping her hands.

"I wanted to look at your beautiful old chest," explained the visitor. "I caught sight of it through the open door."

"You are very welcome, miss," she answered, "and there's a still better one in the kitchen—if you care to see that? We have a good few old things—that came down from Bode's grandmother—Bode was my husband—he's dead, poor man—this ten year."

Nancy followed the woman down a long flagged passage, and found herself in a heavily-beamed, low room,—with a vast fireplace. Here she discovered a fine oak settle, a dresser and a chest,—with the date, sixteen hundred and seventy. Nancy was in raptures, and fell in love with an old blue bowl, that she saw on the dresser. She admired it with such heartfelt enthusiasm, that the woman,—honestly displaying various cracks,—declared that "it had been her grandfather's, but now leaked. If the young lady fancied it—she could have it for a shilling."

But Nancy protested, and said, "I wouldn't dream of imposing on your generosity"—she did not like to use the word "ignorance," and added, "I will gladly give you a sovereign for it"—and produced her purse. The bargain being concluded to their mutual satisfaction, and Sir Dudley having approved of the family chest, and bench, they took leave of the hostess, and returned to the entrance, but here, to their utter and speechless amazement, there was no motor to be seen!

"Where is he?" cried Nancy, looking up and down the road. "Has he taken the car into the yard?"

No, neither car, nor chauffeur were about the premises—they had mysteriously disappeared,—as if dissolved into thin air. Whilst Nancy and her companion stood bewildered, and exclaiming, a youth on a shaggy colt trotted up.

"Dan, did you see a motor?" demanded his mother.

"I did, it passed me just now—going at a great rate."

"What is to be done?" said Nancy, turning to Sir Dudley in despair.

"I understand what's happened; the fellow didn't notice us getting out, he was round in the yard at the time, and, thinking we were still in the car, he has driven off, and left us! Is there any station near this?" turning to the woman.

"Yes, about two miles off, but there's few trains. This is a terrible awkward place to get away from—being a bit out of the way."

"I suppose you have a post-office within reach?" inquired Nancy.

"Yes, in Lofty village,—a mile off."

"Then let us send a wire for the car to return; Auntie Wolfe will be most awfully fussed, if we are not back in time for dinner."

"You can take a telegram, my lad?" said Villars, appealing to the young man.

"Oh yes, sir, for sure," he answered eagerly.

"Then I've got a pencil, and," to Mrs. Bode, "if you'll let me have a bit of paper, I'll just go inside and write it." He retired indoors, and Nancy talked to the colt and Dan, and after a few minutes, Dudley reappeared, and handed a message to the youth, along with a half-crown.

"I'll give you something for yourself, when you come back; be as quick as ever you can. It's half-past seven now," he added, looking at his watch, and then glancing at Nancy, he nodded his head, and said, "There will be no dinner party for you, and me."

"Oh, if they deliver the message at the Court at once, say in half an hour, the car should be here by nine. We will dash home, and appear in time for dessert."

"'I doubt it, said the carpenter, and shed a bitter tear,'" quoted Villars. "Perhaps Mrs. Bode can find us something to eat?" he added.

"I am sorry I haven't got no butcher's meat in the house, sir, but there's fresh eggs, and cold bacon,—and good home-made bread."

"There are worse things!" said Villars, "but I'm not hungry, I was thinking of the young lady."

"A cup of tea, and a slice of home-made bread, is what I should like, if Mrs. Bode will be so kind,—and I shall make the most of my time, in poking about among her nice old things, and there is my nice blue bowl, which I intend to carry home, as a souvenir of this funny adventure. Will you come and help me to ransack the cottage?" said Nancy. "I know you have a *flair* for old oak, and pewter too."

"No," replied Villars, "I'll let you have it all your own way for once; and leave you to gather up the spoil. I'll just stroll down the road for half an hour,—and smoke a cigarette."

CHAPTER XXXV
"EMPTY!"

Meanwhile the merry quartette in the Rolls-Royce had reached their destination rather late, but before she rushed off to dress, Mrs. Speyde eagerly inquired if Miss Travers, and Sir Dudley had arrived?

"No, ma'am, not yet," replied Sutton, the butler.

"Hooray!" she cried, turning to Mayne, "I win five pounds, and I'll gamble it away to-night, on weak, no trumpers."

There happened to be a considerable gathering at the Court that evening. Besides the guests in the house, not a few neighbours were present; and the beautiful old mahogany table loaded with fine silver, and softly shaded candelabra, surrounded by smart and well-favoured young people, looked very gay indeed. The racing party, who had scrambled into their clothes, gradually dropped in between soup, and the second entrée, and heartlessly announced that "the others had evidently lost their way!" It certainly looked like it, for as time advanced, no one appeared to fill the two vacant places;—and vacant places, make a gap, and spoil the symmetry of a dinner table, much as a missing front tooth, mars a pretty face!

"They certainly ought to be here by *this* time," remarked Mrs. De Wolfe, consulting her wristlet watch, "it's just half-past nine."

"Perhaps the car has broken down?" suggested Major Horne, "and they are walking home!"

"A fairly long walk," said Billy Miller, "and a hatefully lonely road."

"Oh! Dudley won't mind *that*," said Josie, in an intimate aside.

It had been a lively and festive meal, the guests were all in high good humour. Dessert had been disposed of, and the ladies were awaiting Mrs. De Wolfe's "eye," when Sutton, the butler, entered with unusual solemnity, and bending his head, made some grave announcement in the immediate vicinity of her left ear.

"Nonsense!" she exclaimed in a startled tone, "nonsense!"

"What is it?" demanded Mayne, and his voice sounded masterful, and imperious.

"Sutton tells me, that the car has come back, and that it is *empty*!"—Meanwhile Sutton stood by, with a face as expressionless as a dinner plate!

"Empty!" echoed Mrs. Horne; "what does he mean?—where are Nancy, and Sir Dudley?"

Sutton cleared his voice twice, and with an overwhelming importance suitable to the occasion, said: "When the footman ran down to open the door just now, there was no one inside the car—nothing but the dust knee cover, and Miss Travers' feather boa."

After a deadly silence, Mrs. De Wolfe pulled herself together, rose and said, as she looked round, "Of course we shall find some ridiculous explanation; meanwhile, let us adjourn,—I will interview Saxton myself."

Whilst the ladies in the drawing-room were whispering, and wondering, and the men in the dining-room were "lighting up" and passing round the port, Mrs. De Wolfe entered the library, there to await her chauffeur. She was accompanied by Roger, and was not a little astonished, when Captain Mayne joined them. He made no excuse whatever, and looked serious, and unlike his usual cheery self. After a short delay, Saxton was ushered in,—a middle-aged, clean-shaven man,—of few words.

"Pray explain, Saxton, where you left Miss Travers, and Sir Dudley?" said his mistress.

"That's more than I can say, ma'am," and there was a moment's silence.

"Well, say *something*!" urged Mayne impatiently (thrusting a spoon into what was not his porridge).

"All I can say, is, that I never laid an eye on either, from the time we left the race stand—till now."

"Where did you stop?" asked Mayne; promptly forestalling Mrs. De Wolfe's anxious questions.

"At a little old farm by the road, to get water for the engine. I ran round to the pump and wasn't away two minutes—later on we had a fairly long wait, maybe a quarter of an hour, at Harraby railway crossing."

"And you never happened to look back into the car?" suggested Roger De Wolfe.

"No, I never does,—I want all my eyes the other way."

"Very true, all right, go on."

"Well I was just staggered, when Fox opened the door of the car, and turned to me, and said, 'Why didn't you go round to the garage? there's no one inside'—and that's all I know!"

"Very well, Saxton, that will do," said his mistress, "go now and get your supper," and with a military salute, Saxton departed.

"It is the strangest, most extraordinary affair," declared Mrs. De Wolfe. "I expect Nancy has done something wild, and giddy, and we shall have her arriving to-night, in the musty old station fly, full of her adventure, and apologies. I'm not really alarmed,—only puzzled. Well!" rising as she spoke, "I must return to the ladies; you two, have not had your smoke. Don't forget that we are playing Bridge,—and want to make up four tables."

Bridge proved to be unusually engrossing, and it was only when the players happened to be Dummy, that their thoughts wandered to the missing couple. Mayne was not among the card party, he seemed restless, and unsettled, and wandered into the big hall, where he concealed himself in one of the largest arm chairs, behind a newspaper. By twelve o'clock, the last lady guests had retired,—early hours were the rule at the Court.

And just about this time, a sinister whisper began to creep up from the lower regions; it reached Mrs. De Wolfe, as she was taking off her pearls. In spite of her attitude, the old lady was painfully anxious. "Thank God," she said to herself, "there was no fear of an accident,—the car and Saxton had come home intact; but where were Nancy and Dudley? Surely they must know the misery their absence was causing."

Turning to Haynes, her confidential treasure, she said, "Is it not extraordinary about Miss Travers? Although I have said nothing downstairs, I am very uneasy, and half inclined to telephone to the police station. I don't think there's much use in my going to bed, for I shall certainly not sleep. Why, Haynes, what's the matter, your face is all blotches,—you've been crying! Don't be foolish, don't you know, that half the troubles in the world, are those that have never happened."

"But this *has* happened, ma'am," rejoined the maid with a sniff. "Martin tells me, that Antonio got a wire from his master about eight o'clock telling him where to bring his own car; and to pack his clothes, and get Miss Travers' warm coat, and a few things in a suit case. He said they were going off to Paris together."

The old lady gave a sharp exclamation, then suddenly sat down. "You must be out of your mind!" she cried.

"Martin wouldn't give him a stitch," continued Haynes triumphantly, "not as much as a pocket-handkerchief; she said she didn't believe a word he said—and I know myself, that I've caught him out in awful lies! However, he went and helped himself to a coat out of the hall—one of *yours*, I think—took most of Sir Dudley's luggage, and went off with the car about ten o'clock: all the men saw him—! Here, wait a second, and I'll get a drop of brandy; keep up, my dear lady, and don't faint if you can help it, and Mrs. De Wolfe did keep up,—although she looked like death.

"I'm too old for these shocks, Haynes," she muttered, after a long silence, "I thought I was hardened! I suppose so far, this story is only known downstairs."

"That's all, ma'am; and I needn't tell you, that not one of the servants would breathe it."

The tale was nevertheless stealing through the house. Mrs. Speyde heard it from her maid; and was at first rudely incredulous. After taking two or three turns up and down the room, she said, "Wait a moment, I'll not undress yet—I've forgotten something downstairs."

"Can't I fetch it, ma'am?"

"No!" waving her back, "I know where it is myself!"

She went softly out along the corridor, and stood looking over the balustrade into the great lounge. Mayne was the only individual below—the other men were assembled in the smoking-room—suddenly he glanced up, and beheld Josie in her flame-coloured garment, drifting down the stairs. She paused half-way, and beckoned to him.

"Derek, I've something to tell you," she whispered, as she halted on the lowest step. Glancing round, she leant forward, and said: "Something *dreadful* has happened!—*Dudley and Nancy have run away to Paris!*"

Mayne stood very still—he might have been a stone.

"His own car, and chauffeur have gone to meet them with their luggage—what a terrible blow for the old lady!"

What a terrible blow for Mayne! This was the second time that Nancy had, so to speak, made him to pass through fire. How false, how treacherous, was that young, and innocent face!

As Mayne remained speechless, Josie continued: "So still waters run deep—not that Nancy was ever very *still*. Although he is my own cousin, I always knew, that Dudley was a bad lot; a regular rotter! but as for the girl, I must confess I'm surprised.—Aren't you?"

"I am," he assented, in a strange dry voice, "surprised in one way, but not in another. It's not the *first* time, that Miss Travers has run away."

Josie opened her great black eyes, to their widest extent.

"And *you* knew all about it—so that is the secret between you!" but Mayne made no reply, and to her great astonishment, walked across the hall, snatched his cap from a peg, opened the great door, and went out.

At this moment, the sound of loud and jovial voices approaching, warned her, that the smoking-room party were about to disperse, so she turned about, ran lightly up the stairs, and disappeared into her own apartment. As for Mayne, he went round into the stable-yard, where men were still hanging about: one of the neighbours had not yet taken his departure; he noticed a group of two or three grooms, and a couple of white-capped women in close conference,—they looked like a gang of conspirators. The doors of the great garage had not been closed, and as the moon made everything as bright as day, he saw, that Sir Dudley's big Mercédès had vanished!

As she had prognosticated, Mrs. De Wolfe never slept that night. She looked a wrinkled old wreck, when Haynes brought her her early tea; nevertheless this Spartan matron, insisted upon getting up and having herself dressed as usual. In spite of Haynes' expostulations, she declared, "I'll go down to breakfast, if it costs me my life! The people upstairs know nothing: so far no one knows the truth, except the servants, and I feel sure that they will keep this terrible matter to themselves. All my guests will have departed by twelve o'clock, and then I shall take to my bed. You may call it a chill, or whatever you like, but I depend upon you, to allow *no one* to come near me."

The old lady's voice was unusually weak: her hands, as she put on her rings, trembled alarmingly. At last she was ready, and just as she was about to leave her room, a familiar figure came flying along the passage, with outstretched hands.

"Nancy!"

"Here I am at last!" she gasped out, "and so dreadfully, dreadfully, sorry, to have tortured you—darling Auntie," embracing her as she spoke.

"Where have you been?" said the trembling old lady, endeavouring to thrust her away.

"Let me come into your room, and tell you all about it." Taking her forcibly by the arm, she added, "Do sit down,—you are shaking all over!"

Mrs. De Wolfe made no reply, but signalled for her to speak.

"I spent last night in a cottage near Lofty.—You've heard about the car having left us behind. This morning, I got up at four o'clock, and walked over the wet fields, to a little station, and caught a milk train; I gave the guard five shillings,—and he dropped me at Haygate. Then I got the old fly,—and here I am!"

"And Dudley,—what has become of Dudley?"

"Haynes," said Nancy, suddenly turning towards her, "would you mind asking Martin to get my bath ready,—I do feel such a grub!"

Yes, for the first time in her life, Nancy appeared positively draggled: her hat was battered, her muslin race-gown torn and soiled, her smart shoes were covered with mud,—whilst her face looked worn, and almost haggard.

As soon as Haynes had departed, she sat down on the sofa by Mrs. De Wolfe, and taking her hand, she said, "Auntie, Sir Dudley has shown himself in his true colours, at last. He is a horrible, false, evil-minded wretch—yes, he *is*," then very rapidly she told how she could not resist the temptation to inspect the old chest, of the departure of the motor, and the wire dispatched to recall Saxton—sometimes speaking breathlessly, sometimes speaking deliberately, always with a great agitation, Nancy related the story of her experience in Mrs. Bode's front parlour;—to all of which her companion listened with an expression of incredulous horror.

When at last Nancy ceased to speak, she said: "Oh, to think of Dudley: Dudley, whom I've almost thought of as a son,—*what* a traitor! If anyone but you, had told me this—I would not have believed it. I must confess, this adventure of yours, has been a terrible revelation, another illusion destroyed. I have lost a life-long belief. Well, what you and I, have now to do, is to conceal this escapade. I shall go down, and announce your return. What cock and a bull story am I to tell them, Nancy?"

She rose as she spoke, and confronted her young friend,—looking terribly old, and shaken.

"Tell them?" repeated Nancy, "let me think! Tell them, that Sir Dudley and I were left behind,—thanks to Saxton's mistake, and that I was obliged to remain at the cottage for the night; but that Sir Dudley made his way to the nearest station, and went up to London. Do you think that will do?"

"It may pass! but what about his sending for his own car?"

"I don't suppose that will come out till later."

"No! Of course the servants will talk,—but their masters and mistresses who are leaving me to-day are bound to believe *my* version of the adventure,—the least they can do after a week's hospitality!"

"Then I shall hurry off and have my bath, and dress," said Nancy, "and come down as soon as possible, and show myself. It will be rather a strain, all things considered, for just at present, I should like to go away, and have a really good comfortable cry."

CHAPTER XXXVI
"TO HIM WHO WAITS——"

Mrs. Bode's motley collection of good old "bits" of glass and china, odds and ends of quaint rubbish—samplers, beads, monster shells, mouldy books of great age, and Mrs. Bode's funny talk, had kept Nancy well amused, and occupied for nearly an hour, and then her hostess insisted on providing a meal, tea, home-made bread, fresh butter, russet apples, and cold bacon. With considerable pomp this simple repast, borne on a huge black tray,—was carried to the front sitting-room, or parlour, and there laid out upon a fine gate table,—flanked by cottage Chippendale chairs. From the deep narrow window, overlooking the road, Nancy leant out, and beckoned gaily to Sir Dudley,—who all this time had been pacing to and fro, smoking endless cigarettes.

As Nancy poured out tea, and he took a place opposite, she wondered if by any chance, Mrs. Bode would take them for husband and wife? Mrs. Bode, having as she considered, "done her manners," and pressed jam, bacon, and apples, in turn upon Sir Dudley, with an excuse about a sick calf, left them to their own devices. Sir Dudley appeared unusually silent and restless, he refused tea, but munched an apple, and then got up and began to pace about the long low room. His manner was that of a man, whose nerves were on edge.

"I can't think what is keeping the car," remarked Nancy, for the third time; "surely that boy took the wire," and she, too, rose, and returned to her post in the narrow deep-set window, through which the moonlight streamed into the room, making everything as clear as day.

"It is five minutes past ten by my watch."

"I expect your watch is fast," said Sir Dudley, as he joined her.

"Did you ever behold a more glorious night? *Dio mio!* What a night for lovers!" he murmured, as he confronted her in the narrow space.

Nancy felt a little uncomfortable; a vague sensation of apprehension came to her. "I think—I hear the car now," she announced, but her voice had an uncertain sound.

"It's just like old times, to have you all to *myself*—even for an hour or two," continued her companion—ignoring her remark—"I'm in no hurry."

"But *I* am," she declared with a nervous laugh.

"Everything comes to him who waits! I have waited nearly a year: and now, Nancy darling—" here Sir Dudley suddenly put his arm round her waist, "I've got you at *last!*"

For a moment she was too paralysed to move; then as she felt his grip tightening, with a tremendous effort, she wrenched herself away, and backed against the shutter, breathless, and gasping.

"What do you mean?" she stammered. "How dare you?"

"A man dares anything, when he loves a woman—as for what I *mean*, I'll soon explain,—it's all I ask," he answered in a husky voice, now seizing both her wrists in a vice-like grip, and devouring her with his burning eyes. "Nancy, my love, I've adored you, from the moment we first met; but Auntie Wolfe's presence, and your own strange cold temperament,—held me in a state of frozen bondage. At first, I swear to you, I strove hard to strangle, and hide my feelings,—because Auntie Wolfe, my mother's friend, *believes* in me; but it was useless. After all, *why* should I struggle against my good angel? and you are cold and undemonstrative, as an angel should be—nevertheless, you *do* care for me."

"No, no, no," protested Nancy breathlessly.—"Never—never—in the way you mean—I think you must be mad! Let go my hands."

"But yes, yes, yes," he reiterated. "To what other fellow, have you ever shown such preference? With me, you are always ready to sing, or dance, or sketch, or walk. I have watched like a lynx,—for I am as jealous as the devil,—and you have favoured *none*! As for Tony Hillside and Lord Lanark, bah!! You and I have tastes in common, we shall spend our lives together; we will go to Greece, to the Far East, to Japan,—and I will be your humble, and devoted slave."

"*Will* you release my hands?" she demanded furiously.

"Presently, darling,—when I have said my say! Listen. Auntie Wolfe will forgive me in time; my wife will divorce me,—it will be merely a question of money."

Nancy endeavoured to interrupt, but it was useless; she was overpowered by a fiery torrent of words, and an emotion, ten times stronger than her own.

"Sometimes you drove me mad," he went on, "I felt inclined to kill you, and myself,—now fate has helped me!"

"I thought you were an honourable man," she broke in, "so this delay about the car deserting us, was all planned."

"No! I swear to you—I'll take my oath it was not," relinquishing her hands at last; "for once, good fortune has befriended me, and thrown me a priceless chance. I should like to pension that silly ass of a chauffeur; for thanks to *him*, you are irretrievably compromised! Yes!" in reply to Nancy's gesture of recoil, "all the world will know, that you and I, have spent the night here together. As Miss Travers, you can never show your face in society; but later, as Lady Villars, you will be welcomed with open arms. The wire I sent, was to my man Antonio, telling him to bring my car and luggage here; I expect him about eleven, possibly earlier; as soon as he arrives, we will start for Folkestone, catch the early boat, and be in Paris in four hours!"

"Surely you do not suppose, that I will go with you," demanded Nancy fiercely.

"I do not suppose you have any alternative!" he answered impressively. "Of course I know, that I have startled you, by this unexpected *coup*, but before long, believe me, Nancy, you will look upon this evening, as the beginning of a new, and splendid life! *You* were not borne to waste your best days with an old woman,—who, much as I love her, saps one's vitality! You cannot deny that I am handsome, well born, wealthy, and adore you,— and if your cold little heart cares for anyone,—it cares for *me*. We were born to be happy together."

"What crazy talk!" cried Nancy, and she made an effort to pass him.

"No! no! my own darling; you shall stay here, and listen to me. Such love as mine, will kindle yours; it will,—it *must*!"

Nancy's lips trembled—but she made no reply; she glanced at him, then round the room, with the eyes of a trapped animal; suddenly she made a dart, and placed the table between them. Oh! if she could but reach the door; but with folded arms, Sir Dudley stood between her, and that means of escape,—eyeing her strangely. At last, she said, in a low faint voice: "You spoke just now, about your wife?"

He nodded. "Yes! a she-devil; she's had serious money losses lately, and I shall have no difficulty in bringing her to terms; my *wife* will be all right!"

"And what of my—*husband*?"

Villars broke into a loud derisive laugh, and said: "My own most exquisite Nancy, why invent a fairy tale? You and I, will live, a fairy tale."

"It is no fairy tale," she answered, "I was married in India before I came home."

"Pardon me,—but I do not believe it."

"I cannot help that,—but it is true! Mrs. Ffinch knows, so does Mrs. Hicks; she saw me married; it was all legal: my father wished it to take place,—as he was dying."

"And who are you?—who is your husband?"

"Captain Mayne."

"*Mayne!* why the joke gets better and better! you don't even speak; could you not think of someone more probable? What a preposterous make-up."

"It's no make-up, on my honour."

"Does Mrs. De Wolfe know?" he demanded sharply.

"No!"

"Nothing will ever make me believe your foolish story; if it were the truth, *why* conceal it?"

"Because"—choking as she spoke—"immediately after the ceremony my father died; I was crazy with grief, I *hated* the sight of Captain Mayne, I wrote, and told him this,—and then I ran away."

"Ah! so you *can* run away! Do you hate Captain Mayne now?"

"No, and if he would ask me, I would go back to him to-morrow."

Villars became suddenly livid—after a second's pause, a great perpendicular vein showed itself suddenly in his forehead.

"You would, would you? Well, from what I've seen of Mayne, he's the last sort of fellow to give you another chance; and anyhow this little episode with *me*, will, if you *are* his wife, choke him off altogether! Listen to me, Nancy, I implore you; why waste your lovely youth? Why not come with me: live while you live, and see the far away beautiful world? And you *shall* come with me," he concluded doggedly.

"I'd infinitely rather die!" she answered with decision.

"Oh, Nancy, when you speak, and look like that,—you break my heart; for months you have been my hope, and star,—my one thought,—my only object in life. Surely you *guessed*?"

"Never! or do you suppose, I should have been so friendly, and sisterly and trustful? Mrs. De Wolfe said your emotional speeches, and impulsive acts, were merely your Italian way,—and meant nothing,—she was mistaken, I see!"

"She was," now approaching, his eyes flaming in a white face.

At this moment, the door opened, and Mrs. Bode appeared in a bedgown and slippers. "There's ten o'clock gone, sir, and I'm thinking, that you and your lady, will have to stop here to-night. I can make up a room: it's not very grand, but,— —" further information was interrupted,—by Nancy, who, thrusting the astonished matron violently aside, dashed out of the door, and ran down the long passage into the kitchen. The sound of Nancy's high-heeled shoes racing along the flags, brought Villars to his senses; he had a marvellous power of recovery and self-control; he had realized from the first, when Nancy recoiled from him against the shutter, that the game was lost! nevertheless, some infernal, perverse, impulse, urged him to persist! He might yet gain her by threats, and alarms—such cases had been known!

What devil had entered into him, and forced him to snatch his opportunity; had whispered into his ear,—as he wrote that telegram in this accursed room? The insanity of half an hour, had cost him the loss of Nancy, and his old godmother. Naturally the Court would be closed to him for the rest of his life. Yes! he had pretty well cooked himself. Well! he must make the most of a bad job!

Meanwhile, Mrs. Bode was staring at him, with her hands on her hips and her mouth half open. At last he turned round, and said: "The young lady and I have had a falling out."

"Looks a bit like it, sir! and I declare, here's the car come back for you at last!" for just at this moment, Antonio glided up to the entrance. Strange to say, neither the man nor motor were the same—this vehicle was a big grey open car, and there was luggage, and a lady's fur-lined coat, which the chauffeur brought in, and handed to Mrs. Bode with a ceremonious bow.

"Will you ask the lady to speak to me?" said Villars, as he pressed a sovereign into Mrs. Bode's horny palm.

"Thank you, sir; it's entirely too much,—entirely too much! I'll go and fetch the young lady," and Mrs. Bode padded off in her roomy felt slippers. She found Nancy, in the kitchen,—looking strangely white, and shaken.

"The car has come, miss," she announced cheerfully, "and here's your fur coat. The gentleman will be thankful, if he might speak to you?"

"No, Mrs. Bode, I will never speak to that gentleman again! If he follows me here I shall run away into the fields, or," looking round, "anywhere!"

"Then you ain't going with him in that lovely car, miss?"

"No, I'm going to stay here to-night, Mrs. Bode; if you can give me a bed or even a chair, and to-morrow morning *very* early, I'll get Dan to show me the way to the station."

"Oh, all right, miss, I'll give you a bed, and be pleased. At first, I thought you were man and wife,—specially as he walked about outside, and left you here by your lone,—but I see you've no ring."

"The gentleman is nothing to me,—nothing, *worse* than nothing," cried Nancy passionately, "we happen to be staying in the same house, that was all; and the car left us here by mistake."

Sounds of a brisk booted foot, coming down the long passage; Nancy looked at Mrs. Bode, who hastily opened a door, and thrust her through. She found herself at the foot of some queer old stairs, that twisted round a huge beam or post, and led up to a low loft-like bedroom, with two windows, flush with the floor. Here was a tester bed, painted washstand, and a beautiful chest of drawers, and here Nancy, exhausted, and trembling, sat upon a low straw chair, her eyes riveted on the grey motor car, immediately beneath them. It seemed to be several hours,—but was really twenty minutes, before the car, and its occupants, moved slowly out of sight.

After a brief interview with her hostess,—who had appeared with a pair of clean sheets,—Nancy lay down on the tester bed, and in spite of a lumpy mattress, and an overpowering smell of old feathers, slept, until a shrill young cock, announced the breaking of another day.

CHAPTER XXXVII
NANCY CARRIES IT OFF!

There was no trace of tears on Nancy's smiling face, when three quarters of an hour later, she appeared among the company, looking particularly fresh, and self-possessed. In answer to eager queries, she gave a vivid description of the lure of the oak chest, her rustic hostess, her unique sleeping chamber, and early morning excursion across meadows steeped in dew.

"And what about Sir Dudley all this time?" inquired Mrs. Speyde, "you haven't *murdered* him by any chance, have you?"

The reply to this question, came in Mrs. De Wolfe's very deepest voice, "Dudley Villars made himself scarce, of course; he is a man of the world and able to cope with awkward incidents. He was leaving to-day under any circumstances,—and has already sent for his car."

By degrees the subject subsided, and lapsed; the guests were more or less engaged in preparations for their departure, there was not much time, for sustained discussion, and as far as Nancy was concerned, an exhausting ordeal, was satisfactorily closed.

Before her numerous friends motored away to the station, or to their several homes in the neighbourhood, Nancy held a short parley with two. Firstly, with Mrs. Hicks, who pounced upon her in the hall, and drawing her into one of the embrasures, said: "My dear child, I've scarcely had a word with you these two days; and I've just been longing and *aching* to hear what you and Mayne said to one another on Thursday evening? I suppose you know that *I* sent him!"

"I suppose I do," rejoined Nancy bluntly.

"Has anything been settled?"

"No, not exactly; I believe he went away early this morning."

"He did," assented Mrs. Hicks, "but he is within reach, and you can easily put your hand upon him. Always remember, my dear child, that whenever I can do anything for you, or him, I will. I've had a most gorgeous time! everyone has been so jolly and friendly, it's almost as if I was back in India, and I'll never forget this tennis week as long as ever I live. Now I must go and get my things together, as I see my train is 12.5, so ta, ta, for the present," and she moved off.

The broad back of Mrs. Hicks was scarcely out of sight, before she was superseded by Billy Miller, who was evidently charged with an important subject.

"Our car has not arrived yet, Nancy," she began, and taking her arm she added, "I want you to come out on the lawn with me,—for I've got something to tell you," and Nancy assenting, the two girls passed through the wide french window, and strolled down towards the tennis courts.

"I should like you to be one of the first to know, that I am engaged to Major Horne," announced Miss Miller. "We settled it last evening, out here in the moonlight."

"Oh, Billy, I'm delighted!" said Nancy. "I always thought it was going to come off. I think he is charming, and you will have a delightful mother-in-law,—but what will become of your family?"

"They will have to look after themselves," was the heartless rejoinder. "I have given them a splendid start; you see Minna is married, Brenda is engaged, there is only Baby left,—and she is the flower of the flock; then you know some of us will always be coming backwards and forwards. The Pater has taken a house in town,—which will be a sort of family hotel. Of course, Nancy, I expect you to be one of my bridesmaids. By the way, my dear, you nearly gave us fits last evening."

"I'm afraid I did, and I cannot say that *I* was very happy myself."

"No; I could see that Mrs. De Wolfe was on tenterhooks, although she did her best, to pretend that your staying out all night, was a mere everyday affair! Next to her, amazing to relate, the one who took your absence most sorely to heart, was a mere acquaintance,—Captain Mayne! He seemed uncommonly abstracted, and silent, and that was not all,—I wish it had been; his room happened to be over mine, and I could hear him walking about the whole night! I would go to sleep and wake up, and there he was, still doing sentry go! At one time I had an idea of getting out of bed, and knocking on the ceiling with an umbrella: perhaps he had toothache?"

"Perhaps he had," assented Nancy, but in her heart she knew, that it was not toothache, but dreadful misgivings with regard to herself, that had made him pace his room! He had warned her more than once against Sir Dudley; and his suspicions, and dislike, had proved to be only too well founded.

When all the guests had departed, a Sunday calm descended on the Court. Mrs. Horne and Roger De Wolfe, still remained; the former as a support and confidante and comfort to her old friend, fatigued by her recent activities, and greatly shaken by Nancy's adventure,—required someone of her own age, into whose ear she could pour her troubles.

The two old ladies wandered about the green lawns, or sat in the shade together, enjoying what is known, as a "good talk." The chief subject of Mrs. De Wolfe's discourse, was Dudley Villars; that catastrophe had dislocated years of happy friendship. "I had hereto always quoted him, believed in him, and look at what he has done!" Mrs. Horne, an unusually noble-minded woman, never attempted to recall their interview, and her warning at Cadenabbia—merely contenting herself with saying, "I never liked Sir Dudley, or trusted him, my dear; but I thought that perhaps, as you were so fond of him, there must be good in him, which *I* could not discover."

Whilst these two friends enjoyed one another's society, Roger De Wolfe went round the farms, and coverts, with bailiff and keepers, more as agent, for his cousin, than with the eye of a man inspecting his future possessions! He was, as Mrs. De Wolfe had said, a good, single-minded, stupid fellow,—forty years of age, and still unmarried. Even his best friends were bound to admit that Roger was a bore;—a silent bore,—which is one of the most trying description. The type that sits, and sticks, scarcely speaking,—obviously waiting to be entertained; absorbing ideas, like a great sponge.

Nancy liked Roger; at least he was restful; and when his two chief topics were exhausted,—prize retrievers, and carpentering—she suffered him to, so to speak, "stew in his own juice." They played croquet, and the girls from the Rectory came up and made a set at tennis; but as a rule Nancy spent a good deal of time with herself; lounging in a hammock, dipping into a novel, or sitting on the rustic seat, at the end of the long turf walk. The two old ladies went motoring of an afternoon, and Mrs. De Wolfe expressed her intention of calling on Mrs. Bode and thanking her in person.

"I daresay you will like to come too, Nancy," she said.

"On the contrary, I don't think I could endure to see that house again; no I really couldn't face it! I have already written to Mrs. Bode and sent her a present, and if she offers you a blue bowl, please say that I have changed my mind,—but you need not add, that I do not wish for anything to remind me of her abode."

The day following her visit to Mrs. Bode, Mrs. De Wolfe declared, that she must go and look up Richard Mayne. "I fancy he is feeling rather lonely, now that his nephew has departed, and I'll ask him over on a little visit. I must confess, I was greatly affronted with Derek: rushing out of the house before breakfast,—just as if it had been an hotel; it would have served him right, if I had sent a stiff bill after him! However, I had a nice note from him,—a note of apology, telling me, that he had been unable to wait to see me that morning, as urgent business summoned him to London, and he hoped that I would forgive him? I expect he will be down again, before long, for the partridge shooting, and then I shall give him a piece of my mind, for although I like the boy, I don't hold with these casual manners."

Nancy did not accompany the two ladies, she preferred to take the dogs out, and as she was crossing the hall, Sutton approached her with a solemn face, bearing a note on the salver, and said, "I am very sorry, Miss Travers, but this note was given to me for you just a week ago. It happened at an awkward time, before dinner, the night of that big party. I put it inside the wine book, in my pantry, and forgot all about it until now; such an oversight has never happened to me before; but I hope you will excuse me, miss, knowing what a lot I had on my mind, and so many things to see to. I trust the note is of no consequence,—I see it was written in the house."

Yes—there on the flap of the envelope was "Newenham Court."

"Thank you, Sutton," said Nancy, "I expect it is all right," then turning over the note, she was startled to find that it was addressed to her in Mayne's handwriting. She tore it open, and read:

Thursday evening.

My dear Nancy,

> It was very unfortunate, that our conversation this afternoon was interrupted, I should much like to have a *talk*. May I find you in the little book room immediately after dinner? I shall be there anyhow, about nine o'clock.

Yours always,
D. Mayne.

This was dreadful; not only had she failed to keep the rendezvous, but she had been absent the whole of the following night; and had not arrived home, until after his departure. Naturally, to him, the whole affair must present the blackest aspect. What would she do? what could she do? She felt almost distraught, as she wandered out into the garden, and walked up and down the long turf track, in much the same frame of mind, as that, which had kept Mayne afoot for a whole night.

She remembered the evening of the tournament—how he had never come near her, but, how she had caught his eyes watching her gravely, as she and Sir Dudley sang duets. She would write to him immediately, and give him a full account of her hateful adventure in Mrs. Bode's cottage, and she would ask him to arrange for them to have an immediate meeting. Her present position, was insupportable, the secret altogether too heavy a burden. She was not playing the game, in keeping such a page of her past from Mrs. De Wolfe, nor was it honourable to pass herself off, as a spinster, among the young men of her acquaintance. If Mayne had not returned home,—and at least if they had not come across one another,—matters might have remained in abeyance for years; but now that she knew him, and time had softened a far away tragedy, she realized that she loved him; yes, to herself, there was no use in thrusting away, or trying to evade the truth.

The question was, did he love her? Perhaps! probably! Yes, a girl has an intuition in these things; of course there was the money; that was still a rock of offence; but many men had married women with fortunes, and the marriages had not been unhappy!—Quite the contrary, by all accounts; and she could point out to him, that when they were married, *he* had been the rich partner, and she as poor as a church mouse. Partridge shooting would begin shortly, she would probably see him in a few days—meanwhile she would *write*. She sat for a long time mentally composing her letter. At last, she heard the motor return, and presently she rose to meet the two old ladies, who were coming towards her across the lawn.

"Well!" she exclaimed, "how did you find Mr. Mayne?"

"Oh, my dear," replied Mrs. De Wolfe, throwing up her hands, "I never saw him in such low spirits,—we really couldn't help feeling very sorry for him,—what *do* you think? Derek Mayne has gone back to India,—he left for Marseilles yesterday morning."

"Gone back to India," repeated Nancy, "but why? I heard he had got an extension of leave."

"Yes, but there is some trouble on the frontier, they say, and Derek is high up among the captains of his regiment, and I have always heard a very keen soldier; Mrs. Horne and I have put our heads together, and come to the conclusion that there's something more in his departure, than meets the eye.—Perhaps we shall all know some day? Well, anyway, Nancy, the news does not affect *you*, for somehow, you and Derek were never particularly friendly."

To this, Nancy made no answer, and if her old friend had not been engaged in returning the caresses of three dogs, she might have noticed that her young friend looked strangely pale.

CHAPTER XXXVIII
THE INDIAN MAIL

When Nancy found herself in her own room, she locked the door, and sat down to face this unexpected situation,—this new trouble. She was well aware of the reason of Derek's abrupt departure, but surely it was impossible for him to believe that she had run away with Sir Dudley? he must have heard from his uncle, that she was still at the Court. However, it was evident, that he had received a bad impression of her character, and would have nothing further to say to her! She immediately determined to write to him, and found wonderful comfort in the conviction, that she could clear herself by pen and paper,—but unfortunately the letter would have to wait for days before it could be dispatched. This important epistle she wrote, re-wrote, corrected, and copied, over and over again. Sometimes she found that it said too much, sometimes too little; sometimes it was too bold, sometimes too formal,—and always too *long*. After many hours of meditation, and changing her mind, and destroying much note-paper, she completed in two sheets, an explanation, which she believed would do,—and leave no disagreeable *arrière pensée* upon her conscience.

With considerable diplomacy she obtained the correct address from Mr. Mayne, motored over to Maynesfort alone, took tea with the old gentleman, entertained him with lively talk, made a casual inquiry, and accomplished her errand! On mail day, the momentous dispatch was duly posted by her own hand.

The next event in Nancy's existence, was the death of Mrs. Jenkins. A sudden seizure of apoplexy carried her off in a few hours; her will proved to be a surprising document, and a bitter disappointment to Mrs. Taylor. To her dear friend Henrietta Taylor, she only left one hundred pounds, to Miss Dolling, fifty pounds,—for the purchase of a mourning ring,—the Pom and a substantial sum were bequeathed to the butler; three hundred a year and her wardrobe, to Baker, her faithful maid; her pearls and her portrait to her dear niece, Nancy Travers, as well as the Travers silver and books; all the remainder—including lease of house and investments—were to his great surprise bequeathed to the nephew of her late husband, Samuel Jenkins.

After all, it was but just and fair, that the Jenkins money, should return to the Jenkins purse? But why should poor Mrs. Taylor be cut off with a hundred pounds?—alas! the sad truth must be disclosed. Although Mrs. Taylor enjoyed prolonged midnight conferences, it was Baker, the maid, who had the very *last* word, when putting her lady to bed. Baker cordially hated Mrs. Taylor,—naturally it was painful for her to witness the valuable presents, and beautiful dresses, that the weak-minded old lady bestowed upon her toady.—By gradual degrees, the crafty woman dropped some poisonous truths into her mistress's ear; she even inferred, that Mrs. Taylor was a double-faced friend; who said one thing to her lady's face, and another behind her back!

"I know for a fact, that she told Mrs. Seymour as how your memory was going," boldly announced Baker,—with her mistress's little rat tail of back hair, tightly clenched in her hand, "and that you really wanted someone like herself, to look after you, and your affairs."

Although Mrs. Jenkins had angrily repudiated this information, and commanded the maid to hold her tongue, nevertheless the dart rankled, and went far to counteract Mrs. Taylor's honeyed speeches, and audacious flatteries. To these, Mrs. Jenkins listened greedily,—but she was a sly old thing, and took notes. One or two of her visitors, had ventured hints respecting Mrs. Taylor and her pretensions,—for her arrogance had become insupportable. It had been whispered, that she had already decided what she intended to do with the house in Queen's Gate, when it was her property; and had more than once rashly intimated, that her dear friend Mrs. Jenkins was "breaking up!"

Nancy, who was much surprised at the news of her legacy, stored the picture, sent the pearls to her bank, and went into slight mourning. In these days, she felt nearly as dull and silent as Roger De Wolfe,—although she made a valiant effort to appear otherwise: she was counting the very hours, until she could receive an answer to her letter,—but perhaps Derek would not reply?

Her hopes went up and down, like a see-saw—at one moment she was sanguine—the next visited by despair. Undoubtedly it was an agreeable distraction to Nancy, and a pleasure to her other friends, when Mrs. Ffinch appeared upon the scene. She looked thin, and weather-beaten, but as active, and energetic as ever. At first she came down to stay with the Hillsides,—and later to the Court,—a much more comfortable abode. She had frequently visited there as a girl, and now made herself thoroughly at home. Naturally she saw a great change in her protégée; here was another Nancy from the flapper of Fairplains,—and the two, had long and intimate talks: having many topics, and one secret in common.

"And so you had Mayne at home," said Finchie.

With this abrupt remark, she had opened their first *tête-à-tête*. "Yes. By accident you fell not 'among thieves,' but, among his friends! That marriage was a terrible disaster. If I had not happened to be away,—it would never have taken place. Just see, what a fix you are in; a girl of your appearance and position, could marry almost anybody,—including my poor Tony. Dear me, Nancy, how much I should like you for a niece! Perhaps it could come off after all; for I suppose you are aware, that Captain Mayne could get rid of you if he liked.—Desertion! but what an *esclandre*! You would have to go back to Fairplains, and bury yourself temporarily among the coffee bushes! You and he have met I know,—and met often, I believe he was actually staying here!"

Nancy nodded.

"And there it ended for the present? I understand he has returned to India. I do not know what he and Josie have been up to,—at least I can guess what *she* has been doing,—flirting for all she is worth,—but she has her knife into Derek Mayne up to the hilt; and for what reason?—the rest is silence! Ah! here is the postman coming up the back avenue, let us go down and waylay him, for this is Indian Mail day, and I am expecting the usual screed from my old man."

As the ladies waited whilst the postman sorted out "the Court letters," Nancy's heart almost stood still; would there be one for her, or not? There *was*! She turned her back upon her two companions, and opened it with trembling fingers.

> Hawari Camp,
> Darwaza Hills,
> N. W. Frontier.
>
> My dear Nancy,
>
> I was *very* glad to receive your letter, which makes everything clear. Fate was dead against that interview, perhaps I may get home when this bit of a scrap is over; we are expecting to have a brush with the tribes at once. If I do manage leave, I shall return immediately, and hope our meeting may come off,—the third time is the charm. I write in desperate haste to catch the Dâk just going down, as I want you to have this

answer without delay. My hands are so frozen, I can scarcely hold my pen; will write again next week.

Yours always,
D. M.

This letter filled Nancy with a glow of happiness and a sense of joy and relief, such as she had not known for many a long day. She hurried up the avenue clutching her treasure, half afraid that Finchie would overtake and cross-examine her, but looking back she noticed, that Finchie, with a large bundle of correspondence in her hand, was still gossiping with the postman.

CHAPTER XXXIX
THE AVOWAL

It was mid October and the woods round Newenham were not now dressed in green, but clothed in various shades of brown, dark red, and deep orange; in the grounds, one no longer heard the continual rattle of the mowing machine; the gardeners were busy with barrows and brooms, sweeping up, and removing, the endless showers of withered leaves. Within, the atmosphere was gay and sunny, here were various congenial guests: Roger De Wolfe and Major Horne had come for the pheasant shooting. Mrs. Horne, Billy and Baby Miller were of the party, and Mrs. Hicks who had rushed down on a flying visit, before she sailed for India, also Mrs. Ffinch, and Mr. Mayne.

The solitary old gentleman, had seemed so dull and depressed, that Mrs. De Wolfe insisted that he should join her circle—even for a few days. To Nancy she said, "I've no doubt that the gossips will think that we are going to be married at *last*; they settled a match years and years ago, and how my boys used to laugh and chaff me! You will look after him, Nancy, the old man is devoted to you, and you are devoted to him, and I must confess, I admire the courage with which you take him on at Bridge; a most hopeless and expensive partner, who doubles and re-doubles, even if he holds a Yarborough; the old gambling spirit re-appearing in a milder form!"

It was five o'clock in the afternoon, the party were collected round the tea table in the hall,—a table laden with rare old silver, a fine Crown Derby tea-service, hot scones—savoury sandwiches and cakes too numerous to mention—and Mrs. Ffinch,—who never lost sight of an opportunity,—had cleverly manœuvred dull Roger De Wolfe into a seat next to lively Baby Miller. In the opinion of this astute matron, it was full time that Roger was married; he was forty, his hair was thinning on the top, his figure was thickening; in short, she was resolved upon this match. Glancing over the girls in the neighbourhood, she found none so suitable to be the future mistress of the Court, as pretty, red-haired "Baby."

She could see that Roger was already dazzled and fascinated, and it would be a most desirable alliance. Roger was plain, silent, and worthy; Baby was a charming chatterbox, and a nice, good, clever girl; some day, she would and should be the châtelaine of this dear old house, and take charge of the precious family treasures, when their present owner had passed away. There was a loud hum of talking, and laughing, Major Horne and Roger De Wolfe were discussing their day's sport, Mr. Mayne and Mrs. De Wolfe were still wrangling about their last rubber, when Sutton entered, salver in hand.

"Your letters have just come, sir," he said, approaching Mr. Mayne. "Are there any orders for Graham?"

The old gentleman took up his letters, glanced at them indifferently, and answered, "No, not to-day," turning to Mrs. De Wolfe he added:

"Only a bill from my saddler, and a letter from Julia Torquilstone. I wonder what the deuce *she* is writing about?" he added peevishly—"sure to *want* something," and he laid it unopened by his plate. "I was hoping to hear from my boy. I know the mail came in two days ago."

Nancy too had hoped for a letter; but her hopes had been doomed to disappointment.

As soon as Mr. Mayne had disposed of Mrs. De Wolfe's argument, and a second cup of tea, he opened the neglected epistle from his sister-in-law,— and read it with a frowning face.

"Here's bad news!" he exclaimed, in a tone which silenced every other voice. "Julia has had a line from the War Office, to say that Derek has been dangerously wounded in some action with the hill tribes. Oh, these little wars, and what they cost us!"

"Are there any particulars?" inquired Mrs. De Wolfe.

"There you are!" handing her an official telegram. "I suppose," and his voice was husky, "he will leave his bones out there, like his father."

When Mrs. De Wolfe had glanced over the slip of paper, she was not a little surprised, to see Nancy rise from her place, and stretch out a trembling hand.

"May I see it too?" she asked. The question was so clear and so unexpected, that every eye was riveted on the pale girl, whose gaze was bent on the telegram,—that is to say every eye, save those of Mr. Mayne, who was apparently engulfed in his own trouble.

"I suppose he will die out there alone!" he groaned. "Of course Julia won't stir, I'm too old,—and there's nobody else to go."

"*I* will go," announced Nancy, steadying herself by a tall Charles the First chair, and looking round the assembled company, with a white and rigid face. "I must tell you all at last, and *now*,—that—that—" and her voice sank till it became a whisper—but an audible whisper, "I am his *wife*!"

"Nancy!" ejaculated Mrs. De Wolfe, in a key of contrasting depth.

"It's true," she continued with livid lips, "we were married by my father's deathbed, two and a half years ago, and——" here she completely broke down.

"Nancy, child, don't, *I'll* tell it," volunteered Mrs. Ffinch, stretching out her arm. "No, she is not raving, as you might naturally suppose," she added, glancing at her companions. "I know all about it,—and Mrs. Hicks was present,—she saw them married!"

"Yes," corroborated Mrs. Hicks, "I did, and it's about the only secret I've ever been able to keep!"

"But why a secret?" demanded Mrs. De Wolfe, who had recovered her composure.

"We were married to relieve my father's mind," replied Nancy, who had also reclaimed her self-possession. "I was alone in the world, and very poor, and he was dreadfully unhappy about me; Captain Mayne and I did not care for one another—in those days! Please!" looking round the circle— "*do* forgive me for deceiving you,—but we agreed to keep the marriage secret, and to be strangers always, and I must confess, that *I* behaved very badly. I was distracted, and I ran away; but I was so young, and so heart-broken! It is different now; I shall leave with Mrs. Hicks on Friday, and pray that I may be in time.—I am going to send off a cable," and looking like the wraith of Nancy Travers, she left them.

The old mahogany door closed upon a long expressive silence, presently to be broken by Mrs. Ffinch, who gladly took up her parable. Here was *her* hour! what an opening for her natural eloquence, and love of dominating a situation! As she unravelled Nancy's past, she had the supreme happiness of knowing, that her listeners actually hung upon her words,—especially old Mr. Mayne, with his head advanced, and hand behind his left and best, ear!

In a few short and telling sentences, she described Nancy's adoration of her father, their ideally happy life,—the terrible scene with the panther, Mayne's bad shot, his rescue by Travers, and how when Travers was dying,

Mayne had come forward, and undertaken the charge of Nancy. How immediately after the funeral Nancy, in a condition of frenzied grief, had written a letter of farewell and repudiation to Mayne,—and taken refuge with her old nurse at Coimbatore.

"Aye, it really was a terrible letter," chimed in Mrs. Hicks, "I was there, when he read it, and he looked knocked all of a 'eap.—First he showed it to Teddy Dawson, and then to me. She said as how she blamed him, and how she hated him,—and so he let her go,—what else could he do?"—throwing herself back in her chair, and folding her arms with an air of finality—then added as an afterthought, "but he made her a good allowance!"

"Which she never touched," supplemented Mrs. Ffinch, "the money has lain all this time in Grindlay's Bank; they held no communication with one another, each went their own way: he as a bachelor, she, as an unmarried girl, until they came to London,—where Fate threw them together, in spite of themselves."

"So all the time, there *was* a girl in the background!—a girl to whom he sent money," said Mrs. Horne,—who had a wonderful faculty for remembering—but not disseminating—scraps of gossip. "There's never smoke without a fire, and to think, that all the time it should be *Nancy*."

"It was a case of a foolish, hasty, wedding," declared Mrs. Ffinch judicially; "had I been at home, I would never have allowed it to take place. Unfortunately I happened to be absent for a few days, and in those few days, occurred Nancy's marriage, and her father's death. I think that Derek Mayne,—though he meant well,—behaved like a lunatic!"

"No," corrected his uncle, thumping on the table, "he behaved like a man of honour! I was always fond of Derek, and now I'm *proud* of him! I'll just go and see what that girl is doing?" and taking his stick, he hobbled out of the room.

When Nancy found Mrs. De Wolfe alone, she said, "Hundreds of times I've wanted to speak, and to tell you,—but I dared not; for I felt, that if I opened my lips, the secret would spread; if I told one, I might tell another; and when I saw Derek, I realized that we were to be strangers,—in fact he said so in the plainest terms. There was nothing for it but silence,—at first."

"And now?" inquired her friend, with grave significance.

"Now,—only for my money,—I believe he would have made it up! Money, or no money, I'm going out on Friday; I have already secured my berth, by telephone,—but oh, dear, dear Auntie, supposing I am *too late!*" — and as she sank on her knees and buried her face on the old lady's lap,—her sobs were heartbreaking.

"Don't meet trouble half way, my child," said Mrs. De Wolfe, "though crying will relieve your poor heart. It is only the *young*, the lucky young, who can weep. Remember that the Maynes are as tough as leather; why, look at that old man downstairs; four months ago, a horse rolled upon him, and broke his leg, and three ribs; to-day, he was out shooting pheasants! Oh, Nancy my dear, how often I've wished that you, and Derek would take to one another,—and only to think, that you were married all the time! Well, in my long, and not uneventful life, you have given me the most stunning surprise, I have ever experienced! *Now* I can understand why Derek never came to the house, and went out of his way to avoid me."

"Everything is my fault. Auntie Wolfe," sobbed Nancy, "I'm afraid you will never care for me any more, nor trust me: everyone will think me so secretive, and deceitful,—and so I *was*!"

"It will be all right, my dear, if only Derek recovers, and you make him happy,—as I believe you can. By and by you will both come home, and settle among us,—and your strange story will be forgotten."

As soon as Captain Mayne was convalescent, he and his wife travelled down to Fairplains, where they were the guests of Mr. and Mrs. Dawson; and in that familiar and unchanged verandah, he once more occupied his favourite shabby chair, and surveyed from his place, the dim blue plains. All the neighbours and employees flocked to the bungalow, to hail and welcome Nancy. Francis received his "Little Missy" with rapturous joy, and a few trickling tears.—As for Togo, that faithful heart was always hers.

When Miss Travers, at a few hours' notice, had hurried out to India, to marry, and nurse, Captain Mayne; it was generally believed that this was but the romantic sequel, to a long and mysterious engagement.

Not more than two or three hundred people are in possession of the truth!